POLYPHEMUS

I0612655

MICHAEL SHEA was born in Los Angeles in 1946. His notable works include *Nifft the Lean* (1982), which won a World Fantasy Award, *The Color Out of Time* (1984), and the collection *Polyphemus* (1987), featuring his best known tale, "The Autopsy," which has been often anthologized and was adapted for an episode of Guillermo del Toro's series *Cabinet of Curiosities*. Shea also wrote a number of works set in H. P. Lovecraft's Cthulhu Mythos, collected posthumously in *Demiurge: The Complete Cthulhu Mythos Tales* (2017). Shea died in 2014.

MICHAEL SHEA

POLYPHEMUS

with a new introduction by
LAIRD BARRON

VALANCOURT BOOKS

CONTENTS

INTRODUCTION

The Return of the Giant

by Laird Barron

I originally met Michael Shea around 2005 in Seattle at Norwescon. Marc Laidlaw, a terrific science fiction and horror author in his own right, introduced us. A big moment for me, new to the scene and a longtime admirer of Shea's. To this day, his "The Autopsy" and "The Angel of Death" remain enshrined in my personal hall of fame alongside Karl Edward Wagner's "Summer's End" and T.E.D. Klein's *Petey*. I hit it off with Michael instantly. He was lanky and rawboned. Nicked, weathered, and tough; a button-up shirt and blue jeans man. Down to earth and garrulous, his devil-may-care smile tempered by wisdom dearly earned. He'd shot to stardom in the 1970s and '80s on the strength of a couple of fantasy novels (*A Quest for Simbilis* and *Nifft the Lean*) and several appearances in *The Magazine of Fantasy & Science Fiction*. *Polyphemus,* Shea's 1987 debut collection, announced his presence on a broader scale and cemented his legacy with the same thunderous boom. Then he fell off the map for the better part of a decade and was, at the time of our meeting, embarked on a third act comeback. Successfully, in fact—he soon inked a book deal with a New York publisher, and one of his finest novelettes, "The Growlimb," snagged a World Fantasy award.

Over the succeeding years, I discovered the man had lived a colorful life. He'd wandered and scrapped, survived rough jobs and close calls; he'd subdued some of his demons and wrestled the others to a draw. In another time and place, he'd have been a skald. In this reality, he was a teacher, poet, husband, and father. And, in my estimate, one of the great horror writers of the 20th century.

Let's back up to the beginning.

The first time I encountered the brutish cyclops known as Polyphemus was probably in grade school in a chapter covering Greek mythology. What's imprinted into my brain, though, is how the giant caught trespassing Greek soldiers in his cave, snatched up a couple and devoured them, then collapsed into a drunken slumber after a snootful of wine. I also remember Kirk Douglas and his boys jamming a sharpened log into the poor bastard's eye before escaping that cave under cover from a stampede of the giant's sheep. That sequence of images, coupled with the more elaborate details in the actual text, greatly affected me as a child.

Years later, toward the tail end of my teens, I encountered Shea's "The Autopsy" in David G. Hartwell's landmark horror anthology, *The Dark Descent*. I began to actively seek out his other works, namely the increasingly rare collection faithfully reproduced herein, *Polyphemus*. Naturally, the title, referencing the carnivorous giant, struck a chord. How would the titular tale ramify, or, more likely, subvert the myth? Well, Shea reimagined Odysseus as a far-future colonist roustabout/guide with a king-sized chip on his shoulder, and the cyclops as an inscrutable carnivorous alien behemoth possessed of malignant appetite; the pair locked in a death struggle, pitting human tenacity, ingenuity, and cunning against the prodigiousness and ferocity of an otherworldly foe. Vintage Shea.

Tragically, Michael passed away in 2014. During the course of another essay, I said of him:

"His memory looms large in the weird fiction and horror fields . . . A deep vein of mystery and noir travels through his work, grounding the fantastical tropes. I'd read him since my latter teens, absorbing the unique cadence of his prose without giving conscious thought to how echoes of the natural world inflected his grimiest urban settings, how the superstructures and sprawl of his version of L.A. and San Francisco were influenced by the ancient earth they occupy."

"Polyphemus" embodies everything I admire in a Michael

Shea story. Biting wit, cheerful, bright-eyed cynicism, a powerful intellect that camouflages itself beneath a pulp aesthetic, and, obviously, an appreciation of mythology. He was a master at synthesizing disparate influences and melding genres, cleaving to well-established traditions while spinning them at unexpected angles. He paired the rococo prose of H. P. Lovecraft and Jack Vance with the punch-to-the-jaw immediacy of hardboiled and men's adventure literature. Shea deftly portrayed rustic locales, densely packed megacities, and their respective denizens, sketching countrified dope dealers, streetwalkers, itinerant confidence men, casual vagrants, and blue-collar Joes. He depicted even his least savory characters with grim compassion rather than condescension. His empathy was a rare gift, even among writers. Taken as a whole, the result is a singular voice, a singular approach to horror narrative. As you travel through the pages of *Polyphemus,* the rugged earthiness of his voice will distinguish itself amidst more ornate flights into poetry. A rough and tumble timbre resonates from the core of his being, a recurring note that hearkens to the classics by virtue of its candidness, and to modern masters, especially the aforementioned duo of Lovecraft and Vance, when his fancy takes a hard left turn into weirder territory.

The road to hell is paved with critics who failed to separate artists from their art. Nonetheless, one can't fully escape one's reflection, one's following shadow, one's lived experience, nor one's influences. Art doesn't manifest from a vacuum, nor do writers spring from Jupiter's skull fully formed; every writer is in conversation with contemporaries and those who came before. Shea embraced his influences joyfully, be it the work of his colleagues, his aforementioned demons, or the geography of California he knew and loved so well. These influences shaped his narrative style and imbued it with a definitive character.

This collection demonstrates a spectrum of his chosen remit: you'll meet a cast featuring misfit space colonists; murderous rednecks and the ghost who haunts them; a homeless amateur sleuth in danger of succumbing to the mind games of a deadly mimic; nimble-minded (and fingered) mercenaries plotting an epic score against a beautiful vampire goddess; galactic anthropologists; ill-starred serial killers; an extra on a dystopian movie set where the director plays for keeps; and a coroner forced to match wits with an unearthly predator.

That's merely a taste of what lurks on your path through Shea's strange wilderness; I can't do his virtuoso imagination justice via a capsule summary. I'm thrilled that Valancourt has elected to revive this title. It was important in 1987 and has since ascended to legendary status in the pantheon of horror luminaries.

It has been a joy to revisit these tales as I prepared the introduction. Now, it's your turn to light a torch and venture into the dark cave where wonders and terrors await.

LAIRD BARRON
Stone Ridge, NY
June 11, 2023

LAIRD BARRON spent his early years in Alaska. He is the author of several books, including *The Beautiful Thing That Awaits Us All*, *Swift to Chase*, and *The Wind Began to Howl*. His work has also appeared in many magazines and anthologies. Barron currently resides in the Rondout Valley writing stories about the evil that men do.

POLYPHEMUS

The sunlight falls bright and strong on the wastes of Firebairn at noon, but the wind is fresh and cuts through the warmth of it. Consequently, murmions usually sun themselves in the lee of the buttes and the eroded volcanic cones that stud those plains. In the lee of one such cone—more like a ragged ringwall really, no higher on the average than a hundred meters, but more than four kilometers in the diameter of its enclosure—a murmion luxuriated on a patch of red sand.

The creatures are rather like baby seals in shape, though a bit smaller, which still makes them among the largest of Firebairn's terrestrial fauna. The lakes (such as the one in the crater behind this murmion) and the sea contain the overwhelming majority of the planet's animal life and all its most impressive forms. Indeed, the colonists there had recently established that the murmion evolved from an aquatic line, the same order to which the economically important and much larger delphs belonged. Members of this order were sometimes called "mammalian analogues," based on their reproductive systems, lungs, and vascular organization, but there was something of the arthropod in all of them, perhaps most noticeably in this little pioneer of the dry land. It had a smooth chitinous hide and primitive eyes—ommatidia, really—like small black knobs, while its "flippers," fore and aft, were rigid and three-jointed, though of an oarlike flatness that proclaimed their ancestral function.

This murmion had chosen an unfortunate spot for its nap. It was dark blue in color, and the reddish sand put it in sharp relief. This had not gone unnoticed by a second organism that now crouched upon the crater's rim, still dripping from the lake within, whence it had just emerged. This, known colloquially by

the colonists as a "gabble" (*Sturtis atrox thomsonia*), was batra-
chian in form, though morphologically a far simpler organism
than any frog, being in fact more analogous to an immense
rotifer or roundworm in its internal structure. Moving on four
pseudopodia, it was a green viscid mass with a vast slot for a
mouth and, above the mouth, a freckling of rudimentary eyes
reminiscent of a spider's. It found prey by a subtle discrimination
of color contrasts, and since it frequently left the water to forage
along the land fringes, one could not help feeling the murmion's
sunbathing habits were singularly maladaptive. The gabble was
easily four times the size of the murmion, and swift and silent as
liquid—properties it now demonstrated as it leapt and flowed
down the side of the crater toward the sleeper. Its final lunge
came from so high that the force with which it smacked down
on the murmion imparted a paralyzing shock to the prey. The
gabble stepped daintily back from the stunned creature, bobbed
and weaved, seemed to shudder with delicate anticipation, and
swallowed the murmion whole.

The gabble settled down for a digestive nap on the warm red
sand. Had it possessed more highly evolved eyes, it might have
been alarmed, for something of immense size was already quite
near, grinding its slow way across the desert toward the crater.
Perhaps not. The gabble had no natural land-dwelling predators
larger than itself.

The wastelands of Firebairn would have inspired awe in
anyone susceptible to nature's grandeur. The genesis of this
continent—and of the planet's only other one—was now well
understood. Both were immense tables of volcanic outflow
produced by several primary magma vents in the sea floor, and
augmented by a multitude of lesser vents.

The period of active vulcanism was a hundred million years
past, and there had long been established a global weather cycle
that seasonally scoured the land with hurricane winds and
hammering rains. Erosion had burnished the buttes and cones,
scoured the obsidian fangs and claws off them, till now they
shone like glazed ceramics in the sun. Of the once-towering
volcanic cones, only the stumps remained, like twisted pots and

cauldron rims. Everything was red, black, olive green, ocher, and orange—not just the buttes and the glassy ramparts of the worn cones, but the rain-polished sands and gravels too. These formed threads, ribbons, whole fabrics of color, all woven and braided by the millennial winds.

And bejeweling this already jeweled terrain were the numberless lakes. Most of the lakes were in the craters, but many were on the flats as well, where their stark, cruel blue shone impossibly intense, framed by the polychrome mosaics of the plains. It was a world of inexorable beauty, through which a man might go in rapture, but only if borne in steel, only in a juggernaut harder than the harshness of that stern paradise.

The sand-hog was such a craft, a great tractor-transport, tank-treaded, that chewed across the gravel, gnawing it with a continuous fifty-ton bite. It bore three boats in its undercarriage, nine men and women in its upper decks. In its middle was a holding tank, a belly that whole schools of delphs could be swallowed into and carried off to sate the hunger of the growing colony. It was now farther from the colony than it had ever gone, not due to any shortage of delphs in the colony's immediate vicinity, but in order to combine forage with exploration and mapping of the continent. As the vehicle drew near the landmark its captain had selected for inspection, Penny Lopez, watching from one of the ports, said:

"Look. There's a gabble."

Several of the others joined her at adjacent ports. The presence of a gabble indicated that the crater indeed contained a lake. More than this, it portended that the lake would contain delphs. Delphs and gabbles were ecological associates. Both inhabited only "ocean-rooted" lakes—those whose surrounding craters had still-open vent systems that connected their waters with subcontinental oceanic influxes.

"Why is it wobbling like that?" asked the group's cartographer, Japhet Sparks. Nemo Jones, one of the two armorers, smiled within his ragged beard.

"He ate something nasty, I expect." Penny looked at him sharply. The uncouth armorer had been a suitor of hers at one time. Repulsing his attentions had not sufficiently expressed

Penny's dislike of him, and the power of even his most innocent-seeming remarks to irritate her was a source of open humor among the colonists. But Orson Waverly, who was the expedition's biologist, glanced at Nemo and shared his smile.

Indeed, the gabble did not look well. Pseudopodia spread, it seemed to be trying to brace itself, while spasms and tremors made it quake like a shaken plate of jelly. One of its sides bulged. From the bulge, something sprouted that looked like a blue, crooked knife blade, and even as it did so, a second identical one erupted from the creature's opposite side. With a synchronized sweeping motion, like oars plied by a boatman, these blades began to cut two jagged incisions through the flanks of the gabble.

"Captain Helion," said Waverly, "would you go at one-third for a moment for a field observation?"

The formality of the request was necessary, for the captain, a tall and statuesquely handsome man, disliked modification of any of his procedures. He arched an eyebrow, nodded coolly, and cut speed.

The observation required little time, for as the gabble ceased its impotent quiverings of resistance, a second pair of angled blades thrust from its sides. With an undulating swimming motion (not unlike a baby seal's) these four trenchant protrusions completed a circuit of the froglike belly. Head and forelegs flabbily collapsed, and from the bloody-edged barrel of the gabble's hindquarters, the snout of a murmion poked into the sunlight. It was a brief exulting gesture, such as a dolphin might make, breaking the surface out of sheer exuberance to dive again—and this the murmion did, greedily, into the nourishing pot of its prey's stomach.

Penny gave the smiling Nemo Jones a brief scowl. She went over to the piloting console, where Helion was already steering a course along the crater's perimeter, seeking an access to its interior negotiable by the tractor treads of the fishing craft the hog carried. She asked him the chances of finding such a break, and he cocked an eye at the crater and murmured a judicious reply. The captain's normal manner of stalwart composure was always faintly heightened by Penny Lopez. To Waverly, who was making a journal entry, Jones said:

"You rarely see that happen on dark sand. Murms always lie upon red or yellow, to show up better for the gabbles."

"Don't tell me," put in Jax Giggans, his fellow-armorer, who was readying the rifles. "You've hunted murmions on Katermand. Katermandian murmions. And you know all their tricks. And when they can't find sand the right color to lie on, they make use of special polychromatic piss glands they have to dye it yellow."

Nemo gave a single bark of laughter, practically a cachinnation from this rather solemn and formal man. Jax's joke might have been offered by any of the colonists. The backward jungled planet of Jones's origin, and his endless repertory of woodsman's tricks and lore, were a favorite target for humor. Nemo's normal reaction, however, would have been a courteous blankness—perhaps a blink of bafflement so straight-facedly feigned that many at first believed him slow-witted. But with Jax, he actually laughed, and riposted:

"No. They always piss green. Diet of gabbles."

"A joke!" said Sari, one of the pilot-gunners. "Nemo Jones has made a joke! Check the ports—the sky may be falling." There was a bitter edge to this sneer that was a little surprising to everyone who heard it, perhaps even to Sarissa Wayne herself. She didn't like the way it rang; it made her sound jealous of Jax's friendship with the Katermandian—which she was.

Sarissa considered punching Jones in the face. No, she would probably have to use some heavy blunt instrument to hurt him enough to get things started. In any case fighting him, as Jax had done, seemed to be the only way to get close to him.

Nemo Jones had been less well liked during his first year on Firebairn. For one thing, when he offered solutions to problems arising in the field, they were often bewilderingly irrelevant to the courses of action everyone else was debating—and just as often, they proved to be the best solutions. Combined with his curious solemnity and the definiteness of his opinions, this was an irritating pattern. And for another thing, while he obeyed most orders (though sometimes with an air of stoic compliance that subtly pronounced them stupid), he would every now and again immovably *refuse* an order. And not always a significant order—sometimes quite a routine one. But he could not be argued out of these strange fits of stubbornness and had spent quite a few weeks in the detention cubicle.

Senior staff had soon determined that his usefulness outweighed his recalcitrance and generally allowed him his quirks. And his fellow-colonists in general quickly worked out the same equation on the social level—but not before Jax Giggans, overhearing Jones refuse some commonplace order, had gotten "fed up with the hairy little primadonna." Helion had been the officer in charge and had allowed the fight.

Jax was bull-bodied, over six feet tall. He shaved his scalp, and his head looked like a battering ram. Jones was a handsbreadth shorter, and lighter by fifteen kilos. He was not unimpressive— lean, wide-shouldered, his knot-muscled arms roped with veins, hairy as a goat. But still the smaller man by far.

It was an eventful fight, though not a long one. Jax lost an upper canine, had his nose broken and a rib cracked, and received a multitude of astonishingly large and vivid bruises all over his body. He was a man of courage and picked himself up no less than four times, but he fell five.

Afterward, he would unabashedly describe the fight to anyone who asked. He told Nemo that anyone who could fight as hard as he could had to have good and sufficient reasons for whatever he did.

And there they were—friends now in a way that Jones was with no one else. Sarissa was not averse by temperament to punching Jones in the face, but was ruefully aware that in any case she wanted something more than Jax had with him. First she wanted his friendship, his respect, and then she wanted to mate with him. The crazy phrase was his own, for ironically Jones had first made his suit to her. Back then, before she had known what to make of him, she had rejected his grotesquely formal gestures of courtship. He had gone on, in his methodical way, to woo the more conventionally beautiful Penny Lopez— with a similar lack of success.

"We're approaching a likely entry point. Pilot-gunners belowdecks, please." Helion, ever official, used the intercom, though he might have spoken over his shoulder and been heard by all. Sari went below with her friends Angela and Norrin, to check the chemical balance of the quarry tanks and see to their harpoon guns. Nemo helped Jax lay out the field kits of the party's other weaponry while Orson Waverly and Japhet Sparks stood behind the captain, watching the terrain from the pilot's port.

Erosion had broadened a crack in the cone wall, creating a gravel-floored defile that could be reached by a few meters' climb from the desert floor. Helion stopped the sand-hog below the defile. "Reconnaissance party stand by to disembark," he said, again through the intercom. He thumbed a switch. The door coughed open and the gang ramp creaked outward, downward to the bright sand. He gave the controls to Penny, took his rifle from Jax, and preceded Jax and Nemo down the ramp. The three of them set out to reconnoiter.

The defile appeared more than adequate for the boats. Before they were halfway through it, they saw the lake: a vast, brilliant arena of water, steep-shored save for a small beach at the defile's foot. Near the water's center, perhaps two kilometers offshore, was a small craggy island.

"There's delph here. No doubt of it," Nemo muttered. As was often his way on unknown ground, he moved tautly, "ready to drop to all fours" as Sarissa had once expressed it. Helion disregarded him, but Jax looked at his friend with an air of inquiry, not so much for the remark as for an undertone of unease he had heard in it.

The boats' access assured, they climbed to the crown of the rim and moved along it. The island seemed to be a volcanic plug, an upwelling of magma that had succeeded the cone's formation by a long time, for it was far less eroded than the wall they stood on, to a degree for which the wall's shelter could not account. They had gone less than a mile when a deep cove in the island's flank was revealed.

"Shit," Jax growled in awe. The cove teemed with delphs, by far the biggest school the men had ever seen. Even at that distance, they didn't need the glasses to see the beasts—scores of them sunning in the shallows, their backs bulging above the water looking like a nestful of silver eggs, and scores more where the cove deepened, playing the leaping game of tag characteristic of the younger members of the species. Helion gazed in silent satisfaction. Nemo Jones said:

"There's something wrong with the way the water moves. Have you noticed it?"

The captain's face changed as if a sourness had touched his palate. Jax asked, "How do you mean? Where?"

"Out in midwater, this side of the island. Twice now it's looked jittery in a way the winds don't account for."

Helion sighed. "For God's sake, Jones. *Jittery?* There's some wind chop, a little swell, the sun dazzle . . . just what kind of ominous subtleties do you think you're seeing?"

"It *is* subtle, Captain, and it's not happening right now. But I've seen it twice since we've been up on the ridge here. Subtle but definite. At the least it means some kind of deep current."

"Jones, you may be sincere, but you are also compelled to concoct frontiersman's intuitions about even the most straightforward good luck. I've been watching the lake, and I saw nothing. What about you, Jax?"

"I can't say I did, but I don't make light of Nemo's eye for things."

"Nor do I make light of it, Jones. It'll go in the log if you wish. Meanwhile our job here seems strikingly clear to me, and I think we'd better get to it."

The Katermandian shrugged, staring not at the captain, but at the lake. "Maybe it's meaningless—how can I say? But it wasn't intuition. It's something I *saw*."

He didn't immediately follow the other two back toward the sand-hog. He watched the water a few minutes more, then tensed.

"Again," he murmured. "Yes, I see you. A convective eccentricity, from some magma vent? I think you're too erratic for that. . . ."

He spat on the ground for luck and hurried to catch up to the others.

The boats, moored at the little beach, rode the soft heave of the waters, their armor-glass cockpit bubbles flashing in the sun. The expeditioners stood on the shingle. Nemo squatted a bit apart from the group, watching the lake, meditatively grinding his rifle butt against the gravel. Captain Helion stood facing the other seven. His stance was more erect than usual, truculent, one might almost have said.

"Captain, I have to question this," Orson Waverly was saying. "If you make a special Command Override of it, naturally I'll obey, but it seems needlessly—"

"Needless, Waverly? We don't need delph roe? We don't need fresh breeding stock for the pens at base? Maybe we should radio home and have our surpluses destroyed. Perhaps we should just relax, have a swim, and go back."

"But, Captain," Jax said, "two boats or three—what's the differential?"

"You tell me the differential, Giggans. With three boats out there, we can dye the cove and drive damn near the whole school to shore in one sweep. With two, we might get a third at the first sweep, and then we could go back cruising and gunning all day and not get more than another third from the scatterers."

"But that's just it," Waverly said. "More than two-thirds of a school that size would put the hog near overload. With the tanks that full, half the live take could die on the ride home. It's roe we need more than meat."

Helion's proposal was a distinct departure from his normal style, undeniably unorthodox. Colony procedure was quite explicitly prescribed on this point: one fishing craft was to remain onshore at standby during any maneuver in unexplored environments. The captain's numerical assessment of the situation was not wrong. For a few minutes after a school had been blinded by a dye grenade, it was panicked enough to be moved en masse if the boats' ultrasonic pulsars could effectively bracket it with their crossfire. Here, three boats might handle it, but two could not. Meanwhile, blinded delphs rapidly reoriented to a sightless defensive pattern—sounded shallowly and dispersed—and individuals that eluded a first sweep would have to be painstakingly stalked and harpooned one by one.

But considering the probable yield of even the two-boat deployment, Helion's insistence on the three-boat plan was unreasonable—gluttonous. Waverly saw that his objection hadn't moved the captain, and he added:

"Listen, sir. I respectfully suggest that you're excited by the size of the find. You want to make a record catch. You're letting pride bend your judgment. I'm not rebuking—it's normal, healthy ambition, but—"

"Thank you, Waverly. Now that you've spit out your bit of malice, we'll proceed. We'll start in Formation Delta, assignments as follows. . . ."

Nemo Jones crouched silent throughout the briefing, somberly grinding his rifle butt against the sand. But as the group dispersed to their boats, he rose and touched Penny Lopez's shoulder.

"Penny, I want you to take special warning. The captain won't agree with this, but I think this lake is dangerous. It . . . smells wrong. I think you should stay especially alert."

Penny scowled. It was hard for anyone to blame her for shortness of temper. Jones had importuned her with his embarrassingly formal attentions long past the time when anyone else would have understood her answer to be an emphatic NO. She turned to Helion. "Captain, Armorer Jones reports a negative olfactory observation on reconnaissance. Should it be entered in the log?"

Perhaps Jones was finally starting to get the message—he sighed and turned away. Sarissa took the exchange less well than he did, though only her fellow-pilot Angela Rackham observed it. Sari was dark, slight, and lean—always tautly poised. Anger in her produced an almost visible vibration in this tautness, like a plucked string, and seeing this vibration now, Angela threw an arm across her shoulders and detained her furious departure with a brief, discreet hug.

"Hey. Sari. The sap's punctilious. He still thinks he's her official suitor! He's riding with you—why would he see the need to give you a warning?"

Sari shrugged off Angela's arm, uneasy over being so accurately understood—but then gave her a kiss before getting into her boat. She hated being splenetic and jealous like this, but she was getting intensely fed up with Jones's dense inability—or his peevish unwillingness?—to see that she'd thought him over and that she just might want him after all. When he and Japhet

Sparks climbed into their seats behind her, she thumbed shut the bubble with a bang and pulled out onto the water without a backward glance.

The three boats—domed ellipsoids—moved out in a triangular formation, sliding noiselessly across the water's softly breathing blue serenity. Their wakes were so slight they scarcely marred the waters, wherein the colossal wall containing them, all glossy carmine marbled with jet black, was repeated.

Japhet Sparks sat amidships, between Sarissa and Nemo. He had a true cartographer's love for physical creation, and he turned his bony face greedily upon the scene surrounding them.

"By God, look at it! I've never seen such a gorgeous lake. A marine vent for sure—probably along the magma vent at the root of that island. And talk about recent vulcanism—if that island's a day over ten million, I'll eat it. Oh, for a week to check it out with a lung!"

Without turning, Sarissa asked, "How does the water smell to you?"

Sparks grasped the allusion, but only granted the gibe an irritated shrug. Nemo stared at the back of their pilot's head. "I didn't say it in jest, Sarissa. What it meant I don't know, but—"

"You gave that stiff-necked bitch a special warning. What about *me*, you brainless idiot?"

At this point an impartial observer would probably have exonerated Jones from any charge of willful unawareness of Sari's changed feelings for him. Deep in the grotto of his shaggy beard and vine-thick hair, a glint of surprise lit his eyes' blackness. Unfortunately the hawk-nosed, fierce-eyed little woman was past noticing such subtleties at the moment. She was so infuriated by the plaintive sound of her own outburst that some extraordinary gesture of anger was now absolutely necessary to her to avoid a meltdown in her emotional circuits. (Sari Wayne had spent a few days in detention herself.) She jerked the joystick, launching their craft on a wide, extravagant excursionary curve away from their prescribed formation.

The island lay between them and their quarry-filled cove on its farther side. Her gesture didn't compromise their mission, though she knew that it was going to enrage Helion. Even so,

when his raging voice burst from the intercom, it angered her
further. She had been pulling back in, but now she cut even
more widely back out. Then with insolent leisure—rubbing
in the redoubled insubordination—she began a slow return to
formation, all the while enjoying Helion's furious diatribe in the
manner of a musical obbligato to her grand gesture.

When Jones moved, it took both her and Japhet Sparks completely by surprise. He sprang from the stern seat and dove for
the communicator, whose reply-switch he threw repeatedly,
signaling the captain that he wished to cut in.

Helion was ordering Sarissa to dock at the nearest shelving
of the island's shore, toward which he already had the other two
boats putting in, and there to yield her helm to Japhet. Nemo's
signals, far from inducing him to open the line, made him flood
it even more furiously.

But in Sarissa's boat he now went unregarded. Both she and
Japhet had just seen what Nemo had seen. With a moan of
horror she accelerated to catch up, zigzagging wildly as she did
so, trying to set up a watery commotion that would draw the
eyes of their friends behind them. The two lead boats were now
at half engine as they neared the island. And just astern of them,
a huge shape bulged beneath the surface of the lake.

It was not a turbulence, but a coherent pallid mass that glided
after the boats perhaps a fathom down in the water. Subtler, but
as horrific, was the wake it left—a greasy surface boil hundreds
of meters broad, bespeaking a bulk far vaster than was visible,
though that blurred globe was many times the size of all three
boats combined.

The two advance craft were scarcely a hundred meters from
the island, and their pursuer half as far behind them, when
Helion's boat accelerated explosively, a full-drive leap that should
have run it straight up onto the shoal. Instead, its thrust snagged
and slowed to the leaden crawl that shackles flight in nightmares.
Black grass sprouted from the water, engulfing both the boats.

Grass that writhed like snakes as it grew, meters high and
dense as on the lushest prairie—a medusa grass, dark as space,
its every fibril clutching and raking the air with a blind and busy
greed. Angela's boat was completely enmeshed, its stern cocked

high above the water, turned weightlessly in the shuddering weave as a bug is turned by the spider wrapping it. Helion's boat, however, was gradually tearing shoreward from the net, whose grip its burst of speed had half foiled.

And now Sarissa had reached them. At ninety knots she swerved obliquely to the uncanny meadow and plowed across its fringe. A shock wave, as of pain, rolled through the field. Helion's boat lurched free, roared through the shallows and plunged, spraying sparks, up onto the island. Sarissa's drive had slowed to fifteen knots before she herself fought free into the shoals that fringed the isle and which the monstrous growth had not invaded. She swung parallel to the shore and tucked the boat into an inlet.

The colonists jumped from their vessels and gathered on the shore. Jax and Nemo broke out the rifles, but those they gave them to held them helplessly, standing in a rapture of horror, watching the struggle. Then, near the meadow's center, the pale bulb rose and swelled up from the water.

It was a titanic eye—a transparent orb of gold, intricately veined within, the pupil a scarlet rhomboid into which five sandhogs could have driven abreast. Deep in the yellow ichor, black shapes moved, whole constellations of them swarming through the kelplike jungle of veins; while outside the globe, round its base, a collar of huge tonguelike tentacles stirred, stretched, and licked the air. With cyclopean sloth the whole orb rolled within this tentacular calyx and aimed the red vent of its pupil upon the captured boat.

And now a dreadful purpose entered the action of the fibrils. Variously, testingly, they turned and tilted the craft, probing and caressing it in every orientation. There was a grinding noise. As a man might open a jar, the creature twisted off the boat's cockpit bubble, inverted and shook its hull. Norrin and, a moment later, Angela Rackham tumbled down into the black seethe. The fibrils heaved and catapulted the boat away. It crashed on the island's shore.

All that the watchers did was as a dream. Jax and Nemo pumped explosive shot against every part of the eye and its corolla. The grenade slugs produced only negligible tatterings of its gelatinous substance. Sarissa struggled to free a coil of harpoon line from the wrecked boat's equipment locker, while Helion and Penny helped Sparks lift Orson Waverly—the only surviving occupant of the captured boat—from the space beneath the control panel where he had wedged himself and where he now lay bleeding and comatose. But all these were ghostly acts, performed in stupefaction, while every man and woman did but one thing—watch Norrin and Angela, and the thing that had them.

The black meadow undulated still, but less chaotically, with an insistent peristaltic surge that brought the victims toward the eye. Like castaways caught in a hideous slow surf, they struggled in the snakish multibrachiate grip—clutched, stroked, raised, and dipped, but always eased inexorably nearer the eye. The colonists saw now Norrin's arm clawing sunward, festooned with serpents, now Angela's back and shoulders, bucking to wrench her head free of the nauseous swell.

The tentacles nearest the victims began an obscene elongation, till finally two of them plunged down and plucked the captives free. Swinging them high, the tentacles brought the women inward and poised them above the alien pupil, which moved below, as with a savoring gaze. The tentacles uncoiled. The women plunged into the red vent and sank kicking down within the golden ichor.

In the eye blink of their vanishing through that red chasm, they entered another world and were transformed to different beings. Drifting down they came within the eye, dancing the drowning agony in a tempo surreally slow, an almost comic pantomime of life's wrenching-free from its frame. Their faces and limbs were bloated, corrupt of color in the amber light. Angela's hair bannered wantonly, slow-motion, while those on the island could see her eyes—black holes in a gape-jawed mask—aimed downward on the swarming deep she sank to. Webbed veins, huge crooked roots now partly screened their fall, which showed in glimpses as the overall organic movement within the eye began to boil with a new energy.

Those on the island watched what followed with an amazement so complete it looked like rapture. At one point, responding no doubt to some impulse to avert his own eyes (though he never did so), Nemo Jones cried out:

"Don't look away! Remember details! We've got to know it to kill it."

His companions needed these exhortations as little as Nemo himself did. Forgetting even to attend to Waverly's serious head injury, they watched as if the universe and all time contained no other thing to see. And there were many details to be remembered.

The group sat in a circle around the camp's field stove. Helion sat closest to its light, more visible, more erect, than the others. But there was less pride of rank in his posture than an air of pained self-presentation, as if in response to a tacit charge lodged against him by the others slouched tiredly in the shadows. He had been arguing with Nemo for the last five minutes. Throughout, his normal inflexibility had been accompanied by an uncharacteristic calm. Now he shook his head definitively, rejecting in the gesture not only all the Katermandian had said, but all that he might say. When he spoke, it was formally, his eyes sweeping the whole group by way of preface.

"You will all, as a body, formally depose me and place me under arrest, to which I willingly accede, or you will do this as I prescribe, and with the personnel I have designated. There is no more to say, Jones. Take it or leave it."

The Katermandian squatted on his hams. The light escaping the shadow pools over his eyes was baleful, and this the captain saw; but it was also—and this Helion did not see—compassionate. He set his words out carefully:

"Listen, I beseech you, Captain. You have all the good of pride, as well as the bad of it. You want to atone for our danger, but you've done no real wrong. If you've been foolish, why, everyone's a fool! I've been one thousands of times—it's a wonder I'm alive! It's my plan. Do you want to throw on me the guilt of having someone else take the risk of it? You *know* that Jax and I are our best swimmers. . . ." He gestured awkwardly, breaking off. He read his failure in the captain's sour smile before he heard the man's answer.

"The plan was yours. The log already so witnesses. Our need for it, our predicament here, is wholly my doing, and the log testifies this as well. My decision is as before."

Nemo stood up. He nodded and stepped out of the circle. The wind was freshening, but he left the shelter of the hollow they had camped in and climbed up to the island's saw-toothed crest and found himself a seat overlooking the delph cove, some hundred meters below. He had not been there long when his fellow-armorer joined him. They sat in silence for a while, watching the stars in the molten black mirror of the lake.

"After we fought—remember?" Jax said smiling. "When I said you had good and sufficient reasons for doing things your own way? I was taking that on faith, just because you could fight so well. Well, now I know I was right. I could've sat down for a solid year and never come up with anything like this plan of yours."

"Jax." Nemo clamped a hand on his friend's arm, as if he had been waiting for this opening. "I'm having bad second thoughts. I'm afraid of this plan now. I think it will fail, if Helion goes. You have to dig your heels in—refuse to go unless you're teamed with me. He has no hunch-nerves. He's brave, but he has no *luck*. Your dissension would have more weight with him than anyone's. Force him to use me."

Jax was smiling, shaking his head. "What a storm of words! You're turning downright chatty lately. I'm sorry, Nemo. I know what you mean about his luck. But if he's denied this chance to redeem himself, it'll break him. He'll be good for nothing after this. And I've always liked the poor stiff-neck."

"Shit." Nemo said this mournfully, looking now more directly below their perch to the cove. Only eyes that had watched the school at dusk, when the beasts found berths in the fissures of the shore and emptied their flotation sacs to sink to their rest, could have found them now in the moonlight—vague torpedoes of silver just under the heave of the black water.

He scowled at them. The austere disapproval of his expression might have been that of some creating deity gravely displeased with what he had wrought. It was Firebairn and its unique biogenerative forces that had made the delphs, of course; Nemo had made only an escape plan that enlisted them.

He looked again at Jax, his eyes bitter, refusing to reiterate his request, but also refusing to withdraw it. For answer, his brawny friend turned his face, wryly, to the island's northern quarter, where all explanation of the morrow's insanity lay.

It looked like an immense planktonic toadstool now, the pale orb still exposed, though half sunk from its former elevation. The field of cilia was similarly contracted. Only the tips of the tendrils showed, bristling the moon-polished waters, a field of thorns. The two men stared at the thing for a long time.

"It *is* watching us," Jax said, speaking his decision in the debate that both had pursued internally. All useful speculations had long ago been traded, mutual conjecture exhausted. "So huge it is, and so sharply *aware.* . . ."

"It had to be Orson blinded," Nemo mourned. "Something this big—it has to be marine, from up this vent. If we knew how it worked, there might be. . . ."

"Be what?"

Nemo shrugged helplessly. "Who's that?" Someone was climbing toward them.

"Sari," the pilot-gunner answered, choosing her handholds on the crag as easy and sure as someone gathering shells from a level beach. "Orson's fully conscious," she told them. "He took some broth. He wants us all to have a talk while the captain is still asleep." Nemo heard the shade of pity in this—Sarissa usually called him "Helion." They followed her back down to the camp.

It was past midnight when Captain Helion was wakened. Jax and Japhet told him the group's proposal. Any innovative consensus among his subordinates could now only strike the exhausted man as veiled mutiny. He gave Jax an *et tu, Brute* look, and stared disgustedly into the glowing coils of the camp stove.

"It's clear you'll all do what you want. Kindly trouble me with no further parades of obedience. Spend the time any way you please between now and tomorrow."

"No! Someone bring me out to him. Captain!"

As surprised as Helion, Jax turned to help Sarissa and Nemo carry Orson Waverly's camp chair into the center of the circle. The biologist's eyes were bandaged. Some few tears of blood had escaped the bandages and tracked his cheeks.

"Captain?" The face scanned, hunting a voice-fix on Helion.

"I'm here, Waverly."

"Listen, Captain. Don't slacken now. Give us strictness here, where we need it. This will have to be a systematic information-pooling, using the log. Make it official to make it strict. This thing is epochs ahead of us in its adaptation to this world. We had better evolve a very sharp and efficient group mind to fight it with, and do it pretty damn fast, or else we're all going to die, and you've seen how we're going to die."

The captain rose to the occasion, but only just. He nodded. "Wake me when it's my turn." He went back to his bed.

It was almost dawn. Nemo and Orson Waverly sat by the stove. Everyone else was asleep. Waverly had just turned off the log, which he'd had on playback, and now he sighed. The two men's ears still rang with all the perplexities the tape had woven round their weary minds.

"Dear God, Nemo. What I wouldn't give for an *image* of the thing, a five-second look at it to give me a nice solid, detailed picture. I'm awash in all these words. My brain is a knot, and all I'm visualizing is a cartoon, a caricature."

"So give it back to me—this caricature."

Waverly sighed deeply. "Two distinct groups of carnivores, patrolling the interior of a huge transparent sphere. The sphere also contains thick growths of kelp. The kelp is rooted in a layer of basal muck that floors the sphere, and the two breeds of cruising carnivores—I see them as sharks and squids—are also rooted in that muck, or at least connected to it by long slender flexible tethers of translucent material, sort of like delicate umbilici that issue from their caudal extremities and trail down behind them to the floor of the sphere."

"Mmmm. What's kelp, and what are sharks and squids?"

When Waverly had explained these terrene forms, Nemo granted the general accuracy of the caricature. "Of course," the biologist went on, "the things you've all described have more tentacles than squids, and a greater variation in tentacle size, and the others, except for the teeth, sound as much like delphs as they do like sharks. . . . You know, I find myself wondering about those tethers. Both groups in constant restless movement—even the ones still waiting their turn to feed—and all that dense growth in there. What kept those caudal umbilici of theirs from getting tangled, snagged—even breaking?"

"Orson! Yes! Now that you say it, I remember I saw exactly that. One of those squids, while they were all circulating, waiting their turn, as you say. . . Nemo paused fractionally here, and Waverly's head lowered—remembering two young women, full of life. "Its tether snagged on a kelp stalk. I think it sensed it—it instantly reversed itself. But not in time, and the tether broke. It stopped cold, and then corkscrewed straight down to the bottom, and I lost sight of it. Actually it's amazing that didn't happen more often. But then their movements were so intricately patterned, so fluid. . . ."

Waverly said nothing, pursuing some thought, and Nemo sat motionless—like cupped hands cherishing a young flame to life within their stillness. But at length the biologist sighed again.

"I keep thinking their tethers could be some sort of alimentary connection with the larger structure containing them. But how could such an important pipeline be so delicate? The whole feeding relationship of the parts to the whole—I'm damned if I can get a handle on it. I want to hear Japhet again."

Nemo keyed up Japhet's testimony from the log. They skimmed through the first few minutes of it, seeking the juncture Waverly wanted. In the snatches of Japhet's voice they heard his anguish, slightly miniaturized by the reduced volume. Angela and Norrin had been well loved by all, and not least by Japhet. Then the biologist nodded, Nemo turned it up, and they listened. First Waverly's voice:

"OK, Japhet. Now let's move to what happened to them on the inside."

"They were still alive—kicking and fighting, but slower moving than you'd expect. Bloating, I think. Swelling a little— like maybe those fluids in there were some kind of enzymes? When they'd sunk to the top of all that . . . seaweed, those first things hit them. Fish-shaped, big saw-toothed mouths. Black eyeknobs set in stripe patterns—a little like delph eyes except for their having so many of them.

"Anyway, they hit them first. Started tearing chunks out of them. Swarmed on them thick as ants, till they looked like just two wriggling clusters of them. Their blood . . ." The ghost of a groan was recorded here ". . . their blood came out in clouds. Like smoke. It hid what went on."

"I'm sorry, Japhet." Now Waverly's mouth made wry corners at the feebleness of his own apology. "Did they keep sinking as they were being fed on?"

"Not much. The feeding activity buoyed them up. And then all those things broke away. Pretty suddenly. For a couple seconds their . . . remains just hung there, then started sinking again. Then the other things—"

"I'm sorry, Japhet, but I need you to tell me just how much—"

"All the flesh gnawed off!" It was a burst of rage evading intolerable pain. "All the skin, major muscle. Just skeletons, held intact by scraps of tendon, ligament. Some of the larger internal organs left . . ."

"So then the others fed? And they were just as numerous?"

"Yes."

"So you've all said. You must forgive my putting it like this. I have to. But this arrangement seems to leave so small a share to feed on to this multibrachiate group."

There was a silence before Japhet answered, not loudly. "I meant yes, they were just as numerous. But I don't think they were *feeding* on them at all. It was more like they embraced them, and clung in a slightly pulsating way. Because Norrin's face, I remember . . . most of it . . . was left intact by those first things. Then the second ones covered her face, like a fur of wiggling feelers—and yet there she still was, looking out at me, when those octopoid ones cleared away."

And now Orson and Nemo sat surrounded by the same kind of silence that could be heard on the tape. During that silence the biologist groped his hand across the log's keys and cut it off before the catechism continued. After a moment he raised both his hands to adjust his blood-crusted bandage, resettling it gingerly against his maimed eyes. When he had done this, he let out the pain of the maneuver in one long breath.

"It may be that they're detritivores—the tentacled things.

You all report organic debris in the basal muck—the trash-heaped hard parts of larger, presumably bathic, prey. Yet none of you saw the squids penetrating the muck. On the other hand, both Helion and Penny saw sharks down there penetrating the muck—sharks, already amply nourished by their lion's share of prey.

"I'm done for the night, Nemo. Right now my brain is a goddamned square wheel. I can't get any kind of interpretation *moving*. It's stupefying, this bizarre complexity. The field of prey-snaring cilia, the central mouthed dome of intestinal structures, surrounded by a calyx of major cilia—there are pseudo-coelenterates they've found over at Base Two that have these features. They're littoral-benthic-zone dwellers—one meter across at the biggest, goddamn it, and with nothing like this kind of endosomatic complexity. There might be bathic varieties that are bigger, but the things are sensorially impoverished; slow, groping, tactile hunters. You say this thing tracked our boats toward the island and is now hemming us in, dodging laterally to catch any move we try to make from shore. This thing sees or smells or hears or all three. Monstrous. Incomprehensible. I need more medicine. I need some sleep. Maybe the answer will come in a dream. But I'll give you one thing to dream on, Nemo. If this thing does in some way follow the model of those little pseudo-coelenterates they've found—if it hangs proportionally deep in the water and is able to expand as broadly in the lateral dimension—then its tail end hangs down into this lake for at least half a kilometer, and its field of cilia is able to hug this island's whole perimeter, or damn near it, in its loving embrace.

"Take me to my cot, Nemo, and God help us all. Helion and Jax are going to die tomorrow. I'm sorry, but this seems to me a simple fact. I've told them what I'm telling you, but I couldn't change their minds. So I say to you now, brutal though it is—choose vantage points from which you can see down into this thing from all possible angles. Have the log's microphone run out on an extension, and issue field glasses. When our friends die, I want it to pay off with every scrap of sight and sound that can be gotten out of it. If Polyphemus takes their lives, it's going to betray itself to us in the process. Wake me an hour after dawn, and don't fail me. By the time they set out, I'll have a list of specific questions I want answered and some final arrangements I want made."

Just after dawn, Sarissa Wayne climbed to the ridgetop where Jax and Nemo had sat the night before. She settled down and watched the preparations, already well along, being made in the delph cove below. She and Penny had begun them. The roll of metallic net that each craft carried had been taken from its spool in the stern of Sarissa's boat and brought over to the cove. One end of it was anchored to the cove's southern spur, and then she and Penny had swum it across the cove mouth.

They had made marvelously silent work of it, and only partly for fear of waking the delphs, which Jax and Helion were already edging up on with the tranquilizer guns. Polyphemus—this was what Waverly, without explanation, had bitterly dubbed their persecutor the night before—Polyphemus had already demonstrated how swiftly it could pour itself around the island's perimeter. The previous afternoon the colonists had done some experimenting. They had driven Helion's boat—only slightly damaged—to the opposite side of the island, choosing a launching spot more than four hundred meters upshore from Polyphemus's visible limit of extension. They detached its harpoon winch, anchored this ashore, and tethered the boat to its cable. They set it on autopilot with just enough fuel in the tanks for a few hundred meters' run. It was making thirty-five knots within the first four seconds of its launching and was snared by the giant's sudden-sprouting tendrils less than seventy meters offshore.

The capture was not resisted—cable was paid out as the titan wrestled its prey toward its central orb. But the craft never reached that organ. Well before the cilia had brought it within the grasp of the larger feeding-tentacles, they froze, still gripping it. A few seconds later they flung it into the air and, by the time it had struck the water, had vanished from beneath it. The colonists hauled the boat ashore, feeling themselves, if potentially wiser, no less baffled and terrified.

Swimming in the black predawn waters with this recollection of the giant's speed, its inscrutable responsiveness, had been the closest thing to a lived nightmare in Sarissa's experience. Her legs could still feel that ticklish expectancy of Polyphemus's caustic, sticky first touch. Her heart still remembered its terrifying, clamoring haste, and her shoulder muscles their springsteel readiness through every second it had taken to string the barricade.

But her mind was now wholly detached from these bodily memories. It was not the scene below that so distracted her. The tranquilizer darts used on captured delphs to prevent their panicking and crushing one another during their transport in cages to the sand-hog had paralyzed six of the creatures in the cove. The men had collared them with cable in two trios, staggered so that the middle delph of each trio was positioned half a length in advance of its flanking fellows. The trios had been tethered to shore, and though the beasts were just waking and getting restive, Jax and Helion were able to slip into the undercarriages they had rigged and test their fit. Their boot heels were just visible through the water, kicking for purchase under the tails of the delphs. Their recirculating respiration packs made no more than a faint boil in the water, and this the delphs' motion, once they were goaded forward, would obliterate.

Sarissa's own life, and those of all the others, depended on this grotesque rehearsal, which did not alter her staring inattention. Her preoccupation was elsewhere, its focus revealed when her eyes narrowed at Nemo Jones's reappearance in the cove. He came down from the knoll that flanked it, where he had been helping Japhet make the two harpoon-gun emplacements she had requested the evening before. He went straight to Penny Lopez, who was working on a release mechanism for rolling back a segment of the cove barrier when it was time for Jax and Helion to make their sortie. Whatever Nemo said to Penny caused her to straighten and face him.

He talked to her for perhaps a minute, and when, with a queer formal bow, he left her, Sarissa's eyes didn't merely fail to follow him—they refused to. Thereafter, she didn't watch anything in particular so much as she avoided watching that sector of the crag that lay between herself and the point from which Nemo had left her view.

"Sarissa. Sarissa. I have something important to say. Will you talk with me?" The question seemed necessary to Nemo, as she had not looked up when he saluted her. Still not looking, she said:

"Whether or not I'll talk to you depends on what you have to tell me."

Nemo nodded at this and sat down at a discreet distance from her so she would not have to strain to keep him out of her field of vision. He looked at the sky a minute before saying, "I've just given Penny Lopez my apologies and told her I was withdrawing my suit for her. To disappoint a woman is always grave, so no lying should go with it. I confessed to her—"

Sarissa snorted, shook her head, and, visibly in spite of herself, began to laugh. Nemo looked at his knees and waited humbly. Sarissa had to make several attempts before she could speak her retort:

" 'To disappoint a woman is always grave.' Nemo, I swear to you. I was watching your exchange with her. After you walked away from her, that poor woman literally jumped into the air and clicked her heels together. If she doesn't live another day, if none of us do, she'll at least have that last day in peace. She's *never* wanted you."

"I agree her feelings are mixed. But I have never entirely displeased her. Once I had stated my case to her, last summer, she became sarcastic and piquish to me. Some of this is a kind of coquetry, for which a woman must be forgiven, as it is a natural defense against capture. But she started out—"

"What did you confess to her?"

"She started out not entirely disliking me. I confessed to her that the woman I first chose, first desired—that I did not pay suit to this woman only because she *did* entirely dislike me, and though I am not fainthearted, it's a fool that sets out hunting impossible quarry."

Sarissa looked at him now. She studied him with wrath, perplexity, relish. "What was this woman's name, this first choice of yours? This select soul, this feminine paragon, this august personage who merited Nemo Jones's initial designation as his mate? Bless my ears with this pearl's name."

"Sari Wayne."

She sat there, grinning a grin of sardonic vindication, nodding slowly, the picture of one who bitterly acknowledges an idiocy she has long struggled with.

"Me. Right. And I remember your first tender gesture. No! I put that too weakly! Your first tender gesture lives—writhes!—vivid as a flame, before my mind's eye."

New movement down in the cove distracted them momentarily. Helion and Jax had begun to goad their "mounts" through some elementary paces. They did not use the sonic pulsars designed for delph herding—all too probably detectable by Polyphemus—but small electric prods that Jax had improvised. The method seemed to be working, though it produced an uncharacteristically jerky movement in the beasts. The sun's edge kindled on the eastern crater rim. Sarissa and Nemo faced each other again. She resumed reminiscingly, mocking the tone of a tale-teller:

"It was that enormous hydra I harpooned on Gamma. A superlative shot, I do confess! But not like your thirty-meter dive from the ringwall! Nor your herculean amputation of the major tentacle—even as it thrashed in its titanic death-throes. Being upstaged like that was not enough, of course. You had to drag the amputated member to me afterward. Everyone relaxing, having a sunset drink, rehashing a fine day's work . . . and up you come, toppling people left and right, blindly tripping them up behind you with the drag of the reeking obscenity you hauled! I, who run from nothing, nor no man alive, fled!"

"It was a declaration!" The Katermandian's tone was both coaxing and exasperated in equal measure. "Embarrassment is for those who do routine work and scorn excessive notice! But love is . . . drama! Excess is . . . called for! Such marksmanship was once-in-a-million marksmanship! Could I do less and fitly show my love? I *meant* you to laugh at me, then *hug* me! Courtship's comedy! Was I supposed to smirk and laugh? I did it for your entertainment."

Sarissa had what in an earlier era had been called the Aha Experience. Why, she asked herself, were women so slow to identify irony or deadpan humor in men? Obviously, she answered, because they unavoidably deemed men to be a little dimmer than they sometimes were in fact. She gave a long sigh.

"Well, that may be true," she admitted—both to what he had said and to what she had thought—"but you're still a miserable idiot. Embarrass them enough and anyone will run. But after that you should have seen how I came to feel. I want you to pay suit to me, and love me, and make love to me, and not to anyone else. Now hasn't that been plain enough, you fucking backwoods dolt? And whether it has or not, well, what about it? Here and now, once and for all."

Nemo nodded energetically, but though his mouth opened, nothing came out of it. Apparently, this ardent inarticulacy conveyed an answer to Sarissa that she found satisfactory. She wrapped her arms around his waist and pressed her face against his chest. He held her, looking over her head toward the sunrise, and clearer than the happiness his face showed was his amazement. All in his world had been craft, the stalking, second-guessing, and teasing-out of quarry from the hostile complexities of its habitat. To have Sarissa, whom he had thought irreversibly inimical to him, holding him with such single-mindedness, was to him in the nature of a prodigy. It was as if, in his native rain forest, an archidand—that wily, toothsome biped, splendid-winged and brazen-taloned—had leapt from its cover in the dense warp-vine and sparx and—far from dodging away with invisible speed—had ambled up to the astonished hunter and dipped its head to nuzzle at his hand. The pair did not notice the two figures approaching them until they were in speaking distance and one of them, Japhet Sparks, hailed them.

Sparks was leading Orson Waverly. The lovers broke their embrace—not out of shame, but from a chilling of their hearts. They knew Waverly's errand. Sarissa helped him to a seat. She, Nemo, and Japhet—all those who must be Waverly's eyes— now looked only at him, not down toward the cove, not at each other.

"I've already briefed Penny. I wanted to do it while they were still in the water. They know what I'm doing and approve, but it's pointless to sicken them with the sight of my actually doing it. So let's be quick. The captain will be assembling us for his own briefing in a little while, as soon as he and Jax make some last adjustments to their undercarriages. Sarissa?"

"Here, Orson."

"The guns from Helion's and Angela's boats are set up. Japhet's wound double cable on the winches and got the guns anchored where you wanted them. Give them both the field glasses, Japhet. Hang these around your necks now. Get them focused for Polyphemus immediately you take up your positions. I want you on the knoll across the beach from Sarissa's, Nemo—Japhet has it worked out. You'll be on the other side of the thing from her and almost as high above it. Penny and Japhet will be shoreside, watching it from different angles. They'll both have mikes we've rigged to the log. I want to get any sound any of us makes correlated with a running account of its moves. We want all its behavior, and every possible synchronicity of that behavior with what happens around it.

"Because of course we can't assume it sees, just because it looks to us like an eye. It twisted our boat open like—someone unstoppering a specimen bottle. But it could have felt organic presences inside vibrationally, electrochemically—we just don't know. I'd been jammed in under the panel, and it missed me. It makes me think the thing does see, and my invisibility to it saved me. If it does, I don't think Jax and Helion have a prayer.

"Here are my specific questions. First and foremost, how precisely does it track us? Every detail of its behavior that we can correlate with any detail of its *prey's* behavior—" Waverly's mouth moved speechlessly a few times. He resumed more quietly. "If we can relate these two spheres of activity in any new way, we may get a key to how to dodge it. Killing it seems to me as good as impossible. Nevertheless, it *has* occurred to me that if we understood its feeding mechanism, we could conceivably poison it. Its whole alimentary setup is one of the things that confuses me most. These quasi-independent packs. By the time they're through with the prey, it's just a carcass, seventy percent reduced in volume, that drifts down to the base of the orb. If they are highly articulated organelles, if they are the digestive apparatus itself, how are they transmitting the nutrients they absorb to the macro-organism? These threadlike breakable tethers seem ludicrously unlikely as transport ducts for nutrients of such bulk. If they are not transferring the nourishment, then Polyphemus itself must be a kind of huge detritivore, nourished by the sharks' and squids' carrion leavings. But then why the gross volumetric disproportion? Why does Polyphemus get forty percent, at most, of every kill, and these . . . predacious saprophytes sixty or more? What service to the whole rates that big a part of the take?

"But to test this, study the basal areas all you can—Sarissa and Nemo especially. That's why I've got you high. Look for . . . feeding debris, its relation to the inner landscape of Polyphemus. What's the structure down there? If motile, how does it behave? Japhet and Penny will be studying the packs more particularly, but I want all of you to be constantly checking the whole, trying to catch overall gestalts of movement, responsiveness and what stimulates it.

"With the squids and sharks, two specific things interest me. Watch for waste excretion in any form. They could be using a selective fraction of their intake and be producing usable wastes that Polyphemus absorbs. Second: you all seemed to be in agreement that the squids didn't appear to consume nearly as much as the sharks, if indeed they actually *fed* at all. Precisely what were they doing? Study that closely.

"That's it. As far as productive guesses go, I've got next to nothing to offer at this point. This thing is completely incredible. God help us to think effectively together, because, so far, I am truly in the dark."

Midmorning on Firebairn is, next to sunset, its most golden hour. The jumbled colors of the igneous wastes blaze, melt, smolder, under the sky's brilliance as if the land were still in its molten nativity. And in this particular place the young sun kindled a special jewel even more dazzling than the vast ringwall or the waters contained by it. As Nemo climbed the knoll assigned him, he looked upon that jewel with loathing and wonder. Within the sphere of lustrous amber, the patrolling packs wove their own distinct colors through the black-and-purple jungle. Those that Waverly called "sharks" were especially striking.

Their torpedo bodies had streaks of pigmentation that flashed iridescent as the things cruised through the filtered sunlight. Nemo thought of the cove—invisible to him now beyond the ridge Sarissa stood on—from which he had just come. Helion, grim and businesslike, had turned directly from the briefing to the water and slipped under, snuggling himself out of sight beneath his harnessed beasts. But Jax had paused by the brink so that Nemo could take his hand. Nemo had said:

"Lucky fellow. In an hour you'll be in the sand-hog, radioing air rescue."

The big man had smiled, glanced at the binoculars hanging against the fur on the Katermandian's chest, drawing their owner's eyes upon them, filling his heart with wretchedness. But Jax had grinned:

"That's right. Use these, and when I climb ashore you can see me waving to you."

Nemo had reached his position, but before he signaled to Sarissa, he looked down on their enemy. He pressed his clenched fist against his chest, which is the way the hunters of Katermand take oaths, and he said:

"Hear me, Polyphemus. My name is Nemo. Nemo Jones. And I am going to rip the life right out of you. We together will find the way, but it's me that's going to do it to you."

He raised his arm and signaled to the short, slight figure manning the guns on the next knoll over. Even as he had turned his eyes away, a detail had snagged at their periphery. He caught up his glasses and trained them on the orb, at a point deep within the anchorings of the kelp.

Sarissa hesitated. Japhet, Penny, Nemo—all were stationed now, but for a moment she found herself unable to pass on the go-ahead to the cove. She checked the welded cable moorings Japhet had rigged for the guns and for the third time reassured herself that the crag she stood on would break before they did. She looked down into the cove, where Orson waited for her word, the barrier-gate's pull-cord in one hand. Jax and Helion held their beasts ready—not near the gate, but by the shore of the inlet, for before they emerged themselves they would drive

out a large part of the school ahead of them and thereafter keep
as many of these as possible around them as they penetrated the
dangerous waters offshore.

The delphs had swum unmolested past Polyphemus; some
of them had even cruised through its peripheral field of cilia.
It was one of the first observations they had made the previous
afternoon, once some measure of organization had succeeded
their initial trance of horror. The plan had seemed good. Now,
without any of Waverly's biological training to reinforce her
pessimism, she felt a gloom as deep as his. It was not going
to work. It would fail because Sarissa now had everything to
lose—not just her life, but Nemo as well. Whenever the heart
prayed entirely for luck, that was when luck failed. She cupped
her hands by her mouth and, in a tone scarcely louder than con-
versational, said:

"Now."

Orson, seventy meters below, pulled the cord. When Jax and
Helion saw the opening, they launched prearranged converging
drives on the gate that cut out about two-thirds of the school
and herded it before them. "Close it," Sarissa said. Orson relaxed
his grip on the cord and let the gate spring back. If the sortie
failed, its survivors would need food.

The shepherding of a protective screen of free-swimming
delphs did not start well. The trios were bulky enough to exert a
local dominance on their unharnessed fellows, but too awkward
of movement to work the group as a whole into any formation.
As the teams edged past the sheltering horn of the cove, the
school began to dissolve before them, individuals and couples—
gamesome with the unpent tensions of their confinement—dispersing swiftly. Sarissa watched the two men's cover bleeding
away, branching out into the lake in quick, silvery trickles. She
ground her teeth and looked to Polyphemus.

The giant was half the island away—the knoll she stood on
walled off the cove from its vision, if vision it had. And with
the captain and Jax angling sharply away from the giant as they
penetrated the open waters, they would be three-quarters of
the island's length distant from it before the shoreline ceased to
mask them. It was not conceivable that two men, the subtlest

shadows of men, really, clinging to the undersides of living screens twice their size, could be detected at such a range. And still Sarissa groaned at the steady shrinkage of the school. As the lure of open water grew stronger, the clumsy goading of the two trios came to seem itself a force of dispersal, an irritation even the nearer members of the school began to flee.

And then it seemed the two men abandoned the attempt to herd the rest of the school and began to make smoother progress outward. They were already a hundred meters offshore, and she watched them make the next fifty as quickly as they had that first stage. As if in illustration of her thoughts about luck, a fair-sized cluster of delphs, uncoerced now, cohered, and stayed just ahead of the escapees.

Sarissa realized that for perhaps the last full minute, the men had been out in the zone of Polyphemus's unimpeded survey. Her head snapped round toward the colossus. The swarming globe was as before—though perhaps a shade farther out from its sector of the shore? She swung her eyes back to the two little silver blurs, the escaping trios, but even before she focused on them she had swept her gaze halfway back toward Polyphemus. Out there, between the monster and the hidden men, some hundred and fifty meters offshore from where she stood, a narrow boil of movement scarred the water. It was the surface track of an underwater thrust whose rate was perhaps thirty knots, and precisely aimed to intercept the trios.

Sarissa stepped over to the gun whose emplacement commanded the coveward sector of the water, kicked up the muzzle for a long shot, and trained it on the spot where the surface scar and the delph trios would impact. Touching the gun, which always calmed her, helped little—her heart was all hollowness and terror. The two men must have seen what was approaching them. The trios veered sharply about three seconds before it struck, and the water all around them sprouted Polyphemus's viperous cilia. Within another two seconds, she had already fired her first shot.

It was well over two hundred meters, at the very limit of the harpoon's effective striking power. Only her elevation made it even feasible. The line's silver arc sang out and down. She held her breath, as she always unconsciously did when she feared to disturb the plunge of a long shot that she already knew, as soon as it had left the cannon, was good. The medusa-tangle had meanwhile gripped the lead trio and propped the silver beasts upward, like three bright tombstones against the sun, while other cilia worked for what was under them. It was the delicate, discriminating motion of a man lifting a trapdoor to pluck something out from beneath it. The line's arc crumpled, shuddered through its 220-meter length as the spear impacted, transfixing the lead delph of the trio. With one hand Sarissa flicked on the automatic winch, and the line pulled straight— one puny machine engaging Polyphemus in a tug-of-war. Her other hand had already re-aimed the gun.

The second trio, while equally entangled, was not held so clear as the first. She fired and knew in the instant of doing it the shot was bad. She writhed through the seconds' wait before she could fire again. From under the trio she had hit, a struggling weave of cilia and human limbs fought its way round to the backs of the beasts. A snake-wrapped arm sought and seized the shaft of the harpoon.

"Yes!" Sarissa screamed. "That's it! Climb the line!" Her second shot dove short of its mark. The instant the cable had ceased to pay out and cleared the feed-out spools, she fired again, and again knew she had it. A tremendous expectancy filled her. To beat this titanic enemy, rob it—never had she felt that the delicate geometry, the fleet calculus of her art, an art of parabolas and pin-sharp steel points, could achieve so much. Far away, a tiny Laocoön, the man wrestled half his body onto his trio's backs, having to fight the panicked heave of the beasts as well as the great leeches woven round his frame. It was Jax. His shaven head, stripped of its respiration helmet, fought clear. Now he had the shaft by both hands.

Her third shot struck, and she winched in the line. As it taut-ened, she saw the trio come loose and thrash freely against its pull—utterly untethered by any cilia. She knew in that sicken-ing instant what she would shortly see—*did* see seconds later: Helion's struggling shape making the now-familiar storm-heaved progress through the black tentacular field, passed from cilium to cilium, moving Eye-ward—for now a field of that black grass sprouted in a long swath, a pathway back to Polyphemus.

Sarissa howled with rage and concentrated furiously on the one she might save. Switching to her magazine of untethered harpoons, she began to pump them down upon the zone surrounding Jax, hoping to scythe down just enough cilia to give him a fighting chance.

And the armorer fought indeed against the giant—himself a giant of relentless will, his big muscles sharp-cut in the morning light with the strain. His struggle had tilted the trio toward him, and he had worked his grip up to the harpoon line itself. Sarissa's shots rained around him, as close as she dared put them, and suddenly it seemed he had several fewer cilia round his chest. He surged up, working two handspans higher up the line—but the cilia had not withdrawn, merely shifted their grip to his shoulders. They bowed him backward, folded him impossibly. Sarissa saw his hands let go before the sharp sound of his breaking back reached her. He collapsed into the meadow, like a wearied man throwing himself back on the grass for a rest. His trio was now also winched easily shoreward. The swath that bore Jax and, farther along, Helion, now began a swift contraction, without submerging. Round the island's shore the two were swept, while the huge orb rolled languorously and turned what she could not help but feel was a lusting gaze upon them as they drew near, the red rhomboidal pupil-mouth contracting and dilating in anticipation.

"When is she coming down?" Orson Waverly asked. "I need everyone's report. It just doesn't cohere yet. What's she doing?"

The other three traded looks.

"She's crying, Orson," Nemo Jones said. "Let her be, just a while yet. She thought for a minute she had saved them."

The biologist sighed. "All right. Let's rake through it again. Penny and Japhet agree they saw both squids and sharks excrete—eject large clouds of fine sediment, of considerable volume, that drifted down to the base of the orb. Meanwhile, early on, Nemo caught sight of some kind of large carcass, a cetaceanoid he thinks, being actively swallowed down, by minute movements, into the basal stratum. Cetaceanoids are bathic lake dwellers, and Polyphemus hasn't left the surface for the last two days. Conclusions: first, it *is* a giant detritivore; second, it's hunting and feeding from deep down even as it sits here, my guess being that it hunts with structures similar to those it uses up here and probably engulfed the cetaceanoid last night. Fine. At this point I see no way those things help us.

"Now to the packs. Very little that's new, essentially. Both Japhet and Penny now agree that when the squids fasten to their prey they show a shuddering movement that might be the reverse of peristaltic. But as to what they might be pumping into the bodies, you caught no clues. What would it *be?*" Waverly sounded petulant, exhorting his own imagination rather than the others. "Digestive fluids? Then what feeds the squids themselves if they just soften up the prey for Polyphemus—and if nourishment flows from it to them, how does it do so? And this about the sharks. You all three now say you saw them dive to the bottom even when their tethers had not been broken— saw more than one of them worming themselves belly-down against the basal stratum and then rejoining their packs above. Were they grazing on some of the detritus there? No one saw them using their jaws down there?"

All shook their heads, and Nemo answered for them: "No."

"Shit! It's too much to cope with! Was there nothing else new, no change in the pattern of the packs' collective behavior, for instance? In the way each group acted together, or the way the two groups interacted?"

"Well . . ." All faces, including the blind one, turned toward Penny. "Look. This is nothing certain, but I had the *feeling,* at least, that the packs, both kinds, were concentrated a little more heavily at one side of the globe just before . . . just before Sarissa started firing." She had started weeping, though she struggled stubbornly against letting her voice break. Nemo laid a hand on her forearm, and she clutched it. She let herself go then, cried in slow, quiet gasps, which Waverly didn't seem to notice. His mind had snagged on something.

"They concentrated on the side nearest the prey? Penny? On the side nearest the prey?"

"Yes. They . . . always kept circulating . . . circulating so much it was hard to say. But, yes. I think so."

Waverly nodded. His face had tightened. His teeth ground slightly, busily, behind his closed lips, a sign of thought in him. The faded blood tracks on his cheeks ceased to resemble tears, looked more like war paint now.

"Japhet. Tell me again about the movement of the squids' tentacles—not while they were on the prey, but well before that."

"But what can I say that I haven't already—"

"Try this on. You've all reported that their tentacles show size differential—some quite short and fine, others thicker and considerably longer. All, you've more or less agreed, 'vibrated all the time.' But are you sure? Absolutely? Did anyone notice, for instance, that sometimes it was the smaller, finer tentacles doing most of the vibrating, sometimes almost exclusively the larger ones, and only sometimes all of them together?"

Nemo's eyes immediately came up, to meet Japhet's. These were similarly kindled. Japhet said:

"Yes. That's precisely right. Nemo saw it too."

Waverly's back straightened, and his palms rested carefully on his thighs. "And the sharks. Someone on the log, Jax I think, said their eyes were reddish-black, in three triangular clusters that tapered back to sharp points on the dorsum. And you, Japhet, said they reminded you of delph eyes. There are three clusters instead of two, but what would you others—"

"Look," Nemo said. "Sarissa. She's seen something."

Even Waverly turned his futile gaze toward the knoll where the gunner stood. Her body was taut, and she had her glasses trained on Polyphemus. She lowered them, raised them again. Then she let them drop to her chest, spun around, and rushed to her as-yet-unused gun, the one trained on Polyphemus's sector of the lake.

Sarissa sighed and wiped her eyes. She had cried this way once before, at the training camp on Cygnus IV. She had been just seventeen and had failed her first gunnery finals. Failed. She had placed third in the class (of over a hundred)—not first. She had gone into the sand dunes fringing the lake where the finals were given each year and thrown herself down like a piece of trash discarded in the wasteland. Then she had mourned her shipwrecked pride and mourned two target floats, grazed but unpunctured, that had bobbed back up to mock her after she had fired on them. Now, two faces grieved her, and these would *not* bob back up from the water they had slipped into an hour and a half before. She faced Polyphemus and spat toward it, feeling hate enough to make her spittle caustic, to make her eyes spout laser beams. She saw what looked like a deep crease forming down in the muddy floor of the giant's interior.

She trained her glasses on it. It was not a stable feature of the stratum. It had not been there before, and now she could see it deepen, as if the whole layer were contorting for some unguessable effort. A few seconds more, and a shudder passed through the titan that made the crystalline walls through which she spied blur in the magnified field of her vision. The puckered place at once began to smooth out again.

Perplexed, she took the glasses from her eyes and it was then, viewing Polyphemus as a whole, that she saw a boil of motion to one side of the globe, halfway out amid the circumambient field of cilia. She brought up the glasses again.

As she focused on the turbulence, its cause popped to the surface: a glassy, opaque ellipsoid, perhaps half the size of one of the fishing boats. One end was more tapered than the other, and at this end, two flagella, perhaps three meters long, were attached. With a slow, labored thrashing, they drove the organism out of the black meadow that fringed the parental hemisphere.

Once the thing had been a few moments in progress, it seemed that it hugged, preferentially, the shallows fringing the isle, for it began to make its way round toward a point just off the knoll Sarissa stood on. The perception and the reaction came in the same instant. She rushed to the nearer gun, swept its muzzle downward, and waited. It was already within range, but she waited for the shot to become absolutely sure, and waited too for the slightest sign of divergence from its course as her signal to fire. She heard the others hailing her but spared no fraction of her attention for a response. This little piece of her enemy she could take from it, and she meant to do so.

It was within a hundred meters when she saw bubbles appearing around its flanks and realized that it had begun to sink even as it thrashed onward. She fired. The line hissed vindictively, the barb plunged to the little orb's center, fierce as a viper. The flagella continued to thrash impotently, but not, it seemed, particularly excitedly. She noted that the main part of the orb was tough only in its sheath and that its contents were gelatinous. So she set the winch going on the first line and planted her second shot at the base of the flagella, where she reasoned a greater muscular rigidity should give her barb a firmer bite. Her aim was surreally true—she saw where the lance would lodge well before it did so, and almost set the winch on the line before it had even struck. She was already hauling her catch along the surface of the lake by the time the others reached her.

"Polyphemus ejected it—its basal stratum seamed up and squeezed it out somewhere on that side, just below the water level."

The winches had dragged it directly below them now and began to lift it from the water. The flagella, with a brainless mechanicity, did not cease to flail as the blubbery mass floundered up the rock wall. Out of the group's watchful silence, Nemo muttered:

"Polyphemus can see it—if it sees. Can hear it—if it hears. But it's not interfering."

"Polyphemus sees and hears," Orson Waverly said. "But it doesn't think. That thing isn't prey if it came out of the giant's body. And what isn't prey our greedy, mindless friend doesn't bother with."

The five people stood around the thing, watching its flagella's movement weakening gradually. Their knolltop group might have been a scene of ancient sacrifice. The things Waverly had called for when the organism had first been lashed to the rock promoted the illusion. Japhet, Nemo, Penny, and Sarissa all held flensing knives, and Japhet had used the little industrial lasers the boats carried to good effect on the plastic oars their emergency rafts contained. A large scoop, fork, and oversized pair of tongs had been fashioned, and a large sifting screen improvised from cable. The log was set up on a rock near the blunt prow of the sacrificial beast. The recorder's console might have been the abstracted face of the deity this druidic cult had gathered to appease: the Group Mind's memory-amplifier. Into this, the blindfolded priest meant to feed each scrap and nuance of the offering he could not see, hoping to purchase with this rite the greater insight that he and his fellow-supplicants sorely needed.

The warm wind washed over the sacrifice, and the propulsive energy slowly metronomed out of its black stern-whips. Its smooth envelope had been faintly translucent, but now had grown waxier and begun to wrinkle. Out of the silence Sarissa said:

"I think it's weak enough to cut. Let's open it."

"Remember," said Waverly. "First the integument. If it has a distinct structure, flense me out sections and separate it as neatly as possible from what's under it."

At first, once their giant scalpels had been at work a few minutes, everyone was reporting that no clearly defined integument existed, but this proved an error. A distinct outermost layer did exist, but it was more than two feet thick. It was a gelatinofibrous material. Its fibrosity was attenuated at the outer levels, but the deeper into the stratum one went, the more sharply articulated, and more darkly pigmented these fiber-bundles became until, at the stratum's interface with the subincumbent tissues, it looked like a tightly packed surface of black-tentacled sea anemones. An embryonic Meadow of Medusa—all question of the thing's identity was settled here.

Within the cavernum lined with this dark pile of fibril-tips was a smooth, elongate capsule perhaps twice the size of a man. Its surface was of a thin, tough material of linked hoop-shaped plates, so that the whole suggested a giant pupal case. The celebrants of the rite exhumed the whole upper surface of this sarcophagus shape. They worked with gusto, scattering the black, blubbery rugs of tissue about them on the sunlit stone, until the core of this biological torpedo lay upon a supporting remnant of the integument—lay on a crude-cut altar hewn from its own protective material.

Waverly, considering a moment, decided, "Cut in thirds,

carefully and gradually, along seams in the plating. Be looking for clear structures, and also be checking with each other as you cut to see how far along the length of the thing those structures run. Then, when you've cut halfway down through it, open it lengthwise, along a lengthwise seam if you can find one."

His vatic crew raised their drenched blades and returned eagerly to work. Their concentration was complete. Their victim could have been as huge as its parent—their every move expressed an unconditional will to sift its secrets out of it. But revelation was quick to come. The pupal case proved thin, easily cut, and all reported that a dense, very delicately fibrous gray tissue underlay the sheath. It was macroscopically featureless, and after they had gone some thirty centimeters down, it began to look like the sheath's sole content. Then Sarissa's blade scraped on something hard.

Japhet and Penny joined her with knives. They scooped a hollow round the object, shaved it free from webs of tissue, pried it out. It was a human skull, which the tissue packed within as it had without, filling its orbits with gray gelatinous pseudo-eyes. Sarissa held it up in the light of the noon sun. Her eyes stared into its jellied gaze, and her face worked as if she was struggling to read a message in its masklike expression. She said:

"It's ... fresh. There's still some cartilage in the ... nose hole."

Nemo came up behind her. He reached around, took it gently from her hand, gave it to Japhet, and gripped her shoulders. His hands strained, as if by the firmness of their grip he could throttle—as with a tourniquet—the grief and horror rising in her. Face blank, she let Nemo steer her to a seat on the rock. She watched the lake.

Waverly was deeply excited by the find and made them bring him to the site of discovery. His hands, tremulous and lustful as a gloating miser's, caressed the socket the skull had lain in, palped the surrounding tissue. A blind augur, he did a thorough divination from the alien entrails.

"It's deep inside a highly specialized structure. It didn't just wander in. Saw it open. Comb out the tissues packed inside it."

The skull had hardly been opened before something was

found: thumb-sized white ovoids, nearly a score of them, embedded in the tissue. Penny helping him, Waverly cut one open, fingered its contents with exquisite thoroughness. "Listen," he said. "Improvise a large comb, fine-toothed as possible. Start with the fork we made while Japhet makes something finer. Anywhere in this tissue, whether it's encased in fragments of prey or not, look for anything that might be an egg—smaller than these, larger, I don't know—but probably on a similar scale and, hopefully, of a recognizably different form. Nemo and Penny on that. I'm going to open a few more of these. Sarissa, I want you to help me with knife and tweezers, but first help me rig a little table. Sarissa?"

Not speaking, she came up, touched him. The augurs went to work.

A bit later, they all sat together on the knoll. Waverly sat at his little bench, where he and Sarissa had unraveled the innards of three more of the objects found in the skull. On the same bench were four black pellets, half the size of those from the skull, which Japhet had just combed from the tissue of the sarcophagus. He had cried, "Orson! I found some. They're black. They're a little like delph roe. Smaller, harder, separate, but shaped like roe." Waverly had straightened then. He had called them all around him, but once they had gathered, had sat quiet a long time.

They waited, the bright, bulky tatters of their butchery scattered all about. The chunks and gobbets of alien blubber surrounded them like the debris of some bizarre biological sculpture they had lately joined in finishing. In a way, this was true. They had hewn out the features, the intelligible form, of the being that imprisoned them. Waverly's face came up, and he smiled slightly, as if with pleasure at the flood of sunlight that bathed him. His mouth groped for speech, but luxuriatingly, as if his mind were rummaging through a wealth of utterances.

"Delph eyes have the incredible motion-detective power of a jumping spider's, and we've recently confirmed to our satisfaction that their resolution of image and detail—of the very subtlest gestalts—that it probably surpasses our own. Polyphemus doesn't eat delphs."

This might have been the gloating introduction of a very hot paper read at an academy meeting. Waverly paused, visibly trying to sober himself. "I think the reason is that independent organisms, evolved more or less directly from the delphinid order, have become functioning saprophytes in the systems of Polyphemus's kind. These delphinids have first crack at their host's prey, and they function as their host's eyes." He talked faster now, rushing to include his fellows in his new overview. "My guess is that the sharks' ancestors were engulfed by polyphemids as food, enjoyed some natural resistance to their digestive enzymes, and learned to thrive on their captors' meals. If polyphemids resembled the smaller littoral analogues I mentioned, they had only tactile sensibilities, with perhaps some primitive olfactory discrimination. Any one of them whose saprophytes could start cueing it to their visual recognitions of prey would surely eat better than its blind fellow-hunters. And the saprophytes, evolutionally speaking, would feel a great stimulus to providing such cues.

"And I'm convinced the squids are similar in their history. Their tentacle activity is discriminative in just the way the cilia of our own organs of Corti are. When the smaller tentacles vibrate, higher frequency sounds are being registered; and when the larger, the lower frequencies, while all are usually in some kind of motion, as would be expected from the mixture of frequencies in most environmental noise. The squids are the giant's ears—grotesque though it sounds, I have no doubt of it. Both these captured species have evolved a caudal nerve-link with the giant's own major ganglia, which I am certain are in that basal stratum. The kelp is part of its own neural system, and perhaps respiratory and alimentary as well. If what's in this egg's yolk is at all analogous, and I think it is, then the giant's basal stratum is a dense neural tangle, the plane of intersection for Polyphemus and its two breeds of saprophyte, as well as being its zone of absorption for nutrients. And when those sensory cooperatives breed, their reproductive packets are planted in that same stratum. The squids embed their eggs in the carrion before it is absorbed there. Quite possibly, they don't feed at all as adults and take in their life's nourishment during some kind of larval phase. The sharks go down and lay their eggs directly in the stratum. These genetic packages are then apparently well located to be included in that of the host itself, and the tidy partnership is perpetuated, while those that are not entrapped in the material of Polyphemus's spores no doubt hatch endosomatically to replenish the adult host's sensory packs. And as for the nutritive disproportionality between host and saprophytes, it's even less than I thought, for as the individual adult sensories die, they surely fall to the basal stratum and feed their master with their own corpses."

Waverly stopped, but with an air of cutting himself short. He sat, a small canny smile on his face, as if challenging his friends to see what he did. Nemo said:

"Then if those sharks are still close enough to being delphs— if their eyes are built the same—our dyes could blind them."

Waverly cackled—it was the most blatant hilarity that any of his fellows had heard from him. Then all five of them were talking at once. But when the first gusts of jubilation and (often fantastic) strategy had subsided, the biologist said:

"Listen. I think we can do it. And if it works, it's surely a start, a great satisfaction if nothing else. But it may not be enough. Because if blinding fails to drive it away, its auditory mechanism may be all it needs to kill us. I've got one or two specific suggestions to add to all you've said. Let's get down to the beach, finalize our plan, and get to work."

The work that began that afternoon lasted most of the night, and decorated the island with a small, unsteady constellation of lights, of flaring and guttering stars. Japhet welded harpoon line into three-strand cables, Nemo and Sarissa toiled by camp lanterns modifying rifle ammunition, Orson and Penny converted the tough hides of freshly slaughtered delphs into a hundred meters of tubing, Orson scrolling the material and holding it for Penny to fuse with the bright needle-fine laser beam.

Just after sunrise, the boat that Polyphemus had rejected once already set out from the island's shore. It was, as before, tethered to a rock, though even more strongly than before. But this time it had passengers: two rather rigid figures with heads of stuffed cloth, painted features, and stuffed wet-suits for bodies. A system of wires, guyed to one of the boat engine's flywheels, imparted a jerky agitation to the lifeless shapes.

Polyphemus reached for the craft the moment it was off-shore. As soon as the creature took hold, Japhet stepped up the winch paying out the cable, to facilitate the giant's speedy taking-in of the prey. A quarter of the island's circumference away, Polyphemus's mouth opened.

And when that red-rimmed trapezoid dilated, there came a series of twelve explosive barks. They sounded from the knoll Sarissa had been stationed on the day before. Their noise, eerily gradual, traveled out to cross and fill the lake's whole vast arena, and before the second had sounded, their effects began to appear: a series of twelve splashes in the lake of ichor bordered by the mouth's rim. Violently expanding clouds of yellow smoke began to bloom within the orb, some near its surface, others deeper down. The coalescence of these roiling masses had stained the contents of the entire globe within a minute and a half. Sarissa and Nemo, whose rifles had launched the missiles, stood with field glasses trained on Polyphemus.

The giant's overall movement had suffered a marked change. The steady peristaltic surge of the cilia faltered—the entangled boat ceased to flow so smoothly toward the orb. It paused, was joggled as by choppy seas. The fibers enmeshing it grew frenetically active, but somewhat less purposive.

"It's groping the boat," Penny shouted up to the two on the knoll. She stood on the beach, the nearest of them all to the captive bait. "It's not pulling it in nearly so fast!"

Nemo and Sarissa probed the thinning mists of dye for clues to the fate of the giant's eyes. The pigment was dispersing according to its normal behavior in lake and seawater, the bulk of it settling out in a harmless precipitate within three minutes of going into solution. The orb's inner jungle melted back into visibility. Sarissa said, thick-voiced as with desire:

"They're scrambling. Panicking."

"Yes. It's their normal patrolling motion, speeded up. Can you make out the eye color?"

"Yes! Red! Check that pack to the lower left." In both delphs and Polyphemus's visual sensories, the eyes' normal color was blackish-red in most light. And now the eyes on the "eyes" of Polyphemus flashed deep ruby as they boiled in their kinetically heated-up patrol movements. This was the color of dye-blinded delph eyes, once the chemical had converted their chromatophore molecules to an isomer that the impingement of photons could not reconvert—that is, once the eyes' retinal substances had been permanently bleached.

"But they're not colliding," Sarissa said. The joy in her voice had diminished several degrees. "Getting snarled more often, but still coordinated. I think they can still hunt and kill. . . ." Nemo knew that the foreboding in her tone related not to this part of their assault, but to a secondary phase of their plan that everyone hoped would not need implementation, but he pretended not to understand this.

"So what? They can't show it the way to its food, that's all we care about."

"The boat!" Penny called. "It's started bringing it in again!"

The action of the cilia, though different in quality, more searching and gradual, was smooth again. The craft wallowed and toppled onward.

And it was, some moments later, consumed by the giant. There was no opening of it, no shaking out of the tasty nutmeat and discarding of the husk. The cilia brought it to the feeder-tentacles, which plucked it up, crushed it like a large shellfish, and hurled it whole into the mouth. As it sank, the sharks, clearly endowed with fine directional control and some form of sensitivity to mechanical vibration, swarmed on it. All took their turns, assaulting hungrily, retiring unsatisfied from the metallic morsel. The squids too took their futile turns, and at length the craft settled to the basal muck, with Japhet still paying out cable to allow its sinking.

The day's agenda was completed a short while later, executed by five rather taut, silent people. A respirator, rigged to a float so that it rode some six feet under water, was set adrift from the cove. A hundred meters of improvised air hose linked it to the shore, where Nemo and Japhet worked a crude bellows of delph hide to produce continuous aspiration in the device. Polyphemus struck it with violent accuracy a short distance offshore.

Sarissa Wayne tilted the muzzle of the harpoon gun a little higher. This brought the grappling hook strapped to the underside of the harpoon up to her eye level. She reached out and touched one of its needle-sharp points, looked at the hook with distaste and unease.

"It's ludicrous," she said. "The more I think about it. How did we ever convince ourselves that it was rational? All of Orson's goddamned *inferences*..."

These words were addressed to no human shape, but to a grotesque manikin, half-beast, half-machine, that stood beside her on the flank of the knoll. The body was a squamous hulk, ensheathed in overlapping plates, shingles, and greaves of a dark leathery substance. The head that crowned it was a metal-and-glass bulb with insectoid mechanical mouthparts, while on its back something like an engine was mounted on a shoulder frame. This Caliban replied in an eerie remnant of a voice, filtered by the respirator mask:

"Don't start doubting it now, Sarissa—you won't function as effectively if you do."

"Horseshit! I'm getting you out of there if I have to spear you and fish you out. Function effectively! You think I'm going to let you down, Jones? All this shit about trusting me, everything you said to me in bed last night, all lies, right?"

Nemo knew she was not really concerned with his words, that essentially she needed to hold him again before he went down. He shook his head, shifted his feet wretchedly in their delph-skin boots, his queer expeditionary armor a torment bottling up his answering need to hold her.

"Dearest love. I'm going in, and I'm coming out."

"Coming out," she said quietly. "That's just it. You won't have any trouble getting *in*...."

They looked at the cable that belted the entire hummock they stood on. From a point just under their feet it dove in a shallow arc to Polyphemus's mouth-corner. Within the orb the cable dangled through the kelp. Down on the neural mulch their eyes could just pick out the wreck of their decoy boat. Sarissa stepped over to the second gun and checked its angle, speaking in a tone so carefully constrained it sounded absent. "If this thing wants to pull away, submerge, all our lines together won't hold it. If it's aroused while you're . . . *deafening* it—if it reacts, it will take you down."

"Listen, sweetness, if we let ourselves go over it all again, we only lose what time we have to talk about our love."

"Talk about our love!" She whirled on him. "Jones, you fool, with all your courtships and vows and declarations. I don't want to talk about our love, I want to *have* it."

Japhet Sparks called from the beach: "It's ready!" He and Orson had slipped their bait into the water. It was the engine of their most seriously damaged boat, mounted on a cut-down raft and anchored to the rock by a length of tripled cable. Sarissa went round the knolltop and called to Penny down in the cove. She sat in the helm of their escape craft—their one good boat, driven in the shallows around the island and hooked to a trailer raft for the two riders who would not fit inside.

"Penny! Bait's up! Here we go!"

"Hit it! I'm standing by!"

Nemo raised his gloved hand to Sarissa. She stood still and nodded, staring him straight in the eyes through his faceplate. Nemo took from the ground a large heavy hook with a handle-gripped bar attached. He eased down to the lower ledge cut for him to stand on, just under the cable where it began its plunge to the giant's mouth. He checked the weaponry in the side racks of his back-frame. The motor the frame supported was one of the small ones with which each boat's emergency raft was supplied. Nemo switched it on briefly for a final assurance of its stability on its improvised mount, and switched it off. Then he hung the hook on the cable above his head and gripped the bar with both hands.

"OK, Sarissa."

She called down to Japhet: "Now!" The noisy little bait-raft fired on and chugged out toward the black meadow.

It was seized by the fibrils and tumbled orbward. Polyphemus's mouth began to open—and then the raft hit the limit of its tether. The cilia began to toil, frustrated, roused. The mouth, as if impatient, gaped fully open. Nemo jumped from the ledge.

As he dove, he felt metamorphosed into a kind of bomb. He wore two wet-suits, and to the outer one his delph-hide armor was sewn with steel wire. A padded, capsuled thing, his body was surreally snug and remote from the dreadful vision into which he plunged. The veined opacity of the orb's wall loomed into sharper focus, and the teeming amber lake in the giant's lips rushed to him. Nemo brought his feet up and locked his knees. With the sense of exaggerated mass his gear gave him, it seemed when his heels impacted that he struck a titanic hammerblow on the bell of his own doom. The true proportionality of the matter was that he was like a sparrow touching down on the flank of a large hill. Even so, when he freed his hook and hacked it for purchase into the orb wall, the suicidal blatancy of the act horrified him. The material was tough, pierceable only with fierce blows. He worked his way up from the mouth-corner along the giant's lip, a swollen, scalloped border of tissue shot with purple fibrosities. He gained his feet and began to stalk along the border of the golden tarn.

From his rack he took a crooked scythe welded from the blades of three flensing knives. He stuck its razor tip into the ichor and vigorously slashed up its surface. Sharks, as fast as rockets, rose and converged on the spot, fangs foremost. Nemo saw that their ragged teeth moved independently in addition to the jaws' movement of them—mouths that worked more like shredders than scissors. The rabid schools milled insistently, their red, poisoned eye-clusters flashing with their sharp, snakish turns. Nemo racked the scythe and took down one of his three rifles. He began to pump explosive shot into the haggletoothed mouths. Outside the orb, at the fringe of its dome just behind where he stood, something huge moved. It was a trio of Polyphemus's feeder-tentacles, beginning to elongate yearningly outward, toward the stubborn bait-raft. Nemo kept firing.

When he had killed perhaps a dozen, he found he was kindling unhoped-for havoc among these blinded sensories. Each one hit, as its head ruptured, went into spasms that snarled the coordination of its pack. Each, as it thrashed, scribbled the ichor with ribbons and wraiths of its blood, waking the appetites of the squadron it jostled. The cannibal frenzy spread as the blood got thicker and made every beast smell like food to its fellows. It was, apparently, some visual cue that normally inhibited this kind of accident—the taste of cannibal food itself certainly did not.

Two other of Polyphemus's feeder tentacles had gone out toward its recalcitrant prey. So far none had reached it, but all showed a slow, inexorable extensibility that was not yet exhausted. Nemo scanned the red uproar beneath his feet. His goal was now the basal stratum, and he sought a window to it through the fanged turmoil. He saw one down along a major strand of the kelp, turned the ignition of the motor on his back, and dove in, rifle first.

They had seen Helion's still-masked face remain unaffected after his engulfment, while Jax's had soon begun to bloat and corrode, but, curiously, it was in his face that Nemo dreaded first feeling some caustic leakage, rather than his hands, which had been left fairly thinly gloved for the manipulation of his weapons. The stalk he followed was as thick as his body, and he kept it just above his back, to force any attacker into a frontal approach.

Down where the stalks coalesced toward their common rootage, while there was still room to navigate between them, he branched off to his first task, where the wreck lay.

The hulk's cable had supported it against complete subsidence. It was sunk in a turgid half-liquid zone just above a more solid neural mulch. Its fractured hull offered many places where the coils of cable he had brought could be threaded through its chassis. Firmly and intricately, he wove the wreck to several major kelp stalks. Yesterday's bait had now set its hook in the prey that had swallowed it. Yesterday's bad luck—that Polyphemus should not flee in panic at its blinding, but feed regardless and wait to feed again—was today's good luck. "Take me down now if you want to," Nemo hissed in the smothered silence of his helmet.

Now came the task that probed luck's spiderweb. They had

observed three distinct basal zones in which the sensories' neuro-umbilici attached. Now Nemo sped to the nearest of these and, trying to stay ahead of his fear, charged into it, scything through tethers in broad sweeps. He found a lateral branching of kelp to stand on and cut his motor.

As the squids came down, he shot them. They rained toward him with the erratic dodging movement of moths or snowflakes, and he shot them as they applied their caudal tips to the mulch to regenerate their tethers. The inner explosions tended to split them lengthwise, and several, in dying, vomited upward from their beaks little clouds of eggs like those found in the skull.

Nemo scythed the remaining tethers. Overhead, the silvery interface of ichor with open sky was visible in patches through the churned gore of the sharks, and Nemo saw it shattered by the impact of one of Sarissa's grappling hooks. The bait-raft's tether must be near breaking. He worked faster, darting upward from his ambush now to meet and kill those that were slow in descending. At least half of the tethers he cut must have been those of sharks, but few of these came down except in bleeding tatters, more mulch for the undiscriminating titan, which now dined upon its own senses.

And then Nemo was on to the second zone. Here he swept zigzag through the field and mowed it all at once. Panic was big in him, trying to split from within the shell of his self-command. His compromise was to push the very limit of recklessness. He stood in the center of the mown patch and fired directly overhead, accelerating his motor periodically against the muddy tug of Polyphemus's appetite at his feet. The sensories came dodging down through the veiny gloom, while from the smoky plane of the higher turmoil shark-meat drizzled ever more continually, trailing wisps of torn tissue. He saw Sarissa's second hook hit the interface and glide toward its purchase in the giant's mouth-corner.

The rent and ragged molluscoidal shapes piled in little drifts around him. When the weapon's fifty-shot magazine gave out, he dropped it and snatched down another rifle. And then no others descended. He waited two seconds, five, then launched himself toward the third attachment zone.

In the same instant that he did so, the floor of his little ocean tore itself from under his feet. In the inertial shock that followed, Nemo sprawled helpless in the turbid boil. He collided with a stalk and hugged it, and then the giant was still. A moment later, the silver ceiling of this living cosmos exploded a third time. The bait-raft, its snapped cable fluttering behind it, dug an effervescent shaft down toward him. Nemo accelerated toward the last of the sensories' anchorages.

Those on shore saw him raise his scythe, dart forward—but then check his swing and pull up just short of the umbilical thicket. There, at the edge of the webwork, the scaly little manshape paused and, from his place in the orb's deepest murk, seemed to gauge how far the thicket towered over him.

"What's he doing?" Japhet called to Sarissa from the beach. She didn't take her eyes from Nemo, and her answer to Japhet was spoken only to herself, almost whispered:

"He's thinking how to kill them from higher up. *Yes.* Get near the exit before you do it—get near as you can!"

The scaly shape probed the kelp adjoining the thicket and separated out from it a slender side-stalk perhaps fifty meters long. Nemo grasped this by the tip and began to drag it in a gradually rising spiral round the thicket's perimeter. He tightened the spiral as he rose, gathering the lower parts of the neural tethers into a sheaf. When the stalk ran out, he tied it to a more massive growth and found another, higher branching one.

Orson Waverly had extrapolated rather extensively from what the previous day's test had shown them: "I think it fell back immediately on a more primitive feeding taxon, probably geared for motile but armored or shelled prey. Maybe it feeds on some of the pseudobrachiopoda—there's some big bathic ones just been found.

"But it's the implications of this behavior that are most significant to us. Totally blinded, and no panic reaction. I think these saprophytes, during their evolution, have maintained a very separable, interruptible kind of sensory feed-in with their host. After all, with tethers routinely broken, that kind of reaction wouldn't be very productive for Polyphemus. But, still, the complete deprivation of an important sensory input? My guess is that as long as the sensories are alive and maintain attachment, they transmit a steady flow of 'white noise,' random neural firings, to the host. It doesn't experience a disruption of sensation so much as a kind of zero-information state, such as it might experience on a dark night, or very deep down.

"I *am* convinced that as the sensories are killed, Polyphemus will feel a cumulative encroachment of sensory deprivation—a state of 'total blank' as opposed to one of 'no news,' and it seems to me this *must* produce a violent reaction of some sort. Now understand that from this point I'm only guessing, but it's often the case that creatures as primitive as Polyphemus is, when you consider it apart from this startling adaptive turn it has taken— that such creatures can be relatively insensitive to extensive physical disruption. For my money, Nemo should have a good chance of killing at least a majority of the sensories before any radical sense of anomaly begins to dominate the giant's behavior."

Now Nemo repeated Orson's words in a snarl—"for my money"—and began firing on the sensories his ploy had aggregated into a desperate snarl no more than twenty-five meters from the titan's mouth. He was prodigal of shot, perforated the bloody, frantic mass from every angle. When his magazine emptied, he let the rifle drop and grabbed his last. After a moment—during which the redundant butchery had him in a kind of vengeful trance—he realized his work was done. It was then that the giant moved again.

It filled Nemo with awe, as Polyphemus's previous lurching movement had not done, for this was an immense concerted muscular effort of the biocosmos that held him. The pressure of the ichor increased upon him as the entire orb tautened and strained to pull itself offshore, out to deeper waters. The message of darkness had at last definitely reached the titan's murk-shrouded ganglia. The giant was alarmed.

And on finding that a quintuple thickness of cable opposed its withdrawal from shore, alarm became the plainest panic. Nemo, who had felt so huge and blatant during his soaring approach to the enemy, now felt he was reduced to a jot of foam in the raging prow of a tidal wave. His motor's effort mouthward, skyward, seemed a ludicrous trivium. Polyphemus had a very powerful—awesome, even—capture-resistance taxon. It had sought to move and found that painful stasis opposed its murky will. It tried again, and a fang of pain on a scale that it could feel was sunk into its core as its efforts to flee tore loose the roots of its own most central nerves. And now Polyphemus was an earthquake. Volcanic clouds of its black blood roiled up from the wounds of its self-violated ganglia. Pain could not vie with the blind will to escape that it had kindled in this colossus—unmolested, no doubt, through centuries of easy gluttony. Polyphemus strove, and an ink storm arose from its tearing entrails.

And when they tore free and the boat, trailing broken trees of nerve cord, came vomiting, rocketing mouthward, Nemo knew he would be trapped in the ichor's inertia—would fall with Polyphemus and join him in his dark retreat, if he failed to reach the boat before it erupted free. He gave up vertical striving and fought to intercept it.

As it erupted he saw he was missing it, was a helpless half-second too slow, but mindlessly he sustained his drive after the craft had passed him. A trailing nerve stalk clubbed his belly, and he hugged it with both arms and legs, while all the fluid volume of Polyphemus strove to strip him off and flush him down. The boat, the stalk, and then Nemo, were into the sky.

The sudden surge into free-fall tricked Nemo out of his grip on the stalks. He could see he was falling free of the sinking feeder-tentacles, but that he was going to dive into the cilium-field sluggishly following the giant's subsidence. He fought to straighten for a sharp hands-first entry so that he could pull the dive shallow as soon as he struck. He hit the vipered foam and arched his back strongly as he entered. As he surfaced, he felt himself pulled short. A fibril had snarled in the screw of his motor.

The field was retiring laterally before it sank under—Polyphemus was pulling its skirts, so to speak, off of the mid-shallows they had overlain. Nemo threw his feet in the air to flop backward where he could get a grip on the cilium. He just managed this, but was too awkwardly folded, legs flailing, to get a scythe free from his snarled rack. A red shock of pain ruptured his left foot.

An instant passed before he had the wit to seize hold of his foot and grab the line of the harpoon that pierced it. He wrapped it round his arm, feeling nothing so much as a vivid embarrassment and indignity in his position as he fought for his scythe with his free hand. He had been dragged past the littoral drop-off before he had it out and went under.

For a brief eternity he expected Polyphemus's full weight to haul against his steel-wound arm, and then he got the scythe tip under the fibril and pulled mightily.

Jones lay on the beach the expedition had first set out from. Japhet had brought the medical kit from the sand-hog and waited at a discreet distance while Sarissa cleaned and bandaged Nemo's foot. She finished the bandage and patted his thigh, smiling absently with an unconscious appraisal and satisfaction in her eyes, such a gaze as a breeder might bend upon his prize beast, knowing it safe after some hazard.

"No artery hit," she said, "a few of the metacarpals broken, I think. At the worst, you'll have a slight limp and that won't make you any the less active."

Nemo nodded gravely and didn't answer at once. "I love you all the more for your . . . determination to save me," he said at last. "No doubt you had an agonizing moment there as you fired, dreading that the shot might be . . . a little off."

"Not the slightest." She said it fiercely. Her large black eyes came up and bull's-eyed his; a distinct frost of impugned expertise gave them added bite. "I knew it before I even saw exactly what kind of fix you would get into: there was no way I was going to miss *you*, Jones."

Nemo nodded. "I see." He looked at the lake and smiled.

Down in its waters, their enemy still pursued its ponderous retreat. Deep in the lake's root, the cold and lightless magmatic shaft, it sought the realms that were the ancient nursery of its evolution. Its encounter with the vertebrate bipeds had reft it of the fruits of five million years' development. It had found the butcher-work of these midgets far cannier than its own, and so it stumbled back down to the night of its origin.

THE ANGEL OF DEATH

A young man named Engelmann, out late one night, entered a phone booth and pretended to search for a number in the book. He savored the booth's little island of light, and his own prominence in it, like a lone glass-cased museum exhibit on the dim street.

Displaying himself thus made him grin with irony, for he knew his rarity and power would not be perceived by anyone who passed. Here, O street, was the man the city lived in fear of! His very shape and substance! Behold, and fail to see! He lifted the receiver, deposited two dimes, dialed a local prefix and then, randomly, four more digits.

He got an old man's voice. "Who is it?" A little angry-edgy, as if to an unexpected knocker outside his door. There was a TV on in the background.

"Hello, sir," Engelmann cried, hearty as an emcee. "I'm glad you tuned in, sir, because, once again, it's Angel of Death time!"

A pause. Just enough to show the name had struck, registered. "What? Is this some radio call? I never listen to the radio."

"No, sir! This is a *hot tip*. I'm letting you and only you know that it's Angel of Death time, brought to you by that ol' Guy in the Sky, the Angel of Death himself, *my*self!"

Now the pause echoed unmistakably with the old man's awareness. "Who is this? Who are you calling?"

"But I'm calling you! And I know you're ecstatic, 'cause only I can satisfy, right? Only I can make 'em die!"

"You're crazy! Who do you want? Leave me alone!"

Engelmann positively shimmied with contained laughter, for the old man didn't hang up! He waited, as if for the reply of Death itself. He waited to argue for mercy, for exemption, as if

Engelmann hovered somewhere above his roof and clutched his very fate in angelic talons.

"Oh, but, sir—*you're* not my Mystery Guest tonight. I'm just calling to *tell* you. You must know about me—how I go light-foot, smoother than smoke, or growl along in my powerful car. I'm that devilish, cleverish, feverish Angel of Death, that snooper and swooper and brain-outscooper. This is a *tip,* sir! I picked you out of the air! Take this down."

The old voice came back, half-begging, half-barking: "You shouldn't be bothering people that don't do you any harm! Is this a joke?"

"Just take this down please, sir. Don't you see it's a news-worthy *tip?* You can send it to that Jimmy what's-his-name. Is it Scheisskiss? The guy who writes the column. Ready now? Take this down:

> *"Those sniggering bitches*
> *Out scratching their itches—*
> *All steamy and sticky,*
> *All teases and twitches—*
> *I shatter their skulls into*
> *Spatters and tatters—*
> *I slug and I slug them*
> *To jumbled red matter!"*

Engelmann hung up crisply and left the booth. He strolled back the way he had come. His body was plump and tall, and he moved with a kind of stately drift—a secret pomp. He was a visiting potentate, again at large in the Cosmos. Tonight, in fact, he was stepping down from his Citadel and into the city's Time and Space, for the eighth time.

During his intervals up in his eyrie (where he lay in timeless power, watching TV) he was also down here among men, of course. Their unflagging vigilance and dread enshrined him everywhere, night after night. He was a Presence here even between those times when he chose, according to the long sweet tidal shiftings of his will, to descend in the flesh.

And now, for the eighth time, he had descended, and moved

among men. Even unto his angelic car he moved, and entered it, and woke the vigor of its engines.

At this point a remarkable coincidence—the first, in fact, of a series—occurred. At the very hour of the Angel's descent into the space and time of mankind, another transcendent individual made a similar entry. That is to say, he plunged from space into the warm, rich atmosphere of Earth.

It wasn't only the timing that made this remarkable. For as the newly arrived entity braked his plunge and extruded an umbrella of rigid cilia so that his sphericity, hanging beneath, began to drift smoothly like a giant thistledown—as he performed these adjustments, he immediately initiated a sensor-probe of relative psychic concentrations throughout the biosphere. And in doing this he quickly identified as his nearest promising target a huge concatenation of vitalities that was none other than the city through which Engelmann then moved.

Engelmann was driving at that moment, gliding down lamplit corridors of parked cars. Humorously, he had chosen a street that was just on the margin of what the press generally designated as his "territory." As he drifted past, his eyes ransacked the cars, front seats and back. Eerie emptiness! Nine months before, a street like this would have offered a dozen pairs of greedy mammals, hutching up, for here was the only escape for the ache of young blood in the crowded apartments everywhere. And it had been he, Engelmann, who, like a scouring wind, had cleansed these streets.

But there was something here. He sensed it. He almost felt the secret rocking, the muffled titter aimed precisely at himself, a snigger of triumph at duping the Angel of Death. He turned and came back down the block. There was a van ahead that, just perceptibly, had moved, or had it? As he passed, his senses crowded up to it, embraced it, passionate for any faint clue of hot, hidden grapplings. And, by his fierce angelic eyes, it moved! The van rocked slightly!

He parked around the nearest corner. His hand, stark and gorgeously remorseless like an eagle's talon, grasped his weapon and plunged it deep in his jacket's side pocket. Ah, the luscious tang of imminence in the night air! They in their grunt-ing swinish scorn of him, thinking themselves safe. To know he could creep near them, pluck off their nasty shell of secrecy, smash to putty their sneering softnesses till they bled and drib-bled, swooning and collapsing in exquisite agonies of remorse and futile repentance!

He stepped out, feeling the swell and tug of mighty wings at his shoulders, and wing-buoyed he moved, his heels treading in creamy silence the would-be-betraying pavements.

He stood at the van's cab door. There were curtains behind the front seat, and even as he stared at them, they shivered. He shuddered, their undulation smoothly continued in his flesh; and looking down with casual sovereignty, he saw that the lock button stood tall and silver within the rolled-up window, obedi-ent to his will.

Then he moved, knowing his own speed and clarity com-pared to the dazed flesh-tranced time he was thrusting into: he, a celestial falcon; they, groggy and a-blush with blood, like vermin too gorged even to flinch. He seized the handle, thumbed home the button, pulled wide the door, and vaulted up to jam his knees into the driver's seat. He swept aside the curtain, and two matted heads popped up from the broken pane of street-light that fell and shattered on two bodies. The Angel of Death squeezed out a bullet from his Magnum and felt the delicious lurch of its velocity jump from him and plunge through the skin and domed bone of the smaller head. With splendid fluid flexions of sinew and talon, with leisurely largess, he hammered both those skulls repeatedly, distributing the roaring gouts of lead to follow his dying targets through their spasms of recoil.

Engelmann drove home wanderingly, whimsically. He went to an all-night market for a six-pack of root beer, doubled back to buy a newspaper at a liquor store, went to a drive-through taco stand, and after elaborate polite discussion with the woman behind the clown-faced intercom, ordered a vanilla shake. These movements were his way of relishing his almost dizzying free-dom—freedom to prowl these streets, or to quit them, to pull up and, in one smooth climb, to exit them, whenever he chose.

Meanwhile, that intercosmic tuft of thistledown was drifting over the very neighborhood that Engelmann had just visited with his wrath. This being had, among his colleagues, a complex personal designation that involved simultaneous articulations in a multiple of electromagnetic frequencies. The phonetic aspect of this designation was, roughly, "Siraf."

Siraf, then, just as Engelmann was ordering his vanilla shake, selected the rooftop of a tall and partly disused building as a covert in which to pass his inert phase. The Archives required that all field-workers, upon entering an alien sphere, lie passive for a time, before engaging in research on the indigenous life-forms. By this tactic the worker could gain some assurance that he had entered a sufficiently stable configuration, before expending valuable research energies on mimicry and transactional involvement. Each worker could carry only limited quanta of metamorphic power, and even in the best circumstances, only brief investigations were possible. Hence the care taken to tele-palp the surroundings thoroughly for any sign of disruptive local phenomena that might abort the worker's researches.

Siraf adopted a spherical shape and rolled himself against the tarry brick parapet of the rooftop. He immediately initiated telescans of the nearest lying indigenes. Although most of these seemed to be dormant, and all were in any case too distant for fine-focused observations, the young scholar was able to add much to the morphological program provided him by the Archives for this race. That program had been in truth the merest sketch, and Siraf improved the hours of inertia by fleshing it out with studious encodements of the data he was able to gather.

But of course, this kind of preparation could only go so far in alleviating the inevitable obscurity and confusion of alien interactions. He could expect to assimilate most of the physical structure, locomotor routines, much vocabulary, and so be able, on emerging from dormancy, to mimic and to initiate transactions with the autochthones. But it would only be *during* that brief and energy-exorbitant period of mimicry and close-range interaction that he could fine-tune his observations.

For example, Siraf had soon enzymatically recorded much of the local speech. But when it came time actually to effect relationships with the natives, he would still have no clue to the motile and behavioral patterns that this vocabulary served. He would know how to express many concepts, but would have no guide to what concepts it was appropriate to express under what circumstances. A field-worker could come onstage in perfect costume, so to speak, but with no hint of his role, or even, in many cases, of what kind of thing a role might *be*.

It should give some sense of Siraf's excellence as a scholar to report that within a few busy hours of assimilations and inferences, he had arrived at a closely reasoned choice of form. Of the two sexes, it appeared that the larger, the "male," enjoyed a significantly greater degree of mobility and social initiative than did the "female." (For example, the dreams of several nearby dormant females were full of this very theme.) To this finding he added the fact that the sexual drive of this race seemed remarkably dominant among its impulses—a circumstance that boded well for his chances of getting much valued insights into its reproductive rituals. Altogether, a young male with high mating potential seemed indicated for a maximum probability of successful interaction. The specifications he arrived at were, in the native units: height, 6'4"; weight, 215 lbs.; age, 24 years; muscular and vascular systems highly articulated; features, Nordic; hair, blond.

Siraf was aware that many of his colleagues would condemn this choice by reason of its exceeding the norms of size, strength, and general aesthetic appeal by local standards. They would point out that an abnormal individual was not likely to elicit normative reactions. His atypicality would distort his findings.

But Siraf's heuristic methods were the reverse of conservative. He reasoned that there was no such thing as "situational purity." To experiment at all was to disrupt, distort. And since there was no way around it, why not *use* slight disruption? Let the field-worker agitate a bit the hive he visits. Not traumatically, but to a degree that might intensify and multiply the scholar's involvements in his all-too-brief time for probing.

Throughout those hours when Siraf lay conceiving himself, it happened that Engelmann was doing very much the same thing. He was in his room on the top floor of an old apartment building. He lay on his mattress before the TV, propped to a half-sitting posture by pillows. He was alternately watching the tube and writing in a spiral notebook that he held against his raised knees.

"Freedom!" (he wrote) "It's a joke / miracle, a staggering simplicity! You just dare to take Justice, and the daring alone fills you with power. The mere daring-to-fly *is* the power of flight. I *can* fly. I *have* power over life, and freedom from death. Even if the Insect-Squads eventually do take me—"

A Jacuzzi ad came on and he stopped writing to watch it, having seen it twice already. It would repeat throughout the program, a late movie on a local channel. Two big-breasted girls in bikinis—one on the edge of the pool paddling her legs, one sitting in the water—laughed with a young man. He was neck-deep, and his trendy mustachioed head bobbed on the bubbles just at the submerged girl's breast level. There was a voice-over pitch, and addresses of the company's outlets rolled across the scene. When the ad was over, Engelmann had to reread what he had written before he could go on:

"I won't be taken to the Poison Room. Oh, no! I'll go to the shining halls of Medicine. I'll be given soul-upholstering drugs. For my freedom itself protects me. It's too 'unreal' for the Little Folk. The very horror of what I do classifies it past the reach of punishment."

He stopped to watch the movie for a while. It was sci-fi, and there were spaceflight shots with starry backgrounds that exalted him. The ad returned. He watched it closely, and afterward he wrote with a heat and fitfulness he had not shown:

"I do what I will. I paint the world as I will. Your skulls are my paintpots, bitches! I empty them with my rude and potent brush. I splash out frescoes of my revenge. Your cheating sneering little world is my palette. I'll make my masterpieces and lay them out to dry. And I'll have them displayed in the press as if it *were* no more than paint I splash around. And so it is! And so it is! I make it so, and so it is!"

Engelmann laid aside his notebook. He found that he ached to go down again, to swoop for another kill. That lovely blind red impetus had returned to him, his heart was engorged with it as with some bodily fluid.

It caused him a painful division of feeling. He had always loved to savor each deed both ways in time, first through a long anticipation, and after, to relish its echo through the expectant desolation of the city's renewed terror. Especially in this latter period he felt his tread to reverberate, gigantically, through the city. Then, spectral, huge, he lived in the hearts of seven million.

But desire was great upon him, and he lusted for a fierce, unparalleled abundance that would fill the air with the red debris of his redundant rage. After brief hesitation, he made the pact with himself to take further vengeance the following night.

Engelmann did not fall asleep until the afternoon of the next day, and he was still in the depths of his sleep when, at dusk, Siraf terminated his dormancy.

He rolled out from the brick parapet to a clear space on the tar and gravel. There, again in compliance with Archivist tradition, Siraf uttered the Field-worker's Vow prior to transmorphing. The articulation involved a phonetic aspect that sounded like lush, melancholy flute solos. Its cognitive content was, roughly:

> Having sworn to be a foundling through the stars,
> I lie on yet another threshold.
> I will remember, though I travel far.
> As treasure I'll store up all I behold.

He extended his mass into a slender ellipsoid six and a half feet long, and transmorphed.

He had perceived that the fiber-envelopes universally adopted by the indigenes were pretty widely available and thus did not warrant the energy expenditure that would be needed to fabricate them from his own substance. He found, as he lay making detailed adjustments of his new material apparatus, that the pebbles of the rooftop painfully disrupted the curvature of his dorsal dermal surface. He sat up and brushed the little stones off the pale ridgings of back and shoulder muscle. His length of limb stretched his sinewing to gothic gauntness. He stood up and did a brisk dance of acquaintanceship with arms, legs, lungs. Then he walked to the parapet, leaned on it, and looked consideringly over the city.

Profitable as his dormant scanning had been, he now faced a demanding struggle for comprehension. The race was a complex one; close-range involvement with it was going to be a matter of frantic ad-libbing, a swift juggling of known variables with the always bewildering influx of new data. A local parallel for his plight would be a man running dizzily ahead to keep a crazy stack of dishes balanced in his hands. Siraf smiled, practicing the facial contortion that would be deemed appropriate to this image.

His first goal must be clothing. He had foreseen that if his stature was unusual, so would commensurate enfiberments be, but he was counting on the abundance of the population to ensure that an appropriate envelope could be found fairly readily. He scouted now for the nearest considerable center of vital activity.

Siraf happened to be in a largely residential neighborhood, but it was a Saturday night, and three streets away was a very thriving stretch of bars, discos, dirty-book stores, and rib joints. It was invisible to him, even from his thirty-story elevation, but he tele-palped the psychic concentration, noting that high emotive levels seemed to prevail. The area should offer a rich field of options, at least. He picked out an alleyway route that would bring him to the middle of the block. Then he found the shadowiest side of the building and walked down the wall, risking this anomalous gravity-orientation because dark had fallen and it saved time.

The last alley Siraf followed debouched on the activity zone. He crouched behind some big packing crates just inside the alley mouth. Across the street he could see an adult bookstore and an Italian take-out stand. Within five seconds of his pausing in this covert, an individual pulled up to the curb in front of the bookstore, and he was not only amply clothed, but just about Siraf's size as well!

Surely this was one of those rare assignments where the field-worker and his target cosmos were in a strange harmony, and luck blessed the scholar's labors. This convenient individual was of a darkly pigmented species that Siraf had rejected as a mimicry choice when he perceived that it enjoyed more limited options of social interaction than the paler ones. The man wore a broad-brimmed leather hat, a pirate shirt of maroon silk, leather pants, and calf-high Peter Pan boots. He also wore a gold watch and a gold pendant and several fat gold rings. The Eldorado he sat in, all burnished chrome, glowed on the pavements. He waited behind the wheel, and after a few moments two brightly and scantily dressed young women sauntered up to speak to him through his half-open window.

The psychic effluvia that flooded these neon-starred blocks were those of highly stimulated organisms. In all directions he detected the perceptual blur and latent vulcanism of alcohol-saturated brains. Even a highly disruptive act, if swift and decisive, should be slow to engender any organized response in such surroundings. Siraf deemed some initial traumatizing of the natives permissible, if it was strictly localized in its impact and if it facilitated entry into full interaction with them elsewhere. He began to increase the density of his hands and arms.

It took several moments to achieve a massiveness sufficient to deal with the glass and steel of the Cadillac. The girls strolled off again. The statuesque black man in the colorful enfiberments sat adjusting his tape deck. Siraf gauged him to be perhaps an inch taller and twenty pounds heavier than himself. He realized that when the man's enfiberments had been removed, he would experience the atmospheric temperature as a great discomfort. The large boxes behind which the scholar crouched were full of shredded wood, and he decided they should answer nicely for insulation. His arms were ready. He straightened up and strode toward the Eldorado.

There was a fair number of people on the sidewalks, but all at some distance. The nearest were the two girls. Both gave amazed shouts, and one of them made a merry, obscene gesture of admiration. The well-dressed man became aware of Siraf a fraction later than his two employees. He was, however, like most successful pimps a quick-thinking man. He took in the nude stranger's sheetings of stomach muscle, the machinelike power of his thighs, his dreamy and absorbed gait—and he locked both doors and twisted the key in the ignition.

Siraf, telepalping the mechanism, inhibited the spark. He plunged his hands through the window glass, took a crushing grip on the steel of the door, and ripped it entirely out of its snug frame. He placed it as neatly as possible on the roof of the car. Then he reached inside for the man, who was just then crawling through the farther door, and seized him by shoulder and thigh. He spoke several reassurances that he had prepared in advance:

"Come along now," he said soothingly. "Nothing to worry about. This won't take a minute, and you'll be plenty warm afterward."

The man gave him a long, horrified glance. Siraf found pressure points in shoulder and leg that canceled resistance and allowed him to lift the man out. "Outsy-daisy," he said, uncertain of the expression. He hoisted the man straight-arm over his head and carried him to the sidewalk. There he sat him down, leaned him against the wall, and started to remove his clothes. A fascinated crowd was forming, at a respectful distance. Siraf took and donned the hat, the shirt, the trousers, and, last, the boots. He left the jewelry on the man.

When he was dressed—and it was done in moments—he picked up the still-quiescent donor and carried him to the alley mouth. There Siraf bedded him snugly amidst the shredded wood in the largest packing crate. He tucked the insulator around him till only the head lay visible, like a set jewel, or shipped fruit, in the midst of the excelsior. Since he had already grossly violated behavioral norms, he took his leave of the crowd, after an amicable salute, by running straight up the wall of the nearest building and disappearing over the top, eighteen stories above.

He knew that the indigenes' communication system was relatively swift and efficient, and so he traveled several miles, overleaping streets, when he had to, at the darkest points and most carefully chosen instants. He did not think a concerted pursuit likely in a place not only populous but rife, as far as he could gather, with transactions of the most intense and violent kind. He fled on nevertheless, conscientiously safeguarding his researches, and it so happened that as he fled across one particular roof, his passage sent down an eerie drumbeat into the sleep of that other alien, Engelmann, the Angel of Death.

Just then he lay in the dense webbing of a lustful nightmare where ghastly sprawling spiders envenomed and sucked away his flesh. The hammering of those feet kicked through and scattered the nightmare like gusts tearing up a sluggish ground mist and sent sad, turbulent dream-reverberations through him. He felt that desperately vital news, cosmic tidings, were being sped by messenger to a distant city, where there would be a vast rejoicing. And meanwhile he, Engelmann, lay in a living grave upon some giant plain, and saw the runner pass him with that news, and struggled to rise and follow, and could not, could never reach that far, vast rejoicing.

As for Siraf, about a mile beyond this new coincidence he slowed and found a high building for reconnoitering. He decided that his entry point would be a park some blocks distant, and when he had approached it and studied it from a new rooftop perch just across the street, he felt fully confirmed in his decision. Singles bars, cabarets, movies fringed the leafy square, whose pathways and benches were as lively as the surrounding sidewalks.

Long unmoving, he spied that scene. With his fine-spun nets of telepulses he trawled and seined the swarming lagoon of psychic life below. His investigative powers were cruelly limited by distance, but such was the emotive unanimity of the crowd that he could read much from its sheer ambience. It was overwhelmingly obvious from what he saw—pairing rituals, symbolic self-exhibitions, musical mimicry of copulatory contortions—that the place was a hotbed of mating-related activities. It seemed the luck that had clothed him was not faltering.

In the Archives, mating transactions were highly prized as data, for among sexed organisms, they often provided a key to many other emotive patterns and social rituals in a given race's repertory. At the same time, they were recognized as the trickiest exchanges for a field-worker to mimic, since cuing behavior and display symbolism were likely to be very subtly elaborated in such crucial interactions. But Siraf resolved that his daring would match his luck. He would take mating for his immediate aim. He adjusted his hat and took the stairs down to the street.

He followed the sidewalk for a short time before crossing over to the park. With every step he modulated more precisely his posture and gait to those prevailing and achieved a fuller acquaintance with the local vocalization system by rummaging in the vocabularies of those he passed. He accomplished, in a few hundred yards, great refinements in the facial and bodily techniques of confronting and moving among others. He also satisfied himself that most of the active pairing was going on in the park, and, accordingly, he soon crossed over.

It happened that a tall, exhilarated grad student named Jeannie Kudajzinsky had entered the park not long before Siraf did. Prior to doing so, she had enjoyed three stiff Bloody Marys at The Elevator Disco-Bar while watching the dancers with increasingly droll approval. She had spent the last five days, ten hours a day, in the library stacks preparing for her doctoral exams in anthropology. And now she lounged in the park, watching the passersby with a jaunty smile, indulging in what she thought of as "contemporary anthropology," an amused survey of current styles in self-decoration and self-preservation. Her overall feeling was that the night was splendid and anything might happen.

It was from Jeannie that Siraf received his first unmistakable lead in the tangle of fleeting ideations he was combing through as he strolled the paths. He noted among her cerebral events his own image undressed and subjected to various erotic attentions. He circled round to pass her again in a few moments.

She wore body-emphasizing courting finery. Her mammary and gluteal bulges appeared precisely to fulfill the normative ideal, but her stature was sufficiently norm-excessive to make it likely that she was deprived of interaction and thus probably the more motivated toward it. She would stand about six feet tall. Fighting that inevitable pang, that forlorn sense of ignorance every investigator felt as he prepared to grapple closely with alien phenomena, Siraf stepped up to her bench and opened with an expression that he felt fairly sure was appropriate:

"Hello, my dear. You're looking lovely tonight."

Jeannie laughed. Her first disbelief at the approach of this beautiful Nordic pimp became a giddy sense of *savoir-faire,* and she promptly countered him:

"You say that like you know how I look other times. You've been following me around, right?"

"Oh, no. I only just now picked you out. Does your appearance change radically with the passage of time?"

"That's putting it mildly. Think how I'll look in forty years!"

Siraf was about to clarify that he meant over short periods, but Jeannie laughed with such gusto at her own retort that he was cued to discount the whole exchange. The image of himself sitting by her on the bench was recurring vividly in her cerebrations, attended by strong though ambiguous affect. Siraf sat down with a reassuring smile. He was aware of a verbal routine apparently designed for such a situation as this, and so he ventured it: "I was just passing, and I thought I'd stop by for a while and see how you are."

The woman's new laughter informed him that the formula did not apply.

"Well, that's wonderful," she gasped. "We don't get to see you much out this way." Jeannie was going to elaborate the joke when she was taken with a guilty awareness that, in her excitement and anxiety, she had done nothing but laugh at the man. "Listen," she said, "are you a foreigner? Your accent is perfect, I mean you have no accent at all, but your ... your idioms are a little funny—Christ! That doesn't sound like I'm putting you down, does it?"

"I'm not the slightest bit put down. In fact, I am a foreigner. I'm Norwegian." Jeannie's turn of speech had given him his cue, and as he spoke he read the nationality in her expectations.

"You certainly look it," she said. "I mean that as a compliment."

"Oh, yes," said Siraf, adopting a grave manner and feeling with new keenness his ignorance. He decided it was safest to answer tautologically and countercompliment: "A compliment is a very pleasant thing to receive. Thank you. You are a very desirable woman. I mean that as a compliment in return."

Jeannie could find no sign in his face that he was joking, and as she smiled incredulously at him, he went on, developing the seemingly gratifying theme of her physical form:

"For instance, something the observer immediately notes about you is the abundant development of your breasts and your posteriors. Your face has a delightful symmetry. It is ... foxlike." He caught a clear suggestion from her here, as he hesitated. "Moreover I see that you are unusually large, and I thought this a wonderful coincidence, because I too am abnormally large-bodied."

From resurgent hilarity, Jeannie had subsided to bemused attention. All shadings of irony or affront were missing from the man's impossible words. There was an honesty, a tender objectivity in them such as she had never heard in a man's voice. An Innocent? A Noble Savage? If this was illusion, as the whole man seemed illusory in his perfection, she decided to rise to it, as on a dare, and take it at face value. Had she only been pretending to believe that anything might happen tonight?

"You are very sweet to tell me the things you do," she answered. "You have this marvelous sincerity. I hate that word, but it's what you have. Furthermore, you're beautiful, physically I mean, as far as I am concerned. What do you say to that?"

She smiled in his eyes, half humor, half suspense. She did not know what to expect, as if she were Baucis in the myth and had just given a nudge of collusion to one of the disguised gods in her house. Siraf, finding no clue, returned her own formula:

"You are very sweet to tell me."

"Most men wouldn't react that way," she said.

Siraf had a swift fear that the woman was objectively rating the credibility of his performance—knew him to be a performer, in other words, though he found no such image in her. "They would not?" he asked, trying to express innocent, grave alarm. It made Jeannie laugh again in spite of herself.

"Don't be so shocked! It's beautiful that you answered that way. See? Again beautiful. See how you're racking up points?"

The game metaphor, which he had noted as a common turn of mind, locally, oriented him, and he recognized that performance here was humorously commented on without signifying doubt of the performer's genuineness. He laughed, and Jeannie felt a burst of *déjà vu*. Long ago, in high school, before she had become (as she liked to phrase it) "a certified giantess," she had often sat in a car with a certain basketball player. There had been in him a similar ease of acceptance, and with him she had felt an exhilarating, unthreatened freedom of thought and body. He would always start by inviting her for a burger and a Coke. . . .

"Well," said Siraf, "how about driving out for a burger and Coke?"

This almost eerie echoing of her reverie at first made her stare and then made her jump up, as if to throw off bodily the last encumbrances of cynicism and disbelief. She snuffed the night air appreciatively, and said:

"Wonderful! I'd love a drive! I'd love a hamburger!"

They walked down the paths to the sidewalk. The curb was parked solid, and Siraf was confident that an adequate vehicle could be procured. As they passed, he telepalped each car for fuel and performance levels and settled on a new black Cadillac halfway down the block. He probed its ignition and, as they approached it, started it up. Jeannie's surprise told him that the performance was anomalous. Hastily he searched out a reassuring tag for such occasions:

"Oh, you know how it is. It sometimes does that."

"Oh, yes," Jeannie nodded emphatically. "I know what you mean. Sometimes they just get eager to get going."

He now made out the proper sequence from her anticipatory ideations and, springing the locks with telepulses, opened the passenger door and let her in.

At just about this time, Engelmann was slowly awakening. He had left the TV on, and its rising to the more hectic pitch of prime time was what gradually wedged him out of his sleep. He stumbled to the bathroom, came back to his mattress only slightly less groggy, and plunged his hand into a cardboard box on the floor near the bed. From amidst candy bars, cheese-'n'-cracker paks, bags of chips, and boxes of cookies, he drew out several packages of cupcakes, some rolls of miniature dough-nuts, and a quart of chocolate milk, which he liked warm.

He breakfasted. Some of his mind followed the beloved food

down to his insides; some of his mind carefully watched the backgrounds of the tired cop-series for streets and locales he knew; but most of it peered queasily back into the dream-tangle he had just crawled out of.

All those Things That Should Not Be—all that spiderous, bristly grappling. Granted, such things squirmed eternally behind the veil of nightmare. But why should he plunge so often into them? Why should his thought so tirelessly conceive the worst it could? Wasn't it after all only the price of his greatness, his terrible freedom? Engelmann licked his fingers and, with a musing air, took up his notebook.

"Lo!" (he wrote) "I've burst from the shadow-show called Human Action. That pantomime! It's all cringing, all shying-away-from, all writhing-to-please! So I've torn free—I've swung at those shadow-manikins and smashed them to tatters, to rags and lust." He paused, corrected "lust" to "dust," and sped on.

"But just for this reason, the shadow-dimness no longer protects me. I see the real infinity of possibility, infinite possibility both dark and light. That's why so many nightmares come with freedom!"

He stopped to savor this high pitch of understanding for a moment, and the feel of archangelic overview quickened his heart to full wakefulness.

"Oh, yes, I pay!" (he wrote) "Power isn't free! It's not just given away! Dues? I guess I know about paying dues!"

He shook his head here with a wry smile of self-admiration.

"Oh, there will be rest at the end! I admit I've had that consolation to stiffen me against the nightmares. Everyone earns a rest, and for me there'll be the long hours of protection and nourishment. Institutional life! All shining and brilliant with the lovely psychic varnishes of drugs!

"But for now, there is still the struggle! I'm not so ready to give up the power of flight—not so fast, whatever it costs! So for now let the dues be reckoned, and I'll just pay up on demand."

All the latent feeling of the nightmare was dispersed now, and the Angel of Death was fully himself, voluptuously stretching out the wings of his oversoaring irony. And, like the splendid sun-burnished cock in the fresh morn, he suddenly craved to tread some squawking, fluster-feathered she-bird and hammer the heat of his blood into her pleasure-devastated flesh.

So the Angel of Death took up the image of his beloved and laid her in a shadowy place behind his eyelids. He laid her so that the shadows concealed her head. Her body cringed and shivered under his taloned regal feasting. She rolled her dark-smeared head with her cherished agony. And her clutching, penetrated flesh—aided by Engelmann's deft right hand—tugged and tugged on the root of his pleasure and at last, powerfully, quite plucked it out of those divine loins.

The Angel of Death rose and washed and changed his clothes. He began to clean his gun, and as he did so, fell to musing again on the ease and quietude of a mental institution. This line of thought shortly led him to so piercing-sweet a mirth that he dropped his work and snatched up his notebook again. He wrote:

"It's like being a giant that no one sees rightly. The doctors will come up to me, and they'll talk to my knees, thinking they see me. I roar down to them: 'Here I am up here, you sniveling jerks!' They nod compassionately to my knees and answer: 'Yes, these inflated ideas—they are your punishment as much as your pleasure. Tragically for others, you've been led to cherish these ideas of exaggerated potency and now you are compelled to enact them.'

"I boom back jovially: 'Doctors! My exaggerations are made true by your sons' and daughters' blood. I *am* gigantic with it. Up here, Doctors! Up here I am!'

" 'Yes,' they say, 'that is the horror of your condition—your utter separateness. You're trapped in a void where others are no realer, no more comfort to you, than furniture.'

"How answer to be heard? This dogged, blind, idiot compassion is of course only the child of fear. Everyone on Earth uses others like furniture, cautiously at first, then abusively, once familiarity sets in. I have made grosser and more daring uses of them and admit it's for my whim, and through this I've reached another order of being, another order of happiness. I could roar out louder than an H-bomb, and they'd still be straining their ears at me to catch the nuances. It's just this simple: I'm the crazy guy who happens to *be* Napoleon. I *am* the Angel of Death."

Engelmann read what he had written, reread it, and at length, took up the gun again. When it was cleaned and reloaded he got up and turned off the TV. He pulled on a jacket and stuffed his Magnum into one pocket of it. Into the other he shoved three candy bars from his cardboard box and turned off his light.

Fearlessly he walked down the dark flights and fearlessly out into the gusty night. He stabbed and twisted with his key, and his deep-chested car came to life. The Angel of Death was again on the city, and he meant to hover wheresoever he would—to stand and stoop with Olympian randomness wherever the covert stirred beneath his eye.

Siraf, for much of their drive, was absorbing navigational procedures and signals, while following Jeannie's ideations closely for clues to his route. Simultaneously, of course, he was encoding everything, for in this he never ceased. Jeannie talked about herself, luxuriating in a sense that she could say anything that came to her, and yet only half attending to what she did say. For her sense of sexual-fantasy-come-true had not faltered. The very turnings of the car had a dreamlike congruence with her desires. All the shopping districts and showpiece streets of the city that she loved to see at night streamed past them now, while through it all Siraf sat stately, beautiful and grave, receiving the details of her life with his odd, earnest answers. The sensation of unreal rightness peaked when he steered them into one of the few old-fashioned drive-ins still operating in the city. In her high school days they had been the norm, before the coming of the drive-through.

Siraf handled the opening meal transactions fairly smoothly, using his foreigner's prerogative to ask for details of procedure when he failed to palp clear indications. He watched her handling of the food when it arrived, and aped it.

"How did you start the car from outside?" Jeannie asked. He read her back the hypothesis she mentally rehearsed in self-answer.

"Remote control," he said and, on a further hint, significantly tapped his empty pocket. He bit into his cheeseburger, far too hard. It ejected a gout of sauce through its greasy diaperings and splattered the chest of his shirt.

When Jeannie laughed, he joined her, causing her to apply her napkin with guilty solicitude and turn on the lights to bring the carhop. She was an older woman. Pointing to his shirt, Siraf told her:

"The cheeseburger squirted it."

"Look, sir. We make them all the same," she said. "They don't squirt other people."

He nodded. "I see. Perhaps I bit it too forcefully."

The woman stared, and seeing his candid gaze, her brow darkened.

"Then, again," he offered, "it is possible that I was holding it incorrectly." Jeannie leaned forward quickly.

"Could we just get some water please?"

She helped him wipe the silk clean, pressing her free hand against his chest to tauten the fabric. The tactile influx she experienced awakened a complex image in her that Siraf noted.

Precisely here—in Siraf's notice and misunderstanding of Jeannie's mental image—was demonstrated an insidious and incorrigible blind spot affecting the judgments of all the Archives's field-workers in their readings of highly evolved conscious forms. Jeannie's image—to which her mind had reverted throughout their meal—was one of copulation in the backseat of a car on a breezy night. The car was parked on a street canopied by big broad-leaved trees and lit by old-fashioned streetlights.

Siraf took this ideation as a simple, projected goal, though Jeannie did not clearly visualize her partner in it. The assumption was reasonable, on the grounds of the image's consonance with their actual situation: it was night, there was a light breeze, they had a car.

In fact, Jeannie was savoring a fantasy. The spilled sauce, the heat of skin felt through a thin shirt, had renewed certain memories of her basketball player. They had never parked in such a place as she pictured, however—the street was added from childhood walks in another city, where she had lived for a time with an aunt. This sensual nostalgic compound, mixing memory and desire, was in no sense a project. Jeannie feared the Angel of Death as much as anyone.

On the theoretical level, the Archives fully recognized the inevitability of such errors. But in the field, the urgent thing was always to identify the subject's dominant psychic configuration. The less articulated strata of consciousness that this emerged from must often be neglected, for simple lack of time to analyze them; the interaction must be kept going above all else, and of course there were the field-worker's ongoing anatomical investigations and his monitoring of the larger environment to be sustained simultaneously as well.

In the present instance, Siraf was lucky. His proposal that they "drive to a tree-lined street, and park there," did not elicit the alarm it might well have done. His unfailing closeness to her thought so emphasized his magic aura that she could not simply recoil in fear from a suggestion that would have to be called insane, in this place and time, coming from anyone else. Coming from Siraf, this offer of her erotic dream made real had the character of one of those crucial choosings offered the heroes of so many of the myths she studied. To the daring, this mythic choice offered revelation. To the daunted, drab endurance. Jeannie, aglow with three Bloody Marys and dawning lust, decided that here was a critical challenge to her faith and recklessness. She must dare to choose enchantment over safety.

And, after she had assented to his proposal—with a grand "Why not?" and a sweep of the arm that scattered a few drops of her Coke on the lap of his trousers—a further, somewhat shabbier, reflection occurred to her that made the risk seem less. After a moment she brought it out, to confirm it to herself:

"I know it's morbid, but you get to where you calculate, you know? I mean about this Angel of Death character. The week just after one of those killings is statistically the safest time, right? Ghoulish way to think, I guess, but there it is."

Siraf was preoccupied with internally reviewing the sexual apparatus he would shortly have to employ, for he palped high oxygen concentrations nearby and guessed they were approaching heavily treed neighborhoods. He gathered, distractedly, that the "Angel of Death" awakened strong avoidance reactions and that he was a kind of public figure. His name was not associated in her with any clear facial or bodily image, but rather with written accounts too elliptically evoked to admit piecing out.

Jeannie had quelled her own fear. Thus easily was this phantom vanquished, whose only reality to her was a series of news photos of meaningless curbsides with police and stretchers. But as fear dwindled to insubstantiality, she was pleased to poke at it with little jabs of theory, noticing the while that Siraf was experimentally stiffening his procreative member. (He was astonished at the rigidity that the flaccid protuberance was capable of attaining.)

"It's really amazing to think that what that character does is essentially a substitute for, you know, sex. It's a classic pattern, I mean apparently it pops up at the time—I mean *all* the time. You've heard of it, the weapon's the symbolic organ, right? He's displaying his potency to the woman by killing her. There's the equation of sex and pain, death is the orgasm he causes. I guess sometimes you feel vengeful, but what's the point of killing someone like that? It would be just as cruel and pointless as what he does to others."

Just then Siraf was busy appreciating for the first time what a powerfully engrossing phase of experience sexual engagement was for this race. As he tested the relevant aspects of his neural apparatus—that is to say, almost all of it—he saw that he faced a turbulent adventure. Perhaps a fit image for this stout spirit, as he faced the strange cerebroneural uproar that would shortly engulf him, would be that of a beginning swimmer facing huge waves that he must, for the first time, ride.

Nevertheless he was, in a half-attending way, fascinated by this strange ritual variant of the mating pattern that Jeannie was so glibly describing. It appeared to be a cultural institution that was abhorred, but of sufficient permanence to generate a theoretical tradition. That he was dealing, on this planet, with a highly symbolic sentience, he had seen immediately. But a symbolic system that could substitute death for the process of insemination would be a startling oddity to add to the Archives' store. Then Jeannie's train of thought became strongly and unequivocally mating-directed. He sought, amidst towering leafy sycamores and old-style streetlights, a place to park.

Thus it was that Jeannie Kudajzinsky became a point of intersection, of convergence, for the two starry nomads abroad in that night. Unburdened by all sense of antecedent and consequence, she enjoyed fluid and explosive embraces and intermittences of warm enclaspment during which she watched the gold-brown sycamore leaves where the sparse lights splashed them with visibility. Of the two who converged on her, Engelmann, even in the instant of his actually seeing her, possessed her only as an abstraction, while Siraf was so busily encoding her (and his own) electrochemical activity that he almost ceased to perceive her simple bodily presence at all. Between these two potencies, she lived her dream of love alone.

Siraf, for his part, was humbly amazed at the extreme aesthetic capacities that were being revealed to him. Their copious, spasmodic exchanges of fluids he found to be among the most dynamic transactions he had ever observed to fall within the repertory of a race's routine behaviors. So desperately focused was his attention that the brief impingement of a strong psychic source outside that focus came as a slight shock to him. The signal he caught, as the pair of them rested, was a very intense ideation of a faceless pair coupling in a car. Siraf found the coincidence striking. The ideator was moving at a vehicular rate and passed from range almost as soon as Siraf had identified his thought. Then Jeannie's slow, rocking demands recommenced.

Siraf reentered the labyrinth of his borrowed form. Jeannie, splendid and abandoned, rode his lap until, all at once, she drove herself greedily to climax. He followed suit.

She lay against him. She spoke thickly into his chest. "It's astonishing. Having exactly what I want so easily. But then you're like a dream. A wet dream."

"A wet dream. Is that an idiom?"

She sat up and laughed. "I don't think so, dear. I don't know what else you call them. Nocturnal emissions, I guess, would—"

The light in the car came on. It was Siraf's doing, and what had moved him to do it had gone unnoticed by Jeannie, so that at first all her startlement was at the sudden illumination. Then, following Siraf's eyes, she saw the gun and squinting face behind it just outside the window. She saw this through the image of herself and Siraf mirrored on the glass—saw how she straddled him and gaped, saw how her gape began to become a scream—all these last readings of the world she took before the gun fired. When it did, alarm had activated only the slightest muscular resistances in her, and the slug's impact snatched her off the scholar's thighs and flung her slack as a doll against the farther door.

For both the superhuman wanderers who were thus brought together face-to-face for the first time, this was a moment almost impossibly charged with meaning. On Siraf's side, so surprised had he been that he was still scrambling along a nano-second behind the attacker's cerebral flow. He had hit the light in a reflexive attempt to maximize data of the transaction he suddenly realized was at hand. During the first shot, and Jeannie's falling, and the subsequent instant that the eyes stared over the gun at him through the hole in the glass, his mind sprinted to get abreast of developments: (a) Jeannie was dead. (b) This was beyond doubt precisely the mating variant, and the practitioner of it, she had spoken of. (c) He himself was just sufficiently entangled with her legs to inhibit by a critical instant his extricating himself. (d) The man was now squeezing the trigger again, and the slug would surely reach Siraf's skull. (e) Therefore, he must of necessity again exceed behavioral norms, to preserve the viability of his mimicked apparatus.

The confrontation found Engelmann likewise somewhat stunned. There had been that sudden blooming of light within the car, just as he was stealing near, infernal yellowish light falling on those splendid lengths of limb, those heroic loins all notched and knotted with the goatish strength of lust; there had been her Atlantean breasts nosing like lilies from the rumpled calyx of her pushed-up clothes, and his Luciferian face. Engelmann felt that he had stumbled upon the very archetype of the crime that it was his divinity to scourge. He had uncovered daemons, or demigods, at the coupling. Here was the two-backed beast itself, the Enemy, divine, in its way, as the Angel of Death was. Here was the test, and he would meet it. Exalted, he raised his massy Magnum at her staring not-yet-fearful eyes, and bravely, steadily, mightily, he smote her with fire and ruin. And lo, she was hurled down by the power of his tool and cast below in blood and darkness. And then Engelmann swung that godly tool on the goatish colossus. Here, for an instant, the Angel of Death bore with his naked eyes the stare of the enemy. In that hawk-browed gaze the Angel saw no fear, only a bright unreadable concentration. Then the Angel of Death gave battle, fearing not, the song of supreme combat in his ears. He pumped out roaring destruction into the eyes of the Enemy.

This was the beginning of the Angel's ordeal. Here commenced That Which Should Not Be. The range was close, and the shot sprayed what seemed to be the whole back of the man's head against the black tuck-and-roll and the windshield behind him. But even as Engelmann turned to flee his triumphant work, that spray of pulverized bone and brain leapt off the upholstery, jumped off the glass, leaving it unmarked save for the bullet's exit hole, and sped back, recohering in air like a convergent bee-swarm, to reconstitute the gold-haired spheroid of the titan's head.

Seeing that face reknit, and the dark shattered eyes resume their stare—seeing this ruptured the very soul of the Angel of Death. A vital tissue of belief, a deep and unsuspected faith, was torn in him. His mind bled horror that flooded thought and swept it down dreadful channels that had long been dug in him, and lain waiting. The Angel of Death ran, flinging away his gun, and making water in his chaotic muscular exertions to escape.

He hauled himself behind the wheel of his car, left idling a half block down the street. He loosed the brake and grabbed the stick shift and . . . waited.

He could not flee, plunge off into the madness now alive in him, as long as a hope remained that he had dreamed. If that black car in his rearview did not stir, if the moments lengthened and nothing happened, he had hallucinated and was free. If not, Engelmann knew with an eerie certainty what would happen: that *thing,* only temporarily a man in form, would burst through the very steel of the car, surge out, and, with a roar of Ragnarök, sprint after him. He waited, the gunfire utterly forgotten. That, and the police it might have summoned, existed in another world, to which he could never return if he did not prove now to himself that only corpses lay in that black car.

Siraf was ready for immediate pursuit but sat still throughout Engelmann's sprint back to his car. He longed to give chase. On this lucky excursion, jackpot on jackpot of data was falling to his lot, and he meant to seize on this second homicidal subject in any way he could, if only by getting a verbal report from the individual on the full meaning of his rite's bizarre symbolism.

But the female, Jeannie, had clearly abhorred in the abstract the fate that had now actually stricken her. Siraf very much wanted to fix her while it was still possible. He touched her long calves, still across his thighs, hating the wastage. The Archives' most fundamental traditions abjured him not to do it—not at the cost of the new data and not when the first subject's loss was completely fortuitous. Siraf's ambition, and his dedication to the Archives, showed him necessity, but he could not bring himself to move until absolutely the last moment, when the other's car should start to move and he must run it down before it lost him.

And, then, it did *not* move! The aggressor waited down the street, visualizing a bizarre form of pursuit by Siraf, ideating with such intensity that the image came through clearly even at that range. Siraf was being invited into the ritual. What an amazingly flexible acceptance of the (to him) impossible on the part of this attacker! For he was now playing the game of retreat and coy pause, and waiting to be chased by his victim!

There would be time then, after all. He began increasing his bodily density. Simultaneously he sought out by thermal palp every least fragment of Jeannie's head throughout the car's interior. The finer fluids had cooled quickly on the glass and metal, but all retained critical traces of warmth. The reassembly was telekinetic, his body motionless in its process of mass-gain. He referred to his enzymatic record for his exhaustive readouts of her craniocerebral morphology. It was a work of delicate correlations, electrically swift. The chips and tissue-shreds each had to be minutely cleansed and neatly relodged in the dense three-dimensional puzzle. It took twenty-seven seconds. He sanitized, sutured, and sealed the countless seams with thermal telebeams, infinitely fine. When he saw her eyes open and struggle for focus, he was content, and as, just then, his density had reached its peak, he propped her on the seat, pulled up his trousers, and hurled himself against the car door.

For Engelmann, the healing seconds of silence and inactivity had almost closed his horror's wound. He breathed deeply and pulled the car into gear, scarcely yet daring to believe he had been delivered from a mythic retribution, delivered from the Impossible. Then in the mirror he saw the Cadillac's side bloom outward and the giant emerge from the tattering steel and spraying glass amidst a roar of Ragnarök. With a howl of acceleration his deep-chested car fled away.

Now inexorably That Which Should Not Be came to pass. Precisely as he dreaded, the giant began to sprint after him, and though Engelmann shortly hit fifty, his Enemy gained. He drove at and beyond the limit of control, sliding and careering through turns that ought by all odds to have destroyed him. The giant gained. The Angel of Death was Phaethon now, dragged broken-limbed among the stars, a mortal suddenly seized by real gods.

"Real Gods!" He screamed it aloud. "No!" Had he not then believed his own godhead? Yes. No. Yes—but *not like this*. It was partly a *game!* Only the deaths had been real—ordinary deaths. His divinity had only been . . . poetic!

But there was no holding on to this late truth, for it was truth no more. He had flown upward on real wings, had for a fact soared up to where the Impossible lodged. For here it was a dozen strides back of him, its face an image of mythic calm while its legs and arms drove it forward as furiously as the connecting rods on a locomotive's wheels. The Angel of Death had been just angel enough, had had just power enough, to damn himself, to bring down on himself a truly divine avenger. At home there was a machine gun, and to that poor scrap of potency, the limit of his defense, Engelmann now bent all his thoughts. He threw a left turn too fast, side-swiped a parked car, and roared on, dribbling glass and clattering with popped chrome.

Siraf stopped. He had by now returned to normal mass, but

even so he found that the effort required to maintain this speed would shortly do serious damage to his adopted anatomy. He had read a clear destination in his attacker's thoughts, including a map thither that the latter had fleetingly rehearsed to himself. The distance remaining to be covered was not great.

So the young scholar settled to an easy jog, husbanding his forces. He had received premonitory glimpses of his quarry's desire—of the scenario that the man waited to play out when Siraf joined him in his room. He foresaw that new mimicries would be required, and that this investigation would almost surely exhaust his research energies—hardly a misfortune, considering the choice insights he had been granted. Especially this second find. Could a rarer, more paradoxical and self-destructive rite exist, than this his recent attacker flew to consummate?

And at length, when Siraf stood in the vestibule of Engelmann's apartment building and read him clearly where he lay seven stories above, the scholar found in full what he had guessed at, an astonishing necro-erotic ritual with himself as co-celebrant. He was indeed expected to transform his body—and how could the man have educed so unerringly his power to do so? More, how could he so smoothly accept it, beyond the capacities of his kind though it was, and incorporate it in his passionate fantasies? Not for the first time in his career, Siraf acknowledged with awe in his heart the endless creativity of consciousness as he had met with it throughout its polymorphic, transgalactic sprawl. He deactivated the lights of the stairwell and caused his form to melt into several smaller ones. Slowly these climbed the carpeted stairs, with a whispery prickly noise, mounting multiply to probe this second earthly mystery.

Could a more dreadful, even tragic, misunderstanding be conceived? It was lunatic expectation, not desire, that powered those intense imaginings of Engelmann's! But how could Siraf, speed-reading his impossibly involved text, be blamed? The Angel's visions sprang from his real (and all too unreal) encounter, but the grafting where hallucination sprouted from fact was missed by the scholar. And since the half-sexual terror that now flooded the man's nerves was not grossly different from the half-sexual rage of his initial assault, here too Siraf saw continuum and concentrated on reading his scripted role in the rite. Repugnance he surely felt, but professionalism squelched it. He had already gathered that no kind of emotional violence should surprise him, coming from this turbulent species.

Somewhat later, near the stillest hour of the night, Jeannie Kudajzinsky stepped through a great hole of shredded steel and stood on asphalt and broken glass, an alien in this ended and continued world. It might have been one of those ritual womb-symbols that she emerged from, she thought, for she found herself reborn—into the Impossible.

She walked along the sidewalk, very slowly. All was emptiness, holocaust hadn't raised a single siren. Had she died in fact, and were all these buildings crypts? An hour and more she had sat in the ruined car, remembering, and no one had passed.

She decided that the most terrible aspect of it all, the thing that could conceivably drive her mad, was that there should be nothing more, that she should now have to walk back into her life and simply resume it. She looked at the big sycamore leaves applauding the wind. Like vile arthritic hands they covetously rubbed the brass-nippled streetlamps. Panic began to radiate from a point-source in her stomach's pit. Just then she was spoken to—distinctly, voicelessly:

"Jeannie. Be comforted. This is Siraf. I am an extraterrestrial and your experiences were simple realities, every one."

She looked straight up—from instinct, as the telepulses bore no directional trace. Ten feet above her, under a vaulting of branches, hung that tuft of transcosmic thistledown, Siraf's traveling shape. Jeannie gazed. After a long and chaotic moment, she *was* comforted. Softly she said:

"You were. . . ."

"In a human shape. We mated. The sexual homicide—his name was Engelmann—killed you. I repaired you. Then I indulged Engelmann in his fantasies. He is dead, my dear. Barring the energy I need for my return, I am utterly depleted, and there was no fixing him. But from Engelmann I learned—too late for him—the proneness of your race to psychic trauma, and so I've taken care to explain things. Do you understand?"

"Yes," she said. "But why . . . ?"

"Scholarship. Please accept my thanks for your time and cooperation. I apologize for the inconvenience involved."

"I'm a scholar too!" she blurted. Sadness, and the lone discoverer's exaltation, stretched her heart between them, while through all else and amazing to herself, she felt a piercing envy.

"Yes," Siraf responded. "And you have taught me much. Goodbye."

He was gone. "Goodbye," she said, an instant too late. And then once more, in a shout, the better to project her voice across the light-years: "Goodbye!"

After a moment she spread her arms and did a sprawling, not to say gargantuan, pirouette under the sycamore trees. She whooped with laughter, and at the quiet, coward streets where gunshots and fury had not raised a single stir of protest or of aid, she shook her fist and shouted: "Revelation! Great! But what the hell can I *do* with it?"

Engelmann sat on his mattress with his back against the corner he'd shoved his bed into, after bolting his door. He had the machine gun across his thighs and the TV on. He couldn't watch the TV, however—only the door, whose terrible flimsiness was like an ongoing horror show that the tube could not compete with. That Which Should Not Be, *was*. Effortlessly, irresistibly, It took Its being and did Its will on man. Not any man. On *him* alone. Engelmann wept and ground his teeth together.

What was there not? What unspeakabilities, glimpsed in dreams, were not proven now? For he knew the true form of that which chased him. It was a trinity, three-in-one. Eight-legged things from the sniggering dark, come scuttling down from the poisonous cobwebby stars. But he had not flown up there! Not truly! Why should they come down? That dreadful three-in-one—one for his face, one for his heart, one for his loins. He'd had no wings, not really! Only a costume made of others' blood, only a god-costume. Was that his crime, blasphemy? What wall, what puny dike of Possibility, was left to stand between himself and chaos now? All the rest of the world was safe in its fortress, only he—*was that a movement outside the door?*

Back inside the Fortress! Back inside! O World, let Engelmann back within the walls! Engelmann wants back in, dear world! Things are coming, things that will pierce his pitiful skin and corrode his precious heart with poisons!

Was that a bulging of the panel of the door?

Oh, here is Engelmann, alone and naked! Take him in, he begs you; he is helpless, his water flows; oh, pick him up and cradle him out of harm! Momma! Not death! Not pain and death!

But something was piercing the door, soundlessly, as if it were clay, or cheese. And a blister was swelling from the ceiling, and another from the wall. Three tarantulas, big as German shepherds, hatched through wood and plaster; their shaggy legs whispered as they came tenderfooting toward him. One for his face. One for his heart. One for his loins. The gun, as they do in nightmares, failed to fire.

UNCLE TUGGS

I

Now you should understand that when Gabe Tuggs offered me this job, I didn't like the idea of working for him. I didn't like getting into any kind of deal with any of those three Tuggs brothers, but right then my bank account was hurtin' for certain. I'd had like a great burst of energy take hold of me when I made so much money landscaping that spring. I started building that cabin Barbara's always bitching about—and with the kids getting so big now, the trailer does seem small, even with all the little rooms I've tacked onto it. Anyway, I'd poured the slab and had the packets of two-by-fours delivered. So right then, early that fall, there was a little freak rain, and the job calls stopped dead. A lot of people are just looking for any excuse to put off having work done till next spring. I'd been two weeks without a nibble. I still owed on the two-by-fours, and we had big dentist bills, and both my stake-bed and my pickup needed new sets of tires.

So. When Gabe Tuggs came and found me in the Eight Ball off Courthouse Square and offered me this job, I said, "Hmmm." I said to him, "Gabe, why don't we have another beer while I weigh it in my mind?"

Gabe used the cast on his left hand for a hammer on the bar. He ordered two beers. "And a shooter of bourbon with mine, Lloyd," I told Lloyd. Gabe didn't say anything, just paid. He was tight-fisted, so I could see now he really meant to talk business. The job was cutting fifty or sixty trees on Uncle Tuggs's place to firewood, and I liked the deal. But I took my time drinking. I didn't want to answer too fast. I sat there a bit like I was just relaxing and savoring Lloyd's god-awful house bourbon.

Of course the truth was, I never could feel very relaxed sitting next to Gabe Tuggs. It's true he was the smallest of the three brothers. He stood not a hair over six feet two and was scarcely a yard wide. And if he weighed an ounce over 240, I'd eat the difference—and a nasty meal it would be. The thing was that what Gabe lacked in size he made up in meanness. His cast covered up one of his gaudier tattoos, but he had plenty of others showing—three-color tattoos with lots of teeth and tails and claws in them. A kind of burnt-leather-and-motor-oil smell came off of Gabe—his ponytail even had a kind of motor-oily look, and he always wore shades that were as black as a bug's eyes. He was the kind of guy that sitting next to him made you uneasy, like sitting next to a bear.

But anyway, I did like the deal. I could take one cord out for every cord I left to them. In October I could already get $140 for a cord that was only half splitters. If I pushed it, I could truck out two of those a day.

I also *trusted* the deal. I didn't trust the brothers, you understand—I trusted their situation, which was plain to anyone who thought about it. Since moving onto their Uncle Tuggs's place to caretake after he disappeared, they would have planted every shed and barn on it cram-full of prime skunkweed. No doubt of it. It'd be safe indoors from theft and law, and it'd be the readiest big cash they could make off the property. So. Waiting for harvest, with the grow-lights working overtime, they'd need cash in the short term for gas, drugs, booze, and food. What to do? Chop up and sell old Uncle's oaks and madronas. The boys would be living off all that wood all through the winter and spring. They'd have to play straight with their cutters and customers. And this was twice as true just now, with both Grant Tuggs, the oldest—and now Gabe, too—injured like they had been, and within a week of each other. Knowing Gabe from high school wouldn't have counted for anything if they'd wanted to cheat me, but their having to depend on that firewood for their octanes and their Jack Daniels and their elephant tranquilizers—that was what made me say to Gabe:

"Well, Gabe, I believe I could take on that job. Do I under-

stand rightly that you've cut some kind of road so I can get my
stakebed down into the draw?"

I knew Uncle's place since high school, from having my cars
up there to be fixed from time to time, like a lot of people. It
was six or seven acres, with the house and barn and sheds on
about a half acre of fairly level ground, not far off the highway.
Behind that the land dropped away to hilly ground with several
draws winding through it with plenty of trees growing in them
with lots of mid-sized scraggly stuff perfect for weeding out for
firewood.

Gabe looked pissed at my question. He hammered the bar
with his cast again. He said, "We got a roadcut down into the
first draw. Goddamn dozer broke down right at the bottom. Still
sittin' there, but you can get around it. Same," he told Lloyd.

I was impressed—I mean that he bought me another drink
like that. I could see the boys really wanted someone they could
trust on this job. I said:

"Boy, that's too bad. You guys really seem to be having some
bad luck lately. How's Grant doin'?" I didn't quite dare ask about
his break, but I looked at his cast when I asked about Grant's.
He gave me that black bugeye like he was considering how it
would be to twist my scalp off like a beer bottle cap. Though I'm
kind of short, my cap's on pretty tight and might give him some
trouble. It would sure hurt like hell to have him trying it out,
though. Finally, not moving his lips much, Gabe says:

"They're changing his cast tomorrow."

Gabe had actually thought Grunt's accident was pretty
funny when he had it—back before Gabe was hurt himself. He
described it to Billy Vale, who he'd sometimes drink with, and
Billy Vale described it to me. Old Grunt (Grunt was what we all
called Grant behind his back)—Grunt decided to split up a heap
of rollers they had by the house, so their own stoves would be
taken care of.

Now Grunt had plenty of back for labor, but he didn't like it
any better than his brothers did, so when he got inspired to some
kind of work, he liked to jump on it, power through it, and get it
over with. So Grunt honked up a couple foot-long rails of crank,
and had five or six shooters of Cuervo Gold, and munched

down some salt and lime slices, and fired up the splitter that old
Uncle Tuggs had left behind, like he'd left behind almost all his
other gear when he disappeared. Grunt starts plunking those
rollers into the splitter and gets such a rhythm going that in no
time he finishes the pile.

Grunt's breathing fire by now. He jumps into Uncle's old
stakebed (which the front brakes are just about shot on, but what
the hell) and goes jouncing down their little roadcut and into
the draw. He lays about him with the chain saw and drives up
another heap of rollers. He does some more shooters, munches
a bunch more salt and lime slices, honks a couple more rails of
crank, and fires the splitter back up. He starts feeding it rollers
from off the truckbed, turning back and forth between the bed
and the splitter. Well, the splitter's wheels are locked, but you
know how they can creep sometimes? Except this one practically
jumps—swings one end all the way around behind Grunt's legs
so that he trips and falls backwards across it as he turns from the
truck with another roller. To top it off, just then the wedge goes
into drive! And Grunt swore he never touched the drive lever
when he fell, and it's hard to see how he *could* have. If he hadn't
had so much crank in him, he'd never have hoisted his legs out
of the way in time, and as it was, one of his feet snagged and the
wedge nipped him just hard enough to crack his shinbone.

Anyway, I just shook my head sympathetically, about Grunt's
cast and all. "Well, Gabe," I said, "I like your offer. I'll want
to leave early enough each day to take my buyers their wood
straight off my truck so I don't have to stockpile."

"Long as you leave the same amount you leave with every
day, I *give* a shit. I want to start tomorrow morning. I'll be out to
mark the trees for you."

I wanted to ask him what he was going to do, take a bite out
of each one he wanted cut? "What about trucking your cords
for you?" I asked him. "Will you want to hire me for that—I
mean, since your truck's out?"

I thought this might make Gabe mad again because that was
how he got hurt, you see, trying to change the front brake shoes
on that truck, but he surprised me. He kind of looked off into
the air. "Who knows?" he said. "Maybe we won't want to sweat

the work ourselves. Let's just get some cut first. And remember, you're making two cords of splitters for us, too."

"No problem. I can use your splitter?"

Gabe shrugged. "If you want."

I wasn't sure I *did* want. I worked on my drink, thinking how it was no wonder the brothers seemed ready to hire out all the work, even selling their own cords. First you had their trouble with that splitter. Then you had Gabe's accident. He'd got that truck's front end up on Uncle's roll-under hydraulic pump-jack, laid under there and started hammering off the front left drum with a blunt chisel and a hand sledge. (He'd told Billy Vale this one, too, but he didn't laugh as much telling it as he did about Grunt's.) All of a sudden, *whoosh,* the pressure blows out of the jack and the truck sits on Gabe's face. He was lying on thick grass and he had the wheel lying under the axle, so his head wasn't mashed, but one of his hands got caught half-raised and he cracked two of the bones in it. And then, on top of all this, there was their grader breaking down, which I hadn't heard about. Put it all together, it was starting to seem like everything old Uncle Tuggs had left on the place was giving the brothers trouble. When Uncle and Cherry (his little honey) and Ralph (his big mean smelly old dog) disappeared early last summer, he took nothing but his old black repair van with him. Every vehicle, tool, or component known to man, or pieces of it, was left on his place, though a lot of it was scattered or rusted or hidden in a pile of parts. And none of it seemed to be doing the boys any good. I got up.

"Well, OK, Gabe," I told him. "I'll see you in the morning. You guys hear anything from the sheriff yet?"

This question actually seemed to startle Gabe for a minute. That might seem odd, since it was him and his brothers that had got the official search for Uncle started in the first place. Of course, they'd been waiting two months now with no results. Add to that the fact that it had been three months longer yet since Grant Tuggs had been the last person to see Uncle alive, and maybe Gabe's reaction wasn't really so odd. The boys must just have given up any hope of ever seeing Uncle again, and must not even be thinking about it anymore.

"Hell," Gabe said after a minute. "They haven't found jack-shit."

As I drove home I thought about the job, and got more and more pleased with it. There were mucho cords in those draws. Once I got home I hadn't been on the phone fifteen minutes before I'd sold three cords, COD, as soon as I could deliver.

II

A little after sunrise I drove my stakebed up to Tuggs's yard. I knew that place pretty well, as I say, and right then, in that early sunlight, it seemed like a lot of years since I'd started bringing my first car up here—an old Plymouth. Hell, twenty years at least, in plain fact. In those days the brothers might be around, but it was Uncle everyone came up here to see. The boys had never lived here before now. When you thought about it, it was kind of funny, actually, that being called Uncle was the old man's own joke, from his kid sister having three such big sons. He'd sure stuck by the joke—I couldn't recall any other name for him—but the thing was, he was just the opposite of a family-minded man. He'd let his nephews hang around his place, but even though their mother did a lot of moving and drinking and remarrying, and they got shuffled around a lot, he'd never take them in even temporarily. He probably figured she'd try to scrape them off on him, and he probably was right, but even so, I could remember thinking it was funny how he didn't even seem to feel like an uncle towards them, even though he'd let them use his tools and fix their heaps at his place. For instance, there was that accident with Ronnie Partlett that had made Gabe Tuggs kind of famous when we were back in high school. He and Ronnie stole a bottle of bourbon from Gabe's stepdad, and took Ronnie's mom's car, and were driving all around one Friday night smashing mailboxes with a baseball bat they'd stolen from the school gym. Well, Gabe was driving, and Ronnie was leaning way out with the bat to smash a bunch of boxes that they were just coming up on, and all of a sudden a cat shoots across the road, and Gabe swerves to mash it, and poor

Ronnie's head is jammed into those mailboxes. Gabe got a year on the youth farm, and I remembered being up here a couple days later and hearing Uncle talking about it with some other old fart that he was fixing his tractor for. The other guy said that Ronnie was no better than a vegetable now, for all intents and purposes, and Uncle laughed and said, yeah, but you had to be fair to Gabe, because Ronnie hadn't had that far to go in the first place. Which was God's truth. What struck me just then was how Uncle said it, like he saw Ronnie and Gabe on a par, and didn't feel any more involved with one than the other.

What Uncle did—even more than working here at his place— was ride a kind of circuit mechanic's route in an old black van jammed with tools. Back when I was a kid, he was already a strange, tall, skinny old guy that everybody's grandfather liked to joke and cackle with and everybody's grandmother disapproved of as being foulmouthed but was also a little secretly tickled by. He was kind of like an old-time circuit preacher that prayed over cars and graders and trucks. He'd stand talking over an engine, jawing with the owner, as long as he ever spent touching it. But then, finally, just here and there, he'd give a little dab with a wrench, a little poke with the screwdriver, and ba-*room!* the thing would be humming. Like a laying on of hands.

Also, the old goat always had some much younger woman (or chippy, as some people's mothers called them) living up here with him. He was a greasy, gangly, bump-throated old guy. He had a big spade-shaped nose that came all the way down past his mouth, or seemed to. His mouth was wide, without all its teeth, and when he wasn't talking—when he was looking at an engine and thinking, his eyes far away—he had this sort of secret lemon-sucking smile that always, as long as I could remember, set my teeth a little on edge. As I got older, and *he* got older, it surprised and irritated me more and more that he always had these younger women living with him. If after a while one of them stopped showing up around his place, no more than a week or so would pass and he'd have another one out there with the same nice big advantages on her as the one before her'd had. What sort of rubbed it all in, you might say, was that he loved to talk about what he did in bed with them. Or talk about what he'd *like* to do in bed with them, or talk about what he'd like to do in bed with any *other* woman who came to mind, or came in sight, at any moment. Old Uncle Tuggs liked to talk about screwing, or possible screwing, or even impossible screwing, in any way, shape, or form. The thing was, he had a *talent* for it. He had such a humorous, greedy, descriptive way of talking about it that you just had to listen, and laugh.

But it sort of hit me just then, looking at his old place, that I'd never really like Uncle Tuggs. It surprised me. I mean, I guess I always knew I didn't like him, but the fact never stood out for me to notice it like it did now. There was something about him that I always thought was just like Ralph, his dog. In the first place, it seemed like Ralph had been old and mangy from the first day I laid eyes on him—and yet there he still was, just last winter, and not looking that much older, when you thought about it. That was just like Uncle himself. And then Ralph was so big, and so bony. That was like Uncle, too. But most of all, Ralph had this sneaky, hungry air about him. I mean hungry in some kind of strange way you couldn't quite put your finger on, with a way of hanging back, circling you, his eyes always spying sideways at you and laughing. And that was definitely like Uncle—that was him to a T, in just a slightly less obvious way.

Gabe came out of the barn. He had two chain saws by their grip bars in one hand and a can of gas under the arm with the cast. As I pulled up to let him in, I could see into the barn, and see where the boys had walled off a back part of it, so I knew they were probably growing dope back there, too, as well as in all the sheds (you could hear a generator going somewhere—Walter had been into town to buy a new one, so the one Uncle'd left must have broken down). Gabe got in, and I drove us down past the old stakebed sitting nose to the grass where the jack gave out, and down to the edge of the nearest draw.

The roadcut down into it *was* rough, and that little John Deere was right bang at the bottom of it, its skip-loader shoved halfway into the dirt for another bite when it died. You had to admit it was bizarre. The last time it had been used before that, it had worked fine. Grant had come up to grade off some old weedy dirt piles from a cellar and septic tank dug years before—I guess Uncle just didn't feel like doing it himself for some reason—and that in fact was the last time anyone had seen Uncle, because when Grunt came back the next day to finish up, he said he found Uncle, Cherry, Ralph, and the van all gone. Anyway, three months later, after the brothers decided it was time the law looked into this (and a lot of people by this time were wondering), and after the sheriff OK'd their caretaking the place, they no sooner fire the John Deere up again to develop the property's cash potential a little, and *bam* it breaks down. I was just able to edge my truck out around it and onto the draw bottom.

"Well, Gabe," I told him, "this gravel feels pretty firm—I shouldn't have any trouble getting down-draw a ways."

"Forget it. You're cuttin' up here. Just get all these fuckers at the head of the draw here."

Old Gabe sure had a friendly, winning way about him. Why the hell did he need to mark the trees at all if that was what he wanted? Turned out—as I was breaking out my twelve-pack of Buckhorn, rolling up my sleeves, and firing up the bigger chain saw—that he didn't bother with marking trees, just took one of my beers and sat on a rock and started watching, like I was free TV.

I went to work. I dropped a half-dozen smaller trees that would be in the way of falling the bigger ones later on. I trimmed the lettuce off them and dragged it out of the way and started cutting them into rollers. All this time Gabe was watching me, looking broody. After a while I see it's the chain saw he's actually watching. After a half hour or so, he gets up, pins the other saw with his foot, and starts it with his good hand.

"Hey!" he tells me, "use this awhile! I don't like that one to overheat."

Well, this is bullshit, the saw was fine. But I didn't want to lose my stride, so I just put the one down, took the other, and kept going. Gabe took another one of my beers, sat down on a madrona I'd cut, and started watching *that* saw. After a while I stopped for a rest.

"Mind if I switch back to the big one now, Gabe?" I asked him. "It goes faster."

Sullen, like it hurt his mouth to ask it, Gabe said, "Seem to you like either one of them pulls?"

"Pulls? Left or right?"

"Left or right!" he shouts—I'm surprised how suddenly worked up he was. "Up or down! Pulls *any* direction!"

I waited a minute. "Why, no, Gabe," I said very calmly. "I've got to say I haven't felt either one of these saws pull particularly in any direction at all whatsoever."

He just grunted, but I could've sworn he looked relieved. I went back to work with the bigger saw, and he didn't mention overheating anymore. Gabe watched and drank my beer. I had figured a twelve-pack would last me till lunch, but the cheap bastard drank three of my beers, and by eleven I'd run dry. I made a big deal about emptying the last can, but hints are wasted on any Tuggs. Just then from up at the house came the sound of someone firing up a car, and I said to Gabe:

"Is that Walter? Going out? Could you get him to bring back another twelve-pack?"

"Walter's not here. That's Grant. He won't be back till late, he's going to get his cast changed."

"Well, have you got any beers in the house, Gabe? It's getting kind of thirsty out, and it looks like I've just run dry."

Good old Gabe just shrugged. "Fuck if I know," he said cheerfully.

I went back to falling some more trees. I decided at noon I'd drive out for another twelver, and this one I was going to lock in my cab and take out can by can so that even a Tuggs would get the point. And then the strangest thing happened that I've ever had happen with a chain saw—and I mean including the time I lost this joint of my finger here, right? I'd started on this little oak, you see. It had two main branchings that pushed out at its neighbors so as to give it a tricky kind of torque, but it had a definite lean out over the draw bottom that should control its fall. Well, what happened was that when I touched the saw to begin the undercut, the saw had an incredible power surge, and ripped clear through the trunk with one backhanded stroke!

Now this can't happen. Certainly not on an undercut like that. The shift and pinch of the trunk as its support gets cut through would trap the biggest saw just like *that*. You have to get the weight of the tree hanging with the undercuts, but then you cut through the back of this stress and the tree snaps forward off the saw—it's the only way to do it.

Except it did happen. Can you picture the kind of acceleration I'm talking about? The blade just roared straight through the tree—I'd still swear that kind of power just physically was not *in* that saw. It sliced the trunk at a crazy angle, and the tree pitches down, flips off the hang-up of one of its boughs on the next tree, and twists sideways as it whops down the rest of the way, bang-square on the tree that Gabe was perched on.

Gabe had lots of fast in him, like all the Tuggs. He'd just jumped off when the oak came down and clamped him face-down across the madrona, chest and right arm pinned, head and left arm poking out on the other side. And as if things weren't strange already, the impact itself was strange. The oak fell on one of its two branchings, which snapped but didn't break off, and acted like a kind of hinge, letting the oak down just enough to pinch Gabe solid, but also giving just enough support so that no more than two or three of his ribs were cracked at most. When his head cleared and his eyes focused again, he started to swear something terrible.

"God*damn,* Gabe," I told him. "You weren't just woofin' when you asked about it pulling! Did you *see* how this thing yawed on me?"

Gabe kept on swearing, and it sounded weird because what he was saying was so fierce and yet his voice was almost quiet at the same time, because it hurt him too much to fill his lungs and roar. I was really sorry a thing like this had happened to a guy like Gabe with me *involved* in its happening. Of course he himself had seemed to suspect his chain saws were acting up, but he was the kind of guy that if you broke a couple of his ribs, he was going to hold it against you no matter what. He'd just spent too many of his years running elephant tranquilizers and crystal meth with other crazy bikers, and *doing* them, to have much sense of the fine points of a case left in him. I studied how to cut him free.

"Look here, Gabe," I told him. "A lot of the weight's from this other side branch here. I'll lop it off and maybe the oak will rise off you some."

"Cut me the fuck outta here, you fuckin' clown! Ow!" Gabe said—he'd shouted too loud. I laid the blade to that side branch, and the saw sank through it smooth and normal as you please. A good three hundred pounds' weight dropped free. But goddamn if that oak didn't lift at all. By some freak twist in it, the trunk actually seemed to press a shade harder on poor Gabe.

"Well, at least this saw's behaving OK now, Gabe," I told him. "I guess I'll try cutting that branch above you, and maybe then I'll be able to—"

"GET—THIS—THING—OFF—ME!" Gabe screeched, and then had to groan, it hurt so much to screech. The branch wasn't a main one but was hefty, and I might be able to push up the oak with it off and just lift it enough for Gabe to pull himself out. His head stuck out just below and to one side of the branch, so I got on its opposite side and reached the blade up.

"Keep your eyes shut," I advised him, "because this sawdust is going to be coming down around your head." Gabe just groaned again and ground his teeth. I gunned the saw and set it to the branch.

Right there—right then—things started to go bad in a big way. It was like when I touched the saw to that branch, a kind of nightmare started, and kept on, getting worse and worse, until—well, I'm going to describe it all to you in just the order it happened in.

I touch the saw to the bough, right? It sinks maybe halfway in, lulling me, getting me off guard—and then it has another one of those unreal power surges! It whips—I mean *whips*—through the rest of the branch in a second. I can't unsqueeze the trigger! I can't let go the grip! *Zip* through the bough and on down— *chonk*-zoom—clean through poor Gabe Tuggs's neck. That saw moved so fast that Gabe's head and the bough hit the ground at just about the same second, and I just had time to free my hands and pull back before the branch hit my arms—and it did hit the chain saw right where I dropped it and smashed it dead.

I stood cursing, but I was in kind of a trance, too. I walked around the trees, and on the other side of them I walked up and down, helpless, shaking my head and swearing. I was using my voice to drown out the awful noise of Gabe's bleeding on the other side of that tree sandwich. From this side he might just be some guy peacefully bent over a fence or something that you were seeing from behind—except for that oak tree on him, of course. But I could still see in my mind the horrible way he was cut off short on the other side. I made myself stand still. I took a deep breath and blew it out.

"Brother," I told myself out loud, "this is the worst luck you've ever had in a long and distinguished *career* of bad luck, and you better get a grip on yourself because now you have really got your ass in a crack."

I never talk to myself out loud like that, and the fact that I was doing it just shows how blown away my mind was, but somehow it helped me, and so I went on:

"You're going to have to hide poor Gabe. Bury him. Because there's no way Walter or Grunt Tuggs is going to accept a reasonable explanation of how this tragic mishap happened. So you're going to have to come in tomorrow, and tell them that after Grunt left for the hospital, Gabe took off somewhere and still hadn't showed up before you left with your wood."

I sounded reasonable to myself, and it got me moving. I went back around the trees. But I was still like in shock. All I could do for a while was stare at those remains and the horrible mess of blood they had sprayed on the ground and a lot of the wood. And then when I made myself move again, all I could think of to do was pick up poor Gabe's head by the ponytail and hide it in a manzanita bush—pretty ridiculous with the whole rest of him still clamped between those trees. The oak lay long-wise on the madrona, almost aligned to it. To keep from binding the saw or from mangling the body any worse, the neatest way to cut him out would be to chop that oak to rollers from its crown, the nearest end.

"All right, then," I told myself, "chop it to rollers, pull him free and bury him, and use the shovel to bury the blood, too. Then get the bloody rollers on the flatbed first, cover them with the clean ones you'll have just cut, and get the hell out of here before Grunt or Walter comes back."

I felt encouraged—I was still making sense. Down the draw a little way was the mouth of a ravine that Grunt Tuggs had shoved the dirt piles into when he graded them off for Uncle. The loose heap spilled right out into the draw and should be easy to bury Gabe in.

My mind felt like it was clicking again. I fired up the smaller saw and set to the crown of that oak, dropping it roller by roller. This saw hadn't acted up yet, but you can bet I kept it well away from me while I worked.

I don't want you to think that all through this I wasn't feeling some personal regret for Gabe as a man. No matter what kind of scumbag a person might be, they have some human characteristics, too, usually, and you should try to come up with these and give them their due when they pass on. So I tried to remember Gabe's high points while I worked, though after high school I pretty much lost touch with him, and only knew his doings by hearsay. I remember while I was still in the service hearing how him and Walter had got together as septic-tank contractors. They and two guys they subbed part of their work to apparently had a knack for getting things out of the houses they worked at. Then there was a divorced lady and her daughters had a big place in the hills where these boys were setting a tank for an extra wing she was adding. Maybe the lady was too trusting, too sociable, but Gabe and the boys, who had some bottles on hand, let the day turn into a kind of wild party and all four got sent up for Rape forcible and Rape statutory and Breaking and Entering and some other things. And from what I heard afterwards here and there, both Walter and Gabe used every opportunity to work on their rape techniques while they were in the joint.

Well, after that? I seemed to remember they all got out of the joint within a year of each other—Grunt was already up-country in another state for a second-degree murder—and got together on something. Yes, that would be the garage they leased near Courthouse Square in Healdsburg. Now there was something you had to give Gabe credit for—he wasn't charged with anything on that one, though there were some Mexican car-clubbers got shot outside of town by someone, and Grunt did go up again, for receiving stolen goods. On the other hand, you couldn't really give Gabe too much credit for that, because everyone knew he would've gone up, too, if they'd been able to get enough evidence on him. Anyway, after that Gabe and Walter were running crank down around LA. I knew that from Billy Vale, who'd met Gabe while he was in jail for it, and went in with him awhile when Gabe went back to it after he got out.

It began to sink in to me how much the brothers tended to stay together in spite of their various adventures. Would they really buy my story that Gabe had just taken off? And wouldn't I have to get rid of his chopper to make them believe it even for a little while? Could I ramp it up onto my stakebed and cover it with rollers? It made me feel a little panicky. Christ! Could I get all this done in time? I raised my saw to start a new cut, and from up near the house I heard the roar of a car pull in.

Oh, perfect! Oh, fine! That had to be Walter! I was so stupefied by this new bad luck, I just kept cutting. I dropped a roller, started another one. I heard Walter's motor cut off, his car door bang shut, then a house door bang. I just kept cutting.

III

It was like one of those nightmares where you're supposed to be hiding from these people, but your cover is just too thin and all the time you're really blatant. And somehow they keep on not seeing you, but at any second they just *have* to see you. I just kept standing there cutting my way towards poor Gabe and the big red splotch on the ground in front of him. Up at the house another door banged. Over the saw, in a pause between cuts, I could just make out the sound of someone sifting through tools near one of the sheds.

I was maybe five cuts from springing Gabe's trunk. Would my luck hold? After I hid him, I'd still have to get a shovel to cover the blood. I heard an engine fire up in the yard. It wasn't Walter's car—it was shriller. And then Walter howled and I heard him screeching and swearing.

It wouldn't be natural for me to ignore that noise—he'd expect me to come running up there to see what happened.

For a minute, though, it was impossible for me to move, every ounce of me was so unwilling to leave the body so obvious like that for anyone to see who came to the edge of the yard. But at last I made myself trot on up to the yard, the chain saw idling in my hand.

There was Walter, standing by a rusty stripped-down V-8 engine Uncle had left sitting on a block of wood in the grass. One of his hands was bloody—Walter was clutching it and cursing a blue streak. And damned if the fan blades on that derelict weren't still spinning!

"What the hell happened, Walter?"

Walter was a lot bigger than Gabe—almost as big as Grunt—but he didn't wear his hair like his older and younger brothers did. His was dude-hair, and his face was shaved, which let you see all the dings and chunks taken out of it. Right now Walter Tuggs looked amazed.

"I was takin' the fuckin' distributor cap! The fuckin' engine fired up!"

"Jesus, Walter! That is *bizarre!*"

Walter looked at me. The whites were showing all the way around his mean little gray eyes. Between each word he said, his jaw kind of sagged, like it wanted to hang. *"Bizarre?"* he said. *"Bizarre?* What the fuck do you *mean* bizarre?"

"I mean *strange,* Walter. I mean, Jesus Christ, that's *strange.*"

"Strange? *Strange?* You're fuckin'-aye-straight it's strange! That sucker's amputated! There's no *gas!*"

What could I say? He was right! That fan had mauled a lot of skin off his knuckles, but it was that kind of thing that is so surprising that it blots out pain for a while. I still didn't like to see Walter Tuggs bleeding like that. In just pure disposition, you'd have to say he was the meanest of the brothers. True, he did skunkweed and reds to such an extent that a lot of the time he seemed more amazed than mean. But he had a way of getting confused, and if he stayed confused about any one thing long enough, then he turned mean. Luckily his memory was so short he usually forgot what was confusing him pretty quick, but bleeding like he was was likely to keep the confusing fact that a dead engine had mauled him on Walter's *mind.*

But he didn't get steamed up. No! Walter surprised me. He looked at that V-8 and said, fairly quietly, "So fuck your fuckin' distributor. *Be* that way! I'll just go trim the fuckin' dope." Then he just turned and walked towards the toolshed. It was the oddest thing, like he had some running argument with that motor, or with something in it—an argument he was so involved in he didn't even notice he'd copped to their dope crop right in front of me.

I figured I should keep an eye on Walter for a few minutes to see that he settled into something. I killed off the saw and set it down. I went to the shed where he was tying a rag around his hand and got out a double-bitted ax.

"I'm gonna do some of your splits now, Walter. Then I'm gonna haul a load of rollers out of the draw for myself."

He just shrugged. I went over to the rollers piled by the back porch near the splitter—which, the way things were going, there was no way I was going to use—and started setting them on end and splitting them. I warmed up to the ax work, and my mind started moving again. How big would their dope be? Two months old, dating from the day they moved in. There'd be some spraying as well as trimming to do, and all those downers made Walter a slow worker. He'd be at it an hour. If I could just get back down to the draw for another twenty minutes, I could spring Gabe and hide him and the worst of the blood. Then I could settle to clean up in more detail, because then even if Walter did come to the edge of the yard, he'd miss anything that didn't outright kick him in the face.

So I kept splitting. I've always liked splitting madrona—it's so red the cross cuts look like steaks. It's crisp and kind of waxy and splits clean with one good stroke: *whack*-plop, *whack*-plop, *whack*-plop. The splitters fell apart rosy and mellow in the sunlight. I was just starting to feel I might get out of this mess if I stayed cool.

Meanwhile Walter had found a pair of hand shears in the shed and was working them to get the rustiness out of them. He worked them and worked them, already looking like his usual vacant self again: *eee*-eee, *eee*-eee, *eee*-eee. In the noon quiet and the fine sunshine, the two of us made a funny, peaceful kind of music: *whack*-plop, *eee*-eee, *whack*-plop, *eee*-eee.

An inspiration came to Walter. He rummaged in the shed again and got a spray can of Liquid Wrench. Holding this, he wandered towards the barn, spraying the shears and still working them as he went: *eee*-eee, *eee*-eee. And right there, just as he got to the barn door, Walter had one of the strangest accidents I've ever seen. Not worst, but strangest, and coming from me that ought to mean something. Maybe the shears were slippery from the Liquid Wrench, but as he worked them faster they suddenly snapped open so hard they flipped out of his grip, spun end over end straight down, and sank one blade all the way through Walter's shoe and foot and it must have been another inch on into the ground.

For a minute Walter froze. He stood and gaped at his foot like it had betrayed him. Then he hoisted the foot, shears and all, off the ground and started hopping around on his other foot and roaring. He roared some things there's no need to repeat, things—and combinations of things—that I'd never even thought of. The kind of things I guess you need a pair of shears through your foot to help you think up. I ran over to him.

"Sit down, Walter. Against the barn here!"

"------- -- ----- ------- ----- -- ----- !"

"That's it, scoot back this way a little more. Lean back on the wall here! That's it!"

"------- --- --------- ------- -----!"

"Hold that knee straight now. Lock it!" I told him. I planted one of my feet against his toes to hold his foot rigid, and then I hauled the shears out of him. He slammed the barn wall with his head, cracking one of the planks. When his eyes had cleared a little, he said:

"In the kitchen. Counter. Jack Daniels."

"Good idea!" I told him. "Get your shoe off, and we can pour some in the hole!"

"Fuck the hole!" Walter screeched. "I'm gonna drink it!"

Just the same he started working on his laces, and I hurried through the back door into the kitchen, and when I got to that JD bottle I took some of Walter's advice and had a long pull off it. I found a sixer of Buckhorn in their icebox and had one of them and half another as a chaser. I watched poor Walter from the window, loosening his shoelaces gingerly, like they were snakes that might bite him. I took another pull, finished my beer, and cracked another.

"Can you believe a day like this?" I asked myself. I felt like I was a stranger I had to give advice to and couldn't think of what to tell him. "They talk about accident-prone?" I asked. "Those aren't just empty words. It seems like every tool or gadget on this place has it in for these boys."

Just then the coldest kind of a shudder went straight through me—up from the floor I stood on and right out through my scalp, and it was like Uncle Tuggs was standing right there with me. I mean, I was still looking out the window, seeing Walter ease his shoe off and get some reds out of his vest pocket and swallow them, but what I was really seeing was Uncle Tuggs's face. I was feeling him in my guts, the smell of his dirty kitchen was the smell of Uncle himself in my nostrils. And he had this particular look on his face that I'd seen there again and again over the years, and it hit me now that it was that look that somehow summed up old Uncle Tuggs—got right at the gist of him. It was the look he'd have when he'd just fixed some immediate problem on whatever car I had at the time. Well, that takes care of that, he'd say, but before long that X or Y of yours is going to go and then you might as well just shitcan the whole rig. And we'd stand there, both of us knowing he was right, and both knowing I'd never have the money to fix that X or Y—and his oily black eyes would be laughing in just this particular way. And now I could feel the meaning in that look like never before—that deep inside, Uncle gloated more over knowing how things broke than knowing how to fix them.

It was truly scary—I could see Cherry, too, in a manner of speaking. I mean with that same feel of the smell and rub of her. A little honey about my age, ex-flower child, with the kind of advantages on her that back in high school it would have blown every zit on my face to get my hands on—but her eyes were missing! Right at the centers they were dead and gone, so that you couldn't picture them. It really went through me. Uncle's other honeys? What about them? Could I remember their eyes? Walter was bellowing for me. As I took him out the whiskey and beer, I told myself:

"Calm down now. Just stay cool. This is actually good luck. He won't go wandering around now and look in the draw."

Walter got out some more reds and washed them down with the JD. Then he drank a beer at one breath. He settled back against the barn and gave me a serious look. "This place, man," he told me, "is trying to *ambush* me. This whole fucking *place.*" He looked off into space, nodding a sort of a just-you-wait nod. He chugged more JD and brooded over his thoughts. Old Walter's thoughts, few though they might be, could often occupy him for hours at a time. Things were looking up. I'd work here just until I saw his reds kick in, then get down into the draw and clean up.

"Listen, Walter," I told him. "You want a ride to the hospital? Because I'll take you down in my truck as soon as I make up a load. I'll split a few more here, and then I'll go down and make up the load." Walter nodded—he looked vague already.

I went back to splitting. This shouldn't take long—*whack*-plop. Then I'd come back here from the hospital after dropping him off—*whack*-plop. Get Gabe's keys and just *drive* his chopper off the place—*whack*-plop. Hide it somewhere nearby and run back—*whonk*.

It was just the ax handle that I hit that one with, and it made my elbows pop. The head had flown off the handle slick as snot. It *whistled,* it spun so straight. It sank its whole length into the center of Walter Tuggs's chest. He'd been sitting with one hand laid sort of loose across his chest, and so two of his fingers got clipped off just as neat as you could imagine and rolled down onto his lap. Walter's eyes and mouth came wide open, he sat up, and then fell back, stone-dead.

IV

It seemed like I'd never move again. Like the sun would set, the moon would rise, Grunt would come home and call the sheriff—and I'd just be standing there through it all, that ax handle in my hands, poor Walter in front of me, and poor old Gabe down in the draw, sandwiched between two trees with his head behind a manzanita bush. Except of course Grunt would just blow me away himself and bury me down in the draw—he'd make no bones about that kind of thing. And it seemed like I *did* stand there forever, and without a single idea in my head how to save myself.

And then, straight out of that like trance, I started to move—to clean things up—and it was bizarre how smoothly I started doing everything, how suddenly I was moving and wasn't wasting a move. I tossed the ax handle in the toolshed, dragged out a piece of carpet Uncle had used to lie under cars on, took it over to Walter, tucked his two fingers into his vest pocket with his reds, and laid him on the carpet. It was amazing how little he bled—I guess because his heart had stopped pumping in a split second. I dragged him over to the road. Big though he was, it still seemed impossible one man could be so heavy.

I dragged him down the road into the draw. I ran back up, got the JD and cans of beer, drained them all, and threw them on a trash heap with a lot of others of their kind. I got the chain saw and a pick and shovel and ran back down into the draw with them. I set them down near Gabe, grabbed Walter's rug again, dragged it as far as the manzanita, got poor Gabe's head by the ponytail and put it on Walter's lap, and dragged both of them still deeper into the draw.

Near where that slide was, where Grunt had dozed a gully full with Uncle's old dirt piles, was a clump of bushes, and I hid Walter and Gabe's head behind it. I ran back up the draw with the carpet, laid it near Gabe's feet, fired the chain saw back up, and started to get the rest of the oak off him.

I couldn't progress so fast in this part of the work. I forced myself to make twenty-inch cuts because I'd need lots of clean rollers to hide the bloody wood in the truck, but I had to clench my teeth to keep from bellowing out the fear that was in me now. It was like being trapped in a film that had slowed down. All the shadows in the draw looked darker and cooler, and I overdrove the chain saw to keep from hearing this bizarre, thick *quiet* that was welling like a flood out of the ground, like it might fill the draw and close over my head and snuff out even the chain saw's noise like a candle flame. Crazy? I *was* crazy! I kept seeing Uncle.

With Grunt, and after him the law to be afraid of, and all the tricky moves I had to plan, it was that old goat that kept pushing himself into my mind. Just like a goat, too—the way one might push its clammy muzzle against your hand, wanting something from you? It *was* a cold, sweaty nudge—his faced shoved against my mind with a scary skin-rub feeling.

For some reason, it was from a particular recent period that I remembered him—from just a few years back when the brothers had their garage scam going down in Healdsburg. Uncle hadn't had any part in the boys' cheats, though he had to know about them—had to know that if some housewife stopped in with a nice new car, she'd drive it off with a big bill and with her carburetor and battery and what-all replaced by used junk. He had to know about those rip-off contracts too, the ones the boys had with those *cholos* that eventually got shot.

None of that had anything to do with why Uncle sometimes hung around their place—why he sometimes donated his talent, and was probably the only reason why the boys had any straight customers at all after the first month or so. No, Uncle was there for something else. *He* was hanging around for the show, giving the boys' setup a shove now and then to keep it rolling—just like he'd give an engine that finicky, kind of disdainful jab with a screwdriver or poke with a wrench. That was how Uncle had fun. People always assumed it was by tinkering things to life, but actually it was by keeping things going so that he could watch them dying longer. I dropped the piece that had Gabe pinned. He sagged down to his knees and flopped back on the carpet.

Even so tragically shortened, Gabe was like an oak stump to pull, but now I felt like the film was speeded back up and I could move ahead of my feelings again. I left Gabe behind the bushes with his head and Walter. I ran back and grabbed the shovel. I started scooping sand from where it was thick on the draw bottom and slinging it over the drag marks and the blood splotches and salting it over the bloody rollers. They looked crusty, but it killed the color. I tossed the smashed saw on the truckbed and started tossing those rollers on after it. Big sugary clots of sand drizzled off that raw-meat madrona as it bounced on the bed, and in that late light it all looked like a nightmare you might have after gorging yourself on rare roast beef and jelly doughnuts. I had to rest before starting to throw the clean rollers on to cover the mess. I looked up and was completely stunned. The sun was setting! Just one red half of it was left, all webbed over by the black branches of oak trees.

I jumped. I spun. I made those rollers rise and fly into the truck, but as fast as I could move wasn't half fast enough. The fear was truly big in me now—and still not of Grunt, or the law, but of Uncle—like he could somehow catch up with me, grab me, and stop me dead in the middle of this awful work of mine. When the clean wood I'd cut was loaded, it wasn't enough to cover the mess, so I started lopping off some more. The first roller I dropped, the sun went with it. The sky was still light, but now all the shadows ran together in the draw. I gritted my teeth and kept cutting, and remembered Uncle's eyes. His eyes as he'd been telling you where he'd like to stick his tongue and his fingers in some woman passing by just then—his little lemon-sucking smile as he told you about it, as he rubbed the balls of his mind against your ears, *tinkering* with your mind just as he tinkered with his nephews' customers' cars, smiling as he watched the boys—so blatant and so dumb—hassle, cheat, steal, and strong-arm their way back to jail. His eyes as he sat in his van, fingering the back of Cherry's neck as they drove by, tinkering with her nerves as he steered. And *her* eyes while he did it, looking empty and disman-tled, like clocks with their hands stripped off. I stopped cutting. I didn't really have enough, but to hell with it. I wasn't going to be able to make myself stay down here much longer.

I killed the saw, loaded my cuts, and set in and bolted my truck's tailgate. I stood there in the quiet that had closed right back in like a pool, and in the shadows that now were also like a pool that I was sunk in way over my head, with my feet turned to lead. I didn't want to go down that draw to do my last piece of work. They lay there waiting for me to take hold of them and wrestle them into the dirt, and I had to say something, to hold their silence off at arm's length.

"OK," I said. "There you boys lie, and I've got to bury you now and get out of here fast. And first I'm going to have to get your scooter's key out of your pocket, Gabe. I *really* hate doing this. But you know, deep down, that all this was a tragic mishap—I mean, if you know anything, you know that it's something *he* . . . something Uncle. . . ."

I knew as I said it that I shouldn't say his name, and no sooner *did* I say it than he was there. Standing right behind me.

My heart nearly sneezed a piston. I screeched and jumped and spun around—and saw the draw was empty. No one was there but me, my stakebed, and that busted John Deere. I stood down in that lagoon of shadows, my heart still thudding back into place, and listened to the cricket noise start nibbling at the edges of all that cold, creaky quiet. I shook myself. I took up the pick and shovel and ran down to where the boys were hidden.

It was eerie getting Gabe's key out of his pocket with his face staring at me from off to one side, where it sat on Walter's lap. But I got it, and stood up. I felt wired to work again, felt like with just a little more hustle I might still get my ass out of here alive. I grabbed the pick and swung it against that dirt slide.

Burying them in that slide was one of those ideas that looks good at a fast glance, but the minute you start doing it you can see why it stinks. The loose dirt kept pouring onto what I dug out, as any idiot would expect from a slide. I swung the pick like a propeller, stabbed out dirt by the bushel with that shovel, ground my teeth and grunted and sweated—and all I was doing was dragging that whole pile farther and farther out onto the draw bottom.

So I tried to put less back in it—ease the dirt out till I'd opened just enough of a notch in the slope to hide the boys in. I couldn't do it! The least little bit I moved them, the pick and shovel seemed to *jump* with it. They seemed to yank at my arms—my shoulders got sore trying to hold back their lunges at that dirt pile. I was staggering, swearing, and losing every single stroke of the battle. It was like fighting the buck of a power tool, and these were just dead wood and steel. Finally I flung that shovel down, kicked it, cursed it, and stomped on it. I stood there trying to catch my breath, and right then, up by the house, I heard a car's engine cut off and its door open.

V

I was petrified. I'd totally missed any sound it'd made coming in. I stopped breathing to listen. I heard the door thunk shut, and heavy limping steps move towards the house. I breathed again.

Let Grunt get inside the house. Let him get inside and shut the door, I told myself. Then sling a pile on the boys just where they lie—enough to keep the flies off. Then fire up the truck and drive the hell out of here. If Grunt comes out to ask, idle just long enough to say Walt and Gabe went off with someone who came by around noon. You were in the draw, didn't see them, just heard a car and some conversation you couldn't make out, then Gabe came to the edge of the draw and said if he and Walter didn't get back here before dark, just to take your wood on out, so that's what you were doing.

All this came to me in the space of a half dozen of those steps I heard moving towards the house. That just showed how wound tight I was. I was so deep in shit I couldn't feel the new waves hit me anymore, just rolled with them. The steps got hollow, climbing and crossing the back porch. Four, three, two more and he'd reach the back door. That was when, right in front of me, the pick jumped off the ground, twirled in the air, and *chunk*—started chopping at the slide all by itself, while the shovel came up on its nose, twirled, and *chonk*—stabbed into the dirt beside the pick. The click and rasp and clank of them rose so biting clear above the cricket noise—such an age-old unmistakable sound—it seemed you could hear it clear to Healdsburg. Up on the porch the footsteps stopped. There was a long pause while those tools worked and nothing else moved anywhere on old Uncle's acres. Then came the footsteps again—creak-*thock,* creak-*thock*—heading back off the porch and down the steps they had just climbed.

I still wasn't moving. I was *with* those god-awful tools, you see, not three yards from where they hung in midair tearing that slide apart. The terrible magic moving them was like a thickness in the air around them, and it held me fast like a bug in jelly.

Not that I didn't finally understand what was happening on this place. I saw it now, I got the gist of it, and I realized that pick and shovel weren't going to bother turning on me, because they had their own row to hoe, but I couldn't move anyway. My legs just wouldn't thaw out. I watched them hack and chew, all alone in the shadowy air, and I listened to Grunt's steps coming back. He stopped, the car's trunk popped open, something clanked slightly, the trunk was shut and the steps came on.

It was dark in the draw now, but straight overhead—where I looked like a drowning man might—the sky was still blue and the first star had just showed in it. There was a little piece of my mind like that star, up there apart from me looking down on the mess I was in, and it told me that when Grunt had paused up on the porch there, that pause had lasted too long. Too long for him just to be identifying what this noise was. This noise meant something particular to old Grunt. Though his steps were nearer now, they were quieter—the little grinding noises of his 280 pounds gimping across the grass to the draw. Meanwhile the pick and shovel had that dirt pouring down like winter runoff onto the draw bottom. Right then as I was watching, like an island in a stream, a corner of black metal poked out of that runoff.

I moved then. I got my feet unrooted, and after that it was easy—I felt so light and small compared to the power that hummed through those tools. I was quick and quiet as a fish in that pool of darkness—I slipped up the opposite slope and behind some oaks. I didn't want to stay even that near to what those tools were uncovering, but there came Grunt Tuggs, limping down the roadcut, a twelve-gauge pump-riot in his right hand, which made that shotgun look no bigger than a breadstick.

Dear Christ, old Grunt was big. Barrel-gutted though beer had made him, his shoulders still made his belly look small. He was balding on top, so his ponytail started from a kind of equator around the back of his head. His face had that full-moon look—puffy with little slitty crafty-mean eyes, like a samurai gone to seed on bad sake. He stopped at the foot of the roadcut and leaned against the John Deere, hoisting the leg with the cast on it so he could dangle and rest it a minute. That cast was so clean and new and white, and the bulk of Grunt was so oily-dark, bristly, and mean, that it was a little comical-looking somehow, like a party hat on a grizzly.

From where he was he couldn't see the tools past those bushes down the draw, but he knew my truck, and he bellowed out my name. The pick and shovel paused, like a man would do that was startled. It made a shiver go right through me. Then they started digging again. They made the dirt river down wider and wider off that black island. It was the tail end of a black van, tilted almost upside down in its grave. If it hadn't been for that shotgun, I would have run. Grunt called out again. His voice was like a grader blade breaking dirt:

"Step out where I can see you, sucker, or I'm gonna cut your ass in half. Willy? You hear me? Stop digging and step out!"

When the tools didn't stop, he started walking down the draw, his moonface bright in the dark, his eyes creased almost shut with his anger. And not just anger, maybe. Maybe a touch of worry, too. Yes. A touch of something I'd never seen on the face of Grunt Tuggs before. And then he stopped, and stared, seeing what made the noise he'd thought was me.

His head came back and his mouth opened a little. A shudder went through him as he watched the dirt trickling off the old black chassis lying wheels-up. Then his hands remembered the shotgun. He shook his head and heaved his shoulders like throwing off weight.

"All right, then, old man!" he shouted. His voice was sharp with a touch of a wild laugh in it. "OK! If that's how you want it! I've *still* got plenty of shells. Plenty left. So whatever it takes!" And he pumped off a wad of double-ought that slammed spang against that shovel's head and set it twirling like a ballerina on its toe.

But just *like* a dancer, it stayed balanced, and spun to a sudden stop. It tipped back once for some thrust and launched itself end over end through the air. That shovelhead swatted Grunt a smack upside the ear that rang like a churchbell, and that I *know* you could hear down in Healdsburg. Meanwhile the pick had swung up like a pendulum and clouted Grunt's head sideways—

clubwise—knocking it halfway back to where the shovel had smacked it from, and dropping him on the ground.

Grunt got up on one elbow, shaking his head. The John Deere fired up. It roared alive. Its lights came on. It clanked into gear and came chugging and grunting like a giant pig down-draw towards Grunt Tuggs.

The pick and shovel went back to working faster than ever. They looked like two pairs now with their long shadows in the headlights, and in those lights I could see Grunt still blinking the glaze from his eyes, staring at that old black van that the dirt twisted and snaked off of like something alive—that van that no one had seen for five months, along with Uncle and Cherry and Ralph, and all of them together last seen alive by Grunt Tuggs himself. Grunt pushed his chest up off the ground, but still couldn't get the rest of his body moving before the John Deere had reached him. His legs lay dead as cordwood as the John Deere stopped and set the bottom teeth of its skip-loader against the dirt a foot from Grunt.

My throat was bulging up towards my mouth, like I was going to puke my heart out. Every square inch of me wanted out of that draw, but I had no more muscle to move than a shadow does. The grader grunted, bit down, chewed loose the plug of gravel Grunt lay on, and hoisted him, its jaw drooling pebbles that drizzled down like hungry spit. The handle of the van's rear door twitched downwards once, then again, and again, and again—and popped the gritty door-catch free. The door shoved open with a noise like broken teeth grinding.

Ralph stuck his muzzle out into the headlight beams. Those beams showed all the detail of him, the fur-clumps dangling from gluey black skin. You could see through the gaps in his snout to the honeycombed bone of him, see the maggots wrestling and crowding and twisting their little tails in there like thousands of tiny flames. Ralph jumped down from the van. His tail, all busy with worms, wagged a little, like he was pleased to see old Grunt. As the dog trotted to him, you could see his left shoulder had a big frayed blast-hole blown out of it—splintered shoulder-bone showed like chalk in the moldy muscle. The John Deere lowered Grunt, like a waiter bowing. He was struggling his shotgun to his shoulder, but when the scoop banged down he rolled out, and as he came face up, Ralph set his huge paws on his chest, jawed him by the throat, and clamped his head down hard as iron to the gravel. That was when Uncle came out—and that was when I ran.

True enough, I looked before I ran. I saw him plain enough, or most of him—how *he* had a blast-hole in the left side of his chest and how the headlights made it look black as a moon crater in the crumbly white cheese of his skin. How he had a pipe wrench in one hand and a pair of bolt-cutters in the other, and how his lizard-skinned fingers had a grip on them like roots on earth. But it was his eyes I didn't want to see. We both knew I was there—I understood that—but I just didn't want to make a personal point of it, eye to eye. So I ran. I was still slick as a shadow. I was scared hollow, and light as air. I cut across that slope to the head of the draw as Grunt's bellowing started. I fired up my truck and gunned up the roadcut. Jouncing, flinging rollers high and wide, I rocketed through Uncle Tuggs's yard, made the highway, and took off for help.

I thought I'd never reach it in time—not before my brain-springs started popping out of my ears—but at last I saw that light up ahead. I swung into the lot and jumped out. I ran in and got a twelve-pack and a pint of Jack Daniels.

Behind the wheel again, breathing a little easier, I took the freeway down to River Road, which I took out to the ocean. I drove slow, and worked on the twelve-pack, and thought about it all. It seemed pretty clear to me, when I added it all up, that Uncle just had no reason to have it in for *me,* especially when I'd helped him so much.

When I got to the coast, I turned south, and I dumped the firewood and the broken saw off of several cliffs along a ten-mile stretch of Highway 1. It was a good three hundred dollars' worth of firewood. Somehow, after all I'd been put through, having to do that really pissed me off.

THE PEARLS OF THE VAMPIRE QUEEN

I

To Taramat Light-Touch
Sow-and-Farrow Inn
Karkmahn-Ra

Warmest salutations, O Prince of Scoundrels! Dear deft-fingered felon, Paragon of Pilferers, Nabob of Knaves—good morrow, good day, or good night, whichever suits the hour this finds you! Do you guess who I am that greets you thus? Eh? Of course you do. Who else but your own nimble, narrow-built, never-baffled Nifft—inimitable Nifft of the knife-keen wits!

Has it been two years since we've been out of touch? That much and more, by the Black Crack! I'm sure you thought me dead or something like it, and I promise you, Taramat, I came close to it, for the haul that Barnar and I made in Fregor Ingens has taken us all of twenty-six months of breakneck squandering to dissipate, and if it had been just a jot richer, we would certainly have died of our vices before we'd wasted it all.

Haul? In Fregor? But of course—you don't know about it yet! Stupid of me ... suppose I write you a nice long letter telling you all about it? It's raining here in Chilia where we're visiting Barnar's family. I've got lots of time on my hands, and we won't be getting back down your way till late this spring. So it's agreed then, and I assure you it's no trouble at all, for I love to reminisce about exploits, especially remarkable ones. Just be sure to share this with Ellen if you see her—you know how she dotes on me and relishes keeping abreast of what I'm doing.

Well, it was swamp pearls, Taramat—*five hundred apiece.* Yes.

You may well gape (as I know you're doing). You know their value, I'm sure, but have you ever seen one? Black as obsidian, twelve-faceted (the runts have six), and big as your thumb. They are dazzling to behold—nothing less—and we never doubted that obtaining some was worth risking the vampire queen's wrath.

Now we knew that Queen Vulvula's divers go down after them in threes—one pearl-picker and two stranglers. But this is because they are anxious not to kill the pearl-bearing polyps. With a pair of heavies, the thing's palps can be pinned and the picker left free to take its pearls. They attack the polyp's strangling-node only as a last resort, to free one of their team from a lethal grip of one of the palps. But a diver can get sufficient diversion from just one strangler if the man is strong enough and goes straight for the strangling-node and squeezes to kill. You try to be quick and not leave the thing dead, as their corpses make a good trail for the archer-boats, but to get by with one strangler, he can't be shy about damaging the things. You know Barnar's strength. I was content to risk the picking with him strangling solo, and he was willing to try it if I was. So we signed up as men-at-arms on a Chilite skirmisher to get passage to Cuneate Bay, and spent three days there in Draar Harbor getting provisions. Then we headed south.

With good mounts the swamps are about ten days' journey inland. It's bad country, but our luck was good right up through the eighth day. Then, on the eighth night, it went bad. We were in the salt marshes near the mountains that flank the swamps when three huge salt beetles attacked us. Luckily, though wood is scarce there, we'd kept enough of a fire going to give us a little light to fight by. We killed them all, but not before they'd killed our mounts. Worse, their caustic blood destroyed both our spear shafts. We still had our bows and blades, but we would rather have lost these than the spears, which would be the only really useful weapons in the swamps. When you're swimming you can't use a bow, so it's no help against lurks, and it's scant help against ghuls because they're so tough-bodied in all but a few places. And swords bring you far closer than you ever want to be, either to a lurk or a ghul.

The swamps begin to the south of the Salt Tooth Mountains. As soon as we reached the upper passes of this range, we were looking across a plain of clouds that seemed to have no end. The range forms a wall the clouds can't pass, and the plains below have been a sump of rains for thousands of years.

Descending the range's swamp side, we were deep in cottony fog most of the way down, but just as we neared the plain we entered a zone of clear air between the clouds and the swamp. In the cold gray light between the cloud ceiling and the watery floor, we could see for miles across the pools and thickly grown mudbars that concealed our illicit fortune-to-be. The bars and ridges of silt are mazelike, turning the waters, which look jet black from a distance, into a puzzle of crazy-shaped lagoons. But the growth on these bars, though thick, is not as lush as you'd expect. It's mainly shrubs and flowers; big trees are rare. The question of cover would be tricky as a result. The place offered many avenues of vision down which a man standing on a flatboat could overlook a dozen lagoons at a glance.

But when we stood on the bog's very rim, pausing before we entered the waters, Barnar snuffed softly and said to me: "It's got that smell, Nifft. There could be a great prize waiting for us here." He was right, too. It had that peculiar stink of threat about it. You looked at that low-riding cloud cover, looking torn and dirty as a stable floor, and then at those endless unclean waters, and you knew that obscene riches lay ripening out there, riches so encumbered with danger that their guards had ceased to believe that they could ever be stolen, not in any big way.

II

The waters only looked unclean. Once you were in them, you were amazed to be able to see all the way down to your feet—and down to the bottom of most of the pools, none of which, even of the broader ones, was very deep. The reason is the soil of the swamps. If you dive for a handful of bottom silt and squeeze the water out, you'll find it hefts like iron, and if you kick at the bottom, you set up a low boil of mud that sinks down very fast. I've been told since that the polyps need this dense earth to nourish the growth of their pearls. While the light was still at its strongest, gray and bleached though that was, we made haste to cut our teeth in this business.

In half an hour we were swimming, nudging our packs before us with one hand and holding our drawn swords before us underwater with the other. We had put cork inside our packs and wrapped them in oilskin, and our sword blades were heavily greased. The best way to survive in the swamps is to turn into a water rat and stay in the water for the whole of your working day, and to crawl out onto the bars only to sleep. For one thing, it keeps your water-adjusted reflexes in top readiness. The clarity gives you a few seconds' warning when a lurk comes off the bottom at you, but if you're in and out, your underwater eye will get fuddled and you'll be too slow to take one of those warnings. For another thing, the lagoons are so interconnected that if you swim a mazy path you can go anywhere and almost never risk the visibility of crossing a bar of land.

The first polyp we found grew alone in a small pool. It stood as tall as a man, its palp-tips almost touching the surface. Neither of us knew if this was big or average. It would have been beautiful, standing there in the pool, its blurred redness seeming to burn, if we hadn't had to fight the thing. The palps began to writhe with exploring gestures the minute we paddled into the pool. Keeping out of range, we sank underwater to view it. Down at the base of its anchor-stalk, right below where the bouquet of its arms began, was the small cluster of exposed fibers that is called the strangling-node, from the use men put it to. At the same point on the stalk, but on the other side of it, were two large lumps—pearl blisters for sure.

We surfaced. "Get well breathed, Ox," I said. "I'll hit the blisters the instant you touch the node and draw its arms out of the way. Breathe up."

Barnar nodded. He tied his sword to his floating pack. I wore mine for lurks, but Barnar was going to have both hands full. He emptied his lungs and filled them, each time more deeply. I did the same. We nodded our readiness, and went under.

We swam toward the polyp, dividing to hit it from opposite

sides. I had to hang back till Barnar had drawn all its palps, and I watched as he swam in low and seized the node. All those blood-red palps whipped together and grabbed for him, faster than you'd believe anything could move underwater. It bent like a bush that's suddenly lashed by a storm wind, and it had him by the neck, trunk, and leg so suddenly that he could keep only one hand on the node and had to use the other to free his throat.

I went in. My contact with the thing was brief, but still it made my skin crawl—for the thing was like stone that lived and moved. This toughness is what makes one's work so hard, for the things are unpierceable by any weapon. I pressed on either side of one of the blisters, and the pearl popped out into the water like a seed squeezed from the ripe fruit. I tried to grasp it, but it kept squirting out of my fingers. Something hit me like a hammer between the shoulders. Catching the pearl with a lucky grab, I crawfished madly through the mud, took two more bone-cracking blows on the shoulder, and was clear. I came up starving for air.

Barnar was still down there, a huge blur in the silt where the red arms were striking like thresher's flails. I pocketed the pearl, took air, and went down. The two of them were deadlocked, because Barnar's one-hand grip on the node distracted just enough palps that he could bear, for a few moments, the assault of the rest. His hands are enormously strong. In the steppes he had taken a piece of rock salt and crushed it in one hand—it was as big as a road-apple. But his lungs were surely fit to crack by now, while the polyp was not weakening. I swam in beside him and added both my hands to the node. It was just enough pain to loosen the rest of the thing's grip on my friend. We scrambled backward. Something tore flesh from my face, and then I was free. Barnar boomed like a whale as he broke back into the air. We swam weakly to the mud bar and rested our upper bodies on it. I showed him the pearl. His face was torn in two places, the kind of raw, nasty wound one gets from rocks. My left cheek was a ruin. I still bear the scar of it.

"Well," said Barnar, "high pay, hard work."

"True," I said. "Still, friend, this may be the hardest work I've ever done." And then we heard a movement, distinct, but perhaps a lagoon or two distant. We drew our swords and towed our bundles round into the adjoining pool. Some bushes atop the farther bar were still shaking. From the lagoon beyond came a flat striking sound, the tearing of water, and the grunts and panting of a man.

We swam to the bar and looked over. A smallish man was thrashing on the surface of the water, driving a spear beneath him against the bottom. Even as we watched, his thrusts grew more methodical and he calmed down. A thick fluid, denser than the water and green in color, was boiling up around him, mixed with bubbles.

I began to think I knew the man. He turned his spear round to prod something down there with its butt—and the head he thus exposed showed a viscous green smear of lurk blood. Then he cursed, spat, and swam to the bar, where some bundles lay on the mud and a sword hung in the bushes. I then remembered he had been at the trade fair at Shapur, where I had first learned of the pearl swamps. He had been in the room where a small group of friends of mine had been talking about poaching. He seemed not to have learned more of the matter than was spoken there, to judge by his spread-out gear. Your goods on a bank are like a promise to any archer squad that happens on them that you yourself are somewhere nearby, and they'll hound you out, even if you've managed to duck them first. As for the sword, even in the dull swamp light its sheath of chased bronze was as good as a signpost.

"I think I know him," I told Barnar. "Best join with him, eh? The work would be easier for three, and if he's not instructed he'll draw patrols into the area."

"All right," my friend said. "But he gets only a quarter share till he shapes up. Obvious amateur. I think he's just lost a partner." He had indeed, as we saw upon swimming into his lagoon. We made gestures of peace. He turned his spearhead toward us and waited warily. Then we had eyes only for what lay under the water.

First, we saw that our polyp had been a small one. This pool was dominated by a nine-footer. Held in its palps was the body of another man, a big one. It was not the polyp, though, that had killed the man—and it was probably not his or his partner's inexperience either, but just bad luck. For a lurk as big as a mastiff also lay on the bottom, its fangs still hooked into the man's leg, its flat eye-knobbed head broken and giving off a green cloud of body fluids. Lurks look just like spiders, except the rear part of them isn't a fat, smooth sac—it's plated and ribbed, instead, like a beetle's body. Their poison balloons a man up a good one-and-a-half times his size. Even allowing for that, the pale sausage of a man down there must have been big enough in life to make Barnar look normal.

Of the three things on that pond bottom, only the polyp lived, and we learned something further in watching it as we swam past: the things have, amidst their palps, mouthparts for animal prey, and if left with a sufficiently inert body in their grip, they will devour it, though with a disgusting slowness. The polyp had the dead man's arm hugged tight in its arms and was working on the flesh with a slow rasping and plucking movement.

The little man's name was Kerkin. He remembered our meeting and knew my name without being told, be it said with due modesty. He was no less impressed with the difficulties of this task than we were, and we reached partnership promptly. Kerkin's hopes would have been defeated without us, and he accepted a quarter share with humility. We gave him some cork and helped him remake his bundle.

"Look there!" he cried. The great polyp was thrashing convulsively. It had more purple in it to begin with than ours had—we were to learn that that was generally the color of the big ones. But now it was amazingly pale, almost white, and its rhythmic stiffening had a helpless, purposeless quality, as of sheer pain. In a short time, it slowed, and ceased to move at all.

"The lurk poison!" said Barnar. Of course that was it. The polyp's toughness would have laughed at the biggest lurk's direct assault. But the poison entered the creature handily through its tainted meal. The thing had four blisters, three of which had full-sized pearls in them, the fourth a runt.

For a while we had a perfect poaching implement. We dragged the body of Kerkin's friend—his name had been Hasp—to several more lagoons. We found that if a polyp was jabbed forcibly in the node, it would attack and ultimately feed on the corpse we thrust into its arms. We took more than a dozen pearls this way, and then Hasp began to come to pieces—due not to the nibblings of the polyps, but to the lurk poison. The skeleton began to fragment and the skin to dissolve with terrible suddenness, filling the water with unwholesome stringy clouds of corroded flesh. In a few moments the whole lagoon was transformed into a disgusting broth from which we swam with desperate haste, keeping our faces clear of the water. It killed two small polyps growing there, but we did not dive for their pearls.

The real labor recommenced. While the takings were so easy, Kerkin had begun to whine. After all, the profitable Hasp had been *his* partner, not ours, and we should share even thirds. Now that it was again a wrestling game he dropped this theme readily. We took three more pearls in the same time we had taken to make our first dozen. We climbed up onto a broad bar in the evening, too tired to eat the jerky in our packs. We worked our way into the bushes and lay like the dead—that is, Barnar and I. Kerkin had the first watch, and in his excitement over the wealth we had already made, sleep was far from him. He would not even let me take mine, but insisted on talking. He showed his eagerness like an amateur, but I couldn't help seeing him with a friendly eye—he might have been a stupider version of myself at that age. So I talked with him awhile.

"Not a single flatboat did we see all day," he crowed. "So few people realize, Nifft, how clear it gets here for poaching at this season—of course if it got around, they'd get poached so hard in the fall that they'd take action and the easy times would be over. But we are here now, that's the great thing!"

"You said it's the Year King ceremony that caused it," I said. "So what's that all about then, friend Kerkin?"

Kerkin was eager to talk of this. In matters of the Queen's government his information far exceeded ours, and every man likes to be expert in something.

"The ceremony's called the god-making of the Year King. It means that the Queen ends his year's reign by immortalizing him, as they say." He paused and chuckled, and so I played along and asked:

"And how does she do that for him?"

"How else? She drains his body of every last drop of his blood, before the eyes of her assembled people. She's very thorough too, for she has to get all of it. If even a cup is lost to her, the charm of the blood is imperfect and its magic fails."

"And what is its magic for her, Kerkin?"

"It erases from her body the entire year's aging! Of course like all great magic it carries a terrible penalty for failure in its execution. Starting from the sacred night, for every single night that she is in default of the Year King's blood, she will age an entire year. And this aging, if subsequently she repairs the charm, can never be erased; thereafter, the Year King's blood will restore her only to the age to which she advanced while in default. A month's default, you see, would then make a hag of her, and a hag she would stay ever after, even with the charm reinstated."

Kerkin was a river of information, and I encouraged him to flow on—it does not hurt to gather what one can, when it's being offered free. The Queen's feeding was not confined to this yearly rite alone, though this was the bare minimum essential to her needs. She fed sporadically on random subjects—seldom fatally, except where some punishment was due. The natives of the swamp had received her as their ruler for over three hundred years now, because she had provided the necessary sorcery to expel the ghul, who are also originals of the swamp, and with whom the swampfolk have been immemorially at war.

Kerkin grew warm with his tale. We should kill a ghul, or take the lurk he'd killed, and go to Vulvula's palace to collect the bounty, he said. The great pyramid at the swamp's heart would be alive with folk. Think of the spectacle, and of the jest of being there with a fortune in poached pearls under our doublets! We could sneak a look at the doomed Year King in his chamber before the god-making, for the guards routinely granted a peek for a small bribe—it was almost a tradition. He rattled on, describing the labyrinthine interior of Vulvula's palace as if he knew it at first hand.

Poor Kerkin didn't live past noon of the next day. He fell behind us as we were seeking the day's second polyp. The first had taken all morning, nearly tired us to death, and yielded only a runt. Kerkin didn't have our stamina, and swam in a tired daze. Having lost sight of us, he took a side channel by mistake, and drifted off his guard into a pool he thought we had crossed ahead of him. The violent splashing he made in his misfortune brought us back. We were stunned by what we found. He had blundered into a very deep pool where grew a grandfather polyp so big it raised the hair of my nape—at least fifteen feet from root to palp-tips. And seemingly it hadn't waited provocation, but had seized Kerkin's dangling leg in palps thicker than his body. We got there just as it pulled him under. It enfolded his head between two immense palps and wrenched violently.

Kerkin's whole body spasmed as if lightning was going through it, then he hung from the thing's grip like a sodden log, and the polyp began to feed with a tearing and grinding that bared his arm bone in a sickening few seconds. We did not even try to get the pearls off his body. We swam to a silt bar and crawled onto the mud.

We felt glum as a northern winter. Now our labors must increase, and we'd begun to appreciate the full range of accidents that could befall a man here. We counted our pearls again. We had enough to live well on for a year—enough to buy expensive magic from the best sorcerers; enough to buy women of the rarest accomplishments. But there was so much *more* all around us. You know the feeling. I was racked by it once before. I had just robbed the Earl of Manxlaw and was passing through his seraglio on my way out of his villa, in the dead of night. I was beckoned by a lovely thing. Reckless with success, I paused to serve her with a will. But as soon as I rose, a half-dozen others had wakened, and they hotly persuaded me in whispers. I was profoundly moved. I felt filled with the power to stay there and serve them all. But I had a king's ransom in my bag, and left with a wrenching of the heart.

This was worse. The pearls are worth far more than gold by weight—a fortune of them is so marvelously portable for a man who lives on the move! Still, we stared at the dirty clouds and each of us waited for the other to be the first to suggest that we rest content with what we had.

"Well," I sighed, just to be saying something, "we have to thank the Queen for making this place as safe as it is. Think if we had ghuls here too!"

"At least they breathe air and have blood," Barnar growled. "They're not this nasty mud-crawling kind of thing. Polyps, lurks, *pah!*" I was only half seeing him as he spoke, for at that moment a plan was being born in my mind. This plan was a thing of unspeakable beauty and finesse; I was almost awed by my own ingenuity.

"By the Black Crack," I said quietly. "Barnar, I have an idea that will make us staggeringly rich. We must get that lurk Kerkin killed, and we must kill a ghul as well, and take them both to the pyramid of the Queen in time for the god-making of the Year King. Kerkin said that would be in five days. We can get there two days early at the least, and that will be perfect!"

III

You might pay me high and press me hard, but I couldn't say which was worse—killing a lurk in a lagoon with a seven-foot spear, or hunting a ghul in the black hills west of the swamps. We had to do both.

What? you'll say, we couldn't find that lagoon again? No, we found it fast enough. Our polyp had turned black, with half its palps fallen off. The lurk was there too. Unfortunately, its whole hind section had been eaten away. We were saved the trouble at least of hunting out another lurk, because it *was* another lurk that had eaten the dead one's body away, and it was still right there. I hope my fate never again puts such a sight as that before my eyes, black as the mud it crouched on, and looking half as big as the whole pond bottom. I was swimming lead because I was quicker with the spear, and that thing came straight up off its meal at me.

Now as to the spear, it was luck we'd met Kerkin and had it at all, but two feet should have been sawn off its haft and the thing should have been rebalanced for aquatic use. As it was, the weapon was too unwieldy, what with the water's drag. If I hadn't been carrying it head-down under water, despite the way it slowed my swimming, I would have died right there. That lurk's fangs were as long as my forearms, and before I could even react they were close enough to my thighs for me to count the thorny hairs they were covered with. I had time only to brace my arms—the lurk's own thrust carried him up and pushed the spearhead through the flat part of his body, amongst all those black knobby eyes. I clung to that spear-haft like an ant to straw in a hurricane, and the buck of that big hell-spider lifted me so far out of the water that I was standing on top of it for an instant.

A handy thing about lurks is that all their hard parts are outside, and these by themselves are not very heavy. They will even moult like snakes, and when they do they leave entire perfect shells of themselves, light as straw. This lurk was a monster, big as a pony, but when we'd bled it we reduced it to half its weight. We milked the bulk of its poison out too—the bushes where it splattered yellowed and died before our eyes.

We towed the carcass out of the swamps to the foothills we had entered from the day before, and scrounged enough dead scrub to make a fire in an arroyo. We found that by slitting the abdomen and shoving coals and heated rocks inside, the rest of its guts could be liquefied and drained out. We worked over it the rest of the day and finally had reduced both parts of the body to a bare husk, mere shells of a tough, flexible stuff that was too dark to reveal its hollowness. The whole thing now weighed no more than a small man, though it was unwieldy. Lashed to the spear, it could be carried between us like game. We carried it all night, moving toward the hills in the west.

By dawn we had reached them. Here the ghuls have retreated, to lurk near the swamp, just outside the reach of Vulvula's sorcery. We hid the lurk in a gully and covered it with stones, even though nothing will eat a lurk but another lurk, and they seldom leave the water. We found a place to sleep nearby, well hidden, though ghuls never come out in the day. They hunt at night, and we slept till then, for that's the time they must be hunted too.

The things can only be pierced through the sternum, which is narrow, while their backward-folding knees give them the quickness and dodging power of hares. You know me as a man who'll take your money at any kind of a javelin match, but for ghuls I ask a good clear set and a chance to launch before it knows I'm there.

We tried an unusual approach. It was Barnar's plan, and a lovely piece of wit it was. He spun it out of the well-known melancholy of ghuls. They frequently commit suicide by flinging themselves against Vulvula's barriers—one finds them, it's said, hanging dead in midair, snared in the Queen's invisible nets of power, and crawling with the blue worms that her spell engenders in its victims. Barnar reasoned that given this sad temperament, a ghul would believe a man claiming to have come to him seeking death.

We found one high in the hills by the light of its cook fire. We studied it carefully from among the rocks. It had a man's leg and haunch on a spit—the skin was flaking away in ash, and the thigh-muscle swollen with its juices. The rest of the man lay in pieces by its side, limbs and head pulled from the trunk like a torn fowl's—for ghuls use neither steel nor stone. The huge hands that had done the tearing were crusted with black blood.

Let's say you were to take our friend Grimmlat. Leave his arms the same length but start his hands at his mid-forearms, and crowd all his muscles into the shortened arm that's left. Give him feet of the same proportions with toes like fingers and knees jutting backward. Double the size of his poppy eyes, undersling his jaw an inch, and give him haggle teeth as long as your thumb, and you've got a ghul.

I picked my position in the shadows. Barnar heaved a loud sigh and called out: "Hail there! Is that a ghul?" He trudged noisily into the ghul's camp, and under the cover of his noise I moved up into the spot I'd picked. The ghul sprang up at Barnar's entry.

"May I sit down, friend ghul?" my friend asked. "I want you to do me the service of ending my life."

Ghuls, for all their ugliness, have a profoundly sad expression due to the way their great eyes droop at the corners, and you rather feel for them when you're not involved. This one was in a defensive crouch, otherwise I would have had my shot at once. In almost all postures the things keep their shoulders folded forward, with their breastbone sunk in between their chest-muscles. They're only vulnerable at the moment of attack. That was the point of Barnar's scheme. He sat down cross-legged, like a man who means to stay. Anger began to replace wariness in the ghul's face.

"Are you deaf?" snapped Barnar. "Why do you hang drooling like an idiot? Kill me!"

The ghul didn't like this. It snorted and sat down again, and resumed turning the spit with a stubborn glare.

"Why should I?" it said. They have small spidery voices, like a hag's.

"Why not?" boomed Barnar. "You could eat me! Are you so stupid you can't see that I'm a man like the one you're cooking there?" He gestured indignantly at the head that lay on its side by the ghul. The man had had an enviable black mustache. "You'd kill me quick enough if I didn't ask—you make no sense!" Barnar complained.

"I'm no idiot, you're one," the ghul quavered bitterly. "You'd rot before I got hungry again. Don't you know anything? And anyway I'll do whatever I please and I won't take orders from you, you big sack of horse-flop!" And it licked its ragged teeth loudly to drive the insult home.

"Insults!" cried Barnar, "and I thought I'd be doing you service for service." He heaved a great sigh and rested his forehead on his hands. The ghul looked interested now.

"Why do you want to die?" it asked grudgingly.

"Why?" Barnar's head came up in disbelief. "The world so gray and spongy and futile and cold as it is—life so short and nasty and poor and hemmed in on all sides by destruction—and you ask why? I've had enough of it all, that's why!"

The ghul looked musingly. It stood up slowly and took its supper's head in its hand—the hand was big enough for the head to roll several times over from the blood-black claws to the heel of the shovel-wide palm. It rolled the head thoughtfully for a moment, and then drew back its arm to throw. That was my shot.

I pinned it so solid that half the haft reemerged from its spine, but ghul vitality is terrible, and it actually finished the throw with my spear in it. Barnar moved in time, and the head struck the rock behind him so hard that it flew in pieces like a burst earthen jar.

We took the ghul back to where we had cached the lurk, getting there by dawn. Now we had to build up the lurk's body. We were sure it could be considerably collapsed, and with some experimenting we found how to fold back the legs over the head part, and flatten and fold the back part. We tied it snugly into this reduced position with thongs, and wrapped the whole thing in oilskin. The finished bundle was about the size of a small man who has folded himself up to sleep. We bled the ghul, too, but didn't prepare it any more than by tying the wrists and ankles together. Barnar slung it crosswise over his shoulder and back, and we entered the swamp again. We walked the mudbars openly now, hustling the lurk through the water where we had to, making fairly quick time.

We soon struck one of the marked routes to the pyramid, a series of yellow poles that followed an almost continuous system of mudbars. We stayed with this, and late in the evening we came in sight of the pyramid. It is truly immense, tall enough to join the flat, dark waters with the ragged cloud ceiling. We laid ourselves down atop a broad bar amidst the bushes. We found it easy to sleep.

IV

In the morning we weighted the bundled lurk and sank it in a pool by the sixth route-marker out from the palace—more than a mile out. Then we headed for the palace.

I've taken these eyes of mine to many places, and have been no jack-out-of-the-way, but I'll tell you I had sense enough to be impressed by that pyramid. It had to be a good three hundred feet high to thrust its upper tiers into the clouds as it did. It was a mighty, terraced hill of a palace. It had quays and docking berths all around its skirts, for it stood in the center of a lake, and water unbroken by solid ground spread half a mile around it on all sides. The lower two-thirds was all of stone, but its upper tiers were built of wood. Those great beams were as massive-looking as the monumental stone under them, and could have come from no nearer than the Arbalest Forest, on the fringe of the Iron Hills. One could read the wet of the fog up at the summit from the wood's deep blackness.

By the time we got to the fringe of the palace's great lake, we'd been passed by several inbound boats. The lake was alive with taxi rafts, for it's quickest to get from one side to another of the palace by sailing round it. The interior is a master maze of corridors and chambers. We saw only one archer-squad going out to patrol. They gave us a wave. Bountymen are liked there, and to be traveling palaceward with a dead ghul over one's shoulder is to go with as much guarantee of welcome as a stranger may expect. At our signal a taxicraft came promptly away from the palace's bustling perimeter.

Our pilot liked bountymen but seemed to think they were a bit stupid for taking on such a hard job. A man never gives away more than when he speaks in friendly contempt. We wore no teeth or fangs and thus had to be beginners, and this gave countenance to very particular questions about the pyramid's interior and the god-making rite. The answers confirmed Kerkin's tale.

"We hear the whole top of it is made of big beams," Barnar said with yokelish awe. We were drawing near. Light leaked down the sides of the pyramid from rifts in the cloud, but it was weak light that was itself just leakage from higher clouds. Still, anything so huge, and alive, and old, raised by the hands of man, must fill you with awe—that's my view. The pilot spat in the water to say it all wasn't that wondrous if you knew it like he did.

"You should see the beams in the vaulted ceilings at the top, where the King begins his pilgrimage," he said. "Some of them weigh a ton each, yet are groined and dovetailed just as neat as a fly's whiskers."

The pilot was most reassuring on every important point. From his description a man could move through the entire top level among the ceiling beams, and never touch or be seen from the floor. And the guard on the King's door was two spearmen, no more—for the King was administered a paralytic beverage in his preparation for the preritual vigil. He sat, immobile and awake, in his windowless cell. And even though the level just below would be sealed off on the night before the rite, barring access to the top, the guard up there would not be added to. For it is part of the ceremonial assumption that the King awaits his god-making eagerly, and that his guard is just an honor guard.

We got off at the west quay, by far the most public one. The Queen's Cabinet uses the entire east quay for military and economic business, while the terraces on the north and south sides are interrupted by several water-level exits—channels let into the palace's foundation, to permit the launching of craft directly from its interior. On the west are all the major markets and bazaars, and more than half of the inns and wineshops.

We loitered in the plazas, browsed at the scarf makers and swordsmith's stalls, and had wine at several different places. We got ourselves seen and made chat with merchants—fitting in. Feeling the mood of the place, and establishing our role, you see. The ghul on Barnar's shoulder was an excellent introduction. Most showed us the condescending warmth the pilot had. Bounty hunting is a common way for the rustic youths of the northern hills to get their first look at the metropolis, and folk are used to finding them sufficiently simple. A man whose eye is awake would have been alerted by our mature age, but as we know, most people don't look at things very closely. At one winestall the tapster overcharged us for the amusement of the other customers, then stopped me as I paid up, smiling, and revealed the joke. We all had a good laugh, and when we left I was able to steal the lidded goblet I'd had my wine in. It was just what we would need.

Next we bought rope and bowstrings. We needed quite a few yards of each; we split up to make the purchases, and both of us went to several different places to make up our halves of the quota. Less professional men would have been lulled by the holiday extravagances all around them, and the amazing number of people. It seemed the whole northern swamp—the drier part where most of the population lived—had joined the already large resident population in the palace. But we knew that all you need is to raise a few doubts in a few chance souls to have your best-laid plans buggered and blasted.

At noon we went to the Audiences, held in the central chamber of the pyramid's water-level. The Queen presided here, tirelessly, most of the year. She was now in her seven days' retirement in the catacombs under the foundations, below even the swamp waters. There she communed with the mummies of Year Kings past. She would ceremonially rise from thence on the eve of the god-making, and at the same time the King would be brought down from his cell on the pinnacle, which was called the "heaven" station of his ritual "pilgrimage." The pair would meet in the same Chamber of Audiences that we now entered. After their meeting, the King's body would be taken down to the catacombs—the "night" station of his pilgrimage—there to join the other Year Kings. There they stand in the dark, all gods together—gods of Night, you understand.

The chamber was vast. There must have been a thousand litigants there, and they did not begin to fill the place. Dozens of underjudges handled lesser cases in stalls round the room's perimeter, while royal causes were heard in the room's center by a tribunal of three of the Queen's priestesses. Theirs was a job normally handled by Vulvula alone—such was her wit and memory and clarity of judgment. And let it be said here: no one we talked with ever denied the Queen's justice is thorough and scrupulous, treating the great as strictly as the small. True, in her domain some dozens of people each year wake sick and groggy after horrible dreams, and must keep their beds a month after, and a dozen or so others each year do not wake at all one morning. Still, fair rule is only had at a cost, eh?

Routine matters like tax payments had their own designated tribunals, and we found the one for bounty payments. The clerk there assigned us a skinner. The man rose from a bench where he sat with two other dirty-aproned men. He led us out of the chamber and through a good half mile of corridors. The building is fascinating. You get no sense of pattern at all, even after moving through it for a quarter of an hour. The ceiling heights vary, and some halls are short with many rooms; while others are long with doorways that are few and large. Residents here—and the halls thronged with them—rarely know more than their immediate "neighborhoods" very well. We came out of the municipal quay on the east side.

The man brought the whole skin off in one piece, so fast I couldn't follow his moves. They make parchment from it, and clothiers use it for rich men's slippers and ladies' dagger-sheaths. The guts and bones he threw in a bin on a raft, to be used for baiting the lurk-traps around the lake's perimeter. The head he threw in also, after breaking the jaws with a sledge and removing the teeth for us. It had ten—big grinders with cutting edges. He gave us a runt-pearl in payment.

On the same quay an old coppersmith sat on a stool. He offered to bind our teeth with wire for wearing round the neck. His work was cheap and quick, and we came away wearing our trophies—a five-tooth row apiece. This established our role, with a small disadvantage. Accomplished bountymen wear "jaws"—ten-tooth strings, row under row. They tend to be rough with novices of their own guild—they give them the treatment that greenness gets everywhere, and a bit more besides, if you see my meaning. There were surely some ace bountymen in this convocation. It would just have to be taken as it came.

We did next precisely what a pair of bumpkins *would* have: we went up to the peak of the pyramid to bribe the guards for a gawk at the Year King in his cell.

V

As I've said, the pyramid's top is in the clouds. From its outer terraces you can't see anything but sweating-cold whiteness—above, below, all around. Standing there gave you a desperately lonely feeling. That blind whiteness made it a place without time, a kind of Death. You felt as if you might have been dead without realizing it, that all your busy actions had been grave-dreams, and you yourself a skeleton, a rack of hard white bones that had stood there without moving for a thousand years. We went inside and ascended to the last and highest level, which can only be reached from inside the second-to-last.

There were others coming and going, but the custom of peeking at the King still had enough of the illicit about it to keep people brisk and quiet up here. As rustics turned bounty-men, we had some countenance for moving slower and staring around us.

The place was perfect—it alone of all the levels was simple in plan: a hollow square of halls with three doors to a side. A Year King must not have his vigil in a predecessor's cell before twelve years of purification have passed. Each year therefore the King waits in a different room. The halls were gloomy. They had very deeply vaulted ceilings because the tier is built to adorn the pyramid with an elegantly roofed crown, though it's never clear enough for this to be seen from below.

Our greatest encouragement was to see the two guards posted at the end room of a corridor, near a corner. Barnar muttered to me:

"I can do it. I'll want a catwalk of ropes from just over the door and running round the corner and sixty feet up that next hall."

"I'll string it tonight then," I said.

We looked the guards over as we waited our turn at the door's barred window. They were scarred veterans—blank, observant-eyed, and ready of movement underneath their practiced immobility. They would be good men. The post was lucrative, and the palace guard had elimination bouts just before the rite to determine who would get the King's Watch. I paid one of them, and we took our turn at the window—we'd already noted the door had no lock.

The cell was windowless, the plainest little box of bare wood you could imagine. By the far wall was a heap of cushions. A young man sat on the floor with his upper body leaned back on them. His legs were sprawled loosely on the floor with his lower body. He wore only a breechclout and moccasins. The garments were silver, signifying moonlight and Night, of which he was soon to be a deity. He was well made, muscled like a runner. It was eerie to see a body so molded, ridged and knotted with the habit of life and activity, yet lying so unstrung and strengthless. He seemed powerless even to sit upright. His eyes moved slowly and without aim, but for some reason he suddenly fixed them on our faces at the bars. He knit his brow, and his hand stirred from the cushions as if to reach up and touch his own face, but fell back before it could. I wonder now what kind of dreams or portents we were to him. If he had known the truth, he would have known that we would neither harm nor help him.

We came back down to the lake-level without directions. It cost us two extra hours of blundering around, but it sharpened our wits to the place and it taught us a fairly direct route in a way that guaranteed our remembering it. I didn't come out onto the quay with Barnar. In a dark turning I transferred to his pack all my share of the bowstring we'd bought, and all my gear except for my rope. He gave me all the rope he had. We had already chosen the wineshop where we would meet later that night. He went off to find an apothecary. I retraced the route we had just figured out, and returned to the upper levels.

I found an inn and killed an hour with wine and smoked eel. It was full dark when I reentered the dim halls of the Year King's vigil. They call me Nifft the Lean nowadays, but when I first earned myself a name, I was called Nifft the Nimble. I did the hardest work of this whole glorious nab right there in the next two hours. Right at the door where I entered, I slung up a line I had weighted with my dagger, and hauled myself up among the ceiling beams. I did it with a gaggle of revelers climbing the stairs just behind me, and several others, to judge by the footfalls, just about to round the next corner of the hallway. I was up in a blink, and my line after me.

I moved through the beams to within fifty yards of the guarded door, perfecting my movements and learning the pattern of the joists and rafters. Then I sat down to prepare my ropes. I suited them to the beam intervals where I was, which of course would be the same everywhere. I tripled the ropes, braided them loosely, and knotted them, three knots per interval. The finished hundred feet of catwalk, when I had it coiled round my shoulder, was half my own bulk. Now came the true feat. I proceeded toward the King's door, and coming directly over the guards, I began to anchor the catwalk.

I strung it high, with two levels of beams between me and them. Though the regular spacing of the beams made me visible enough to anyone who was looking, I was well in the shadow and being seen was not the danger. The risk was in the fact that a mere fifteen feet of empty air separated me from the ears of those guards. I worked slower than a miser's hand moving to his purse to pay. Gawkers at the King came steadily, and I managed to coincide the loudest part of my work with the advent and the murmurs of these. This was the knot tightening, for the catwalk must not sag and creak when Barnar used it, as then the halls would be barred to visitors and the silence complete. But rope noise being sharp, and the noises of the visitors subdued, it took agonizingly long to get even one knot firm.

The pressure eased as I got round the corner and down the next hall, but I was soon sweating so hard I was amazed it didn't drizzle down into the corridor and give me away. By the Black Crack, there's no work like hanging frozen for indefinite periods, again and again, unpredictably. It's lizard's work, to tell the truth. But when I had done, I'd left a catwalk up there neatly paralleling one of the longitudinal beams, such that with one foot on that beam and the other on the ropes, Barnar could move along a good broad-stance support with both hands free for his special task.

The palace is mortal cold, and drenched as I was I nearly took a chill on my way down. A noisy fit of rheum would have ruined our next night's work. I hurried to stay warm, and at the wineshop out on the quay, where I found Barnar sitting, I ordered a hot posset.

Barnar gave me his afternoon's purchase: a healing gum used by pearl divers to seal wounds that might draw lurks to them. It was twisted in a scrap of ghul skin. I pocketed it and ordered a second posset, feeling much better. I began to observe that our table was getting respectful clearance from other customers, and interested looks. Barnar explained in a murmur:

"When I've gone you may inherit a quarrel. A pair of bountymen, with two jaws apiece. Biggish men—the one with a pair of lurk fangs over his jaws is the troubleseeker. I didn't quite break his right arm, thought it would bring too much notice if the man had to be carried off. People will tell them you're with me, and if they underestimate you, you'll be getting trouble."

"All right," I said, "any hints for procedure?"

"He's on the strong side, but very slow. His friend plays the jackal, follows him up."

Barnar's mention of leaving told me that he had not yet accomplished the most important errand that fell to his share today. We had rather expected that it would have to be done tonight, as sorcerers are a nocturnal breed.

"You found no one to consult, then?" I asked.

"Just getting a name was much," he rumbled. "It takes a lot of drinking around and rumor-gathering to begin to get a fix on someone reliable. There seems to be a consensus about a certain swamp-witch. I'm going to her now—she lives in the northern swamp. I've hired my guide, and he's standing ready with his raft."

"Then you'll go from her to get the lurk?"

"Yes. I'll see you just after dawn at the dock we landed at this morning."

"Good luck, Ox. Bargain hard. If you offer more than one pearl, she'll take you for green and pass you off with nonsense."

I sought out an inn almost as soon as he left, meaning to be out of trouble's way. I was spotted and followed even so, it seems. They were the truest kind of cutthroat, waiting for the dead of night, so at least I had a couple hours' sleep—it was in a great barracks of an inn, with more than thirty pallets—before I was wakened. A heavy boot-toe kicked me hard against the soles of my feet.

I had laid the spear, which Barnar had returned to me before leaving, along my right side under the blanket, with the head at my heel. This is the way you should do it, so you can lift it straight into action against anyone attacking from your bed's foot, which they must do if you've lain with your head to the wall, as I did. After the kick, it took me one second to sort out the two shapes in the darkness, and another to be sure of the rattle and gleam of teeth at their chests.

Then one further second passed during which the man who kicked me said the word "Get" in a fierce whisper, very distinct. He probably meant to say more than just "Get," but the passage of my spearhead through his heart supervened.

I used just enough thrust to strike heart-deep and no more,

because I knew I'd have to have my spear free again quick; a man doesn't get to be a two-jaw bountyman by being slow on his feet. Sure enough, the other bolted quick as a rat. I used one and the same jerk to free my spear and pull myself to my feet. That man was fast. It took all my force to cock and throw before he got to the door, and I pinned him through the side of his rib cage below his arm just as he was sprinting through it. My spear was just sinking into him before the first man I'd stabbed hit the floor—I swear I was just in time to catch him and kill the noise. I laid him on my pallet, and went quietly after the second one. Some people were awake but feigning sleep, seeing that the scuffle was already settled. I carried the second bountyman back to my pallet, laid him by his colleague, and covered them both with my blanket. I took up my things, wiped my spearhead, and left. At another inn I caught three more hours' sleep.

VI

Early morning is a graveyard kind of hour in the swamps—there's no clear air under the clouds then, because the mist is rising from the waters. It moves in slow, torn columns across the quays, and if you're standing at the waterside, you can't even see the pyramid. I found Barnar at the dock. We carried the bundled lurk across the terrace, and into the palace.

Inside there was some activity—here and there a tavern door opened, and you could see the tapster within kindling the public-room fire. We went as quickly as we could without running, and feared no questions. Since the Chamber of Audiences would be closed now until the god-making, bountymen arriving with a catch would be expected to wrap it up and take it to an inn for the duration.

But at the highest levels there were neither inns nor taverns, and outlanders ascending here with a large burden would draw scrutiny from any guardsman. Here we went even quicker, prepared to kill, counting on the hour to spare us the necessity. We met no one, and gained the outside staircase leading up to the second level from the top.

From the head of these stairs I crept to the door. Inside there was a guard strolling down the corridor, at the end of which was the staircase to the King's level. He passed the door and turned the corner. He was followed by another walking the same way about twenty seconds later. So it went—I watched five more minutes, but there was no gap in their circuit long enough for us to get to that staircase unseen. We would have to kill one.

I conferred with Barnar, then memorized the face of the next guard who passed. We took the one who followed. Barnar seized him from behind as he turned the corner and broke his neck. We hauled him back out to the staircase. We were going to tie his body to its underside, but I found a flask on him, so we chose a less mystery-creating plan. We drenched his beard and doublet with the liquor, replaced the flask in his belt, and Barnar lifted him high overhead. There was a gardened terrace about six levels down—invisible now, but I remembered its location and directed my friend. He heaved, grunting softly. The guard arched outward, seeming to hang sprawled in the fog, staring upward openmouthed, and then was swallowed in the whiteness. After a moment there was a soft crash of broken shrubbery. Barnar, as a last touch, wrenched the staircase's heavy bannister loose and left it hanging. When the guard whose face I had memorized passed, we entered and dashed down the hall with our load.

I got into the rafters, and Barnar threw up the lurk so that it landed across a beam. He came up, and we pulled our line after us. The level below would be sealed off by a full guard at midmorning, to begin the King's two-day preritual isolation, and just after the breakfast hour there would be a last-minute rush of gawkers. We rested, saving our work for that noisy hour.

When the folk began arriving, we carried the lurk within fifty yards of the King's door, and unwrapped it. I inserted crossed sticks into its body through the slit in its abdomen, and this swelled it out perfectly. Barnar prepared three thirty-foot lengths of bowstring and hooked one end of each into the body—one to the rear part, and one to either side of the flat head part, amid the base joints of the legs. Then, with as little left to do as possible, we carried it to just above the King's cell. We stretched it lengthwise atop a beam, tying its forelegs and rear body to two daggers pushed into the wood. It would have a whole day to lose the last of its creases. We laid the coiled bowstrings on top of it, and got out of there.

I have the trick of sleeping to kill time, and Barnar had been up all night. We found perches two full corridors away, in case we made sleep-noises.

When we woke, my time sense told me we had an hour or so to wait until our chosen time, the pit of night. The guards were under oaths of silence during this part of the vigil, but they ignored them. We listened to the small shapeless sounds that were all that was left of their conversation by the time it reached us. Their talk wavered feebly, like the flame of an ill-made candle in a gusty room. You could read their oppression of spirit in the way their voices blurred, ceased, and then, doggedly, started again. Barnar and I traded our thoughts with a look: they would be jumpy, all right.

It was a man like themselves they guarded, and he lay at the threshold of a grisly journey. When humankind make covenants with the more-than-human, or the less-than-human, you may buttress them with traditions and rites as you will, but there remains an unacknowledged horror that is never quieted in men's hearts. At last we moved, and as we came closer, our movements got as deft and still as the creeping of rats, minus even their tiny noise of nails. We entered the perilous silence above the King's door, and looked down upon the two polished domes of the guards' helmets. Their talk had stopped again. You could almost feel their gloom. They were ripe for our game.

We undid the lurk from the daggers—it had straightened nicely. Barnar took the coils of bowstring and tucked them under his arms, then picked up the lurk by the three lines, holding them near the hooks. I crouched on one side of the gap in the beams and fastened a line to a rafter. Barnar stood on the other side of the gap, one foot on the catwalk and the other on the beam, and poised the lurk over the opening. Remember the weight of the thing, my friends! He looked to me, and I nodded that I was ready. He began to pay out line through his fingers, letting the legs drop foremost and bringing the whole thing almost flush with the wall, so that it looked like it was crawling down it. It appeared real enough to stir your hair, its black legs flung out in their six-foot spread, its jointed barrel of a body taut and poised behind. If I had been standing twelve hours in the empty half-dark gnawed at by unhealthy thoughts, and had turned to see such a thing a foot above my shoulder, I would have done just what the guards did.

This is not to detract from Barnar's masterful handling. When he had the thing positioned, he let it drop a good four feet and scuff the wall as it did so. This brought their faces up at just the right instant to see the monster lurch to a murderous poised halt an arm's length above them. They peeled themselves from the doorway and spilled across the corridor, one man losing his spear as he sprawled. Barnar was already hauling the lurk back upward with a marvelous smooth speed that made it seem to be scuttling in reverse motion up the wall.

Holding the lurk straight-armed before him, he danced along the beam and catwalk to the next large gap in the rafters, and cast it down through. The throw was perfect. The skeleton struck with a rattling splash right next to the men, who were just struggling to their feet. He was playing dangerously near them, for the bowstrings were far from invisible, but his speed and timing were such that the men were kept in a state of maximum panic. The second throw sent them stumbling round the corner. I had dropped my line, slid down and entered the King's cell before I heard the sound of Barnar's third cast down the next hallway. Things couldn't be better—they had only one spear and so they wouldn't risk a cast with it, and Barnar could play them several moments more while they gathered their wits and the puppet's reality was put to a test.

I moved as quick as a dodging, darting fly. I had cup, salve, and poniard out, and the King by the ankle in an instant. I cut him under the bump of the ankle, where you'll get a good half-cup of blood and the bleeding will then peter out. I pocketed the goblet, wiped the wound clean, and sealed it with the salve. I scarcely spared a glance for the King's face—he was staring at me with strange sad intensity, as if he knew me and I had somehow disappointed him. Then I was shutting the door, shinning up the rope, and drawing it after me.

I rushed along the catwalk past the corner and signaled through the beams. Barnar was just drawing up the lurk. He unhooked the lines and set the great spider-thing on a beam so that its forelegs hung down into the guards' range of vision. Then Barnar was with me and we were dancing through those beams almost as fast as a man can jog on level ground, going the opposite way round the square of halls from the point where the reinforcements would be entering. Our two guards had been shouting for them for some time—for it was death for them to leave their post on this floor—and we heard boots thundering on the stairs already.

We had left our plans vague at this point, counting on turmoil but unable to foresee its precise form. We had included the possibility of revealing ourselves as practical jokers, since there would be enough guards there who were jealous of our two victims' special post to raise a laugh and some sympathy for our game. But this being the eve of the god-making, and the swamp-folks' prime night of revel out of the whole year, when the pyramid was alive with drinkers and singers from top to bottom, we'd seen at least a good chance for a cleaner escape. This we got. The downstairs guard flooded up into the hall where their colleagues were, and after a brief interval a stampede of more miscellaneous footfalls came pounding up the stairs. We got down from rafters in time to be in the hall as the red-faced citizenry rushed in. They eddied at the head of the stairs, prevented from entering the hall where the action was by the crowd of guards there. We jumped from round the corner and waved excitedly.

"This way! We can get through over here!" I shouted. Threescore of men and women cried out and pounded after us. We let the crowd overtake and surround us, falling back into it as we all rushed round the other way. As they rounded the last corner before the King's cell, we dropped out of the rear of the rout and ran back to the stairs.

VII

On the next night we stood by the dais in the center of the
Chamber of Audiences. It had cost us our runt-pearl from the
ghul to buy this place from one of the chamber guards. Those
near us had paid as much. The whole vast hall was packed with
folk, hot and close, from wall to wall. We had taken our place
hours early, and heard the tale of the "puppet-show upstairs"
passed among the folk around us, variously distorted. People
enjoyed it hugely. A new jocose tradition might have gotten
started, had we not spoiled the humor of the idea for the Queen
a short time later.

She appeared in the great doorway at midnight. Lines of
guards held clear a broad aisle from the doorway to the dais,
where the altar stood, and she remained in the doorway at the
end of this aisle, not moving for a long time. She wore a coarse
white robe that covered her entire body. Her long black hair was
unbound, and her face had a terrible beauty, meaning both those
words. It was a northron face—nose large and strong, eyes set
both shadowy deep and wide apart, a marvelous wide mouth
with lips of infinite expression.

There was a weight and power in the way she stood, a *realness*
that made that whole human multitude seem a shadowy and
passing thing. She stood in her straightness and silence and six
hundred years of life—for she was ancient when she came to this
place—and all of our thousands surrounding her seemed brief,
fugitive, whispering—like a host of dead leaves. Truly my friends,
aren't our lives as quick in their passing as a thief's shadow across
a wall? Queen Vulvula's hand moved to her throat, and her robe
fell from her nakedness. She moved forth down the aisle.

She had a body to stir and stiffen you: big guava breasts,
hanging-ripe; thighs round and strong; hips like a bulging vase
for milk or scented oil. But as she drew near the dais, we saw
it was an autumnal body. The breasts were frost-nipped, beginning to dwindle from within as apples will. Her thighs moved
with a chilled slowness, and the veins were beginning to map

themselves out on the backs of her hands. And as she mounted toward the altar we saw that at the corners of her plump and flexible mouth dark nets of wintery erosion were spreading out across her jaw.

As she stood on the dais I felt her presence fully, like a gust from the icy gulf of her heart. She looked over us as a harvester looks over a great stubborn field that he has made to yield him fruit. She knew her alienness in her people's minds; their unspoken horror and the danger she lived in because of it. And she relished it. The risk and care of empire gratified her centuries-deep mind. She smiled very slightly. Looking at her mouth, you knew that it would have a small frosty atmosphere all its own around it, and that its kiss would suck your soul out in a blaze of cold fire. She moved to the head of the altar.

Literally its head, for the altar was a big statue of a man in a wrestler's bridge, that is, supporting himself on his feet and hands but face upward, so that his thighs, stomach, and chest formed a long level surface. The Queen spoke some words in a language I have never heard. Her voice was mellower than you expected, soft at the edges. Effortlessly it filled the whole hall. As she spoke she pointed overhead, then to the altar, and then floorward, meaning the catacombs below, no doubt. Then she spoke for our understanding:

> *"Your sons have fattened in my rule.*
> *Your rafts go laden with peaceful trade.*
> *There's no man's wife need fear the ghul.*
>
> *Your pearls are spared the poacher's raid—*
> *They're farmed by laws that spread their worth,*
> *And keep ensheathed war's wasteful blade.*
>
> *You've had what good men get on earth—*
> *Now grant your Queen does nothing cruel*
> *Who, dead with craving, ends her dearth.*
>
> *Her year-long lord, with year-long Heaven paid,*
> *Comes now to her to see her thirst allayed."*

The King appeared in the doorway, borne on a litter by two bearers. He slouched, still strengthless, in the seat, but the set of his head showed his wits more awake than before. He wore a sacrificial fillet of graven bronze round his brow, and as they carried him forward, you could see his eyes moving restlessly under its line.

The bearers set the litter before the altar. They were powerful men, of Barnar's type. One grasped the King's wrists and the other his ankles. The Queen spoke again, and there was a tenderness in her voice:

> "Rise to me now, my love, a king,
> And descend from me as a God.
>
> You will sit in Eternity with your line,
> And rule the ever-after-living hosts.
> You will wield the scepter of the shadow-kind,
> You will be judge and shepherd of the ghosts.
>
> Rise to me now, my love, a king,
> And descend from me as a God."

When she had said this, they lifted the King onto the altar. He looked to this side and that as they pressed his legs against the stone legs, his back against the stone chest, his arms and shoulders against the arms and shoulders of stone. And as he looked here and there, I thought for a moment that he looked at me, and smiled, ever so faintly. I don't insist on this—I half think it was a dream myself—the air was so charged, and the silence crawled all over the skin of the multitude like a swarm of ants. But do you suppose he understood what had been done, and took some last small comfort, some revenge in the thought?

She knelt beside him, and her face was taut, refined by a tension of icy love, made younger before our eyes by her passionate anticipation. She lowered her face—worshipfully, kissing—to the muscled juncture of his neck and shoulder. And then there was a crisp, liquid sound of horrible distinctness, her hands clutched his shoulders, and the King's body rose and convulsed upon the stone with the raw coiling power of a speared eel.

The two giants holding him grunted with strain, and the Queen's head rode with the youth's surging body as if it were a part of it. He hammered the rock like a beached dolphin pounds the wet sand, slowing with suffocation, and as he stilled, the Queen clutched and nuzzled with a weasel's self-forgetting lust. Her shoulders worked like pumps as she sucked, and her hands kneaded his torso as if it were a great udder of blood. She almost drowned herself in her hunger, and had to tear her face up from its feeding to breathe with all the desperate speed of a diver breaking the surface. She reared her crazed glass-eyed face before the crowd—her lips smeared, her chin drizzling red. Her breasts were actually fuller now—they jutted youthfully, and I saw a thin thread of blood-red leakage from both her nipples. She leaned and drank again. The King barely moved. His skin tightened over the muscles, while the muscles themselves seemed to be slowly dissolving.

She grew calmer, methodical. She drank from both his wrists next, and then from inside of both his thighs, to empty him efficiently. She licked her mouth clean, then cupped and lifted her breasts and licked her nipples. A priestess ascended the dais with a silver laver in which she washed herself a second time, and then drank off the water. Another priestess brought her a robe of scarlet. She put it on and, flanked by the priestesses, stepped down. It was done.

When she had exited, the littermen laid the King's husk on the litter and bore it from the hall. The Queen would spend the night above, in the King's cell, where the priestesses would install for her a large mirror framed in gold. The King would go to the catacombs, where other priestesses waited with the sacred taxidermy tools.

VIII

The next morning, on the western quay, we waited for the expected to befall. We had hired a taxi raft, and had it standing by. Then the commotion came boiling out of the palace, borne by scores of hurrying folk. The Queen had been heard to waken, rise, and a moment later, scream.

We boarded at once. An hour later we had reached a certain great mudbar near the fringe of the swamp—one so large it amounted to an island. Here we waited, sending the pilot back well paid and at double speed with a small scroll for the Queen. We'd chosen a shrewd man who would have the savvy to get himself into the Queen's hearing in an uproar like the one you would expect in the pyramid. The scroll's marking would help. We had written on the outside: "Concerning the Year King's Missing Blood." A glance at this added vigor to his plying of the stern oar, and he was soon out of sight.

This was the most ticklish step of all. Having two thousand prime swamp pearls put into our hands was going to be a simple matter now. But remaining alive for even an instant after the King's blood was back in the Queen's control—this was going to strain both wit and nerve to accomplish.

Barnar's interview with the swamp-witch was made with this difficulty in mind. If you're going to guarantee your safety with sorcerers—and the vampire queen was a very great one—you've got to get them to protect you with their own thaumaturgy. The trick is to make them give you magic that they cannot themselves afterward over-pass. You've got to ask for the best thing in their repertory.

The swamp-witch was no Vulvula. But it was worthwhile having her professional opinion as to what is the fastest thing that wizardry can call to the aid of man. I would have guessed, all by myself and without paying a pearl, the answer that she gave my friend. Still, it was something to have a confirmation. She told Barnar that the fastest being, in the upper world and the subworlds alike, is a basiliscus. I can almost see you nodding wisely, Taramat. Read on a bit.

So we demanded, along with the pearls, a ring charmed to command the service of a basiliscus. Then we sat down, had a bit of jerky and wine, and waited.

The priestess of the Queen came almost impossibly soon. When we saw she had two archers on the raft with her, I quickly waded into the water. The King's blood had dried into a grayish biscuit, full of little holes like lava-rock. I held it up and called out:

"Throw your bows in the water—double quick! Otherwise the Queen is going to have to drink this whole swamp to save her youth!"

The bows went overboard. The men kept their spears, but this was fair, as we had one, and we couldn't expect them to risk our robbing them. The raft came up to the islet. We gestured the soldiers back. The priestess stepped ashore with two leathern bags and stood staring at us, rage in her eyes, her mouth impassive. I stayed in the water, as the soldiers were so near. Barnar said:

"Time is short, woman. Give us the ring. We'll make the exchange when we're on the creature's back." She nodded wordlessly, and tossed him a small silver ring. Barnar put it on his smallest finger and raised his hands. The spell the witch had taught him was brief. He intoned it with great verve and authority. First there was a long silence.

Then the earth began to wrinkle and crack, like pottery glaze, along a thirty-foot seam that crossed the width of the islet. The cracks darkened and grew, the fragmented clay began to buckle, and even I, standing in the water, felt a giant mass jerking and slithering underfoot. A lizard-foot that could have held me like a doll reached out of the tormented mire. A second followed, as a polished scaly snout appeared. The seam bulged and gaped, and the vast reptile heaved clear, hurling blocks of clay to all sides and raising waves from which I was barely quick enough to save the blood-cake. With imperial self-absorption the basiliscus hauled itself into the water on the other side of the islet, and unfolded its wings to bathe them. They were no bigger, fanned out, than the raft the soldiers stood on—curiously stunted-looking, given the body's bulk. In its own good time it crawled back into the islet and aimed its obsidian eye, big as a target-shield, attentively at Barnar.

The basiliscus isn't a true demon because it can barely use speech at all, but it falls under the compulsions of the Great Age of Thaumaturgy and is part of our inheritance of power from our forebears. You tell it where you want to go. It takes you there and you feed it the ring in payment, allowing it to return to the subworlds. And you'd better feed it the ring, and ask for no further trips. Magic compels it just so far, and then its nature asserts itself. Into its ragged pit of an earhole, Barnar whispered the name of our destination, then mounted its back. I jumped from the water and vaulted on behind him, keeping the blood-cake poised for a throw at the lagoon.

The priestess approached and opened the mouths of both bags for our inspection. I don't know which felt more unreal, to be sitting on the back of that lizard or to be looking at the oily luster of two thousand perfect swamp pearls. The priestess stepped nearer, the bags in one hand, the other extended for the blood. I made the exchange with pickpocket deftness, hugged the bags to me, and Barnar shouted: "Away!"

A slow gale of breath entered the cavelike chest under us. For a moment nothing happened, and fleetingly it bothered me that in that time, neither the priestess nor the soldiers stirred. They didn't make a move, and yet had time enough, if they were good, to spear us both from our mount. Then we were fifty yards away.

The basiliscus's scales were big as flagstones and smooth as wax. Luckily there was room in their interstices for you to sink half your hand in, because its back was far too broad to grip with your legs. It took exactly three running leaps, crossing lakelets like puddles and using big mudbars as stepping-stones. Its wings hammered once, twice, and then suddenly they were winnowing cottony fog, and there was no swamp to be seen.

We swam thundering up through clouds and mist for several moments, knuckles cracking with the strain of our climbing speed, and then we were in clear sky, with the clouds a level white broth below, hemmed in a bowllike rim of ragged peaks. Beyond the hills, where we were headed, the salt steppes lay parching under the hot blue emptiness. Then, through the rush of wind and the creaking leathery toil of the vast wings, we heard a whine far to our rear.

We looked back, and learned in one glance that there *is* something faster than a basiliscus. Whatever its name is—for that we never learned—there was one of them bursting from the cloud-broth just where we had exited. It had one human rider. Even at that moment I marveled that any man should venture to sit astride the spiny neck of such a thing.

I have seen its kind in little—stilt-legged bugs with long bodies and two forelegs it uses as arms, barbed along their insides for piercing what they snatch. Their flat triangular heads have two globelike eyes and dainty greedy mouths, whose hunger the barbed arms must constantly serve. This one's head was big enough for a man to dance on, and it was dead white all over. Only the furious power of its wings—two shining blurs at its sides—set off its form against the white background of clouds. The thing was big enough to kill our basiliscus, though it probably wouldn't be able to eat more than two-thirds of him. Of course it would start with us.

There was no hurrying our mount, which sped its maximum as a matter of course. Meanwhile, the Queen's rider guided the huge pale insect into a long sloping climb that would intersect our course, for we had leveled off. I remembered seeing the lightning deftness of the little cousins of this thing—they can snatch a spider out of its web without leaving a tremor among the silk threads. This thing would have a fifteen-foot reach if an inch, and to cap the mess, I could only defend our rear with one hand; it was imperative for both of us to keep one hand dug into the lizard's scales, or the wind of our passage would sweep us off.

We were over the steppes now. Hopelessly I chose a stabbing-grip on our spear with my free hand. The look of the hell-bug as it rose behind us was all fragility and grace. Its two lower pairs of legs hung trailing in dainty curves under its long body, which looked as smooth and balanced as the war-canoes of the southeastern savages. It was getting so near you could make out the faceting of its eye-globes, a taunting reminder of the pearls in our bags. I could even see the face of the soldier guiding the thing.

It's strange to see a man's face through the screaming wind of that speed, with the whole sky around you and the whole world beneath, a barren floor, and still to get as clear a feel for his past and his character, as if the two of you were sitting at mugs in a cozy tavern. But I did feel I knew the man in that glance—plain sense said that it would be a tough and tried soldier, for an important mission like this. The face said that and more—the scars above and below the steady bright eyes, squinted against the wind, the mouth shut and thoughtful. It added up to a sturdy, cool professional who thinks ahead and then kills you without slipups when it's his job to do so and he has the edge.

Good soldiers stay alive by being unsentimental and having a quick eye for the main chance. There was no time to chew it over. That quirky peek into the man's nature showed me our only long-shot hope, and without a pause for thought I did the hardest thing I've ever done. I grabbed a bag by the bottom, and with a snap of the arm that forced open its drawstrings, I flung its whole contents into the air behind us. I groaned as I did it, looking back. The pearls sped earthward in a glistering black clot, scattering slowly, seeming to swarm as they fell like bees do before hive-making. Our speed and theirs made the jewels flee the faster from sight, and I still see them sometimes in memory, a thousand black stars, tumbling down through the wide blaze of noon.

If betrayal of his Queen was on the soldier's mind before, I do not know. Perhaps if he'd caught us and had the whole two thousand, the habit of loyalty would have stayed firm and he would have smoothly completed his mission. But seeing the pearls there, stark and dazzling in the sky, and knowing that they could be his or they could be who knew whose—it shocked him into realizing the wealth he was pursuing. If he did not follow them down, and finished the chase, they would be leagues behind, and he might never find them. Almost without hesitation, he reined his mount into a dive.

It had to be a whole thousand, you see, for some would be lost, and there must be enough even so to purchase swift escape and a new life. The Queen would eventually work a spell of recall on the mount he rode, and in the meantime he could use it to his advantage. Luck go with the man, I bear him no grudge! Still, as I say, I see them tumbling, tumbling, those thousand dazzling jet-black pearls, sometimes in memory.

Ah well! Having a share of a full thousand would simply have meant more squandering to do. The soldier was a career man, a maker of plans and investments, and is probably cherishing his coffers right now, and dreading thieves. For me, it was work enough to rid myself of the five hundred I came away with. Think—I did it in two years! Surely, that's a feat as great as any involved in the winning of those black beauties!

THE HORROR ON THE #33

O f those grim events I find it difficult, even at this late date, to write. Strictly speaking, they did not even involve me, but Knavle, my dear friend, from whose voluminous correspondence alone I know of them. But we are close in soul, Knavle and I, and through his accounts, hellishly circumstantial as they were, I can say that I too, in a manner, lived those moments of horror with him.

When that first dread encounter befell him, Knavle had been a wino for almost exactly a year. He was in fact observing the anniversary month (he had already lost his memory for exact dates) of his choosing that bibulous career.

I must confess that all of us who knew him sought to discourage him from following this alcoholic vocation. Even I, his closest confidant, had been so unsupportive as to call his choice of life-style a "downward path." He had mildly replied that his was no smooth downhill way; that it was far easier, in fact, to be a short-order cook (for example) or a bank president, than to be a wino; that, moreover, in being an object of compassion, he was performing a vital moral service for those more fortunate than himself who would otherwise, lacking such flagrant specimens of misery, pity only themselves.

Fortunately, over the months Knavle's happiness and dedication persuaded me of the narrowness of my prim response, and by the time I write of, our breach was well healed. In the last letter I had from him before the one detailing his encounter, my friend had written with calm gaiety of his simple rituals of anniversary: apart from drinks cadged from others' bottles, over whose nature he had no control, he was drinking, throughout the month, only Santa Fe White Port—his first "poison" (so he fondly called it) as a fledgling sot.

Ah, the contrast of that letter with the next! The former closed with an airy reference to von Schecklestumpff's remark that religious faith lies more in small observances than grand beliefs, and in the postscript Knavle put the bite on me for five dollars. But even as I was sealing my reply, with a two-dollar money order, his next letter was dropped through my door slot, thick with Knavle's scrupulous detail. About its pages hung— not the festive fragrance of Santa Fe—but the light stink of sweating fear!

Knavle is slight and short—in general, large-bodied winos don't survive well. Knavle was one of those who could fold themselves out of sight to take their doses of oblivion. An important concomitant of this skill is the habit, on waking, of lying perfectly still until one has rediscovered one's surroundings. This Knavle did on the night in question.

He climbed up out of the chasm of two quarts of White Port to find himself folded up, vibrating. He lay on a taut surface of ocher-colored plastic whose texture parodied skin, and which had a scorched smell. He was, he realized, on a bus. That it was late at night, he judged from its being interiorly lit, and from the absence of voices. And by the fetid hum beneath him Knavle knew he was over the bus's motor, at the rear of the great rattling fluorescent barn of a vehicle. Knavle turned his face up, and looked above.

He could see the contents of the bus without sitting up, because it was a new model, with yard-square windows that, when it was dark outside and light within, formed facing walls of mirrors. Out either side, the bus's interior, in hologram, lay adjoining itself. Thus Knavle saw all just by twisting his head slightly, and the image-quality was excellent, even down to the striates of the red rubber aisle-mat and the felt-tipped graffiti on the aluminum screen up front concealing the driver.

As plainly mirrored were the bus's two other passengers, closer to the front. One was a small elderly oriental man, sitting motionless, wearing a suit and tie, his skull appearing as soft as the thin ashen hair slicked down across it. And the other, some seats behind him, was an old woman, a trashbagger.

She was, with her three bulging handbags and two doubled grocery sacks of junk, one of the shopping-cart crazies, the trash can scavengers who wheeled their wealth, mumbling, through just such parks and public squares as Knavle frequented. This one he had never seen. Her hair was a frozen yellowish thorn-ball, like tallow radiating in spikes from her dirty nut-hard face. Even as Knavle studied her, she rose and carried her baggage up the aisle to the little oriental gentleman's seat, muttering to herself as she went. He turned up to her, inquiringly, his smooth bulged brow that suggested infant frailty; the frecklings of age around the deep orbits of his eyes gathered into the constellations of a painful smile. The old woman plumped down beside him and began mumbling with more purpose, almost audibly to Knavle where he lay.

My friend watched, expecting the old man's attempt to extricate himself. The little person made none. His mouth widened —a smile now of absorption in what the old she-crazy was saying. Tenderly, absently, he almost-touched the careful knot of his tie, and replied something. The white spike-radiating head rocked, nodding.

Knavle's neck was cramped, and he was just deciding to sit up when he saw the old woman throw a look round the bus. There was something in the alert competence of the look that chilled him. He felt sure she had not seen him, and that look made him know that she must not. The bus increased speed, plowing down a long slope between sparse lines of streetlamps just visible through the interior reflections in the windows. The motor went into a higher, sighing key, and the boom and hustle of the great chassis erased all traces of what the trashbagger was now saying to her seatmate.

As she spoke she began actually to touch the little man, to groom him here and there—pat his tie knot, smooth the hair like fine dead grass at his temples, stroke his lapels. While she did these things, the man's head drooped forward, he gaped at her and seemed to want to deny something that she was saying.

Then all at once the old woman shifted in her seat and went

straight to work on him. She unknotted his tie, dragged it out of his collar, and wadded it into one of her bags. She reached down, seemed to fumble obscenely for a moment, then sat up, tucking one of his shoes into a different bag. Lastly, she rousted the comb from one of his back pockets and snagged it decoratively in her waxy locks. The old man gazed at her, rapt, with the expression of one who wants to smile politely, but finds what has been said a bit too difficult, or shocking.

As what seemed a finishing stroke in this senseless touch-up, the trashbagger tilted the man's head slightly to one side. Then she set all of her parcels down in the aisle, reached up and took hold of her own throat with both hands, and stripped her face clean off her skull. However, it was not a skull that was revealed, but the head of some huge wasp, or great carnivorous fly. Its merciless oral machinery sank into the old man's neck. For perhaps fifteen seconds, the trashbagger fed.

Then she pulled her face back on, swept up all her goods in one arm, and supported the little body like some drunken crony on the other. Staggering down the aisle to the head of the bus as the vehicle suddenly slowed for a stop, she tendered a small something to the unseen driver. The doors gasped open, and the spiky head descended.

Knavle could not resist sitting up to peer outside. They were at an in-town park he knew, at an intersection where the neon of an all-night coffee shop added to the light of the signals, set to idiotic pulsations of red and yellow. From the intersection, he knew he was on the #33 bus.

She set the small gentleman's body on a bus-stop bench backed by the park's dark wall of foliage. She walked on toward the crosswalk, leaving him sprawled in a slovenly way that the neatness of the man himself would never have tolerated. Knavle looked at him and saw that across the street a bored waitress, leaning at her counter in the coffee shop, stared at him too. Then he glanced back at the corner and saw that he himself was being studied by the trashbagger. She had paused in her hobbling departure and now looked Knavle straight in the eyes. They stared at each other a long moment across the disjointed figure that slouched in the poison-candy-colored light. Then the bus pulled away. With a groan my friend shrank back down in his seat. Alas! In a world of glass, where can a man lie hidden?

II

A person without experience of the wino perspective could easily miss the peculiar dismalness of Knavle's position. He and his caste inhabit the waste corners of the world and have therefore the least power to hide of any class of men. Only a man who possesses things has any power to rearrange his life, to avoid or defend; as for the resolutely destitute, they are already clinging to crannies and last possibilities. There are only so many places to sleep for free, or to get a morning's work distributing supermarket advertisers, and to these places Knavle had to go.

In his account of the day following the incident his style was firm and factual, but the activities he reported betrayed how disturbed he was. In the first place, around noon, he bought and ate, not only two hot dogs, but an order of fries as well. In the second place, after his meal, he went and reported the murder on the bus to the police.

The food alone was very telling—any serious wino dislikes buying it. Wine is a corrosive that reduces and disposes of one's time. Nothing is expected of it, it commits one to nothing—its purchase expresses not even the bare assumption that the morrow will dawn. How different the act of buying food, a stark confession of belief in the future! I needed no more than this to tell me that Knavle was contemplating positive action and might even go so far as to try to save his life in a coherent and serious way.

But of course I *had* further and far more startling evidence of this. To go to the police! Knavle! He was himself shocked that he had gone to this extreme, as his letter ended by expressing. Here follows Knavle's own account:

> I went to the central station, McPittle, instead of one of the local tanks where I'm known, because I reasoned that such

heavy news should go straight to the heart of the organization, for promptest action.

The central station is a square glass building at least twenty-five stories high. It's a mirror-shaft, it reflects everything around it—sky, neighboring buildings, street traffic.

Inside the building, though, total transparency takes over. There are some floors where you can see the entire width of the place through hundreds of glass cubicle dividers. A forest of heads bobs in and out of view among the window-maze, round black heads as numerous as the acres of little round black holes in the ceilings. These, like a field of boringly orderly stars, are hung with ugly fluorescent moons—square aluminum grids like ice-cube trays. The slightly chilled air has a mausoleum smell, I think from the presence of so much underarm deodorant.

The first man I saw asked me if I had a record. I expected this, what with my good suit off at the cleaners, and having left my shave and my shine in my other pants. I said I had a record, but I hadn't done anything lately and that I had come to report a murder I'd witnessed last night after midnight on the #33 bus, Airport to Flanders Heights. The murder was of an elderly Japanese or perhaps Chinese gentleman, and by an even more elderly woman of a vagabondish, addled appearance. The man I spoke to turned to his partner and said, thumbing at me: "Get this individual's name and data. I've got a feeling he has a record."

The partner took my name and data, and I waited for about an hour on a cushioned bench without a back. Finally the report came up from downstairs that yes, I did have a record. They gave me my file number and sent me up two floors to see a detective. All the detectives were busy, so I waited in the detectives' waiting room for about two hours. At last they called me to the bench. The girl asked for my file number. I had lost it.

They telephoned downstairs, but the file-number department was closed. They told me to come back in the morning, and I left, blessing my luck, for I'd managed to work out of my system this strange compulsion to report this thing and without having actually to do it. More important still, I'd thought about the trashbagger through all those hours waiting and come to realize something about her: she would never let herself get caught, and no human power would ever take her against her will.

After this, Knavle's fatalism returned—or so I believed. His letters pointedly excluded mention of the incident, and the life they reported, divided between the usual parks and missions and neighborhoods, was his old life unaltered. It would have been tactless to applaud the stoic bravery of this. We both knew that he had confronted an entity of the direst kind, which now knew him as a witness to its act. But to live on in spite of this, to make, after his initial excited folly, no move to hide or defend himself—this was no more than his wino's code of honor required. To praise an integrity that he would want his friends simply to assume him to have, would have insulted him.

But I was misled, and his behavior was in fact *not* perfectly fatalistic. After several letters he "let slip" that, not only had he not cut down on his bus riding—he had increased it and had begun to ride the #33 with especial frequency. This was a converse species of betrayal of his ethics. I wrote him so at once, my real concern, of course, being greater for his life than his code of behavior. But I stressed this point—to seek the inevitable was as mad as to flee it. What had happened to his sot's detachment? I knew his desert-fringed city well enough to realize that he could get around it quite adequately without using the #33 line, and told him quite forcefully that this he ought to do. His reply was rather airy. He insisted the #33 had always been one of his entertainments. Aside from its offering, if taken round-trip, three hours of warm lodging, its cross-town course gave one an excellent panorama of the city—from its spectacular glass-and-girders heart, through successive ethnic zones, through the outlying bean fields, orchards, and eucalyptus windbreaks on the town's fringe, out to the airport. Moreover, he added, he never took it at night anymore. Small protection! For Knavle's second encounter was soon enough in coming. And it happened on the #33 in broad daylight, at high, glorious noon!

On the #33's return ride from the airport, the farmland is succeeded by a black-and-Latin ghetto whose streets are broad, their asphalt striped with grass-tufted seams, and on whose plank fencing or raw cinder-block walls *cholo* writing jostles the styleless black graffiti. The land rises into minor hills after this, where the streets are crowded with taller, more Victorian frame structures. Chinese, Korean, and aged white people live here. And here, as the bus topped a rise, the cloud cover that had dimmed the whole first half of Knavle's ride broke up before a fresh breeze. Tons of honey-colored sunlight were poured upon the steep shingled rooftops; the winter-scoured pavements glowed white and dry. My friend rejoiced in the sight and wondered if his sole fellow-passenger did likewise. She was a little chicken-necked biddy, wattled with age, and wearing a small round Sunday hat *cum* nonfunctional fragment of blue veil. She sat near the front, Knavle the rear; he could not determine if she even saw beyond the window glass beside her. The bus, just past the rise, pulled into a stop, its big new-model brakes making barely a squeak. The door wheezed and clapped. A thornball of tallowish hair rose, like a malign jerky sun, from the step well. Paying nothing, the old leather-faced trashbagger mumbled up the aisle as the bus pulled away. Had there been a hum of revolution from the roll of identifying plaques set in the bus's brow? Perhaps to NOT IN SERVICE?

Oddly, Knavle did not feel directly endangered, though he was perfectly visible. Without knowing why, he felt sure from the first that the biddy was to be the old vagabond's prey. Just so. The trashbagger gasped to a seat just two aft of the biddy. She sat mumbling, rummaging without system among her multiple tacky baggage. Knavle watched, with no slightest concern to conceal the focus of his attention. The crone had not met his eyes as she came up the aisle.

Now she got up and advanced to the lady's seat—she sat, as many of them like to do, on its aisleward edge. The old nomad stood there in a bearish slouch, hugging her bags and sacks of trash, muttered down, and made a vague uncouth movement with her head. The biddy looked up at her, and Knavle could feel, though not see, how her knobby hands fretted with the gloves they doubtless held in her lap. Yet with the disquiet, there was also in that biddy's brow the same knit of fascination Knavle remembered from the little Japanese gentleman. Her thrifty, bony chin hung slack an instant, then she positively smiled, tightening the threads of age across her lean jaw. She moved in to the window, and the trashbagger plumped herself down in her place.

The she-tramp set her bundles down in the aisle, then leaned forward to massage her legs, speaking in a steady rumble the while. The biddy, whom Knavle saw in profile, wore as she listened a beaming church-social smile that he was sure was the liveliest in her repertory. She nodded to some remark, then lifted her hand with a little gesture that suggested the sliding-aside of some intervening panel. Leaning close to this aperture of special confidence she had created, the biddy murmured an eager sentence to the trashbagger, who, sitting up from rubbing her ankles, nodded deliberately.

They sat bent in closer conference. The spiky head spoke; the biddy's; again the spiky. And as she spoke, the trashbagger casually reached up and plucked one of the biddy's earrings off of her earlobe and pocketed it. The biddy nodded dazedly—seemingly, more at something said than done. The trashbagger muttered and plucked down the second earring.

Knavle, for no clear reason, expected the old vagabond to take the Sunday hat as one of her trophies, but she did not. She took the coat of the biddy's blue knit suit off her with surprising address and, as with the Japanese gentleman, a shoe last of all. Knavle had been asking himself if he would watch to the end. Now he sat powerless to look away as the crone seized her own throat and wrenched off the rubbery bag of face and scalp, freeing the huge insect head with its black nodular eyes and the compact surgical apparatus of its mouthparts.

It was not the busy, multiple scissoring movement of these that Knavle watched as they sank into the biddy's neck—but rather the eyes. Since each of them was a hemisphere and they faced opposite directions, he knew that they had wraparound focus and saw the bus's whole interior. Nevertheless he had the overwhelming feeling that they were aimed at himself, centrally and exclusively, in the manner of a human gaze.

For fifteen seconds he and the immense arthropod stared at each other while the latter fed. The exuberant unpent sunlight poured through the all-admitting windows and lit those compound eyes with a rainbow coruscation. Knavle marveled at the radiance fractured on those hundred thousand lenses; the creature seemed gilded with immortality in those moments, with the gorgeous streets and sky passing outside.

Then the trashbagger was pulling back on the wigged sack, shouldering the biddy and her bundles on either side, and shuffling out, as the bus sighed curbward for its first stop since she had gotten on. She tendered something at the driver's stall and got off. She set the biddy on the bus-stop bench and shuffled away, round the corner, gone. The biddy sat askew—coatless in her lace-throated blouse, but still wearing her Sunday hat—and seemed to sleep with a faintly abandoned air, publicly, shamelessly, like an old wino in a park.

III

After receiving Knavle's account of this second confrontation, I awaited his next letter with dread. I hoped he would decide to abandon that city, but had too much reason to expect him—not only to stay—but to seek out the Trashbagger again.

When his next letter came, it brought not only the disappointment of seeing my fears justified, but a more subtle unease as well. I present that brief epistle in its entirety. Knavle's unsettling degree of intuition about the Trashbagger, the particularity with which he surmises the Trashbagger's aims and her laws, strongly suggested to me that my friend was already to a critical extent subject to a kind of hypnotic influence exerted by the creature. I subjoin the document:

March 17

To Mr. J. Bradley McPittle

Dear McPittle:
    A wino is a frontiersman, a romantic. He lives squarely

in the wasteland that most men so furiously deny, though it surrounds them. For all our best mirrors and lenses, aimed star- or atom-ward, tell the same tale: motes of matter wheeling in gulfs of black space.

Anyone who takes a walk on the desert at night, on a clear night, can see this truth without lenses. I've often insisted, McPittle, on the fact that my city stands on a desert. Even lacking this, any big city at night is in itself a good facsimile of a desert, and a good wino is the official desert rat of all such wastelands.

Any wino who is not merely a timeserver inhabits the desert out of pride, because it is the truth, or at least the truth's image. He scorns the glass mazes of responsibility, wherein so many well-upholstered heads bristle and bob and keep the ever-deepening streams of data creeping through the crooked course of systems!

But I digress. I'm on the bench at the park stop of the #33 line. It's late afternoon now—near rush hour. I'll stay on the bus all night if need be. I distributed advertisers yesterday— endless miles of advertisers! I have with me both fare and provisions. In a nice stout paper bag I have a quart of Santa Fe White Port, a quart of Italian Swiss Tawny Sherry, a quart of Thunderbird, and a pink bottle of Pagan Pink Ripple. I've got three packages of cracker-and-peanut-butter sandwichettes, fifty cents' worth of beef jerky, two Three Musketeers bars, and a package of Beer Nuts. Also, in a separate bag made out of red plastic netting, I have five pounds of oranges.

For the past half-hour I was wondering why I got the oranges, which I don't like—but I just remembered that we used to take them with us as kids when we rode the bus to the beach.

I'm petrified. But I am also strangely sure of one thing: it's in that last conversation you have with the Trashbagger that all is won or lost. Only if she outtalks you there, only if she hypnotizes you, does her face come off. If you outthink her and resist her will, you win your freedom.

I wish I had a gun! I couldn't even afford a kitchen knife!

There's something else I know too, McPittle. I'm

convinced I'm not the only man in this city to have witnessed the Trashbagger's crimes. And I feel that her other witnesses have been as powerless to testify as I was, perhaps through fear of madness, or torpor of the will. How many of those people in that coffee shop across from me, eating there doggedly, docilely, on display, how many of them have seen and are saying nothing? Their fat, freckled earlobes, their veiny noses, move slightly in mastication. Their neckless profiles are a trifle stiff with the pretense of invisibility to the roaring street. . . .

Whatever else, I won't hide. I won't—the bus, two blocks off. Must seal and send. May luck sit on my shoulder!

Yours,

Knavle

IV

I intended to present a digest of Knavle's subsequent letter—the last he ever wrote. But despite the vagaries of my friend's style, and the rather baroque imagery to which he was addicted, I feel it would be unfair of me to interpose myself between the reader and what must be the sole firsthand account of the Trashbagger extant.

I here present then, with the most poignant feeling, the letter itself, intact as before, despite its length:

March 1?

Dear McPittle:

Taking the #33 at rush hour is a kind of drowning, an immersion in breathless waiting men. Children, or an occasional addled vociferous type, will send ripples of response through the mass, but then all our engines return to *idle*. The feel of all those idling psychic dynamos around one causes at moments an unbearable suffocating suspense. How can we all wait like this, you think, packed, paralyzed? You think of the thousand unguessable impulses that any one of us could explode with at any moment. The fact that we don't, that we all sit and stand, drowned in silence—it becomes amazing, awe-inspiring in itself.

As the light fails in the sky and the interior lights come on, then we, a fluorescent-lit thicket of the drowned, go more minutely on display to the sidewalks we pass. We are they, shown them as plainly as are the manikin displays in plate glass. We flee, a little copse of shadows, across the concrete. Perhaps we look like an exhibit in some future museum of our culture. We are quietly posed, seemingly intent, unaware that our world lies buried a millennium deep in time past.

We were all agreed to sit and wait in silence. Most of the other passengers had other agreements going, such as about taking baths and washing their clothes. They resented anyone's waiting in silence with them, who had not entered these other covenants too.

Therefore, since I was already in bad odor with the company to begin with (so to speak), I didn't aggravate matters by sneaking any sips. I ate my cracker sandwichettes, and then an orange, as quietly as possible in the window seat I had gotten. I waited.

Around eight it was safe to start getting a gloss on, and I did so. I wasn't yet afraid, because I really expected nothing until the post-eleven thin-out of riders. Now I nursed my wine and enjoyed the sense of being on a cruise. A bus has the same rock and surge as a boat, and at night it contains you in an alien element—the dark—just as a boat does. I peered through my reflection at the streets outside, or followed the easy-paced changes of the faces of my fellow-travelers—augmented at one door, eroding away at the other. I did the latter discreetly by watching the windows. I had the contented feeling, as I did this, of guaranteed distraction, such as watching TV can give—though this, of course, had far more variety than TV.

My wine ran out at about ten-thirty. Since we were nearing the outbound end of the run, I decided to get down at the last intersection before the bus entered the airport. I could replenish at the liquor store that stood there and get the bus again as it came back out of the airport.

Just after I got down, I realized I hadn't gotten a clear look at the driver's face. I hadn't remembered to do this on the previous encounters and had told myself to keep track of the drivers this time out.

But when I got back on, I was startled by the bus's being completely empty, and when I took my seat a ways back, I still hadn't noticed the man behind the wheel.

The bus almost never left the airport without someone aboard—not before midnight, anyway. The implication of its being empty did not escape me. I sat literally on the edge of my seat, meaning to face the Trashbagger standing if she got on. This was irrational. I knew she could only be escaped through debate and that no physical dodging could save my life, failing in this. Still I sat poised.

But absolutely no one got on. Not at the lonely stops in the rural stretch, where the dead light of the brown-vapor highway lamps lay on the black rank and file of identical orange trees. Not in the ghettoed hills, where the intersections were lit by the Coors sign of a ten-stool bar, the traffic signals, and an old-fashioned streetlight on a pseudo-Corinthian column of cement. And not in big-money downtown, in whose glass-box megaliths the ceiling lights formed shapeless mosaics, hanging like white larvae in hives. Not for over fifteen miles. We got onto the freeway for the last short stretch to our turn-around downtown.

This was nothing short of impossible. It was a minor order of impossibility, but it *was* one nonetheless. Not once did the bus pause to fall back into the schedule that it must surely be getting ahead of, barreling stopless on, as it was. The longer I delayed saying something to the driver—going up, for instance, and making a jocular remark about its being a busy night—the more powerless I was to speak. The bus spun through the turnaround in the downtown terminal and roared back out and onto the freeway again.

The certainty—panicky and insistent—that if I pulled the cord, the driver would not let me off, almost drove me to try, though I was resolved so fiercely to come face to face with my enemy, and though this was so clearly a premonition of our confrontation. We roared through the recrossing of the city. Once more, absolutely no one got on.

I got numb enough to my suspense to open the bottle of port I had bought when I got off. We turned through the airport without a pause, and with a deepening hum of gears, charged out on our return. I heard a snort, a cough, and a stir behind me.

I turned. Six seats back, near the rear, a tousled unshaven face—toothless though relatively unsenile—sprouted into view, scrubbing gummy eyelids with a blackened hand whose dirtiness was so deep-lying that it was glossy. It was a fellow-wino, just ending a nap that must have been going on for hours. As I stared at him, as blank as his own scarce-wakened mind, the bus braked with a whistling gasp, and its door clapped open.

I will relive that moment of waiting for as long as is left me. We sat in that weird triptych of the interior adjoined by its differently tilted selves on either side. There we were, six winos, waiting, amid six rows of chrome arcs on the empty seat-backs, like shiny rib cages. Up from the doorwell rose, dodderingly, the spiky tallowish planet. The Trashbagger passed the driver without paying, and waddled toward me— *me* now, I was sure!—as the bus pulled out. I could not move. My nerves cried *rise* to my legs, but the electric impulse fell down into a bodiless gulf where no legs were.

Her body was a squat mass of dowdy brown overcoat, a matronly nonshape. Over this her burst of electric hair—like a dirtied dandelion seed-puff—and her brown face as etched with line as an oak's bark, floated with a faint tremor that suggested inner voltage, fierce, secret meditation. I looked at my reflection in the window beside me, asking myself why I did not rise, stand ready, fight, or flee.

But as she stood near my seat, looking at me, I found that I feared not so much for my life, as lest I should make a mistake. It was something like stage fright that I shook with, an overawing sense that in this interview I must make my ultimate and all-determining account of myself and that my subsequent fate should be precisely as good as my performance now. The urgency of escape was muffled by this dread. The Trashbagger set her parcels down on a seat across the aisle and, with a whispery concussion, dropped onto the seat next to me. With the panic of a nervous child who blurts the first thing he can think of, I asked her:

"Do you push around a shopping cart?" For I had seen many like her who did.

The old face aimed itself at me—the hair gave off a whiff of something like shoe polish with the movement. The walnut-shell topography of skin gullied and rivered more deeply with the tightening of a smile:

"Yes. You bet I do."

"Why?" I croaked.

"Why, to collect everything that's mine."

"And what . . . is yours?"

"All trash."

I nodded. I did not want to ask my next question:

"And what's trash?"

"Why, don't you know that? It's everything, sooner or later."

Her answers came with serene clarity. Yet I could not be sure, as I stared in her face, if her lips in fact moved, or even if she used a voice.

And each answer astonished me. Not in itself—but simply that I had received it. Without expecting for an instant that she would spare my life, I felt a mellow pang of faith in her. Her aura irresistibly inspired it. For despite her poverty and dirt, her agedness had taken on a wild-old-wicked-man quality. Hers, I felt, was the crusty, careless age of genius— Einsteinian, Whitmanesque, vital and bookish and humane.

It struck me then. To the old gentleman she had surely seemed benevolent, Confucian. To the biddy she must have been deaconish, and oozed a pastorly unction.

But realizing this did not free me from the spell. I found it impossible to recall what her head looked like when stripped of its living mask. I felt, and could only feel, that she was wisdom itself, that she was the very center of my hope and held the key to my salvation.

"But listen, ma'am," I said—carefully, hushedly—"I am not trash."

She shook her head very slightly. "But you will be."

"Tell me," I said, "just give me a hint. What must I argue? What line of defense must I take? I only want a clue."

"But what *can* you argue?" she said. My heart moved with a despairing assent to this. I saw through the reflection in the window that in this seeming-short time we had almost recrossed the city and were not far from the freeway stretch. In my stomach I felt an antlike crawliness. I remembered the maggots I had found, with horror, in the belly of a dead cat I had turned over as a boy.

"I think I understand you," I said. "All lives are chance-formed electrochemical engines, vastly isolated in space. Then entropy . . . atrophy . . . death . . . trash . . ."

Each word I said sank me deeper in fear, till I felt I was suffocating in my speech. Conversations with the Trashbagger led to a single end. I'd seen it. This conversation too was a brief maze leading to the same door.

"But isn't there something more, something else, that doesn't become trash?" I cried. It took great effort to say this. She exerted a kind of gravity, causing the mind to fall into her mode of thought. It was like physical toil to formulate an idea alien to her. The words came out of my mouth stillborn. Her old eroded face was a desert my question got lost in.

"Something more? Something else?" she echoed, with remote sad humor. Again I wondered—had she spoken with her voice, or had her eyes answered, cold black stars above her desolation of a face? She leaned forward and scratched at a varicosity through a hole in her filthy socks. "Motes in space," she sighed as she sat up, "wound up by accident, running down by necessity."

I might have been speaking myself, so simple and direct was my assent to what she said. I heard a concluding note in her tone and sensed our talk was ending, but could not for my life deny what she had said.

"You've got to tell me," I blurted. "Are you going to take it off?"

She bent to scratch her other leg. "Take what off?" she asked me.

"Your face."

"My face?" she asked, sitting up. She looked into my eyes for a long moment. "Yes," she said, putting her hands to her throat.

I saw the seam in the skin—crosswise to the esophagus—split cleanly, like withered lips parting. A thinner neck was unveiled within, bristling with black chitinous hairs and barbs. This could not be. There was, however, no other reality—only these three bus interiors and, outside, the arc-lit sixty-mile-an-hour emptiness of the freeway, which we had just entered. With a flabby friction the empty bag of the old woman's face slid completely off the instrument-cluster of the Trashbagger's feeding apparatus, and off the vast compound eyes.

I looked in the window beside me and beseeched my image to move, not to sit there and die, but somehow to rise. My image did nothing. Behind me the black multilensed planets, lit by a fluorescent sun, loomed near.

I did the impossible. I tore myself loose from my reflection. It remained still, stupefied, looking on, while I wrenched myself round to face the immense hymenopterous head. I felt as powerless to move as if there were no space around me, or as if I had become completely insubstantial. But with the same furious blind contradictiveness, I *did* move. I heaved, and brought upward arms and hands that held something. With this something, desperately, I smote the Trashbagger.

It was my plastic bag of oranges. It weighed several pounds, and the flexible neck of the bag made blackjacklike blows possible. The fruit had a meaty sound against the stiff and surprisingly tough globes of the Trashbagger's eyes.

It was a groggy-enough blow, given her mass and strength, but it had enormous effect. The Trashbagger rocked back on the seat, and in the same moment the bus swerved sharply; this, combined with her recoil, dumped her straight out of the seat. I had a glimpse of the wino staring on round-eyed from the rear, and then the sudden emergence of the driver's head from behind his aluminum screen brought me around.

He was a young black man with a goatee and a half-length natural. The bus still roared forward down the freeway, and yet he had brought his head and shoulders completely around, to stare back at me in outrage and shock.

"Are you crazy, man!" he shouted. "What you *doin*'? Don't you know who that is?"

"Jesus Christ!" I screamed back. "Look out!!"

The freeway poured toward us through the windshield behind the driver's head, and there I saw a big two-trailer truck drop sluggishly from an on-ramp and into our lane ahead. It was barely doing thirty yet, and we were at sixty-five.

The driver looked around and, in slow motion, it seemed, pulled himself back behind the screen. Both trailers of the truck were heaped with oranges. As the vehicle struggled toward forty with dinosaurian effort, and as we began—too late, I saw—to brake and swerve aside, it seemed I saw each individual orange—dewy, porous, luminous in the freeway's arc lights. Our wheels locked before we could quite pull out of the lane, and the bus skated sideways against the trailers of the frantically accelerating fruit truck.

A rain of oranges drummed on our roof, and then our whole long rattling frame whirled through a half-circle and crashed rear-first against one of the legs of an overpass.

I clutched the seat through the impact, which sent the Trashbagger rolling down the aisle to the rear of the bus. Then we were motionless, and with a cough, the pneumatic doors flapped open. I sprang up, crossed the aisle, and jumped out onto the freeway. I took three running steps toward the on-ramp the truck—now sprawled ahead of us—had entered by. From behind the bus the Trashbagger stepped out and stood in my way. I stopped and lifted my sack of oranges again.

One of her antennae was bent, half-folded sideways. In the arc light her great eyes seemed to brim with sight, each one of them like a cosmos of individuals—lenses innumerable as the tiny relentless lives of coral in an acre of archipelago. I realized with astonishment that, save for the orange truck beyond the bus, the freeway was perfectly deserted.

"There is no place to run," the Trashbagger said. Unmistakably, it was a voice, the creature's true voice—a dry chitinous whisper that made clicks and slotting noises serve for its consonants. "No place. Not in time. Not in space. Nowhere. Are you quite mad?"

"Yes!" I shouted, desperately eager to agree. "Yes! Stand back! Stand back, or I'll hit you again!"

The Trashbagger's mouthparts, a black and green bouquet of rasps and pliers, worked, clicking and twiddling with a curious energy. As if she did not have wraparound focus, she tilted now one and now the other globe of lenses at me, with a movement like a bird's, or a mantis's delicate head-cocking. Her shoulders shook. She made a low pneumatic commotion. I realized that she was *laughing.*

The laughter raised every hair on my body. It had the nasty final sound of a quarter falling into a glass box. It had some of that blind wild energy, that booming clatter, of an empty bus doing seventy on a midnight freeway. The locking tomb was in it too, the gasp of the closing door. I ran past her—she made no move to stop me. I ran straight up the ivied slope of the embankment, through the lamp-lit smog-oily leaves, cold and wet with the fog. At the top there was a chain link fence. I climbed over it, and I ran. My God, McPittle, how I ran!

Knavle

V

Knavle never wrote another letter, as I have mentioned. He said it was a morbid habit, and abandoned the practice.

He also abandoned the wino's life. He has become an itinerant juggler, and as a result I see him much more frequently. And though he speaks wistfully of his days as a drunkard, he realizes that their attraction is largely a matter of that fortuitous beauty all things have when they are past. He is sincerely devoted to juggling, the art of which he first assayed using those same oranges that saved his life that night.

He was here just recently, for an engagement at the local Senior Citizens' Center, and he spoke of his new calling:

"Juggling, McPittle," he told me, "has given me something I never had as a wino. It is a defiance of gravity of the most beautifully direct kind. Everything that lives is a defiance of gravity! Everything has a dance in it which it is my joy to liberate, and I mean to specialize in precisely this, until my next meeting with the Trashbagger. Everything must dance, you see—everything—until it winds up in her shopping cart, that rattling jail!"

THE EXTRA

What made me decide to go down and sign up for a movie? It was as casual as could be. One day the notion was nowhere near my mind, and the next morning I was doing it.

I was hanging out at the zoo—where else?—with all the other monkeys. I was leaning against the wall between Vic's Liquors and Freddie Photon's Fast Holo Hut, and listening as hard as I could to try to catch what I was thinking, which seemed to be nothing much. And a friend of mine steps up, Japhet Starkey, white dude, a big grin on him.

"Hey, Professor," he says. "You look deep, Babe. What's the haps?"

"Hey, Blood. You look high and bright. Doing yourself some good?"

He gives me a wise look, lots of heavy eyebrow. "You just said it, Rufus. That's exactly what I'm doing."

Down along the wall from us a peaceful little shakedown that had been going on struck some sparks and flared up in a brawl. The crowd swelled out to make some watching room. It picked us up and washed us along the balcony, past the Holo Hut all the way to the Digital Dominoes Den. Japhet shouts in my ear: "Now we can grab some rail!"

So we worked our way across the balcony. I never swam before I got here, but it was like swimming. Your moves had to be firm but smooth, you had to stroke your way through. Otherwise someone you stepped too hard on might pull you under and stomp you. We made it to the shaft and leaned on the rail. A brawl or shooting farther in always cleared spaces out at the rail.

"So what it is," Japh tells me. "I'm going down tomorrow and sign up for a movie."

Now I was the one making eyebrows. "Fool! Why you wanna do that?"

And he just laughed and waved his arm at the shaft. Not that I needed the answer. Thirty more stories of balconies over us, twenty below, all the rails jammed with welfare monkeys like us, all the walkways crisscrossing the shaft at every level jammed with more of same. Even the air in the shaft was jammed, packed so tight with zoo noise you could reach over the rail and tear off a handful of it. You could hear gunshots over it pretty well, though, and we did, just then. We look up and see a guy come sailing over the rail six or seven levels up.

"Third one down!" Japh shouts.

"Fourth down!" I shout, because I judged the guy's arc to be a little flatter than Japhet did. But he was right, guy jounced off the rail of the third walkway below us before he snapped back out and kept falling. So I double-palmed Japh and gave him a food credit.

"So what's the flick?" I asked him.

"*Alien Web.*"

"Sure," I say. "Pluton Studios. Historical sci-fi, set in the late twentieth, alien invasion flick." I had a kind of name for always being in the library, and I liked to play up to it. I only read the dailies now and then, but I liked the entertainment news and kept pretty good track of it. Japhet looked pleased, and sly.

"That's it, Rufus. That's my ticket. And you could do it too, hey? Why not?"

"You some kind of crazy, Japh?—Motherfucker!" This I didn't say to Japh, but because there was a hand in my pocket that wasn't mine. I whipped around punching, and some sorry little blood in snakelocks backed off. He had a friend, but Japhet stepped in beside me and they faded back into the crowd.

"What are you sayin' to me?" I say to Japh. "You might be desperate, but I'm not. Not nearly. *I'm* not tired of living."

"Not tired of living here?" He's smiling. He looks serene. And I realize then that he's going to do what he says, he really is.

It rubbed me two ways at once. I admired him, jacking his spirit up for a gamble like that. It made me restless, made me want to do something for myself too. But I like to come up with things on my own. I don't like being jerked around by other people's inspirations.

"Not that tired," I tell him. "Tell me you ain't serious. You even got tube fare out to the studios, fool?"

"I, my good spook, have got tube fare for *two*."

It moved me. You couldn't count on staying together once you got into a movie, but it would make him feel a little more lucky not to be walking up to something like that alone. It would me too. The whole proposition was starting to seem realer now, but I still felt too jacked around by it. I shook my head.

"I got my Aunt Harriet to look after. Got to pick her up any minute now at the Hut."

"Hey. Rufus. Buy her a decade in one of the Cinetrons. In two days, if you come back, you can buy both yourselves five or ten years on the farm."

"What station you be at? What time?" And I stand there asking myself did I just *say* that? Japhet laughs, whacks my shoulder, and tells me.

"Don't wait if I don't show," I tell him.

And that's how simple it was, really. My mind couldn't swing with it without a fight, of course. I hadn't swum halfway back across the balcony before I shook my head and decided, fuck this, there was no way I'd show tomorrow. But I couldn't leave the idea alone. In the Hut I hung around watching the seniors triggering away at their last games before the three o'clock escort left. You've met Aunt Harriet—she's pushing eighty, was my momma's oldest sister of nine. It always made me smile to see her blasting those fast holos, a mean, peppery old lady full of fight. If she'd still had legs for running, *she* would've gone straight down to Pluton Studios. What was I doing that had good legs, the last ones left in our family, that was down to just the two of us?

The Hut had good escorts—well paid and would show some fight—which was why it was one of this level's senior hangouts. You can't stay in your eight-by-ten all day, video and pap stamps or no video and pap stamps. I usually walked my aunt back anyway, like a lot of the seniors' family would do, because the escorts might be tough but there was still only twelve of them.

I didn't have to use my sap today—no one tried to get past their shields and prods. We all stood on the belt out to our complex and my aunt was raging and bitching about all her ailments and I was scoffing and cussing her for being a sissy the way she likes me to do, and meanwhile what do you think I was thinking about? About all the graffiti in the library books.

That's right. The tapes can't be messed with, except for all the reading terminals being kicked to shit and half out of focus, but I liked to read the old books too. A lot of them hadn't been put on tape and never would be. The past's so vast and the world's so wide, right? The strangest things would pop out of those books and swell up around you if you pried at the dim parts here and there with a dictionary. I won't get started on it—it was a thing with me, a place where I could go to breathe. But that graffiti. I got a knack for reading somehow, and I could follow text through so many layers of *fuck yous* and *eat mes* you wouldn't believe it, but I didn't have X-ray. And there was no way around it, either, when you'd be reading along hot on something and come to that six or sixty pages that had been razored right out. So now I stood there thinking about those books, how trying to see what was in them was like trying to see out a dirty window. And that's what staying here was—spending your life trying to see something, anything, out of a cracked, dirty window.

"Auntie," I said, "I'm gonna buy you a decade at one of the Cinetrons."

"With what?"

"My pap script. I be eating out tomorrow."

"Huh! You gonna leave me your sap? You know how mine hurt my hand now with this damn arthritis."

"Nope. I'm gonna leave you my roscoe."

"What?! Where the hell you goin', Rufus, leavin' your roscoe?"

"To a safe place, don't need any gun. Can't take one in there anyway."

I think that probably told her. "Huh! Safe place!" But she didn't say anything else. She understood.

Early next morning I took her to a Cinetron where she'd only seen four of the ten flicks running. I checked the food pack they gave her, went in and checked that her seat's potty worked. One of the guards of her section was a dude I knew, and I gave him my last two credits to keep an eye out for her. I gave her a kiss just before the lights went down. I had to say something, so I said: "When I come back, maybe we go to the farm for a while."

She wouldn't look at me, and damn if there weren't tears in her eyes. "You a good boy, Rufus," she said.

"You a nasty crusty little old lady," I told her. My eyes got a little wet too, going out of there, but I felt good, light and ready. So we just go down and see what happens, I told myself, but either way, fuck this zoo for good. I went on down to the station and found Japhet, and the way he grinned to see me made me feel better yet.

When the tube pulled in we hooked arms, saps in our free hands, and avalanched in with the crowd. We had good position, in line with the door. We were squeezed up off our feet and poured straight into the car. When the crowd spread to fill it, our feet touched down and we hugged a pole and held it.

The tube took off. There was just enough room for someone to work a hand free and start messing with my unit. I stomped some toes at a guess, and the hand pulled back. I helped Japh evict another hand from his pocket, and then we hit the next station. The big padded pneumatic packers gently wedged another fifty people on board, and we didn't have to protect anything after that because no one could move anything. We floated peacefully at two hundred klicks per, the weight-shifts playing our ribs like squeezeboxes on the curves.

The studio had shuttles at the Seventh South Exurb station. Half our trainload seemed to be going to Pluton. The shuttles filled up in five minutes and drove off with us.

It was always great to get outside. There it was all over you—the sky! It was pale yellow, and you could make out little clouds in it—real ones—here and there. There was even a breeze. It made my mind feel wide open, lucky.

Some of that leaked away as we got near the set. The set has to scare you, whatever it looks like, if you're an extra. This one was about a klick and a half square, late-twentieth office buildings and highrise apartments sticking up out of it along with church steeples, powerpoles, billboards, big trees here and there. You couldn't really see into it because it was walled, and also pretty well surrounded by the studio buildings. A bunch of small aircraft were swarming around above it—two different styles, the aliens and the home team. Special Effects was limbering its robots for the air battle.

They let us off at the studio canteen just outside one of the big gates in the set's wall. The call was for two thousand extras, and the shuttles could bring back the quota in one more trip to the station. They drove back, and we went in to breakfast. I had bacon and coffee. Real! I can't tell you. Japh and me sat there chewing and staring at each other, stupefied. Other people had eggs, pancakes—no one could believe it. The noise was happy. People kept shouting jokes like: "Hey, I don't got a copy of the script yet!"—and everyone laughed at them over and over.

The Costume Department had big processing trailers pulled up outside when they filed us out. We went in raw at one end and came out ready at the other. First a strip search. Then repairs on people looking too outrageously zoo—oldstyle shirts to hide tit rings, hats to bag snakelocks, scrapeoffs for facepaint. You got shoes if you thought yours weren't good for running. The crews were ace, sized you at a look. I was out in twenty minutes—I just needed my dayglo throat-tattoo painted over. The second load of extras was already in the canteen when they sent us on out to the bleachers.

The bleachers were set up near the gate with an empty speaking platform in front of them. There wasn't all that much to watch while we waited for the rest. A lot was going on around us, but mostly in the buildings where all the communications and monitors and master controls were. There were crews of techs zipping around in their little carts, and maintenance trucks driving in and out the gate. Some of the camera rafts were testing their air cushions, dropping fast to the ground on a big whoosh of blowers. They don't land outright for payoffs. They can get back up to hover a fraction faster off the air cushion, and camera time's everything in these big one-take shoots.

People in the bleachers wanting to sound pro about being an extra kept calling the rafts moneyboats. If any were vets, they weren't passing out any tips. How could it help here anyway, what they'd found on other sets in different stories?

Now the last of the second load was taking seats and the costume trailers were closing up. Everyone was talking about the script and what the aliens might be, and since no one knew shit about either one, it made lively conversation. Two trucks came out of the gate, and a team of Actors' Guild reps and studio people got out of the first one. They stood around the platform, and the Guild's mediator walked up onto it.

She was a young honey, dressed very zoo, hair in snakes and all her tattoos on one arm with a see-through sleeve on it and her other arm bare. I wanted to laugh. For sure, she had a condo somewhere uptown.

"Man!" Japhet grinned. "A nice, fat, do-nothing *job*."

That was the truth. Guild reps never got sweaty driving a bargain. Where was the room for parley with the studios? It was simple economics, like this: For some reason, all you chimps on these benches want money, and furthermore not a chimp of you'd *be* on these benches if you had any kind of job at all or any chance to ever get one. Right? Right! So here's the terms.

The honey said she and the rep team had just finished their drive-through and the set was up to the contract's specs. She gave us the wise eyeball saying it, like we were all zoo together and no one snuck any shit past *her*. She skinned down the specs to us from her pocket display.

We learned plenty, but it was the apps, the refuges, and the weapons that made up the gist of the odds. The Anti-Personnel Properties, or apps, were the aliens. There were a thousand of them. They weighed eighty-five kilos and ran as fast as a healthy man. They had no projectile weaponry and had to get hold of you to kill you. Then the refuges. In the set, one out of ten of all the doors, gates, and other entryways could actually be opened. Half of these led into actual rooms that were "viable for defense," and three-quarters of these contained "some implement viable as a weapon."

We'd get a half-hour preshoot run-through of the set to

spock out resources and survival plans. The shoot would last an hour. The pot was twenty million, split by the survivors. The bonus for killing an app was ten thousand, paid at the scene by the camera rafts when you gave them your kill's claim tag. Any cash already in the pockets of survivors when they reached the paygate was theirs, no questions asked. This was an arty touch. You say you want *real* turmoil in those streets? Muggings in the middle of alien death?

A cart pulled up a trailer with a whole rack of terminals mounted on it. They called us down by rows to feed in our IDs and give the screens our thumbprints. So technically we were signing before reading the contract, because they gave us our copies of it at the same time, but no one was going to read it anyway—damn few even could. The last people had barely got back to their seats with it when she said: "OK. Everyone's read it? So fine. This is last call. Back out now if you're going to, and we'll erase your consent. Notice the police vans pulling up over there. It's a felony, ten to fifteen, to break contract after you hear the buzzer. All right, then." The buzzer buzzed. "Time to get to work. Mr. Martini from the studio is going to run one of the apps through its paces for you now. Best of luck to each and every one of you."

Martini was a real studio sweetie. He had a waxed scalp and trendy green jumpsuit, a twinkly smile, and a down-to-business voice. "All right, gang. These apps home on body heat, a standard infrared perception kit. They've got crude vibrational pickups, but they don't mean much in heavy activity zones. George, will you open the truck? They've got about the same mass as some of you bigger guys, but they can exert a lot of leverage in the clinch."

George opened the tail of the second truck, and out of it jumped a big flop-eared dog. It busted up the bleachers. Relief, right? I mean it was a huge dog, but it was a dog. Another studio man called it over in front of the bleachers and told it to sit. It sat without a twitch. Then George did some keying on a little unit at his belt, stepping back from the truck, and Martini said, "It's on override now, kids, so keep your seats and save your energy."

And a spider jumped out of the truck. It was a little bigger than a man on all fours would be, but with a much wider spread to its legs. It was covered with spiky brown hair except for the flat front section where all the legs and eyes were attached, and that was a shiny black. It moved ticklefoot, light as a dancer.

"This is about two-thirds speed, and the leap at the end is its usual attack mode," Martini said, and the thing ran straight at the dog and jumped it from about two meters off. "The fangs hypo it with a paralytic, then with a powerful solvent, and then suck out the solute."

The forelegs snatched the dog off the ground, and as the fangs sank in, the dog gave a huge twitch that would have knocked a big man down, but didn't budge the spider. Then the dog went stiff, and hung there with just little tremors of its head and paws. That was a seventy-five-kilo dog. Martini wasn't kidding about leverage in the clinch.

The bleachers were empty-quiet. I heard someone swallow two rows away. "The feeding cycle takes about five minutes. They will complete their cycle unless a new quarry comes very close to them, so don't just go charging cavalierly past apps you find feeding." The dog had puffed up, and its tremors died out. Now it started shrinking back down, the app tilting it this way and that for better drainage. "Each one has two call tags—they're the biggest eyes at the front of the cluster. Tearing either one free will call a raft. Throw it into the raft, and they'll throw you your bonus. A final caution. See the tag-along?"

Probably no one had till then—a little fist-sized antigrav unit above and behind the belly bulb. It started making wide circles over the app. "When the app goes into attack mode, the tag-along camera starts circling for angles, so we don't get too much footage that's strictly from the aliens' point of view. It's got collide/avoid, but if you jump in its way it can give you a knock. A very remote hazard, but we feel a responsibility to advise you of it."

"Stop!" someone shouts. "I'm getting all choked up!"

That cracked the ice on the bleachers a little. People started talking, their eyes on that shrinking dog, and Martini looked patient and let them. It was cold, scared talk, leading nowhere, just telling each other what was right in front of us, trying to make our minds grip hold of it, like hugging poison thorns.

"Two-thirds speed," Japh said.

"Yeah. I wish I been doing three hours a day on the treadmill, Japh. For the last solid year."

"I have been, the last week anyway. You're in shape, Rufe. Better wind than me."

"Christ Creeping Jesus."

"Yeah."

The dog looked to weigh about twelve kilos now, all hollows and folds. Like you could tack his paws to a pole and he'd flap in the wind like a flag.

"OK, gang! We'll show you full speed now. George?"

The spider dropped the dog, spun, ran back to the truck and jumped in. You never heard such quiet. Four thousand eyeballs scoping that burst of speed, two thousand brains asking their legs: Well? Can you? Those studio techies had calibrated it right to the hair between hope and horror. I *can*, I thought. But around turns? Zig and zag? For an hour? But with a head start and hideouts . . .

Some people found a more definite answer than I did. While we were lined up for the transports to take us to the run-through, fifty or sixty people walked straight over to the cops and got in the prison vans. Our driver standing by his door said:

"That's the biggest walk-off I ever heard of."

"You're breaking my heart," the guy in front of me said.

" 's OK, they called a hundred over need."

"Extra extras," I said. "Man, you making me feel *super*fluous."

He stamped our hands with our transport number. The four of them would send us in at four different gates, then we'd reboard and go to a new gate. Whatever you'd scouted on the run-through you'd have to find from a new angle going in for the shoot. Everyone colliding on crisscross paths to some piece of hope they've got squirreled away, if they can just get to it in time. Establishes the perfect *ambience* of impending holocaust, don't you think?

Just inside the gate we turned and drove into a big fluorescent utility tunnel built into the set wall. I kept thinking: *zoo meat.*

This phony city in a box was like a zoo—the old kind, I mean. Caged specimens of urban history. This zoo just rented its inmates—we gave a short, peppy demonstration of the habitat's hazards, and fed some of the other tenants. We were zoo food, zoo-bred for that authentic flavor.

And we'd all spent years of our lives scanning flicks like this one would be. They'd been our main brain food. So in a way, we owed the studios. It was just common karma to end up doing our bit for the Product, or maybe it was like reincarnation. And, hey—what else were we qualified for? Being streetmeat is the only job you can get with a Ph.D. in Urban Horror. And somehow it scared me hollow, this nagging feeling I belonged here.

We passed several gates before we stopped at ours. They got us out and formed us up in front of it. We could try any entry we saw—door, gate, or window. But any refuge we found, we could only check out for ten seconds and then had to get back in the street—the rafts would be dogging us. Japh and I both judged that covering ground and scoping layout came first. Why weasel out refuges you couldn't find again from your shoot gate? We would split left and right just inside, run the rim for five minutes or so, then swing out across the set, come back up along the far wall, and try to come straight back across to our gate. We'd hunt hideouts once we got some feel for the blueprint, but would waste no attention on blocks that blinded at the wall, which we meant to stay out of. Back in the transport we'd stitch our two maps together. There was a siren. The gate slid up.

We ran out onto a block of shopfronts and office buildings— ten and twelve stories, mid-twentieth style. Parked cars packed the curbs, and as many more stood in the lanes. We looked back at the closing gate as we ran. Display screen surfaced this side of it, and its image fit neat as a jigsaw piece into a video masking the wall and extending the street for blocks behind us. It was a work of art. It was seamless. Even this close you were only sure where the wall was because the video already had apps chasing the crowd on its sidewalks, and its traffic was rolling, and tangling in smashups. And no top edge to the wall—projection holos caulked the seam with yellow sky. At the first cross-street, Japh ran left and I ran right.

I'd read cities in the eighties and nineties had jumbled ground-plans and no-logic layouts, but they couldn't have been this radical. I ran between fifty-story buildings with glass-and-steel walls, like huge mirrors, crossed a street and was in rat-brown wooden slums with weed lots, then between an amusement park and a block-long video of beach and surf and spider-pinned sun-bathers kicking the sand, then past car lots webbed over with acres of bright plastic flags. No block clued you to what was around its corners. You'd come to a crossing that looked like a main line, six lanes and blazing with signals, but to the right you'd find a parking lot continued on into a wall-video of a stadium standing in a sea of parked cars, and to the left would be thirty meters of blind alley full of trash bins.

Those wall-videos scared me. They were too fucking good, and I tried for a brainprint of each one I passed. I wasn't trying doors till I left the perimeter, but most of the others were trying everything in sight. The fighters were sparring higher now to let the rafts ride herd at roof level. The rafts bullhorned count-downs at refuges people had found and gone in to check out. Without slowing down, I tried to keep track of the finds I saw made, especially parked cars, which people were giving a lot of their action. One out of five had doors that worked, and half those had motors and five minutes' gas in them. The rub was the cars *in* the streets. They were robots. For the shoot they'd start driving themselves into fancy collisions. They had plastic people in them wearing scream-twisted going-to-die faces for the close-ups. Those faces were reading us the traffic forecast for this afternoon. On the other hand, running down apps with some wheels looked like the only painless bonus buck to be made.

I turned in from the wall, started my zigzag across the set, trying doors now. I had my pace, and a nice sweat oiled my moves. It was tricky to keep a straight heading because it turned out that wall-videos blinded off some streets in the inner set too. That really dimmed my outlook. In a hurry you could really start losing track of where the perimeter was at all. I felt better when I'd made a few finds. A working car in a shopping mall's lot. A movie house with outside stairs to a working door—the room was bare, no door latch, but I could shoulder it shut. And best of all, in a block of houses with lawns and trees, a cellar door with stairs down to a room with only one thing in it—but that was a chain saw. It occurred to me maybe it was the riskier doors—ones that might trap you down a hole or up some stairs—that the studio liked to put its refuges behind.

When the rafts called twenty-five minutes, I'd already swung back up to the latitude our gate ought to lie on. I headed back, swinging left down a wide street of burger stands, gas stations, liquor stores. I'd try to beeline, see how close I'd gauged the lay of things. If I reached the wall within a couple blocks either side of our gate, I could trust how I'd read the ground-plan so far.

In the garage of a gas station up ahead I saw a jacked-up car and a man's legs sticking out from under it. The legs started kicking and hammering. A spider crawled out, dragging the guy on his back, just as a car turned onto the street at eighty klicks, skated over, jumped the curb, rammed the pumps, and blew up the station. Even before my balls had dropped back into their bag, it clicked that none of this had made a sound. I was twenty meters short of trying to jog down a video street. I doubled back, tried the next street over. Another video. Third try the same. This was the perimeter wall! Already?

The rafts called the return. We were supposed to start following the first raft we saw flagged with our transport number. I could see two of mine, both headed exactly opposite to me. I'd gone looking for my gate on the far side of town from it.

They gave us ten minutes to sit in the transport, rest and talk, before pulling out. Did we talk! Almost everyone was buddied or teamed up. No big groups, though. You'd only share lucrative lifesaving info with a few people you trusted to help you. Japh had gone half as wrong as I had, just ninety degrees confused at the end. We didn't try for a map, just described each other the refuges we'd found and their neighborhoods, and hoped to steer each other if we hit stretches either of us knew.

The driver shut the doors. He used the p.a., his back to us but his voice bright and sociable. "Ladies and gentlemen. Pluton

Studios reminds you of clause Sixteen C. Any props you use for defense or escape you use at your own risk. The stated refuge and weapons quotas are a hundred percent present and available out there, but so is a lot of nonviable stuff. Extras misled by appearances and utilizing nonviable properties are solely responsible for all consequences of that misuse, so a word to the wise. Pluton Studios, in the sincere hope that you will return to work for them again, would also like to give you a handy rule of thumb. Team up, cooperate—that's fine. But keep in mind that the bigger the group, the stronger the heat signal and the farther it carries. I'm sure you see the point. And lastly. Pluton Studios would like to remind you that there *is* an air battle in progress throughout the shoot. The fighters are built to fragment minutely, minimizing danger to people working on the set. But there will be those occasional one- and two-kilo fragments coming down all over the area, and there are scheduled those two dozen or so collisions of entire aircraft with set buildings, which are going to generate a certain amount of fast, sizable debris. So heads up, ladies and gentlemen, and the best of luck to you all on the shoot."

As we pulled away, an even bigger transport than ours pulled up in our place, a tractor cab towing a big wire cage full of spiders. It boiled with them, climbing and wrestling and tickling each other. The sight killed all the talk in our transport. All those bristly sensors in that boil, all restlessly touching and tasting the air and each other. You can't turn off the heat of your own meat, can't hide it either. And you got hotter the harder you ran from them—your escape shouted out to them, *Here I am, here!* Were we really all going to jump bare-assed into the zoo with those things?

We drove past several gates. From outside, the set had looked square, but this tunnel took a lot of slight bends and never seemed to turn a real corner. The driver kept changing our speed too, and when we got to our shoot gate we just couldn't decide how it related to the run-through gate's place on the rim. Our spiders were already there. They formed us up at the gate, but our eyes kept flickering back to the apps. They swarmed walls, roof, and floor of the cage, thinning here, clotting up there in clumps, and then dropping off like fruit. Exploring machines, groping the world nonstop for a piece they could bite. With nothing better to work on, they groped each other over and over, trading tickles with the tips of the two shortlegs next to their fangs. You saw them at it everywhere.

"Attention, please." The guy at the gate controls used his bullhorn. "You will have three minutes' head start. When the gate opens, wait for my signal." He hit a switch, and the gate slid up.

We were looking down a five-lane freeway, walled by huge videos of cityscape seen from thirty or forty meters off the ground. A light flashed on the gateman's controls; he said, "*Now!*"—and we ran.

The freeway stretched ahead out of sight, but after a few hundred meters we broke through a wall of color, and suddenly we were running between a mall and a drive-in movie with some highrises just ahead. The holo we'd crossed was just a faint haze from this side, and the blind block of freeway videoed on out to the vanishing point behind us, except that right now it had a square hole in it, a cube of real space full of apps.

Japh and I ran straight for three blocks to get good and clear of the rim, then branched right when Japh thought that way looked familiar. We'd agreed to go flat out till the apps were in, build maximum lead, and hope a refuge we knew turned up in the process. Once they started in after us, we'd have to decelerate enough to hunt hideouts as we went. Japh didn't look like this street still felt familiar.

"This it?"

"No."

"Steeple there . . . Try left."

"Right."

The fighters just hung in a standby pattern now. Under them, the rafts fidgeted around in their sectors for perfect position, or cruised to scout how the meat-stampede was branching into the maze.

It wasn't the same steeple, but the church faced a park that had a rack of bicycles in it, no chains on them. We veered over. No chains, and no moving parts. Nothing looked familiar from here, so we ran to get deeper in from the wall, down a brick-paved mall with fountains. One second there was just the hammering of our feet on brick as we got near the other end, then someone started cranking steel girders through a giant meat-grinder in the sky. It was the fighters' cannons, all at once, and their engines howling into battle drive. And then a gravel truck jumped the curb and dinosaured into the mall at us.

"They're in!" Japh screeched, and the truck blew up against a fountain. We dodged past it and down a street of banks and hotels where the robot traffic rolled at full roar.

In one block we saw two head-ons, and a bus broadsided a transit mix at the intersection. It stunned my wits all the worse because knowing the game was on now had just made it click for me: we came in from four gates, but what about the apps? Were there forty in that cage? Fifty? Why hadn't it hit me? They'd be coming from twenty gates, and in no time at all every turn was going to be a wrong one. We saw a woman fire up a curbside car and ace it out into a traffic gap—but then take a big chunk of fighter square on the glass, jump the line and wrap her ride onto the nose of a tank truck that wore it all the way down the block like a hood ornament. Hot fighter crumbs drizzled little holes down through my hair. A guy running ahead of us reached the corner, braked on his heels, spun around, and *wham*—dropped flat down under a spider. His hand stuck out from the legs that jailed him and clawed the sidewalk, and a raft coasted down to suck up a zoom-shot. I would've pissed myself at the sight of that first app, but my water was all gone in sweat.

We ran back to the last corner and took it wide, went pounding down a street of highrises. A spider danced out of an alley-mouth and came pistoning toward us. Japh howled, flung himself on the nearest parked car, and it opened. We piled in and shut the doors—no controls, a dummy. The app jumped onto the hood, bellied up over the windshield, and worked its fangs into the front edge of the roof. Its bulb waggled and bobbed with the work, flattening its hair on the glass like the fur of a petted dog. Its fangs were oily black with a pinch like bolt-cutters. They shredded off a strip of roof. The fucking chassis was barely thicker than foil!

"Out both sides at once!" Japh said. I grabbed his arm.

"Wait. When it's more tied up in it."

The rest of the block looked clear of apps. Some extras tore around the far corner. The lead guy waved his arms, and they all started kicking at the window of a hardware store. The window caved in, and they climbed through as the app tore a second little strip off our roof and then hooked its fangs in around the windshield's frame and strained backward. Cracks webbed the glass, and the frame's corner started tearing free.

"Now!" Both of us screamed it. We shouldered our doors out and dived. Mine was the street side, and a robot van's driver was aiming his permanent scream at me from almost point-blank when I tucked and rolled hard for the centerline, hit it, hugged it, and made myself narrow with all my might while big tires hissed intimately in both my ears. The same instant a gap made room on my left, I jumped up and jammed down the line, one eye out for an opening to break right for the far curb, and the other eye watching the app launch itself from the hood, clear—by a bristle—the boom of a very fast tow truck, and plop on the line behind me.

I broke right through *half* an opening, a taxi polished a corner of its bumper on my pants-leg, and my shoulder slammed a coffin-size dent in a parked mobile home. I heard a fat smack and a mushy crunching and saw a robot limousine proceeding on past the spot where the app had tried breaking right after me through *less* than half an opening. You couldn't tell how I hated touching it, to see me run tear off that eyeknob.

I jumped on the sidewalk waving it, screeching, "Bonus! Bonus!" looking for other apps and for Japhet at the same time. A raft had been splitting its cameras between me and the hardware store and was already slanting down to me when I spotted both at once: Japh, facedown near our car, and another app, feeding on his back—and right then three more apps took the far corner in a commotion of peaked, pumping legjoints, and swarmed in through the hardware store's broken glass. And as the raft came down on its air pad with its fat little director squeaking: "Beautiful sequence! Such moves!" I took a new look at the block's other end, and there was still another app high-stepping around that corner.

"Throw me the fucking bonus!" I screamed.

"Throw us the fucking tag!" squeaked Fats. I flung it up, but had to take off in the same move because my new app had twiddled his shortlegs and rushed me. "Keep running!" Fats called. OK, no problem. OK with you, legs? "Here it comes!"—this was from overhead. A packet of bills dropped past my eyes, but not past my hands. Near the hardware store I veered into the street, and passing saw two apps inside crouched on struggling man-parts, and a girl jabbing the third one with a pitchfork that snapped like candy in her hands. My app was angling out to jump me at the intersection when a big woman powering in from the right tangled into its legs and tumbled it out into the street with her. Me, I danced. Danced stop-go, left-right, neck-deep in robots missing me from four directions. My brain swelled up and just ballooned away as my feet found sidewalk and danced me off into the Zoo-Meat Ballet, that marvelous new must-see from Pluton, now playing citywide.

Panic doesn't quite say it. It was like Japh's being killed had shrunk me. When we'd have to put our backs together in the zoo, I trusted his eyes and sap back there like my own, felt doubled for trouble. Now I felt a dead, shriveled patch between my shoulders, right where Japh hadn't been covered. I couldn't stop spinning around in midrun, couldn't look one way without checking everywhere else the next second, tried every door one minute and forgot doors the next. I ran blocks I might have known or not. I was too scaled down to scope a whole street, my eyes at short focus and clock on split seconds. Now I was nothing *but* an extra, a scrambling detail in someone else's big-screen thrill.

The action got thicker. The apps' ring was closing us in toward the heart of the set. Pluton had programmed the heaviest traffic, gaudiest smashups, thickest air battle here. We were running in dozens now, in streams you had to veer with wherever a spider leapt out or crashing fighter dropped a dam. We came pouring into the biggest open space I'd seen yet.

It was a long downtown park with a half-dozen streets branching off it. The traffic ran solid all ways at once, like a band-saw strung through a maze and thrashing to slash down the walls of it. Down every street you saw inbound apps and extras, but everyone coming in one street was running to leave by the others. All those pumping legs and arms contradicting each other, all their directions canceling out. The people made one big explosion that couldn't spread its outline by a hair—that was shrinking. Spiders fed everywhere, peeling roofs off cars, picnicking under the trees. The rafts skated all over it, making greedy dives and dips, like spoons at a stew, and blown fighters salted the pot with hot debris.

The scope of it bounced me back, knocked some of myself back into me. It was mass paralysis in motion. Running into that would be like climbing through the big screen, saying, *Hey boys, write me all the way in, I'll run till the freeze-frame and end with the credits.* No. Try a door at all costs. Any door. That door.

It was near a corner, a glass door with stairs behind it up to a second-story dress shop with quaintly dressed dummies in the window. It opened. Like a fool, I charged right up the stairs inside, charged right up through the blind turning halfway up, where an app might have crouched for all I knew. But there was nothing, and I jammed on up to the door at the head of the stairs, which also opened.

Except for the dummies in the window, the room was bone-bare of any kind of furniture. It had one object in it, though, right in the middle of the floor. It was an ax. I grabbed it. It was heavy! I swung it and *whunk*—it bit the floor just fine. A *real* ax! I breathed a long deep sweet breath, and let it out. I did a happy little dance to shake the knots from my leg muscles. I was dressed! I was naked steak in track shoes no more!

The door was another matter—less reassuring. It was wood, not thick, and had no latch. I could shoulder it shut against an app's first shove . . . and then what? Then the app would chew it right off its hinges, and I'd have to fight. Could I swing an ax as fast as I'd seen apps jump? Probably . . . but did I really want to check it to find out for sure?

All right, so I should rig up an exit from that display window. That way I could stay right here and run out the shoot clock to the last possible second—that is, right up till an app had its fangs sunk in this door to tear it out. Then I'd bolt for the window and be gone. So I crossed the length of the room and joined the three dummies in the window. That made four of us.

I didn't like being the room's length away from the door, which I would have to be leaning against with all my might to keep anything out of the room. Standing here, I should have a view of anything approaching my street door, but I couldn't see the door itself because the window was bayed and overhung it. On the other hand, the apps had hard little hooks for feet that you could hear clearly on pavement, let alone coming up wooden stairs.

So I went to work, ripping the dresses to strips, sawing through the seams with the ax bit, knotting the strips into a rope. I didn't need much length—just halfway down and I could drop the rest without risking an ankle—but it had to be stout because I was going to be hitting it on the run with all my weight at once.

I should have been keeping my eyes strictly on the sidewalk below me, but I just couldn't. There was too much going on out in that park and the streets surrounding it. The Big Movie kept pulling at my eyes, my mind, trying to suck me into itself.

You couldn't help looking for angles, that was part of it. You try to learn survival Dos and Don'ts from others, right? Especially the Don'ts. I saw these two guys find a parked bus they were able to force the doors of. A knot of other people with some apps hot on their tails saw them make the find, and veered over to crowd in after them. One of the two guys fought them off, but half a dozen swarmed past him anyway. Meanwhile his partner has got behind the wheel and actually got the bus to fire up. I can just make out his face through the windshield, and I see him suddenly look surprised and start twisting and thrashing like he's trying to move his hands from the wheel but can't. The bus lurches out into the traffic stream, jams it up to seventy clicks, and throws a sharp left turn at the park corner without even a touch of the brakes. The bus topples and skates on its side, spewing sparks, smashes into a powerpole, and lies there. Apps start climbing it, and its doors flop open. The apps tilt themselves through and plop down on the groggy meat inside. *Knots,* I say to my hands. *Make knots.*

Now that kind of shit was contract violation! It had to be!

Violation at least of the basic covenant of nonentrapment. It was one thing to have fake pitchforks with breakable handles hanging in hardware stores. It was another thing to have robot vehicles waiting for passengers to have their smashups with!

But who ever actually read the wording of the contract itself, to sniff out what tricks might be hidden in it? And there was other shit, subtler than that bus, that raised the same questions. For instance, I saw a girl charge straight into a duckpond in the park, and the app that was chasing her cringe from the water and sit twiddling at her from the bank. In no time a second, third, fourth refugee splashes into the pond with her, and their apps stop at the brink too, and just crouch there twiddling their shortlegs like the first one.

At just about that same moment, I see a guy start hugging his way up a lamppost. I watch him while my hands make knots—almost immediately two other guys, that have apps on their ass, jump on it too and start humping their way up after him. Well, the pursuing apps stop at the base, baffled and twiddling, like the ones by the pond. *Hey,* I tell myself. *Not one, but two angles.* I don't mind getting wet, and I could hug one of those poles all day if I had to.

But then that first guy inches his way to just above my eye-level on the lamppost—making room for the guys under him—and just as he gets to my height, the pole starts to tilt. It tilts very slowly at first, very gradually. Then faster, faster—and smoothly, it drops sideways, so smoothly it might have been hinged at the base.

And I've scarcely taken this in when that pond catches my eye again. There's a dozen people waist-deep in the water now, and even more apps circling the brink of it, and just as I look that way, those apps start to move. All of them, simultaneous as on a signal, rush into the water. They showed no trouble wading through the water—none at all. And they showed no trouble feeding in it, either.

My rope was done, and I'd anchored one end of it to the bolted-down base of one of the dummies, but I just stood there holding it for a minute, thinking. Now was that legit? Did the water just damp the heat signal momentarily, until enough people got concentrated in the pond? Or were there guys out in the monitoring sheds, studio techies who were watching until—

By the barest luck it caught at the lower corner of my eye: the hairy last half of a spider just then pussyfooting its way in out of view toward my street door.

The sight changed my mind then and there. Fuck running back and holding the door to buy a few extra seconds! Time to break the glass and be gone—the rest of the sidewalk was clear just now. As I hoisted my ax, the black-and-red star of a blown fighter filled the sky just above me. It sent down a smoking fist of debris, quick as thought, straight at my window. I hadn't half ducked when it hit the glass—and bounced off it with a clang like hammered steel!

For a heartbeat I was stunned. I almost wasted precious time giving the glass another smack with my ax, but then I sprinted for the door, and with not a second to spare. But as I jammed my shoulder against it, I could still hear the hammering sound my feet had made. But I wasn't moving now! No—it was outside. Someone else was charging up the stairs from the street.

That scrabble of dainty hooked feet was just beyond my door when I heard it freeze. As the footsteps pounded up toward the turning, I heard, just inches outside the door, the bristly noise of a hairy bulk shifting, and little hooked feet clickety-clacking through a turnaround.

I heard the feet hammer up to the landing, and heard—it seemed all to come at once now—a stumble, a scream, a heavy impact, and the clatter of shoes kicking and kicking and kicking against the walls of the stairwell. And then, a second later, there was a long deep groan that froze to silence halfway through.

None of me moved, but if I'd squeezed that ax handle any harder, it would've oozed out between my fingers. Then, slower than slow, I opened the door.

The app was down on the turning, its bulb cocked up toward me. In its forelegs it held a man jailed, a brother. He was perfectly stiff as the legs delicately tilted him this way and that for added injections here and there, but for the longest time his eyes stared knowingly into mine, asking for help. And all through the feeding, the app's tag-along camera swooped near his face and then circled away, like a pestering fly sucking up his image.

And then I heard the street door creak. It creaked, and new spiderscrabble came mounting the stairs.

When the new app reached the landing, it froze. Its shortlegs twiddled tip to tip with the shortlegs of the first app, which never stopped feeding as it high-fived the newcomer. Then the new one wheeled and scrabbled back down the way it had come. I shut my door and ran back to the window in a sneaking sprint. The intruder was hustling away down the sidewalk, tickling the air for new business.

I knew what I had to do, and if I hesitated now, I'd think it over and never do it, so I charged back, flung open the door, and jumped.

Ah, the leathery squish of its flat little headsection under my soles! All its knees jerked up in spasms around me and froze in a hairy crown of jagged angles. Now—out for the bonus and right back inside again. I'd do just fine here for the rest of the shoot. I knew how to defend the place now! I ripped off one of the eye-knobs and ran outside to flag a camera raft.

I tried to stay near my street door, shouting and waving my kill tag. But the raft that answered me insisted on hovering in the middle of the avenue so that its bow-cameras could keep shooting the action out in the park. And as I moved out to throw them the tag, two new apps took the nearest corner and cut me off from my door. For the second time, I had to catch my bonus on the run.

They were chasing me away from the park—but running in this direction no longer led you head-on into a bunch of inbound apps. The ring had been closed, and the extras were scattering back out now as survivors wormed free and made for the perimeter. That's what I did. I gained lead on my apps at every corner, till they swung after people who crossed the gap between us. It wasn't my tired legs I had to thank, but a lag in the apps themselves—I saw it in others as well. Hauling forty kilos of zoo-meat puree loads down the old springs.

I saw lots of what I wanted—dead apps—but always too much on the run to take advantage of them. I turned on a street that wasn't promising at all, extras running toward me just ahead of apps. Then a fighter dragging a rope of smoke knifed down across them into a brick wall. And then I was looking at a quarter-block hill of bricks with the front half of an app sticking out at one edge. I ran to it and started chopping a shortleg off. *Whap, whap, whap*—it plopped off. A bullhorn voice and a blast of air hit me together. I didn't jump more than a meter, and saw a camera raft slam down on its air cushion right beside me.

"What the hell are you doing? Just take the tag, asshole!"

The director was a sleek little sweetie with micro 'staches crimped to bracket his mouthcorners, waving his free arm for emphasis. I stared. I tossed him a tag. He flung me the bonus packet with a shoofly follow-through of his arm. I pocketed it, then I took the ax to the second shortleg. The studio cop fired a shot past my ear. The director waved both arms, forgetting the horn now: "Stop that! You're vandalizing studio property! That's a felony!"

"Fuck you mean?" I shouted. "We can do what we want to them! Whatever we can!"

"It's dead already!"

"I'm trying a trick with these things. This app's mine! I turned in the tag!"

"What kind of retard are you? We can't have some asshole running around with pedipalps in his hands! You're screwing with the realism!"

I had something, I knew it from his face. "You not thinking, fool! These aliens don't see like we do, have to recognize each other with these things—say some guy cops the trick and saves his ass with it? What a plot twist, fool! What a cameo!"

He was pure studio hack, and for just a second it snagged him, thinking he might be missing an angle that could jack him up the ladder. He got that sweaty studio-hack look, like he was thinking about farting but scared he might crap his pants. But he shook himself. No black zoo-meat going to tell *him*. "Touch that palp again, and you're under arrest here and now for deface-ment of studio property."

Under arrest for defacement of studio property. Somehow the idea of it just made my brain seize up. It jammed my wheels so hard my head rocked like I was punched. "You graymeat booger!" I screamed. I grabbed a brick and flung it at him with all my might.

I threw wild, way too low, and the brick punched through the screen of the suck-vent for the air cushion. I was almost killed! The raft flipped like a coin—*wham,* top-down on the street and *blang*—bounce-flipped back over and sat on a car. The crew was flung out—Jesus, what a mess!—but the director's foot caught in a camera support and he dangled head down off the raft's edge. A big billfold slicked from his pocket and smacked the pavement. And a spider crawled over the top of the brick hill. Hand to wallet—fat!—to pocket. Ax to second palp, one stroke. Grab the pair. Run.

I had more than the app to run from, and more to run for now. Rafts cut their cameras for setdowns, except for those aimed at action in some other direction. I wasn't sure how long a dead app's tag-along kept shooting before switchoff and touchdown on the corpse. Had my donor's been buried? They were so hard to spot. But either way, tag-along footage wasn't monitored, it was retrieved with the units and culled later. I might be on the run this same day, but I could get out of here—walk this cash and my split right through the paygate. But only if no raft saw me with these palps. I had to get out of sight from the air.

But this spider wasn't carrying any puree in it—yet. Or my legs were fading. I couldn't build lead to search cover, or even to turn and stand. We seemed to be out in the fringes, streets nearly empty—but then two rafts showed not far off, cruising for stray action. I made the next turn before they saw me.

Into a blind alley full of barrels and trash bins. I slung a barrel in the app's way, crouched, stuck out both palps with one hand and raised the ax in the other.

It was coming in, frontlegs high to take me. It stopped, lowered them, and got all twiddly. Now it came ticklefoot, gently bobbing. Its palps pinched together to grope mine with their tips. To me it felt like stopping a tube train with a pap straw, to hold off so much nightmare with those crooked little things. Its fangs slicked in and out. It arched and hunkered, waggled its bulb. Was it grooving? Did I give good palp? How hard could I bring down this ax with an arm that had hot welds instead of joints? That was when the app I didn't know about stepped out from behind a trash bin.

It dragged a half-shriveled woman out with it and stood tickling our air. It dropped her and ran toward us. I stood nearest. I had to drop the ax. It was the hardest thing I ever did, and the fastest. I took one of the palps from my left hand and whipped it on app-two as it crowded up on my other side. App-two started feeling it up.

I wasn't giving good palp now—all three of us felt it. Their bobbing got sharper till they were both doing something more like pushups—arch, squat, arch—and they frisked my tips faster and faster. I had cute shortlegs, sure, but something was missing from our relationship. They swung and checked each other out.

Ah! Now here was some rich full-bodied palp! Twiddle high, twiddle low, swing in a circle and twiddle as you go. They had each other straight before I'd edged three steps toward the alleymouth—they had to check this gimp with the half-tickle again. App-one was closer and I poked it my pair, we twiddled high, twiddled low—but here was app-two and I panicked, and split the pair between them again. More pushups and frustrated frisking. We swung in a circle, then halfway back. All systems still not *go*. They had to check each other again, cutting me off from the alleymouth now.

I had to get in character! I'd had my stroke of insight into their motivation, but I had to take off with it, had to make it play. Apps themselves made heat-blips in the size range of prey, so they'd had to be given some professional ethics: never eat a heat-blip with palps. But palps made patterned moves that clicked their eat-switches all the way off and sent them after something else. I had to feel app, move app, now or never. Back they came.

App-two first—I gave it both. Up, down—but now *I* swung us sideways and as one came up blocked it off with two's body. As one recircled, I broke and jumped it the pair—up, down, swing and block out two, still eager for more. Better! They still weren't sure, but now they phased into my rhythm. Two came in for more—and app number three danced into the alley.

That did it. I'd tried my best, but here I went, into the movie for good and final. I only needed music now to dance what was left of my mind away as the credits rolled down and sealed me in video forever. As number three ran up, there was the first high hornblast of our theme, and it didn't surprise me at all. But it held and held, and all three spiders sagged to a crouch, and froze.

In all the sixty minutes of my film career, that last dance with the apps was my greatest role. It's lost to posterity now. I took all three of their tag-alongs and processed them with my ax until they were at the desired consistency—about like sand. I shucked the director's billfold from my wad of bonuses and filled it with the sand, and on my walk to the paygate I leaked it out all along the way and ditched the billfold. But the palps I snuck out in my pants-leg. You've seen them over the fireplace back at our house. I bet you wondered what they were.

All that was a lot to do in the short time after the trumpet called the shoot's end, with all the rafts cruising to roust the survivors out of the set, but it wasn't all I did. I also chopped every fucking leg off those three spiders. Just for fun.

THE AUTOPSY

Dr. Winters stepped out of the tiny Greyhound station and into the midnight street that smelled of pines. The station's window showed the only light, save for a luminous clock-face several doors down and a little neon beer logo two blocks farther on. He could hear a river. It ran deep in a gorge west of town, but the town was only a few streets wide and a mile or so long, and the current's blurred roar was distinct, like the noise of a ghost river running between the banks of dark shop windows. When he had walked a short distance, Dr. Winters set his suitcase down, pocketed his hands, and looked at the stars—thick as cobblestones in the black gulf.

"A mountain hamlet—a mining town," he said. "Stars. No moon. We are in Bailey."

He was talking to his cancer. It was in his stomach. Since learning of it, he had developed this habit of wry communion with it. He meant to show courtesy to this uninvited guest, Death. It would not find him churlish, for that would make its victory absolute. Except, of course, that its victory would *be* absolute, with or without his ironies.

He picked up his suitcase and walked on. The starlight made faint mirrors of the windows' blackness and showed him the man who passed: lizard-lean, white-haired (at fifty-seven), a man traveling on death's business, carrying his own death in him, and even bearing death's wardrobe in his suitcase. For this was filled—aside from his medical kit and some scant necessities—with mortuary bags. The sheriff had told him on the phone of the improvisations that presently enveloped the corpses, and so the doctor had packed these, laying them in his case with bitter amusement, checking the last one's breadth against his chest before the mirror, as a woman will gauge a dress before donning it, and telling his cancer:

"Oh, yes, that's plenty roomy enough for both of us!"

The case was heavy, and he stopped frequently to rest and scan the sky. What a night's work to do, probing pungent, soul-less filth, eyes earthward, beneath such a ceiling of stars! It had taken five days to dig the ten men out. The autumnal equinox had passed, but the weather here had been uniformly hot. And warmer still, no doubt, so deep in the earth.

He entered the courthouse by a side door. His heels knocked on the linoleum corridor. A door at the end of it, on which was lettered NATE CRAVEN, COUNTY SHERIFF, opened well before he reached it, and his friend stepped out to meet him.

"Dammit, Carl, you're *still* so thin they could use you for a whip. Gimme that. You're in too good a shape already. You don't need the exercise."

The case hung weightless from the sheriff's hand, impart-ing no tilt at all to his bull shoulders. Despite his implied self-derogation, he was only moderately paunched for a man his age and size. He had a rough-hewn face, and the bulk of brow, nose, and jaw made his greenish eyes look small until one engaged them and felt the snap and penetration of their intelligence. In the office he half filled two cups from a coffee urn and topped both off with bourbon from a bottle in his desk. When they had finished these, they had finished trading news of mutual friends. The sheriff mixed another round and sipped from his, in a silence clearly prefatory to the work at hand.

"They talk about rough justice," he said. "I've sure seen it now. One of those . . . patients of yours that you'll be working on? He was a killer. Christ, 'killer' doesn't half say it. A killer's the least of what he was. The blast killing *him,* that was the jus-tice part. Those other nine, they were the rough. And it just galls the hell out of me, Carl! If that kiss-ass boss of yours has his way, the rough won't even stop with their being dead! There won't even be any compensation for their survivors! Tell me—has he broke his back yet? I mean, touching his toes for Fordham Mutual?"

"You refer, I take it, to the estimable Coroner Waddleton of

Fordham County." Dr. Winters paused to sip his drink. With a delicate flaring of his nostrils he communicated all the disgust, contempt, and amusement he had felt in his four years as pathologist in Waddleton's office. The sheriff laughed.

"Clear pictures seldom emerge from anything the coroner says," the doctor continued. "He took your name in vain. Vigorously and repeatedly. These expressions formed his opening remarks. He then developed the theme of our office's strict responsibility to the letter of the law, and of the workmen's compensation law in particular. Death benefits accrue only to the dependents of decedents whose deaths arise *out of the course of* their employment, not merely *in* the course of it. Victims of a maniacal assault, though they die on the job, are by no means necessarily compensable under the law. We then contemplated the tragic injustice of an insurance company—*any* insurance company—having to pay benefits to unentitled persons, solely through the laxity and incompetence of investigating officers. Your name came up again, and Coroner Waddleton subjected it to further abuse. Fordham Mutual, campaign contributor or not, is certainly a major insurance company and is therefore entitled to the same fair treatment that all such companies deserve."

Craven uttered a bark of wrathful mirth and spat expertly into his wastebasket. "Ah, the impartial public servant! What's seven widows and sixteen dependent children, next to Fordham Mutual?" He drained his cup and sighed. "I'll tell you what, Carl. We've been five days digging those men out and the last two days sifting half that mountain for explosive traces, with those insurance investigators hanging on our elbows, and the most they could say was that there was 'strong presumptive evidence' of a bomb. Well, I don't budge for that because I don't have to. Waddleton can shove his 'extraordinary circumstances.' If you don't find anything in those bodies, then that's all the autopsy there is to it, and they get buried right here where their families want 'em."

The doctor was smiling at his friend. He finished his cup and spoke with his previous wry detachment, as if the sheriff had not interrupted his narrative.

"The honorable coroner then spoke with remarkable volubility on the subject of Autopsy Consent forms and the malicious subversion of private citizens by vested officers of the law. He had, as it happened, a sheaf of such forms on his desk, all signed, all with a rider clause typed in above the signatures. A cogent paragraph. It had, among its other qualities, the property of turning the coroner's face purple when he read it aloud. He read it aloud to me three times. It appeared that the survivors' consent was contingent on two conditions: that the autopsy be performed *in locum mortis,* that is to say in Bailey, and that only if the coroner's pathologist found concrete evidence of homicide should the decedents be subject either to removal from Bailey or to further necropsy. It was well written. I remember wondering who wrote it."

The sheriff nodded musingly. He took Dr. Winters's empty cup, set it by his own, filled both two-thirds with bourbon, and added a splash of coffee to the doctor's. The two friends exchanged a level stare, rather like poker players in the clinch. The sheriff regarded his cup, sipped from it.

"In locum mortis. What-all does that mean exactly?"

" 'In the place of death.' "

"Oh. Freshen that up for you?"

"I've just started it, thank you."

Both men laughed, paused, and laughed again, some might have said immoderately.

"He all but told me that I *had* to find something to compel a second autopsy," the doctor said at length. "He would have sold his soul—or taken out a second mortgage on it—for a mobile X-ray unit. He's right, of course. If those bodies have trapped any bomb fragments, that would be the surest and quickest way of finding them. It still amazes me your Dr. Parsons could let his X-ray go unfixed for so long."

"He sets bones, stitches wounds, writes prescriptions, and sends anything tricky down the mountain. Just barely manages that. Drunks don't get much done."

"He's gotten that bad?"

"He hangs on and no more. Waddleton was right there, not deputizing him pathologist. I doubt he could find a cannonball in a dead rat. I wouldn't say it where it could hurt him, as long as he's still managing, but everyone here knows it. His patients sort of look after *him* half the time. But Waddleton would have sent you, no matter who was here. Nothing but his best for party contributors like Fordham Mutual."

The doctor looked at his hands and shrugged. "So. There's a killer in the batch. *Was* there a bomb?"

Slowly the sheriff planted his elbows on the desk and pressed his hands against his temples, as if the question had raised a turbulence of memories. For the first time the doctor—half hearkening throughout to the never-quite-muted stirrings of the death within him—saw his friend's exhaustion: the tremor of hand, the bruised look under the eyes.

"When I've told you what we have, I guess you'll end up assuming what I do about it. But I think assuming is as far as any of us will get with this one. It's one of those nightmare specials, Carl. The ones no one ever does get to the bottom of.

"All right, then. About two months ago, we had a man disappear—Ronald Hanley. Mine worker, rock-steady, family man. He didn't come home one night, and we never found a trace of him. OK, that happens sometimes. About a week later, the lady that ran the laundromat, Sharon Starker, *she* disappeared, no trace. We got edgy then. I made an announcement on the local radio about a possible weirdo at large, spelled out special precautions everybody should take. We put both our squad cars on the night beat, and by day we set to work knocking on every door in town collecting alibis for the two times of disappearance.

"No good. Maybe you're fooled by this uniform and think I'm a law officer, protector of the people, and all that? A natural mistake. A lot of people were fooled. In less than seven weeks, six people vanished, just like that. Me and my deputies might as well have stayed in bed round the clock, for all the good we did." The sheriff drained his cup.

"Anyway, at last we got lucky. Don't get me wrong now. We didn't go all hog-wild and actually prevent a crime or anything. But we *did* find a body—except it wasn't the body of any of the seven people that had disappeared. We'd taken to combing the woods nearest town, with temporary deputies from the miners to help. Well, one of those boys was out there with us last week. It was hot—like it's been for a while now—and it was real quiet. He heard this buzzing noise and looked around for it, and he saw a bee-swarm up in the crotch of a tree. Except he was smart enough to know that that's not usual around here—beehives. So it wasn't bees. It was bluebottle flies, a goddamned big cloud of them, all over a bundle that was wrapped in a tarp."

The sheriff studied his knuckles. He had, in his eventful life, occasionally met men literate enough to understand his last name and rash enough to be openly amused by it, and the knuckles—scarred knobs—were eloquent of his reactions. He looked back into his old friend's eyes.

"We got that thing down and unwrapped it. Billy Lee Davis, one of my deputies, he was in Viet Nam, been near some bad, bad things and held on. Billy Lee blew his lunch all over the ground when we unwrapped that thing. It was a man. Some of a man. We knew he'd stood six-two because all the bones were there, and he'd probably weighed between two fifteen and two twenty-five, but he folded up no bigger than a big-size laundry package. Still had his face, both shoulders, and the left arm, but all the rest was clean. It wasn't animal work. It was knife work, all the edges neat as butcher cuts. Except butchered meat, even when you drain it all you can, will bleed a good deal afterwards, and there wasn't one goddamned drop of blood on the tarp, nor in that meat. It was just as pale as fish meat."

Deep in his body's center, the doctor's cancer touched him. Not a ravening attack—it sank one fang of pain, questioningly, into new untasted flesh, probing the scope for its appetite there. He disguised his tremor with a shake of the head.

"A cache, then."

The sheriff nodded. "Like you might keep a pot roast in the icebox for making lunches. I took some pictures of his face, then we put him back and erased our traces. Two of the miners I'd deputized did a lot of hunting, were woods-smart. So I left them on the first watch. We worked out positions and cover for them, and drove back.

"We got right on tracing him, sent out descriptions to every town within a hundred miles. He was no one I'd ever seen in Bailey, nor anyone else either, it began to look like, after we'd combed the town all day with the photos. Then, out of the blue, Billy Lee Davis smacks himself on the forehead and says, 'Sheriff, I seen this man somewhere in town, and not long ago!'

"He'd been shook all day since throwing up, and then all of a sudden he just snapped to. Was dead sure. Except he couldn't remember where or when. We went over and over it, and he tried and tried. It got to where I wanted to grab him by the ankles and hang him upside down and shake him till it dropped out of him. But it was no damn use. Just after dark we went back to that tree—we'd worked out a place to hide the cars and a route to it through the woods. When we were close, we walkie-talkied the men we'd left for an all-clear to come up. No answer at all. And when we got there, all that was left of our trap was the tree. No body, no tarp, no Special Assistant Deputies. Nothing."

This time Dr. Winters poured the coffee and bourbon. "Too much coffee," the sheriff muttered, but drank anyway. "Part of me wanted to chew nails and break necks. And part of me was scared shitless. When we got back, I got on the radio station again and made an emergency broadcast and then had the man at the station rebroadcast it every hour. Told everyone to do everything in groups of three, to stay together at night in threes at least, to go out little as possible, keep armed and keep checking up on each other. It had such a damn-fool sound to it, but just pairing-up was no protection if half of one of those pairs was the killer. I sent our corpse's picture out statewide, I deputized more men and put them on the streets to beef up the night patrol.

"It was next morning that things broke. The sheriff of Rakehell called—he's over in the next county. He said our corpse looked a lot like a man named Abel Dougherty, a mill-hand with Con Wood over there. I left Billy Lee in charge and drove right out.

"This Dougherty had a cripple older sister he always checked back to by phone whenever he left town for long, a habit no one knew about, probably embarrassed him. Sheriff Peck there only

found out about it when the woman called him, said her brother'd been four days gone for vacation and not rung her once.
He'd hardly had her report for an hour when he got the picture I
sent out, and recognized it. And *I* hadn't been in his office more
than ten minutes when Billy Lee called me there. He'd remembered.

"When he'd seen Dougherty was the Sunday night three
days before we found him. Where he'd seen him was the Truck-
er's Tavern outside the north end of town. The man had made
a stir by being jolly drunk and latching onto a miner who was
drinking there, man named Joe Allen, who'd started at the mine
about two months back. Dougherty kept telling him that he
wasn't Joe Allen, but Dougherty's old buddy named Sykes that
had worked with him at Con Wood for a coon's age, and what
the hell kind of joke was this, come have a beer old buddy and
tell me why you took off so sudden and what the hell you been
doing with yourself.

"Allen took it laughing. Dougherty'd clap him on the shoulder, Allen'd clap him right back and make every kind of joke
about it, say, 'Give this man another beer, I'm standing in for
a long-lost friend of his.' Dougherty was so big and loud and
stubborn, Billy Lee was worried about a fight starting, and he
wasn't the only one worried. But this Joe Allen was a natural
good ol' boy, handled it perfect. We'd checked him out weeks
back along with everyone else, and he was real popular with the
other miners. Finally Dougherty swore he was going to take
him on to another bar to help celebrate the vacation Dougherty
was starting out on. Joe Allen got up grinning, said goddamn
it, he couldn't accommodate Dougherty by being this fellow
Sykes, but he could sure as hell have a glass with any serious
drinking man that was treating. He went out with him, and
gave everyone a wink as he left, to the general satisfaction of the
audience."

Craven paused. Dr. Winters met his eyes and knew his thought,
two images: the jolly wink that roused the room to laughter,
and the thing in the tarp aboil with bright blue flies.

"It was plain enough for me," the sheriff said. "I told Billy
Lee to search Allen's room at the Skettles' boardinghouse and

then go straight to the mine and take him. We could fine-polish things once we had him. Since I was already in Rakehell, I saw to some of the loose ends before I started back. I went with Sheriff Peck down to Con Wood, and we found a picture of Eddie Sykes in the personnel files. I'd seen Joe Allen often enough, and it was his picture in that file.

"We found out Sykes had lived alone, was an on-again, off-again worker, private in his comings and goings, and hadn't been around for a while. But one of the sawyers there could be pretty sure of when Sykes left Rakehell because he'd gone to Sykes's cabin the morning after a big meteor shower they had out there about nine weeks back, since some thought the shower might have reached the ground, and not far from Sykes's side of the mountain. He wasn't in that morning, and the sawyer hadn't seen him since.

"After all those weeks, it was sewed up just like that. Within another hour I was almost back in Bailey, had the pedal to the metal, and was barely three miles out of town, when it all blew to shit. I *heard* it blow, I was that close to collaring him. I tell you, Carl, I felt . . . like a *bullet*. I was going to rip right through this Sykes, this goddamned cannibal monster. . . .

"We had to reconstruct what happened. Billy Lee got impatient and went after him alone, but luckily he radioed Travis—my other deputy—first. Travis was on the mountain dragnetting around that tree for clues, but he happened to be near his car when Billy Lee called him. He said he'd just been through Allen's room and had got something really odd. It was a sphere, half again big as a basketball, heavy, made of something that wasn't metal or glass but was a little like both. He could half-see into it, and it looked to be full of some kind of circuitry and components. He hadn't found anything else unusual. He was going to take this thing along with him, and go after Allen now. He told Travis to get up to the mine for backup. He'd be there first and should already have Allen by the time Travis arrived.

"Tierney, the shift boss up there, had an assistant that told us the rest. Billy Lee parked behind the offices where the men in the yard wouldn't see the car. He went upstairs to arrange the arrest with Tierney. They got half a dozen men together. Just as they came out of the building, they saw Allen take off running from the squad car. He had the sphere under his arm.

"The whole compound's fenced in, and Tierney'd already phoned to have all the gates shut. Allen zigged and zagged some but caught on quick to the trap. The sphere slowed him, but he still had a good lead. He hesitated a minute and then ran straight for the main shaft. A cage was just going down with a crew, and he risked every bone in him jumping down after it, but he got safe on top. By the time they got to the switches, the cage was down to the second level, and Allen and the crew had got out. Tierney got it back up. Billy Lee ordered the rest back to get weapons and follow, and him and Tierney rode the cage right back down. And about two minutes later half the goddamned mine blew up."

The sheriff stopped as if cut off, his lips parted to say more, his eyes registering for perhaps the hundredth time his amazement that there was no more, that the weeks of death and mystification ended here, with this split-second recapitulation: more death, more answerless dark, sealing all.

"Nate."

"What."

"Wrap it up and go to bed. I don't need your help. You're dead on your feet."

"I'm not on my feet. And I'm coming along."

"Give me a picture of the victims' position relative to the blast. I'm going to work, and you're going to bed."

The sheriff shook his head absently. "They're mining in shrinkage stopes. The adits—levels—branch off lateral from the vertical shaft. From one level they hollow out overhand up to the one above. Scoop out big chambers and let most of the broken rock stay inside so they can stand on the heaps to cut the ceiling higher. They leave sections of support wall between stopes, and those men were buried several stopes in from the shaft. The cave-in killed *them*. The mountain just folded them up in their own hill of tailings. No kind of fragments reached them. I'm dead sure. The only ones they *found* were of some standard charges that the main blast set off, and those didn't even get close. The big one blew out where the adit joined the shaft, right where, and right when, Billy Lee and Tierney got out of the cage. And there is *nothing* left there, Carl. No sphere, no cage, no Tierney, no Billy Lee Davis. Just rock blown fine as flour."

Dr. Winters nodded and, after a moment, stood up.

"Come on, Nate. I've got to get started. I'll be lucky to have even a few of them done before morning. Drop me off and go to sleep, till then at least. You'll still be there to witness most of the work."

The sheriff rose, took up the doctor's suitcase, and led him out of the office without a word, concession in his silence.

The patrol car was behind the building. The doctor saw a crueller beauty in the stars than he had an hour before. They got in, and Craven swung them out onto the empty street. The doctor opened the window and hearkened, but the motor's surge drowned out the river sound. Before the thrust of their headlights, ranks of old-fashioned parking meters sprouted shadows tall across the sidewalks, shadows that shrank and were cut down by the lights' passage. The sheriff said:

"All those extra dead. For nothing! Not even to . . . *feed* him! If it *was* a bomb, and he made it, he'd know how powerful it was. He wouldn't try some stupid escape stunt with it. And how did he even know that globe was there? We worked it out that Allen was just ending a shift, but he wasn't even up out of the ground before Billy Lee'd parked out of sight from the shaft."

"Let it rest, Nate. I want to hear more, but after you've slept. I know you. All the photos will be there, and the report complete, all the evidence neatly boxed and carefully described. When I've looked things over, I'll know exactly how to proceed by myself."

Bailey had neither hospital nor morgue, and the bodies were in a defunct ice-plant on the edge of town. A generator had been brought down from the mine, lighting improvised, and the refrigeration system reactivated. Dr. Parsons's office, and the tiny examining room that served the sheriff's station in place of a morgue, had furnished this makeshift with all the equipment that Dr. Winters would need beyond what he carried with him. A quarter-mile outside the main body of the town, they drew up to it. Tree-flanked, unneighbored by any other structure, it was a double building; the smaller half—the office—was illuminated. The bodies would be in the big windowless refrigerator segment. Craven pulled up beside a second squad car parked near the office door. A short rake-thin man wearing a large white stetson got out of the car and came over. Craven rolled down his window.

"Trav. This here's Dr. Winters."

" 'Lo, Nate. Dr. Winters. Everything's shipshape inside. Felt more comfortable out here. Last of those newshounds left two hours ago."

"They sure do hang on. You take off now, Trav. Get some sleep and be back at sunup. What temperature we getting?"

The pale stetson, far clearer in the starlight than the shadow-face beneath it, wagged dubiously. "Thirty-six. She won't get lower—some kind of leak."

"That should be cold enough," the doctor said.

Travis drove off, and the sheriff unlocked the padlock on the office door. Waiting behind him, Dr. Winters heard the river again—a cold balm, a whisper of freedom—and overlying this, the stutter and soft snarl of the generator behind the building, a gnawing, remorseless sound that somehow fed the obscure anguish that the other soothed. They went in.

The preparations had been thoughtful and complete. "You can wheel 'em out of the fridge on this and do the examining in here," the sheriff said, indicating a table and a gurney. "You should find all the gear you need on this big table here, and you can write up your reports on that desk. The phone's not hooked up—there's a pay phone at the last gas station if you have to call me."

The doctor nodded, checking over the material on the larger table: scalpels, postmortem and cartilage knives, intestine scissors, rib shears, forceps, probes, mallet and chisels, a blade saw and electric bone saw, scale, jars for specimens, needles and suture, sterilizer, gloves. . . . Beside this array were a few boxes and envelopes with descriptive sheets attached, containing the photographs and such evidentiary objects as had been found associated with the bodies.

"Excellent," he muttered.

"The overhead light's fluorescent, full spectrum or whatever they call it. Better for colors. There's a pint of decent bourbon in that top desk drawer. Ready to look at 'em?"

"Yes."

The sheriff unbarred and slid back the big metal door to the refrigeration chamber. Icy tainted air boiled out of the doorway. The light within was dimmer than that provided in the office—a yellow gloom wherein ten oblong heaps lay on trestles.

The two stood silent for a time, their stillness a kind of unpremeditated homage paid the eternal mystery at its threshold. As if the cold room were in fact a shrine, the doctor found a peculiar awe in the row of veiled forms. The awful unison of their dying, the titan's grave that had been made for them, conferred on them a stern authority, Death's Chosen Ones. His stomach hurt, and he found he had his hand pressed to his abdomen. He glanced at Craven and was relieved to see that his friend, staring wearily at the bodies, had missed the gesture.

"Nate. Help me uncover them."

Starting at opposite ends of the row, they stripped the tarps off and piled them in a corner. Both were brusque now, not pausing over the revelation of the swelled, pulpy faces—most three-lipped with the gaseous burgeoning of their tongues—and the fat, livid hands sprouting from the filthy sleeves. But at one of the bodies Craven stopped. The doctor saw him look, and his mouth twist. Then he flung the tarp on the heap and moved to the next trestle.

When they came out, Dr. Winters took out the bottle and glasses Craven had put in the desk, and they had a drink together. The sheriff made as if he would speak, but shook his head and sighed.

"I *will* get some sleep, Carl. I'm getting crazy thoughts with this thing." The doctor wanted to ask those thoughts. Instead he laid a hand on his friend's shoulder.

"Go home, Sheriff Craven. Take off the badge and lie down. The dead won't run off on you. We'll all still be here in the morning."

When the sound of the patrol car faded, the doctor stood listening to the generator's growl and the silence of the dead, resurgent now. Both the sound and the silence seemed to mock him. The afterecho of his last words made him uneasy. He said to his cancer:

"What about it, dear colleague? We *will* still be here tomorrow? All of us?"

He smiled, but felt an odd discomfort, as if he had ventured a jest in company and roused a hostile silence. He went to the refrigerator door, rolled it back, and viewed the corpses in their ordered rank, with their strange tribunal air. "What, sirs?" he murmured. "Do you judge me? Just who is to examine whom tonight, if I may ask?"

He went back into the office, where his first step was to examine the photographs made by the sheriff in order to see how the dead had lain at their uncovering. The earth had seized them with terrible suddenness. Some crouched, some partly stood, others sprawled in crazy free-fall postures. Each successive photo showed more of the jumble as the shovels continued their work between shots. The doctor studied them closely, noting the identifications inked on the bodies as they came completely into view.

One man, Roger Willet, had died some yards from the main cluster. It appeared he had just straggled into the stope from the adit at the moment of the explosion. He should thus have received, more directly than any of the others, the shock waves of the blast. If bomb fragments were to be found in any of the corpses, Mr. Willet's seemed likeliest to contain them. Dr. Winters pulled on a pair of surgical gloves.

Willet lay at one end of the line of trestles. He wore a thermal shirt and overalls that were strikingly new beneath the filth of burial. Their tough fabrics jarred with the fabric of his flesh—blue, swollen, seeming easily torn or burst, like ripe fruit. In life Willet had grease-combed his hair. Now it was a sculpture of dust, spikes and whorls shaped by the head's last grindings against the mountain that clenched it.

Rigor had come and gone—Willet rolled laxly onto the gurney. As the doctor wheeled him past the others, he felt a slight self-consciousness. The sense of some judgment flowing from the dead assembly—unlike most such vagrant fantasies—had an odd tenacity in him. This stubborn unease began to irritate him with himself, and he moved more briskly.

He put Willet on the examining table and cut the clothes off him with shears, storing the pieces in an evidence box. The overalls were soiled with agonal waste expulsions. The doctor stared a moment with unwilling pity at his naked subject.

"You won't ride down to Fordham in any case," he said to the corpse. "Not unless I find something pretty damned obvious." He pulled his gloves tighter and arranged his implements.

Waddleton had said more to him than he had reported to the sheriff. The doctor was to find, and forcefully to record that he had found, strong "indications" absolutely requiring the decedents' removal to Fordham for X-ray and an exhaustive second postmortem. The doctor's continued employment with the Coroner's Office depended entirely on his compliance in this. He had received this stipulation with a silence Waddleton had not thought it necessary to break. His present resolution was all but made at that moment. Let the obvious be taken as such. If the others showed as plainly as Willet did the external signs of death by asphyxiation, they would receive no more than a thorough external exam. Willet he would examine internally as well, merely to establish in depth for this one what should appear obvious in all. Otherwise, only when the external exam revealed a clearly anomalous feature—and clear and suggestive it must be—would he look deeper.

He rinsed the caked hair in a basin, poured the sediment into a flask and labeled it. Starting with the scalp, he began a minute scrutiny of the body's surfaces, recording his observations as he went.

The characteristic signs of asphyxial death were evident, despite the complicating effects of autolysis and putrefaction. The eyeballs' bulge and the tongue's protrusion were, by now, as much due to gas pressure as to the mode of death, but the latter organ was clamped between locked teeth, leaving little doubt as to that mode. The coloration of degenerative change—a greenish-yellow tint, a darkening and mapping-out of superficial veins—was marked, but not sufficient to obscure the blue of cyanosis on the face and neck, nor the pinpoint hemorrhages freckling neck, chest, and shoulders. From the mouth and nose the doctor scraped matter he was confident was the blood-tinged mucus typically ejected in the airless agony.

He began to find a kind of comedy in his work. What a buffoon death made of a man! A blue pop-eyed three-lipped thing. And there was himself, his curious solicitous intimacy with this clownish carrion. Excuse me, Mr. Willet, while I probe this laceration. What do you feel when I do this? Nothing? Nothing at all? Fine, now what about these nails? Split them clawing at the earth, did you? Yes. A nice bloodblister under this thumbnail, I see—got it on the job a few days before your accident, no doubt? Remarkable calluses here, still quite tough . . .

The doctor looked for an unanalytic moment at the hands—puffed dark paws, gestureless, having renounced all touch and grasp. He felt the wastage of the man concentrated in the hands. The painful futility of the body's fine articulation when it is seen in death—this poignancy he had long learned not to acknowledge when he worked. But now he let it move him a little. This Roger Willet, plodding to his work one afternoon, had suddenly been scrapped, crushed to a nonfunctional heap of perishable materials. It simply happened that his life had chanced to move too close to the passage of a more powerful life, one of those inexorable and hungry lives that leave human wreckage—known or undiscovered—in their wakes. Bad luck, Mr. Willet. Naturally, we feel very sorry about this. But this Joe Allen, your co-worker. Apparently he was some sort of . . . cannibal. It's complicated. We don't understand it all. But the fact is we have to dismantle you now to a certain extent. There's really no hope of your using these parts of yourself again, I'm afraid. Ready now?

The doctor proceeded to the internal exam with a vague eagerness for Willet's fragmentation, for the disarticulation of that sadness in his natural form. He grasped Willet by the jaw and took up the postmortem knife. He sank its point beneath the chin and began the long, gently sawing incision that opened Willet from throat to groin.

In the painstaking separation of the body's laminae Dr. Winters found absorption and pleasure. And yet throughout he felt, marginal but insistent, the movement of a stream of irrelevant images. These were of the building that contained him, and of the night containing it. As from outside, he saw the plant—bleached planks, iron roofing—and the trees crowding it, all in starlight, a ghost-town image. And he saw the refrigerator vault beyond the wall as from within, feeling the stillness of murdered men in a cold yellow light. And at length a question formed itself, darting in and out of the weave of his concentration as the images did: Why did he still feel, like some stir of the air, that sense of mute vigilance surrounding his action, furtively touching his nerves with its inquiry as he worked? He shrugged, overtly angry now. Who else was attending but Death? Wasn't he Death's hireling, and this Death's place? Then let the master look on.

Peeling back Willet's cover of hemorrhage-stippled skin, Dr. Winters read the corpse with an increasing dispassion, a mortuary text. He confined his inspection to the lungs and mediastinum and found there unequivocal testimony to Willet's asphyxial death. The pleurae of the lungs exhibited the expected ecchymoses—bruised spots in the glassy enveloping membrane. Beneath, the polyhedral surface lobules of the lungs themselves were bubbled and blistered—the expected interstitial emphysema. The lungs, on section, were intensely and bloodily congested. The left half of the heart he found contracted and empty, while the right was overdistended and engorged with dark blood, as were the large veins of the upper mediastinum. It was a classic picture of death by suffocation, and at length the doctor, with needle and suture, closed up the text again.

He returned the corpse to the gurney and draped one of his mortuary bags over it in the manner of a shroud. When he had help in the morning, he would weigh the bodies on a platform scale the office contained and afterward bag them properly. He came to the refrigerator door, and hesitated. He stared at the door, not moving, not understanding why.

Run. Get out. Now.

The thought was his own, but it came to him so urgently he

turned around as if someone behind him had spoken. Across the room a thin man in smock and gloves, his eyes shadows, glared at the doctor from the black windows. Behind the man was a shrouded cart, behind that, a wide metal door.

Quietly, wonderingly, the doctor asked, "Run from what?" The eyeless man in the glass was still half-crouched, afraid.

Then, a moment later, the man straightened, threw back his head, and laughed. The doctor walked to the desk and sat down shoulder to shoulder with him. He pulled out the bottle and they had a drink together, regarding each other with identical bemused smiles. Then the doctor said, "Let me pour you another. You need it, old fellow. It makes a man himself again."

Nevertheless his reentry of the vault was difficult, toilsome, each step seeming to require a new summoning of the will to move. In the freezing half-light all movement felt like defiance. His body lagged behind his craving to be quick, to be done with this molestation of the gathered dead. He returned Willet to his pallet and took his neighbor. The name on the tag wired to his boot was Ed Moses. Dr. Winters wheeled him back to the office and closed the big door behind him.

With Moses his work gained momentum. He expected to perform no further internal necropsies. He thought of his employer, rejoicing now in his seeming-submission to Waddleton's ultimatum. The impact would be dire. He pictured the coroner in shock, a sheaf of Pathologist's Reports in one hand, and smiled.

Waddleton could probably make a plausible case for incomplete examination. Still, a pathologist's discretionary powers were not well-defined. Many good ones would approve the adequacy of the doctor's method, given his working conditions. The inevitable litigation with a coalition of compensation claimants would be strenuous and protracted. Win or lose, Waddleton's venal devotion to the insurance company's interest would be abundantly displayed. Further, immediately on his dismissal the doctor would formally disclose its occult cause to the press. A libel action would ensue that he would have as little cause to fear as he had to fear his firing. Both his savings and the lawsuit would long outlast his life.

Externally, Ed Moses exhibited a condition as typically asphyxial as Willet's had been, with no slightest mark of fragment entry. The doctor finished his report and returned Moses to the vault, his movements brisk and precise. His unease was all but gone. That queasy stirring of the air—had he really felt it? It had been, perhaps, some new reverberation of the death at work in him, a psychic shudder of response to the cancer's stealthy probing for his life. He brought out the body next to Moses in the line.

Walter Lou Jackson was big, six feet two inches from heel to crown, and would surely weigh out at more than two hundred pounds. He had writhed mightily against his million-ton coffin with an agonal strength that had torn his face and hands. Death had mauled him like a lion. The doctor set to work.

His hands were fully themselves now—fleet, exact, intricately testing the corpse's character as other fingers might explore a keyboard for its latent melodies. And the doctor watched them with an old pleasure, one of the few that had never failed him, his mind at one remove from their busy intelligence. All the hard deaths! A worldful of them, time without end. Lives wrenched kicking from their snug meat-frames. Walter Lou Jackson had died very hard. Joe Allen brought this on you, Mr. Jackson. We think it was part of his attempt to escape the law.

But what a botched flight! The unreason of it—more than baffling—was eerie in its colossal futility. Beyond question, Allen had been cunning. A ghoul with a psychopath's social finesse. A good old boy who could make a tavernful of men laugh with delight while he cut his victim from their midst, make them applaud his exit with the prey, who stepped jovially into the darkness with murder at his side clapping him on the shoulder. Intelligent, certainly, with a strange technical sophistication as well, suggested by the sphere. Then what of the lunacy yet more strongly suggested by the same object? In the sphere was concentrated all the lethal mystery of Bailey's long nightmare.

Why the explosion? Its location implied an ambush for Allen's pursuers, a purposeful detonation. Had he aimed at a limited cave-in from which he schemed some inconceivable escape? Folly enough in this—far more if, as seemed sure, Allen had made the bomb himself, for then he would have to know its power was grossly inordinate to the need.

But if it was not a bomb, had a different function and only incidentally an explosive potential, Allen might underestimate the blast. It appeared the object was somehow remotely monitored by him, for the timing of events showed he had gone straight for it the instant he emerged from the shaft—shunned the bus waiting to take his shift back to town and made a beeline across the compound for a patrol car that was hidden from his view by the office building. This suggested something more complex than a mere explosive device, something, perhaps, whose destruction was itself more Allen's aim than the explosion produced thereby.

The fact that he risked the sphere's retrieval at all pointed to this interpretation. For the moment he sensed its presence at the mine, he must have guessed that the murder investigation had led to its discovery and removal from his room. But then, knowing himself already liable to the extreme penalty, why should Allen go to such lengths to recapture evidence incriminatory of a lesser offense, possession of an explosive device?

Then grant that the sphere was something more, something instrumental to his murders that could guarantee a conviction he might otherwise evade. Still, his gambit made no sense. Since the sphere—and thus the lawmen he could assume to have taken it—was already at the mine office, he must expect the compound to be sealed at any moment. Meanwhile, the gate was open, escape into the mountains a strong possibility for a man capable of stalking and destroying two experienced and well-armed woodsmen lying in ambush for him. Why had he all but ensured his capture to weaken a case against himself that his escape would have rendered irrelevant? Dr. Winters watched as his own fingers, like a hunting pack round a covert, converged on a small puncture wound below Walter Lou Jackson's xiphoid process, between the eighth ribs.

His left hand touched its borders, the fingers' inquiry quick and tender. The right hand introduced a probe, and both together eased it into the wound. It was rarely fruitful to use a probe on corpses this decayed; the track of the wound would more properly be examined by section. But an inexplicable sense of urgency had taken hold of him. Gently, with infinite pains not to pierce in the softened tissues an artifactual track of his own, he inched the probe in. It moved unobstructed deep into the body, curving upward through the diaphragm toward the heart. The doctor's own heart accelerated. He watched his hands move to record the observation, watched them pause, watched them return to their survey of the corpse, leaving pen and page untouched.

External inspection revealed no further anomaly. All else he observed the doctor recorded faithfully, wondering throughout at the distress he felt. When he had finished, he understood it. Its cause was not the discovery of an entry wound that might bolster Waddleton's case. For the find had, within moments, revealed to him that, should he encounter anything he thought to be a mark of fragment penetration, he was going to ignore it. The damage Joe Allen had done was going to end here, with this last grand slaughter, and would not extend to the impoverishment of his victims' survivors. His mind was now made up: for Jackson and the remaining seven, the external exams would be officially recorded as contraindicating the need for any external exam.

No, the doctor's unease as he finished Jackson's external—as he wrote up his report and signed it—had a different source. His problem was that he did not believe the puncture in Jackson's thorax *was* a mark of fragment entry. He disbelieved this, and had no idea why he did so. Nor had he any idea why, once again, he felt afraid. He sealed the report. Jackson was now officially accounted for and done with. Then Dr. Winters took up the postmortem knife and returned to the corpse.

First the long sawing slice, unzippering the mortal overcoat. Next, two great square flaps of flesh reflected, scrolled laterally to the armpits' line, disrobing the chest: one hand grasping the flap's skirt, the other sweeping beneath it with the knife, flensing through the glassy tissue that joined it to the chest wall, and shaving all muscles from their anchorages to bone and cartilage beneath. Then the dismantling of the strongbox within. Rib shears—so frank and forward a tool, like a gardener's. The steel beak bit through each rib's gristle anchor to the sternum's centerplate. At the sternum's crownpiece the collarbones' ends were knifed, pried, and sprung free from their sockets. The coffer unhasped, unhinged, a knife teased beneath the lid and levered it off.

Some minutes later the doctor straightened up and stepped back from his subject. He moved almost drunkenly, and his age seemed scored more deeply in his face. With loathing haste he stripped his gloves off. He went to the desk, sat down, and poured another drink. If there was something like horror in his face, there was also a hardening in his mouth's line and the muscles of his jaw. He spoke to his glass: "So be it, your Excellency. Something new for your humble servant. Testing my nerve?"

Jackson's pericardium, the shapely capsule containing his heart, should have been all but hidden between the big blood-fat loaves of his lungs. The doctor had found it fully exposed, the lungs flanking it wrinkled lumps less than a third their natural bulk. Not only they, but the left heart and the superior mediastinal veins—all the regions that should have been grossly engorged with blood—were utterly drained of it.

The doctor swallowed his drink and got out the photographs again. He found that Jackson had died on his stomach across the body of another worker, with the upper part of a third trapped between them. Neither these two subjacent corpses nor the surrounding earth showed any stain of a blood loss that must have amounted to two liters.

Possibly the pictures, by some trick of shadow, had failed to pick it up. He turned to the Investigator's Report, where Craven would surely have mentioned any significant amounts of bloody earth uncovered during the disinterment. The sheriff recorded nothing of the kind. Dr. Winters returned to the pictures.

Ronald Pollock, Jackson's most intimate associate in the grave, had died on his back, beneath and slightly askew of Jackson, placing most of their torsos in contact, save where the head and shoulder of the third interposed. It seemed inconceivable Pollock's clothing should lack any trace of such massive drainage from a death mate thus embraced.

The doctor rose abruptly, pulled on fresh gloves, and returned to Jackson. His hands showed a more brutal speed now, closing the great incision temporarily with a few widely spaced sutures. He replaced him in the vault and brought out Pollock, striding, heaving hard at the dead shapes in the shifting of them, thrusting always—so it seemed to him—just a step ahead of urgent thoughts he did not want to have, deformities that whispered at his back, emitting faint, chill gusts of putrid breath. He shook his head—denying, delaying—and pushed the new corpse onto the worktable. The scissors undressed Pollock in greedy bites.

But at length, when he had scanned each scrap of fabric and found nothing like the stain of blood, he came to rest again, relinquishing that simplest, desired resolution he had made such haste to reach. He stood at the instrument table, not seeing it, submitting to the approach of the half-formed things at his mind's periphery.

The revelation of Jackson's shriveled lungs had been more than a shock. He had felt a stab of panic too, in fact that same curiously explicit terror of this place that had urged him to flee earlier. He acknowledged now that the germ of that quickly suppressed terror had been a premonition of this failure to find any trace of the missing blood. Whence the premonition? It had to do with a problem he had steadfastly refused to consider: the mechanics of so complete a drainage of the lungs' densely reticulated vascular structure. Could the earth's crude pressure by itself work so thoroughly, given only a single vent both slender and strangely curved? And then the photograph he had studied. It frightened him now to recall the image—some covert meaning stirred within it, struggling to be seen. Dr. Winters picked the probe up from the table and turned again to the corpse. As surely and exactly as if he had already ascertained the wound's presence, he leaned forward and touched it: a small, neat puncture, just beneath the xiphoid process. He introduced the probe. The wound received it deeply, in a familiar direction.

The doctor went to the desk and took up the photograph again. Pollock's and Jackson's wounded areas were not in contact. The third man's head was sandwiched between their bodies at just that point. He searched out another picture, in which this third man was more central, and found his name inked in below his image: Joe Allen.

Dreamingly, Dr. Winters went to the wide metal door, shoved it aside, entered the vault. He did not search, but went straight to the trestle where Sheriff Craven had paused some hours before. He found the same name on its tag.

The body, beneath decay's spurious obesity, was trim and well-muscled. The face was square-cut, shelf-browed, with a vulpine nose skewed by an old fracture. The swollen tongue lay behind the teeth, and the bulge of decomposition did not obscure what the man's initial impact must have been—handsome and open, his now-waxen black eyes sly and convivial. Say, good buddy, got a minute? I see you comin' on the swing shift every day, don't I? Yeah, Joe Allen. Look, I know it's late, you want to get home, tell the wife you ain't been in there drinkin' since you got off, right? Oh, yeah, I hear that. But this damn disappearance thing's got me so edgy, and I'd swear to God just as I was coming here I seen someone moving around back of that frame house up the street. See how the trees thin out a little down back of the yard, where the moonlight gets in? That's right. Well, I got me this little popper here. Oh, yeah, that's a beauty, we'll have it covered between us. I knew I could spot a man ready for some trouble—couldn't find a patrol car anywhere on the street. Yeah, just down in here now, to that clump of pine. Step careful, you can barely see. That's right. . . .

The doctor's face ran with sweat. He turned on his heel and walked out of the vault, heaving the door shut behind him. In the office's greater warmth he felt the perspiration soaking his shirt under the smock. His stomach rasped with steady oscillations of pain, but he scarcely attended it. He went to Pollock and seized up the postmortem knife.

The work was done with surreal speed, the laminae of flesh and bone recoiling smoothly beneath his desperate but unerring hands, until the thoracic cavity lay exposed, and in it, the vampire-stricken lungs, two gnarled lumps of gray tissue.

He searched no deeper, knowing what the heart and veins would show. He returned to sit at the desk, weakly drooping, the knife, forgotten, still in his left hand. He looked at his reflection in the window, and it seemed his thoughts originated with that fainter, more tenuous Dr. Winters hanging like a ghost outside.

What was this world he lived in? Surely, in a lifetime, he had not begun to guess. To feed in such a way! There was horror enough in this alone. But to feed thus *in his own grave*. How had he accomplished it—leaving aside how he had fought suffocation long enough to do anything at all? How was it to be comprehended, a greed that raged so hotly it would glut itself at the very threshold of its own destruction? That last feast was surely in his stomach still.

Dr. Winters looked at the photograph, at Allen's head snugged into the others' middles like a hungry suckling nuzzling to the sow. Then he looked at the knife in his hand. The hand felt empty of all technique. Its one impulse was to slash, cleave, obliterate the remains of this gluttonous thing, this Joe Allen. He must do this, or flee it utterly. There was no course between. He did not move.

"I *will* examine him," said the ghost in the glass, and did not move. Inside the refrigeration vault, there was a slight noise.

No. It had been some hitch in the generator's murmur. Nothing in there could move. There was another noise, a brief friction against the vault's inner wall. The two old men shook their heads at one another. A catch clicked, and the metal door slid open. Behind the staring image of his own amazement, the doctor saw that a filthy shape stood in the doorway and raised its arms toward him in a gesture of supplication. The doctor turned in his chair. From the shape came a whistling groan, the decayed fragment of a human voice.

Pleadingly, Joe Allen worked his jaw and spread his purple hands. As if speech were a maggot struggling to emerge from his mouth, the blue tumescent face toiled, the huge tongue wallowed helplessly between the viscid lips.

The doctor reached for the telephone, lifted the receiver. Its deadness to his ear meant nothing—he could not have spoken. The thing confronting him, with each least movement that it made, destroyed the very frame of sanity in which words might have meaning, reduced the world itself around him to a waste of dark and silence, a starlit ruin where already, everywhere, the alien and unimaginable was awakening to its new dominion. The corpse raised and reached out one hand as if to stay him—

turned, and walked toward the instrument table. Its legs were leaden, it rocked its shoulders like a swimmer, fighting to make its passage through gravity's dense medium. It reached the table and grasped it exhaustedly. The doctor found himself on his feet, crouched slightly, weightlessly still. The knife in his hand was the only part of himself he clearly felt, and it was like a tongue of fire, a crematory flame. Joe Allen's corpse thrust one hand among the instruments. The thick fingers, with a queer simian ineptitude, brought up a scalpel. Both hands clasped the little handle and plunged the blade between the lips, as a thirsty child might a Popsicle, then jerked it out again, slashing the tongue. Turbid fluid splashed down to the floor. The jaw worked stiffly, the mouth brought out words in a wet ragged hiss:

"Please. Help me. Trapped in *this*." One dead hand struck the dead chest. "Starving."

"What are you?"

"Traveler. Not of Earth."

"An eater of human flesh. A drinker of human blood."

"No. No. Hiding only. Am small. Shape hideous to you. Feared death."

"You brought death." The doctor spoke with the calm of perfect disbelief, himself as incredible to him as the thing he spoke with. It shook its head, the dull, popped eyes glaring with an agony of thwarted expression.

"Killed none. Hid in this. Hid in this not to be killed. Five days now. Drowning in decay. Free me. Please."

"No. You have come to feed on us, you are not hiding in fear. We are your food, your meat and drink. You fed on those two men within your grave. *Their* grave. For you, a delay. In fact, a diversion that has ended the hunt for you."

"No! No! Used men already dead. For me, five days, starvation. Even less. Fed only from need. Horrible necessity!"

The spoiled vocal instrument made a mangled gasp of the last word—an inhuman snake-pit noise the doctor felt as a cold flicker of ophidian tongues within his ears—while the dead arms moved in a sodden approximation of the body language that swears truth.

"No," the doctor said. "You killed them all. Including your

... tool—this man. *What are you?*" Panic erupted in the question that he tried to bury by answering himself instantly. "Resolute, yes. That surely. You used death for an escape route. You need no oxygen perhaps."

"Extracted more than my need from gasses of decay. A lesser component of our metabolism."

The voice was gaining distinctness, developing makeshifts for tones lost in the agonal rupturing of the valves and stops of speech, more effectively wrestling vowel and consonant from the putrid tongue and lips. At the same time the body's crudity of movement did not quite obscure a subtle, incessant experimentation. Fingers flexed and stirred, testing the give of tendons, groping the palm for old points of purchase and counterpressure there. The knees, with cautious repetitions, assessed the new limits of their articulation.

"What was the sphere?"

"My ship. Its destruction our first duty facing discovery." (Fear touched the doctor, like a slug climbing his neck; he had seen, as it spoke, a sharp spastic activity of the tongue, a pleating and shrinkage of its bulk as at the tug of some inward adjustment.) "No chance to reenter. Leaving this body takes far too long. Not even time to set it for destruct—must extrude a cilium, chemical key to broach hull shield. In shaft was my only chance to halt my host."

Though the dead mask hung expressionless, conveyed no irony, the thing's articulacy grew uncannily—each word more smoothly shaped, nuances of tone creeping into its speech. Its right arm tested its wrist as it spoke, and the scalpel the hand still held cut white sparks from the air, while the word *host* seemed itself a little razor-cut, an almost teasing abandonment of fiction preliminary to attack.

But the doctor found that fear had gone from him. The impossibility with which he conversed, and was about to struggle, was working in him an overwhelming amplification of his life's long helpless rage at death. He found his parochial pity for Earth alone stretched to the transstellar scope this traveler commanded, to the whole cosmic trash yard with its bulldozed multitudes of corpses; galactic wheels of carnage—stars, planets with their most majestic generations—all trash, cracked bones and foul rags that pooled, settled, reconcatenated in futile symmetries gravid with new multitudes of briefly animate trash.

And this, standing before him now, was the death it was given him particularly to deal—his mite was being called in by the universal Treasury of Death, and Dr. Winters found himself, an old healer, on fire to pay. His own, more lethal, blade tugged at his hand with its own sharp appetite. He felt entirely the Examiner once more, knew the precise cuts he would make, swiftly and without error. *Very soon now*, he thought and coolly probed for some further insight before its onslaught:

"Why must your ship be destroyed, even at the cost of your host's life?"

"We must not be understood."

"The livestock must not understand what is devouring them."

"Yes, Doctor. Not all at once. But one by one. You will understand what is devouring you. That is essential to my feast."

The doctor shook his head. "You are in your grave already, Traveler. That body will be your coffin. You will be buried in it a second time, for all time."

The thing came one step nearer and opened its mouth. The flabby throat wrestled as with speech, but what sprang out was a slender white filament, more than whip-fast. Dr. Winters saw only the first flicker of its eruption, and then his brain nova-ed, thinning out at light-speed to a white nullity.

When the doctor came to himself, it was in fact to a part of himself only. Before he had opened his eyes he found that his wakened mind had repossessed proprioceptively only a bizarre truncation of his body. His head, neck, left shoulder, arm, and hand declared themselves—the rest was silence.

When he opened his eyes, he found that he lay supine on the gurney, and naked. Something propped his head. A strap bound his left elbow to the gurney's edge, a strap he could feel. His chest was also anchored by a strap, and this he could not feel. Indeed, save for its active remnant, his entire body might have been bound in a block of ice, so numb was it, and so powerless was he to compel the slightest movement from the least part of it.

The room was empty, but from the open door of the vault there came slight sounds: the creak and soft frictions of heavy tarpaulin shifted to accommodate some business involving small clicking and kissing noises.

Tears of fury filled the doctor's eyes. Clenching his one fist at the starry engine of creation that he could not see, he ground his teeth and whispered in the hot breath of strangled weeping:

"Take it back, this dirty little shred of life! I throw it off gladly like the filth it is." The slow knock of boot soles loudened from within the vault, and he turned his head. From the vault door Joe Allen's corpse approached him.

It moved with new energy, though its gait was grotesque, a ducking, hitching progress, jerky with circumventions of decayed muscle, while above this galvanized, struggling frame, the bruise-colored face hung inanimate, an image of detachment. With terrible clarity the thing was revealed for what it was—a damaged hand-puppet vigorously worked from within. And when that frozen face was brought to hang above the doctor, the reeking hands, with the light, solicitous touch of friends at sickbeds, rested on his naked thigh.

The absence of sensation made the touch more dreadful than if felt. It showed him that the nightmare he still desperately denied at heart had annexed his body while he—holding head and arm free—had already more than half-drowned in its mortal paralysis. There, from his chest on down, lay his nightmare part, a nothingness freely possessed by an unspeakability. The corpse said:

"Rotten blood. Thin nourishment. I had only one hour alone before you came. I fed from my neighbor to my left—barely had strength to extend a siphon. Fed from the right while you worked. Tricky going—you are alert. I expected Dr. Parsons. The energy needs of animating this"—one hand left the doctor's thigh and smote the dusty overalls—"and of host-transfer, very high. Once I have you synapsed, I will be near starvation again."

A sequence of unbearable images unfolded in the doctor's

mind, even as the robot carrion turned from the gurney and walked to the instrument table: the sheriff's arrival just after dawn, alone of course, since Craven always took thought for his deputies' rest and because on this errand he would want privacy to consider any indiscretion on behalf of the miners' survivors that the situation might call for; Craven's finding his old friend, supine and alarmingly weak; his hurrying over, his leaning near. Then, somewhat later, a police car containing a rack of still wet bones might plunge off the highway above some deep spot in the gorge.

The corpse took an evidence box from the table and put the scalpel in it. Then it turned and retrieved the mortuary knife from the floor and put that in as well, saying as it did so, without turning, "The sheriff will come in the morning. You spoke like close friends. He will probably come alone."

The coincidence with his thoughts had to be accident, but the intent to terrify and appall him was clear. The tone and timing of that patched-up voice were unmistakably deliberate—sly probes that sought his anguish specifically, sought his mind's personal center. He watched the corpse—over at the table—dipping an apish but accurate hand and plucking up rib shears, scissors, clamps, adding all to the box. He stared, momentarily emptied by shock of all but the will to know finally the full extent of the horror that had appropriated his life. Joe Allen's body carried the box to the worktable beside the gurney, and the expressionless eyes met the doctor's.

"I have gambled. A grave gamble. But now I have won. At risk of personal discovery we are obliged to disconnect, contract, hide as well as possible in the host-body. Suicide in effect. I disregarded situational imperatives, despite starvation before disinterment and subsequent autopsy being all but certain. I caught up with the crew, tackled Pollock and Jackson microseconds before the blast. I computed five days' survival from this cache. I could disconnect at limit of my strength to do so, but otherwise I would chance autopsy, knowing the doctor was an alcoholic incompetent. And now see my gain. You are a prize host. Through you I can feed with near impunity even when killing is too dangerous. Safe meals are delivered to you still warm."

The corpse had painstakingly aligned the gurney parallel to the worktable but offset, the table's foot extending past the gurney's, and separated from it by a distance somewhat less than the reach of Joe Allen's right arm. Now the dead hands distributed the implements along the right edge of the table, save for the scissors and the box. These the corpse took to the table's foot, where it set down the box and slid the scissors' jaws round one strap of its overalls. It began to speak again, and as it did, the scissors dismembered its cerements in unhesitating strokes.

"The cut must be medical, forensically right, though a smaller one is easier. I must be careful of the pectoral muscles or these arms will not convey me. I am no larva anymore—over fifteen hundred grams."

To ease the nightmare's suffocating pressure, to thrust out some flicker of his own will against its engulfment, the doctor flung a question, his voice more cracked than the other's now was:

"Why is my arm free?"

"The last, fine neural splicing needs a sensory-motor standard, to perfect my brain's fit to yours. Lacking this eye-hand coordinating check, only a much coarser control of the host's characteristic motor patterns is possible. This done, I flush out the paralytic, unbind us, and we are free together."

The grave-clothes had fallen in a puzzle of fragments, and the cadaver stood naked, its dark gas-rounded contours making it seem some sleek marine creature, ruddered with the black-veined gas-distended sex. Again the voice had teased for his fear, had uttered the last word with a savoring protraction, and now the doctor's cup of anguish brimmed over; horror and outrage wrenched his spirit in brutal alternation as if trying to tear it naked from its captive frame. He rolled his head in this deadlock, his mouth beginning to split with the slow birth of a mind-emptying outcry.

The corpse watched this, giving a single nod that might have been approbation. Then it mounted the worktable and, with the concentrated caution of some practiced convalescent reentering his bed, lay on its back. The dead eyes again sought the living and found the doctor staring back, grinning insanely.

"Clever corpse!" the doctor cried. "Clever, carnivorous corpse! Able alien! Please don't think I'm criticizing. Who am I to criticize? A mere arm and shoulder, a talking head, just a small piece of a pathologist. But I'm confused." He paused, savoring the monster's attentive silence and his own buoyancy in the hysterical levity that had unexpectedly liberated him. "You're going to use your puppet there to pluck you out of itself and put you on me. But once he's pulled you from your driver's seat, won't he go dead, so to speak, and drop you? You could get a nasty knock. Why not set a plank between the tables—the puppet opens the door, and you scuttle, ooze, lurch, flop, slither, as the case may be, across the bridge. No messy spills. And in any case, isn't this an odd, rather clumsy way to get around among your cattle? Shouldn't you at least carry your own scalpels when you travel? There's always the risk you'll run across that one host in a million that isn't carrying one with him."

He knew his gibes would be answered to his own despair. He exulted, but solely in the momentary bafflement of the predator—in having, for just a moment, mocked its gloating assurance to silence and marred its feast.

Its right hand picked up the postmortem knife beside it, and the left wedged a roll of gauze beneath Allen's neck, lifting the throat to a more prominent arch. The mouth told the ceiling:

"We retain larval form till entry of the host. As larvae we have locomotor structures, and sense buds usable outside our ships' sensory amplifiers. I waited coiled round Joe Allen's bed leg till night, entered by his mouth as he slept." Allen's hand lifted the knife, held it high above the dull, quick eyes, turning it in the light. "Once lodged, we have three instars to adult form," the voice continued absently—the knife might have been a mirror from which the corpse read its features. "Larvally we have only a sketch of our full neural tap. Our metamorphosis is cued and determined by the host's endosomatic ecology. I matured in three days." Allen's wrist flexed, tipping the knife's point downmost. "Most supreme adaptations are purchased at the cost of inessential capacities." The elbow pronated and slowly flexed, hooking the knife bodyward. "Our hosts are all sentients, ecodominants, are already carrying the baggage of coping structures for the planetary environment we find them in. Limbs, sensory portals"—the fist planted the fang of its tool under the chin, tilted it and rode it smoothly down the throat, the voice proceeding unmarred from under the furrow that the steel ploughed—"somatic envelopes, instrumentalities"—down the sternum, diaphragm, abdomen the stainless blade painted its stripe of gaping, muddy tissue—"with a host's brain we inherit all these, the mastery of any planet, netted in its dominant's cerebral nexus. Thus our genetic codings are now all but disencumbered of such provisions."

So swiftly that the doctor flinched, Joe Allen's hand slashed four lateral cuts from the great wound's axis. The seeming butchery left two flawlessly drawn thoracic flaps cleanly outlined. The left hand raised the left flap's hem, and the right coaxed the knife into the aperture, deepening it with small stabs and slices. The posture was a man's who searches a breast pocket, with the dead eyes studying the slow recoil of flesh. The voice, when it resumed, had geared up to an intenser pitch:

"Galactically, the chordate nerve/brain paradigm abounds, and the neural labyrinth is our dominion. Are we to make plank bridges and worm across them to our food? Are cockroaches greater than we for having legs to run up walls and antennae to grope their way? All the quaint, hinged crutches that life sports! The stilts, fins, fans, springs, stalks, flippers, and feathers, all in turn so variously terminating in hooks, clamps, suckers, scissors, forks, or little cages of digits! And besides all the gadgets it concocts for wrestling through its worlds, it is all knobbed, whiskered, crested, plumed, vented, spiked, or measeled over with perceptual gear for combing pittances of noise or color from the environing plentitude."

Invincibly calm and sure, the hands traded tool and tasks. The right flap eased back, revealing ropes of ingeniously spared muscle while promising a genuine appearance once sutured back in place. Helplessly the doctor felt his delirious defiance bleed away and a bleak fascination rebind him.

"We are the taps and relays that share the host's aggregate of afferent nerve-impulse precisely at its nodes of integration. We are the brains that peruse these integrations, integrate them with our existing banks of host-specific data, and, lastly, let their consequences flow down the motor pathway—either the consequences they seek spontaneously, or those we wish to graft upon them. We are besides a streamlined alimentary/circulatory system and a reproductive apparatus. And more than this we need not be."

The corpse had spread its bloody vest, and the feculent hands now took up the rib shears. The voice's sinister coloration of pitch and stress grew yet more marked—the phrases slid from the tongue with a cobra's seeking sway, winding their liquid rhythms round the doctor till a gap in his resistance should let them pour through to slaughter the little courage left him.

"For in this form we have inhabited the densest brainweb of three hundred races, lain intricately snug within them like thriving vine on trelliswork. We've looked out from too many variously windowed masks to regret our own vestigial senses. None read their worlds definitively. Far better then our nomad's range and choice than an unvarying tenancy of one poor set of structures. Far better to slip on as we do whole living beings and wear at once all of their limbs and organs, memories and powers—wear all these as tightly congruent to our wills as a glove is to the hand that fills it."

The shears clipped through the gristle, stolid, bloody jaws monotonously feeding, stopping short of the sternoclavicular joint in the manubrium where the muscles of the pectoral girdle have an important anchorage.

"No consciousness of the chordate type that we have found has been impermeable to our finesse—no dendritic pattern so elaborate we could not read its stitchwork and thread ourselves to match, precisely map its each synaptic seam till we could loosen it and retailor all to suit ourselves. We have strutted costumed in the bodies of planetary autarchs, venerable manikins of moral fashion, but cut of the universal cloth: the weave of fleet electric filaments of experience that we easily reshuttled to the warp of our wishes. Whereafter—newly hemmed and gathered—their living fabric hung obedient to our bias, investing us with honor and influence unlimited."

The tricky verbal melody, through the corpse's deft, unfal-

tering self-dismemberment—the sheer neuromuscular orches-
tration of the compound activity—struck Dr. Winters with the
detached enthrallment great keyboard performers could bring
him. He glimpsed the alien's perspective—a Gulliver waiting in
a Brobdingnagian grave, then marshaling a dead giant against
a living, like a dwarf in a huge mechanical crane, feverishly
programming combat on a battery of levers and pedals, waiting
for the robot arms' enactments, the remote, titanic impact of
the foes—and he marveled, filled with a bleak wonder at life's
infinite strategy and plasticity. Joe Allen's hands reached into his
half-opened abdominal cavity, reached deep below the uncut
anterior muscle that was exposed by the shallow, spurious
incision of the epidermis, till by external measure they were
extended far enough to be touching his thighs. The voice was
still as the forearms advertised a delicate rummaging with the
buried fingers. The shoulders drew back. As the steady withdrawal brought the wrists into view, the dead legs tremored and
quaked with diffuse spasms.

"You called your kind our food and drink, Doctor. If you were
merely that, an elementary usurpation of your motor tracts
alone would satisfy us, give us perfect cattle-control—for what
rarest word or subtlest behavior is more than a flurry of varied
muscles? That trifling skill was ours long ago. It is not mere
blood that feeds this lust I feel now to tenant you, this craving for
an intimacy that years will not stale. My truest feast lies in com-
pelling you to feed in that way. It lies in the utter deformation
of your will this will involve. Had gross nourishment been my
prime need, then my grave-mates—Pollock and Jackson—could
have eked out two weeks of life for me or more. But I scorned a
cowardly parsimony in the face of death. I reinvested more than
half the energy that their blood gave me in fabricating chemi-
cals to keep their brains alive, and fluid-bathed with oxygenated
nutriment."

The corpse reached into its gaping abdomen, and out of its
cloven groin the smeared hands pulled two long skeins of silvery filament. The material looked like masses of nerve fiber,
tough and scintillant—for the weave of it glittered with a slight
incessant movement of each single thread. These nerve skeins

were contracting. They thickened into two swollen nodes, while at the same time the corpse's legs tremored and faintly twitched, as the bright vermiculate roots of the parasite withdrew from within Allen's musculature. When the nodes lay fully contracted—the doctor could just see their tips within the abdomen—then the legs lay still as death.

"I had accessory neural taps only to spare, but I could access much memory, and all of their cognitive responses, and having in my banks all the organ of Corti's electrochemical conversions of English words, I could whisper anything to them directly into the eighth cranial nerve. Those are our true feast, Doctor, such bodiless electric storms of impotent cognition as I tickled up in those two little bone globes. I was forced to drain them just before disinterment, but they lived till then and understood everything—*everything* I did to them."

When the voice paused, the dead and living eyes were locked together. They remained so a moment, and then the dead face smiled.

It recapitulated all the horror of Allen's first resurrection— this waking of expressive soul in that purple death mask. And it was a demon-soul the doctor saw awaken: the smile was barbed with fine, sharp hooks of cruelty at the corners of the mouth, while the barbed eyes beamed fond, languorous anticipation of his pain. Remotely, Dr. Winters heard the flat sound of his own voice asking:

"And Joe Allen?"

"Oh, yes, Doctor. He is with us now, has been throughout. I grieve to abandon so rare a host! He is a true hermit-philosopher, well-read in four languages. He is writing a translation of Marcus Aurelius—he was, I mean, in his free time. . . ."

Long minutes succeeded of the voice accompanying the surreal self-autopsy, but the doctor lay resigned, emptied of reactive power. Still, the full understanding of his fate reverberated in his mind as the parasite sketched his future for him in that borrowed voice. And it did not stop haunting Winters, the sense of what a *virtuoso* this entity was, how flawlessly this mass of neural fibers played the tricky instrument of human speech. As flawlessly as it had puppeteered the corpse's face into that ghastly smile. And with the same artistic aim: to waken, to amplify, to ripen its host-to-be's outrage and horror. The voice, with ever more melody and gloating verve, sent waves of realization through the doctor, amplifications of the Unspeakable.

The parasite's race had traced and tapped the complex interface between the cortical integration of sense input and the neural output governing response. It had interposed its brain between, sharing consciousness while solely commanding the pathways of reaction. The host, the bottled personality, was mute and limbless for any least expression of its own will, while hellishly articulate and agile in the service of the parasite's. It was the host's own hands that bound and wrenched the life half out of his prey, his own loins that experienced the repeated orgasms crowning his other despoliations of their bodies. And when they lay, bound and shrieking still, ready for the consummation, it was his own strength that hauled the smoking entrails from them, and his own intimate tongue and guzzling mouth he plunged into the rank, palpitating feast.

And the doctor had glimpses of the racial history that underlay the aliens' predatory present. Glimpses of a dispassionate, inquiring breed so advanced in the analysis of its own mental fabric that, through scientific commitment and genetic self-sculpting, it had come to embody its own model of perfected consciousness. It had grown streamlined to permit its entry of other beings and its direct acquisition of their experiential worlds. All strictest scholarship at first, until there matured in the disembodied scholars their long-germinal and now blazing, jealous hatred for all "lesser" minds rooted and clothed in the soil and sunlight of solid, particular worlds. The parasite spoke of the "cerebral music," the "symphonies of agonized paradox" that were its invasion's chief plunder. The doctor felt the truth behind this grandiloquence: the parasite's actual harvest from the systematic violation of encoffined personalities was the experience of a barren supremacy of means over lives more primitive, perhaps, but vastly wealthier in the vividness and passionate concern with which life for them was imbued.

The corpse had reached into its thorax and with its dead hands aided the parasite's retraction of its upper-body root system. More and more of its livid mass had gone dead, until only its head and the arm nearer the doctor remained animate, while the silvery worming mass grew in its bleeding abdominal nest.

Then Joe Allen's face grinned, and his hand hoisted up the nude, regathered parasite from his sundered gut and held it for the doctor to view—his tenant-to-be. Winters saw that from the squirming mass of nerve cord one thick filament still draped down, remaining anchored in the canyoned chest toward the upper spine. This, he understood, would be the remote-control line by which it could work at a distance the crane of its old host's body, transferring itself to Winters by means of a giant apparatus it no longer inhabited. This, he knew, was his last moment. Before his own personal horror should begin, and engulf him, he squarely met the corpse's eyes and said:

"Goodbye, Joe Allen. Eddie Sykes, I mean. I hope he gave you strength, the Golden Marcus. I love him too. You are guiltless. Peace be with you at the last."

The demon smile stayed fixed, but, effortlessly, Winters looked through it to the real eyes, those of the encoffined man. Tormented eyes forseeing death, and craving it. The grinning corpse reached out its viscid cargo—a seething, rippling, multinodular lump that completely filled the erstwhile logger's roomy palm. It reached this across and laid it on the doctor's groin. He watched the hand set the bright medusa's head—his new self—on his own skin, but felt nothing.

He watched the dead hand return to the table, take up the scalpel, reach back over, and make a twelve-inch incision up his abdomen, along his spinal axis. It was a deep, slow cut—now sectioning, just straight down through the abdominal wall—and it proceeded in the eerie, utter absence of physical sensation. The moment this was done, the fiber that had stayed anchored in the corpse snapped free, whipped back across the gap, and rejoined the main body that now squirmed toward the incision, its port of entry.

The corpse collapsed. Emptied of all innervating energy, it sagged slack and flaccid, of course. Or had it . . . ? Why was it . . . ? That nearer arm was *supinated*. Both elbow and wrist at the full upturned twist. The palm lay open, offering. *The scalpel still lay in the palm.*

Simple death would have dropped the arm earthward, it would now hang slack. With a blaze, like a nova of light, Winters understood. The man, Sykes, had—for a microsecond before his end—repossessed himself. Had flung a dying impulse of *his* will down through his rotten, fading muscles and had managed a single independent gesture in the narrow interval between the demon's departure and his own death. He had clutched the scalpel and flung out his arm, locking the joints as life left him.

It rekindled Winters's own will, lit a fire of rage and vengefulness. He had caught hope from his predecessor.

How precariously the scalpel lay on the loosened fingers! The slightest tremor would unfix the arm's joints, it would fall and hang and drop the scalpel down farther than Hell's deepest recess from his grasp. And he could see that the scalpel was just—only just—in the reach of his fingers at his forearm's fullest stretch from the bound elbow. The horror crouched on him and, even now slowly feeding its trunk line into his groin incision, at first stopped the doctor's hand with a pang of terror. Then he reminded himself that, until implanted, the enemy was a senseless mass, bristling with plugs, with input jacks for senses, but, until installed in the physical amplifiers of eyes and ears, an utterly deaf, blind monad that waited in a perfect solipsism between two captive sensory envelopes.

He saw his straining fingers above the bright tool of freedom, thought with an insane smile of God and Adam on the Sistine ceiling, and then, with a life span of surgeon's fine control, plucked up the scalpel. The arm fell and hung.

"Sleep," the doctor said. "Sleep revenged."

But he found his retaliation harshly reined-in by the alien's careful provisions. His elbow had been fixed with his upper arm almost at right angles to his body's long axis; his forearm could reach his hand inward and present it closely to the face, suiting the parasite's need of an eye-hand coordinative check, but could not, even with the scalpel's added reach, bring its point within four inches of his groin. Steadily the parasite fed in its tapline. It would usurp motor control in three or four minutes at most, to judge by the time its extrication from Allen had taken.

Frantically the doctor bent his wrist inward to its limit, trying to pick through the strap where it crossed his inner elbow. Sufficient pressure was impossible, and the hold so awkward that even feeble attempts threatened the loss of the scalpel. Smoothly the root of alien control sank into him. It was a defenseless thing of jelly against which he lay lethally armed, and he was still doomed—a preview of all his thrall's impotence-to-be.

But of course there was a way. Not to survive. But to escape, and to have vengeance. For a moment he stared at his captor, hardening his mettle in the blaze of hate it lit in him. Then, swiftly, he determined the order of his moves, and began.

He reached the scalpel to his neck and opened his superior thyroid vein—his inkwell. He laid the scalpel by his ear, dipped his finger in his blood, and began to write on the metal surface of the gurney, beginning by his thigh and moving toward his armpit. Oddly, the incision of his neck, though this was muscularly awake, had been painless, which gave him hopes that raised his courage for what remained to do.

When he had done the message read:

PARASITE
CUT ME
TILL FIND
1500 GM NERVE
FIBER

He wanted to write goodbye to his friend, but the alien had begun to pay out smaller auxiliary filaments collaterally with the main one, and all now lay in speed.

He took up the scalpel, rolled his head to the left, and plunged the blade deep in his ear.

Miracle! Last accidental mercy! It was painless. Some procedural, highly specific anesthetic was in effect. With careful plunges, he obliterated the right inner ear and then thrust silence, with equal thoroughness, into the left. The slashing of the vocal cords followed, then the tendons in the back of the neck that hold it erect. He wished he were free to unstring knees and elbows too, but it could not be. But blinded, deaf, with centers of balance lost, with only rough motor control—all these conditions should fetter the alien's escape, should it in the first place manage the reanimation of a bloodless corpse in which it had not yet achieved a fine-tuned interweave. Before he extinguished his eyes, he paused, the scalpel poised above his face, and blinked them to clear his aim of tears. The right, then the left, both retinas meticulously carved away, the yolk of vision quite scooped out of them. The scalpel's last task, once it had tilted the head sideways to guide the blood flow absolutely clear of possible effacement of the message, was to slash the external carotid artery.

When this was done, the old man sighed with relief and laid his scalpel down. Even as he did so, he felt the deep inward prickle of an alien energy—something that flared, crackled, flared, *groped for*, but did not quite find its purchase. And inwardly, as the doctor sank toward sleep—cerebrally, as a voiceless man must speak—he spoke to the parasite these carefully chosen words:

"Welcome to your new house. I'm afraid there's been some vandalism—the lights don't work, and the plumbing has a very bad leak. There are some other things wrong as well—the neighborhood is perhaps a little *too* quiet, and you may find it hard to get around very easily. But it's been a lovely home to me for fifty-seven years, and somehow I think you'll stay. . . ."

The face, turned toward the body of Joe Allen, seemed to weep scarlet tears, but its last movement before death was to smile.